USA TODAY bestselling author **Heidi Rice** lives in London, England. She is married with two teenage sons—which gives her rather too much of an insight into the male psyche—and also works as a film journalist. She adores her job, which involves getting swept up in a world of high emotion, sensual excitement, funny and feisty women, sexy and tortured men and glamorous locations where laundry doesn't exist. Once she turns off her computer she often does chores—usually involving laundry!

Rachael Thomas has always loved reading romance, and is thrilled to be a Mills & Boon author. She lives and works on a farm in Wales—a far cry from the glamour of a Modern Romance story, but that makes slipping into her characters' worlds all the more appealing. When she's not writing, or working on the farm, she enjoys photography and visiting historical castles and grand houses. Visit her at rachaelthomas.co.uk.

CLAIMED FOR THE DESERT PRINCE'S HEIR

HEIDI RICE

A SHOCKING PROPOSAL IN SICILY

RACHAEL THOMAS

MILLS & BOON

First Published in Great Britain 2019
by Mills & Boon, an imprint of HarperCollins*Publishers*
1 London Bridge Street, London, SE1 9GF

Claimed for the Desert Prince's Heir © 2019 by Heidi Rice

A Shocking Proposal in Sicily © 2019 by Rachael Thomas

ISBN: 978-0-263-27800-2

MIX
Paper from
responsible sources
FSC® C007454

This book is produced from independently certified FSC™ paper
to ensure responsible forest management.
For more information visit www.harpercollins.co.uk/green.

Printed and bound in Spain
by CPI, Barcelona

CLAIMED FOR THE DESERT PRINCE'S HEIR

HEIDI RICE

To Daisy,
thanks for the fabulous brainstorming session that
turned Raif from a desert rogue into a Modern hero!
Mwah! xx

CHAPTER ONE

KASIA SALAH SQUINTED at the heat haze on the horizon and the ominous cloud of dust that shimmered above it, then glared at her mobile phone.

No service.

She breathed the swear word she'd learned during her years at Cambridge University as sweat collected on her upper lip and trickled down her back beneath her T-shirt and the voluminous robe she wore to stave off the heat and dust of the desert landscape. It was the sort of swear word she would have been punished by her grandmother for even knowing—let alone saying—once upon a time. She tucked her smartphone into the back pocket of her shorts, taking several more frustrating moments to locate it under the miles of fabric. Then transferred her glare to the engine of the black SUV—and swore again, louder this time. After all, there was no one within a fifty-mile radius to hear her—and it felt empowering, even if it wasn't going to help.

Why hadn't she thought to take a satellite phone with her before leaving the palace for this research trip? Or a companion? Preferably one who knew a bit more than she did about car mechanics? She sighed and kicked the tyre of the broken-down Jeep.

It had been reckless, over-confident and overly optimistic…her three favourite flaws.

Then again, she hadn't intended to break down in the middle of nowhere with no phone signal.

Sheikh Zane Ali Nawari Khan, her best friend Catherine's husband, the ruler of Narabia and, nominally, her boss, had worked long and hard to bring internet connectivity and a cellphone network to large parts of the kingdom. But she suspected she was too close to the borderlands here—an undeveloped desert, flanked by the mountain region in the south, populated only by the Kholadi nomads. From what she could remember, the Kholadi didn't even have running water, so the chances of them needing a phone signal were fairly slim.

Using the robe to cover her hands, so she didn't burn them on the hot metal, she unhooked the defunct vehicle's bonnet. It slammed down, the sound echoing in the febrile air. Luckily, she had given Cat and her assistant Nadia a detailed itinerary of her day trip, so when she didn't return this evening they would send out a search party.

But that still meant spending a night in the Jeep.

Wasn't that going to be fun, especially when the temperature plummeted as soon as the sun dipped below the desert floor.

The hot, dry wind swept a sprinkle of sand into her face. Tugging the robe's head scarf over her nose and mouth so she didn't inhale the gritty swirls, she peered towards the horizon. The cloud she had spotted earlier had grown, spreading across the land in both directions and blotting out the shimmering heat haze like a malevolent force.

Adrenaline kicked at her ribs like one of Zane's thoroughbred Arabian stallions. And the anxiety she'd been keeping a tight rein on rippled down her spine.

Was that a sandstorm?

And was it headed her way?

She'd never experienced one before, having been cloistered in the luxurious safety of the Golden Palace's women's quarters for most of her life.

But she'd heard about the sandstorms. The carnage they wrought could strike terror into the hearts of grown men and women. Her grandmother had whispered about them in hushed reverential tones; how the worst of them had laid waste to the kingdom, turning farmland back into desert and causing numerous fatalities.

She swallowed down the panic threatening to overwhelm her.

Stop being a drama queen.

It was another one of her flaws. Seeing everything too vividly.

Her grandmother, for all her innate wisdom, had been a drama queen, too. Kasia had been only four years old when she'd gone to live with her, eventually becoming part of the palace staff herself when the old Sheikh had died, and the new Sheikh, Zane, had hired Catherine Smith, a Cambridge scholar, to write a book on the kingdom.

Getting a job as Catherine's personal assistant at the age of nineteen had changed her life—especially when Cat had married Zane and become Narabia's Queen, opening Kasia's eyes to an exciting world beyond the palace walls. She wasn't that over-eager, over-imaginative and overly romantic teenager any more—hiding all her insecurities behind a veil of unfulfillable dreams. She was a grown woman now with dreams she was already achieving of becoming an environmental scientist who would save Narabia's agricultural land from the desert that threatened to consume it.

Some sand and a night in a Jeep wasn't going to faze her…much. In fact, a night spent in the desert might afford her some useful research data.

And who said this was even a sandstorm? There had been no reports of any adverse weather, because she'd checked both the local and the satellite reports before she'd left the palace. She might be reckless, but she was not an idiot.

She repeated the reassuring words, but her gaze remained superglued to the horizon.

The dark, impenetrable cloud grew, blocking out the sun. It had to be at least thirty or forty miles wide, and although it was still a mile away it was advancing fast. The noise cut through the desert silence. Tiny creatures—a lizard, a snake, a rodent—scurried and slithered past her boots, rushing to burrow into the ground. The bright, cloudless sky darkened.

Fear clawed at her throat as her mind tried to engage. Should she get into the SUV? Should she get under it?

Then she saw something—a blot on the horizon—emerge from the cloud like a bullet. It took a while for the shimmering blot to solidify into a silhouette. It was a person, on a horse, galloping fast.

Panic and anxiety tightened around her throat.

Black flowing robes lifted in the wind behind the charging figure, like the wings of a giant predatory bird, as the horse's hooves became audible over the roar of the sand.

The rider was a man. A very big man. His outline broad and strong, the fluid graceful movements powerful and overwhelming as he seemed to become one with the stallion as it galloped at full speed. He wore a headdress, masking most of his face.

The panic wrapped around her heart, the thundering beat matching the clump-clump-clump of the approaching hooves—as she saw the horse and rider change course and veer straight towards her.

Then she noticed the rifle strap crossing his broad chest. A bandit. What else could he be, miles from civilisation? *Run, Kasia, run.*

The silent scream echoed inside her head. The howling winds lifted the sand around her. Then in her grandmother's voice—a voice she had always associated with salvation—*Stay calm. Don't panic. He's just a man.*

But even as she tried to rationalise the fear, liberate herself from the panic—reminding her of the sight of her mother walking away for the last time—a strange melting sensation at her core plunged into her abdomen.

A shout rang out, muffled by his scarf, in a dialect she didn't recognise.

He was almost upon her.

For goodness' sake, Kasia, stop standing there like a ninny and move.

The call to action helped drown out the fear of being alone and defenceless, a fear she had spent years conquering in childhood.

You're not that little girl who wasn't good enough. You're brave and smart and accomplished.

She scrambled round the Jeep, wrenched open the passenger door, and dived into the stuffy interior. The sand peppering the windows sounded like rifle shots as her hand landed on the pistol in the passenger seat.

Zane had insisted she learn to shoot before he would allow her to go into the desert alone. But as her fingers closed over the metal, her heart butted her tonsils.

She knew how to shoot at a target with some degree of accuracy, but she had never shot a living thing.

The charging horse came to an abrupt stop only inches from the SUV's bumper. Scrambling out, the sand slicing her cheeks like a whip, Kasia lifted the pistol in both hands and pressed a trembling finger to the trigger.

'Stop there or I'll shoot,' she shouted in English, because it had become her first language after five years in the UK.

Chocolate eyes narrowed above the mask—glittering with intent and fury. The warmth in her abdomen became hot and heavy. And all the more terrifying.

The bandit swung a leg over the horse's neck and jumped down in one fluid movement without speaking, those dark eyes burning into her soul.

She jerked back a step and the pistol went off. The pop

was barely audible in the storm, but the recoil threw her down hard on her backside and she saw the man jerk back.

Had she hit him?

Before the thought had a chance to register, the stallion reared, its hooves pawing the air above her head. The bandit caught the horse's reins before the animal could trample her into the desert floor, and she felt a rush of relief. Within seconds, though, he loomed over her again and the relief that she hadn't killed him turned to panic. She scrambled back on her bottom, kicked out with her feet.

'Get away from me.'

Where was the gun?

She searched for it frantically, but her vision was all but obscured by the swirling sands. He had become the only focus, the ominous outline bearing down on her.

Long fingers shot from the storm and gripped her arm. He hauled her up, bent down and hefted her onto his shoulder with such speed and strength she could barely grasp what was happening before she found herself straddling the huge black horse's sweat-soaked back.

She lifted her leg, trying to dismount, but before she could get her knee over the pommel, he had mounted behind her.

He grasped the reins with one hand and banded his other arm around her midriff, pulling her into the unyielding strength of his body.

She let out an 'Oomph…' as the air was expelled from her lungs. The iron band of his forearm pressed into her breasts. Then suddenly they were flying, her bottom bouncing on the saddle—abandoning the Jeep, which was already half-buried in sand. Her body was forced to succumb to the will of his much bigger, much stronger one as he bent forward, his robes shielding her from the sand stinging her eyes. She tried to cry out, to fight the lethargy wrought by terror, the visceral heat coursing through her body making her too aware of every place their bodies touched.

He's kidnapping you. You must fight. You must survive.

The words screamed in her head, but her breathing was so rapid now it was painful, her whole body confined, subdued, overwhelmed by his and the storm of sand and dust and darkness raging around them.

They seemed to ride for ever through the swirl of sand—until eventually her fear and panic stopped crushing her ribs and her body melted into exhaustion. The rhythm of the horse's movements seeped into her bones, the man's unyielding strength cocooning her against the elements.

Was this Stockholm syndrome? she wondered vaguely, her tired mind no longer capable of engaging with the terror as her body succumbed to the impenetrable darkness, the controlled purpose of her captor's movements and the stultifying heat coursing through her.

As her eyes drifted shut and her bones turned to water, she dropped down through the years, until she became that little girl again. But this time she was no longer alone and defenceless, her mother gone without a backward glance, but sheltered in strong arms against the storm.

CHAPTER TWO

KASIA WOKE AGAIN in fits and starts. First the bristle of cold on her face, and the heavy weight at her back, both suffocating and warming her. As Kasia opened her eyes, her heart swelled into her throat.

Red light glowed on the horizon, starlight was sprinkled overhead. Shooting stars shot across the sky, illuminating the desert dunes. Her thighs trembled and she became aware of the large warm bulk between them.

A horse. She was on a horse.

His horse.

Memory flooded back.

Kidnapped!

She'd been kidnapped by the man whose muscular forearm banded around her waist. And whose body radiated heat as it cocooned hers.

All the inappropriate dreams she'd had about him returned, too. She shoved them to one side and tried to free her arms.

You're not in Stockholm any more!

A grunt sounded next to her ear, making her aware of the unearthly quiet of the night, the chill of the evening breeze. The storm had passed.

And she was alone, in the middle of the desert, with the bandit who had captured her. And saved her. But why?

Whatever. Now it was time to save herself. From him.

The horse's hooves thudded patiently against the rocky dunes as they rose over a hill. An oasis came into view in the valley below. The horse picked its way down the slope as sure-footed as a cat. The mirrored expanse of water reflected the dying red of the sunset, palm trees and plants grew in profusion around the water's edge. The rasp of her kidnapper's breathing echoed in her ears, making her heart thunder against her ribs.

Was that arousal she could hear in his rough breathing? How would she know? She'd never been in a man's arms before when he was aroused.

Not the point, Kasia. Focus. For goodness' sake.

The numbness in her fingers as she gripped the saddle horn tingled, her thighs quivered and burned, sore from what had to have been several hours on horseback. She became aware of the stinging pain where the sandstorm had abraded her exposed skin and got into her eyes.

She gulped, trying to force her tired mind to come up with a plan.

If he'd saved her from the storm, maybe he wasn't planning to hurt her, now would be a good time to start talking to him.

'Thank you for saving me from the sandstorm,' she said, with as much authority as she could muster with her throat raw and her body brutally aware of the solid chest imprinted on her back. 'I'm a close friend of the Queen. She will pay you handsomely for returning me to the palace now.' The words flowed out, sounding impossibly loud in the quiet night.

But he didn't reply, his body pressing heavily against her as the horse approached the water. She spotted a large tent erected in a copse of palm trees. The horse loped to a stop in front of the tent, and her heartbeat careered into her throat.

The scent of fresh water dispelled the fetid odour of horse and the salty scent of the man. She pushed his chest with her shoulder, freeing her arms from their confinement.

He grunted again, the sound trailing off into a moan, but strangely the panic from earlier didn't return.

He was big and clearly very strong, having ridden for miles to escape the storm, but the way he was holding her didn't feel threatening. It felt protective.

Unless that was just her cockeyed optimism taking another trip to Stockholm.

But he'd made no move to hurt her. So she clung onto her optimism—cockeyed or not—and repeated her promise of riches again in Narabian, but still got no response.

They sat together on the horse in silence, her whole body brutally aware of each subtle shift in his.

She could feel the thigh muscles that cupped her hips flex, sending a shaft of something hot and fluid through her. The wave of arousal shocked her. How could she be turned on? When she didn't even know if this man was a good guy or not?

He shifted again, his moan shivering down her spine. But then the arm around her waist loosened. And his body began to slide to one side.

What the…? Was he dismounting?

She squeezed the horse's sides with her knees and grasped the saddle horn. The rush of air at her back as his hot weight slid away was followed by a loud thud.

She gazed down to see the man lying on the ground beneath the horse.

'Whoa, boy,' she whispered frantically, scared the horse might bolt. But after stamping its hooves far too close to the man's head, it settled, its tail swishing.

How could he have fallen off the horse? Was he asleep? Was that why he hadn't replied? He had to be even more exhausted than she was after their ride.

The questions whipped around her brain. Relief and confusion tangled in her belly.

Leaning over the horse's neck, she grasped the dangling

reins. She hadn't ridden a horse since leaving Narabia for the UK, and certainly never one this enormous, but as she went to kick the horse with her heels, she glanced down at the man again. He hadn't moved, the lump of his body just lying there on the ground. Her legs relaxed and, instead of spurring the horse on, she found herself scrambling down from the huge beast.

Perhaps she was nuts—a cockeyed optimist with a side order of starry-eyed romantic—but she just couldn't bring herself to ride away and leave him lying there. Not after spending what had to have been several hours sleeping in his arms while he'd ridden them both to safety.

Landing on the other side, she grasped the reins and drew the animal further away from the rider's inert form.

She tried to lead the horse to the tent in the trees, but it wouldn't budge, simply snuffling and lifting its muzzle. 'You don't want to leave him, is that it?'

The horse bounced its head as if it was nodding.

Oh, for... Get a grip, Kasia. Horses don't speak English—especially not Narabian bandit horses.

Eventually she gave up trying to coax the horse away. And stepped closer to the man's prone figure. He hadn't moved, but still she approached him with caution. He'd looked enormous on the horse, and being flat on his back didn't seem to diminish his stature much.

A shooting star lit up the dark sky, and she gasped as bright light exploded above her, shedding its glow over the man at her feet. The black headdress covering his head and his nose and mouth had fallen off. He had wavy, dark hair, which stood up in sweaty tufts, but it was his strikingly handsome face that stole her breath.

The sight was imprinted on her retinas as the light died and the shadows returned. High slashing cheekbones, black brows, and sun-burnished skin pulled tight over the perfect symmetry of his features. He had several days' worth of stubble covering the bottom half of his face, but even with the disguising beard, she'd never seen a man as gorgeous. Even Sheikh Zane couldn't hold a candle to him, his features less refined than the Sheikh's but so much more compelling.

So not the point, Kaz. Who cares if he looks like a movie star? He's still a bandit.

But he was the movie star bandit who had saved her, so there was that.

Gathering every ounce of purpose and determination she possessed, she knelt beside him, close enough to make out his features in the dying light. Why did he look familiar?

Another meteor trailed across the night sky, illuminating his face. Shock combined with the heat burning low in her belly as recognition struck.

She gasped. 'Prince Kasim?'

Ruler of the Kholadi. He had attended Zane and Cat's wedding five and a half years ago. She knew all the rumours and gossip about this man—that he was the illegitimate son of one of the old Sheikh's concubines, thrown out of the palace as a boy when Zane, the Sheikh's legitimate heir, had been kidnapped from his American mother in LA and brought to Narabia as a teenager. The story went that Kasim had crawled through the desert only to be treated with equal contempt by his mother's nomadic tribe—until he had forced his way to the top of the Kholadi using the fighting skills he'd honed as he'd grown to manhood.

She'd adored all those stories, they'd been so compelling, so dramatic, and had made him seem even more mythic and dangerously exciting, not that she'd needed to put him on any more of a pedestal after setting eyes on him as a nineteen-year-old at Zane and Cat's wedding.

Clothed in black ceremonial wear, he'd strode into the palace at the head of a heavily armed honour guard of Kholadi tribesman, and stolen her breath, like that of every other girl and woman there. He'd been tall and arrogant and magnificent—part warrior, all chieftain, all man—and much younger than she'd expected. He must have been in his mid-twenties at that wedding because he'd only been seventeen when he had become the Kholadi Chief. After years of battling with his own father's army, he had negotiated a truce with Narabia when Zane had come to the throne.

Observing him from afar during the wedding and a few other official visits before she'd left for Cambridge, Kasia had become a little obsessed with the warrior prince. His prowess with women was almost as legendary as his skill in combat and his political agility. She'd adored all the stories that had trickled down into the palace's women's quarters after every visit—about how manly his physique was unclothed, how impressive his 'assets', how he could make a woman climax with a single glance. Like every other piece of gossip in the quarters, those salacious stories had been embellished and enhanced, but every time she'd had a chance to assess his broad, muscular physique or that rakish, devil-may-care smile from afar, she would fantasise that every word was true—and want to be the next woman on whom he bestowed that smile, and so much more.

He'd been a myth to her then, an object of her febrile adolescent desires, who had been larger than life in every respect. But he was just a man now.

The ripple of heat that she had been trying and failing to ignore sank deeper into her sex.

They didn't call him the Bad-Boy Sheikh for nothing.

She stared at him, unable to believe she'd pointed a gun at him. Thank goodness she hadn't actually shot him. Despite his wicked ways, he was a powerful prince. Plus, he'd rescued her. From a sandstorm.

As she pondered that far too romantic thought his eyelids fluttered.

The dark chocolate gaze fixed on her face and the heat in her sex blossomed like a mushroom cloud.

'Prince Kasim, are you okay?' she asked, the question popping out in English. She repeated it in Narabian. Did he even speak English?

He grunted again and she noticed for the first time the sheen of sweat on his forehead, and that his gaze, so intense earlier, now looked dazed. Then he replied in accented English.

'My name is Raif. Only my brother calls me by my Narabian name.' The husky rasp was expelled on a breath of outrage. 'And, no I'm not okay, you little witch. You shot me.'

The bullet *had* hit him?

'I'm so sorry,' she yelped. But before she could say more, his eyes closed.

The darkness was descending fast, but gripping his robe she tugged it away to reveal bare skin beneath. Scars—so many scars—and a tattoo marred the smooth skin, making the bunch of muscle and sinew look all the more magnificent.

She ignored the well of heat pulsing at her core.

So, so not the point, Kaz.

She pressed trembling fingers to his chest, felt the muscles tense as she frantically ran them over his ribs up to his shoulder to locate the wound. Her fingertips encountered sticky moisture. She drew her hand away, her eyes widening in horror at the stain of fresh blood. The metallic smell invaded the silent night.

She swore again, the same word that had made her feel empowered several hours ago when she'd found herself alone in the desert with a broken-down Jeep.

Now she was alone in the desert with a bleeding man. A bleeding, unconscious warrior prince, who had saved her from a sandstorm and whom she'd shot for his pains.

She'd never felt less empowered in her life.

CHAPTER THREE

'YOU'RE NOT MY SON—you're not anyone's son. You're nothing more than vermin—a rat, born by mistake.'

The angry memory ripped through Raif's body, his heart pounding so hard it felt as if it would gag him. His father's face reared up, the cruel slant of his lips, the contempt in his flat black eyes, the cold echo of the only words he'd ever spoken to him cutting through the familiar nightmare like a rusting blade.

'I clothed and fed you for ten years. You are a man now—any responsibility I had is paid. Now, get out.'

'No…' The desperate cry came out of his mouth, shaming, pathetic, pleading.

The crack of his father's hand sounded like a rifle shot, although the ache wasn't in his cheekbone this time but his arm. He shifted, trying to escape the cruel words, the bitter memories. The echo of remembered pain, too real and so vivid.

'Shh… Prince Raif, you're having a bad dream. Everything is okay, really, it was just a flesh wound.'

Soft words in English drifted to him through the cloaking agony. Something cool and soft fluttered over his brow. Like the wings of an angel.

'Not a prince…a rat,' he whispered back in the same language.

An exotic fragrance—jasmine, spice and female sweat—floated through the night on a cooling breeze. His nostrils flared like those of a stallion scenting its mate. The warmth of the night settled into his groin, swelling his shaft. He concentrated his mind on the pulse of pleasure, let it flow through him, to dull the aching pain always left by the nightmare in his heart.

Not a rat. You're a prince... And a man now, not an unloved boy.

He thought the words but swallowed them, remembering even through his exhaustion that he should never admit to a weakness. Not to anyone.

Soft fingers touched his chin, then something cold pressed against his lips.

The urgent female voice spoke again but he couldn't hear what it said because of the blood rushing in his ears. And the heat hurtling beneath his belt.

The taste of fresh water invaded his senses. He opened his mouth, gulping as the liquid soothed his dry throat.

'Slow down or you'll choke.' The voice was less gentle, firm, demanding—he liked it even more. But then it took the refreshing water away.

He dragged open his eyelids, which had rocks attached to them.

The pleasure swelled and throbbed in his groin.

'Who are you?' he whispered in Kholadi.

The hazy vision was exquisite, like an angel, or a temptress—flushed skin, wild midnight hair, and large eyes the same colour as precious amber, the shade only made more intense by the bruised shadows under them and the wary glow of embarrassment and knowledge.

I want you.

Had he said that aloud?

'I can't understand you, Prince Raif. I don't speak Kholadi.' The lush lips moved, but the address confused him. Why was she mixing his Narabian title with his tribal name?

'Beautiful,' he whispered in English, his fatigued brain

not able to engage with the vagaries of his cultural heritage. He wanted to touch her skin and see if it was as soft as it looked, to capture that pointed chin and bring her mouth down to his, trace the cupid's bow on the top lip with his tongue, but as he lifted his hand, the twinge of pain in his arm made him flinch.

'Lie still and go back to sleep, it's not morning yet, Prince Raif.'

Prince Raif? Who is that? I am not Prince to the Kholadi. I am their Chief.

He gritted his teeth as her cool fingers brushed his chest, an oasis in the midst of the warm night.

'Not an angel…' he said, trying to cling to consciousness, wanting to cling to her, so the nightmare would not return. 'A witch.' Then the sweet, hazy vision faded as the rocks rolled back over his eyes and he plunged back into sleep.

Beautiful.

Kasia stared down at the man she'd been lying beside for several hours now.

Lifting the cloth out of the bowl of warming water beside the bed, she squeezed out the excess liquid with cramping fingers. Placing it on his chest, she brushed it over the contours of muscle and bone shiny with sweat. The now familiar prickle of awareness sped up her arm as she glided the cooling cloth over the taut inked skin of his shoulder.

The red and black serpent tattoo that curled around his collar bone and covered his shoulder blade shimmered in the flicker of light from the kerosene lamps she'd lit as night fell.

She blinked, forcing herself to remain upright and focused. His cheeks above the line of his beard were a little flushed but he didn't have a fever, thank goodness.

Surely the rambling that had woken him up had just been a nightmare.

As he sank back into sleep, his breathing deepened.

He'd managed to swallow a fair portion of the water this time.

She re-dipped the cloth and continued to sweep it over the broad expanse of his chest, her gaze drawn to the scars that had made her wince after wrestling him out of his bloodstained robe the night before.

How could one man have sustained so much damage in his life? And survived?

Heat flushed through her as she followed the white puckered mark of an old wound into the sprinkle of masculine hair that tapered into a fine line and arrowed beneath his pants.

Her gaze connected with the prominent ridge pressing against the loose black cloth—the only piece of clothing she hadn't been brave enough to take off him.

Soaked with sweat, his pants didn't leave much to her imagination as they clung to the long muscles of his flanks and outlined the huge ridge she'd noticed several times during the last few hours.

A sight that managed to both relieve and disturb her in equal measure. Surely he couldn't be badly hurt if he could sport such an impressive erection? But what kind of man could be aroused after getting shot, however superficial the wound had turned out to be?

Look away from the erection. Maybe it's a natural state for a man suffering from exhaustion? How would you know? You've never slept with a man before, and you've certainly never shot one.

The blush burned as she dipped the cloth once more and concentrated on wiping the new film of sweat from his skin. And not getting absorbed again in his aroused state.

She ought to be used to that mammoth erection by now.

After all she'd spent rather a lot of time trying to gauge its size.

Seriously? Look away! And stop objectifying a stranger.

She forced her wayward gaze back to his upper torso.

The bandage she'd applied several hours ago remained unstained.

Thank goodness the bullet had only grazed his upper arm. Her first-aid skills did not extend to conducting emergency surgery in a tent. She'd lost her own phone when he'd rescued her. And she hadn't been able to find anything resembling a satellite phone or communication equipment in the tent.

Although tent was far too ordinary a word for the lavish construction where they had been cocooned since nightfall.

She glanced around the structure, astonished all over again by the luxurious interior she'd discovered after managing to rouse her patient to get him off the desert floor and into his dwelling.

A dwelling more than fit for a desert prince.

Rich silks covered the walls of the chamber that held the large bed pallet and an impressive array of hunting equipment, chests full of tinned and dried goods, clothing and even a battery-powered icebox packed with meat and perishable food. Thankfully she had also discovered medical supplies, which she'd used to clean and bandage his wound. She had even found a goat tethered at the back of the encampment where there was a corral and a shelter for his horse and a smaller pack pony.

How long had Prince Raif, or Prince Kasim, as she had always heard him addressed before he had corrected her, been living here, and why was he living here alone? Or was this simply an emergency shelter the Kholadi kept stocked for tribespeople caught alone in the desert?

Stop asking questions you can't answer.

She dumped the cloth in the bowl and sat on her

haunches, a wave of exhaustion making her feel light-headed.

She examined her patient, and pressed the back of her hand to his brow. She released a breath. Still normal, no sign of any adverse effects from his wound.

After several hours of getting intimately acquainted with this man's face and body, hearing the strange plea she couldn't understand in his nightmares, she had no desire to hurt him more than she already had.

The guilt had crippled her at first. But as the minutes had stretched into hours, her vigil had morphed into something strangely cathartic.

Prince Raif fascinated her, he always had even from afar. But he fascinated her even more now, bandaged and virtually naked, flushed with what she suspected was a mild case of heatstroke from their exhausting escape and with the evidence of his own mortality—and the harsh reality of his life—visible in those scars and that striking tattoo. Awareness prickled and glowed, making her skin tighten over her bones and her heart thump against her ribs.

The crack of a log in the fire outside the tent made her jump. She shook her head, trying to dispel the fugue state into which she seemed to be descending.

He'd called her a witch and—while he had a valid reason to think she was one, after all she *had* shot him—she'd also seen hunger in his eyes. A hunger that had disturbed her as much as it had excited her.

The visceral intimacy that had been created by his rescue and her recent vigil was an illusion.

Prince Raif was famous, or rather infamous, for seducing any woman he wanted and then discarding her.

Another crackle from the fire forced her tired mind to unlock.

Getting a bit ahead of yourself there, Kaz.

Worrying about how she was going to explain shooting

him when he woke up made more sense than worrying about how she was going to resist a seduction that hadn't happened.

She forced her gaze away from his mesmerising body and out towards the desert. The shimmer of light on the horizon as dawn began to seep over the dunes was gilded by the orange and gold flames leaping from the fire pit.

The desert was another world, wild and beautiful and sophisticated in its own way—especially its eco-system. But it was a world she had never been a part of, cocooned as she had been in the Sheikh's palace and then the world of UK academia.

She had never known a man like Prince Raif, however well she might once have wanted to know him, or how well she now knew the contours of his harsh body, the design of his tattoo.

Forcing herself to her feet, she stumbled out of the tent, absorbed the glorious beauty of another desert sunrise, then walked to the corral, watered the horse and brought back an armful of wood. She fed the fire, aware the temperature would remain low until the sun rose fairly high in the sky.

As she staggered back into the tent her gaze tracked inexorably to the Prince's broad chest. She watched it rise and fall in a regular rhythm, the nightmares no longer tormenting him. The serpent tattoo coiled around his shoulder in the flicker of lamplight—as vibrant as the man it adorned.

Her heart lifted and swelled with relief. He would be fine. She hadn't hurt him too badly.

He looked peaceful now—or as peaceful as a man as large and powerful as he was could ever look.

She lay down, curled up beside him and dragged the soft blanket over the T-shirt and shorts ensemble she'd been living in for nearly twenty-four hours as the night's chill seeped into her weary bones.

She needed sleep. And however frivolous or foolishly

romantic the urge, she wanted to stay beside him, just in case he had another of those nasty nightmares.

She placed her hand over his heart. She absorbed the steady rhythm and the sharp tug of awareness. She could feel the puckered skin of an old wound. Okay, maybe she didn't want to lie beside him just for the sake of his health or well-being. But what harm could it do?

She'd never get another opportunity to touch him like this, and maybe she owed this much to the fanciful girl she'd been, the girl she'd thought had died during all those hours of reading and studying, a world away. She was glad that girl hadn't died completely, because she'd always liked her.

'Sleep well, Prince Raif,' she whispered.

As soon as her lids closed, she dropped into the deep well that had been beckoning her for hours. Vivid erotic dreams leapt and danced like the flames in the fire pit and the shooting stars in the desert night, full of heat and purpose, both dazzling and intoxicating.

But the dreams didn't disturb her any more, because with them came the fierce tug of yearning.

CHAPTER FOUR

RAIF JERKED AWAKE, then slammed his eyes shut again as the light from the sun shining into the tent seemed to burn his retinas.

Why was he lying in bed at midday?

But as soon as he shifted, he felt the twinge in his arm, and he knew. The memories assailed him all at once. The deafening sound of the storm, the pop of gunfire, the sharp recoil as a bullet glanced off his flesh. The scent of jasmine and sweat during the endless ride to safety, the long night of exhausted sleep and nightmares, the sound of voices—his father's sneering contempt from many years ago and the pleas of an angel to lie still, to drink, not to drink too fast...

She'd been quite a bossy angel now he thought about it.

Not an angel, a witch. She'd tried to shoot him—the fierce look in her eyes as she'd pointed the pistol at him both arousing and infuriating. A rueful smile edged his mouth, but then he hissed as his dry lips cracked.

He closed his eyes and became one with his body—a process he'd learned as a boy through brutal experience—to assess his injuries.

His arm was a little stiff, but not as stiff as when he'd been kicked by his stallion Zarak a week ago on his first trip back to the tribal lands in over five months.

The gap had been too long since his last return, and the stallion—always high-spirited—had thrown a temper tantrum.

Zarak had missed him, but not as much as he'd missed

Zarak, and the landscape, the culture, the people who had saved him as a child—and turned him into a man.

But this trip had been fraught with surprises. After leaving the desert encampment, in the outskirts of the tribal lands, to spend time alone at his private oasis, to enjoy the challenge of being a man again—instead of a chieftain, or a prince, or a business tycoon—the sandstorm had struck.

He moved his arm, testing its limits. The mild ache that had woken him during the night was gone now. Unlike the more pressing ache in his groin.

A gust of breath raised the hair on his chest and made the pounding in his groin intensify. He blinked, letting his eyes adjust to the light, and turned, to see the vision he had encountered the night before.

It was her. The angel. The witch.

She lay beside him, fast asleep. Her wild hair, tied in a haphazard ponytail, accentuated her exquisite beauty—high cheekbones, kissable lips, and those large eyes, closed now as she lay sleeping.

How old was she? Early twenties? Definitely more a woman than a girl. Bold enough to aim a gun at him.

And where was she from? The dust-stained T-shirt stretched enticingly over her breasts bore the insignia of the same British university Catherine, the Queen of Narabia, had attended. With her colouring, the girl could be a native of this part of the world, but she was dressed like a student in LA or London.

The swell of arousal grew as he examined the toned thighs displayed by her shorts.

The colour in her cheeks heightened and her breathing became irregular. Her eyelids flickered, the rapid eye movements suggesting she was having a vivid dream. Could she sense him observing her?

He had to stifle a smile when she moaned—the sound so

husky it seemed to stroke his erection. Was she dreaming about him? He hoped so, because he had dreamed of her.

She mumbled something in her sleep, shifted and then her small hand, which had been resting on the bedding, reached out to touch his chest. He gritted his teeth as her fingertips slid over his nipple and down his ribs, trailing fire in their wake, and turning his erection to iron, before getting tantalisingly close to the waistband of his pants. Her touch dropped away abruptly as she rolled over—giving him a nice view of her pert bottom.

He wetted his lips, struggling to quell the brutal pulse of unrequited desire and ignore the stab of something else at the loss of her touch.

Disappointment? Regret? Longing?

He remembered the same feeling from the night before when he'd had the recurring nightmare, and he'd clung to her compassion. Which was not like him. He didn't need tenderness from anyone.

He'd been alone all his life, had been shot at many times and had survived much worse than a sandstorm. He had made it his mission never to rely on the kindness of others. If his life had taught him one thing—both as a boy in the desert and as a man in the boardrooms of Manhattan—it was that no one could be trusted. That life was brutal and survival was all that counted. That weakness would destroy you.

Dragging his gaze away from the girl's perfectly rounded backside, he sat up. Taking a deep breath, he got a lungful of his own scent.

Damn, he smelt worse than Zarak after a day-long ride. His stomach growled so loudly he was surprised he didn't wake the girl. He must eat and wash. And tend to Zarak, and the goat and the pack pony. He could decide what to do with the woman later. If she came from the Golden Palace, the seat of his brother Zane's power in the neighbouring kingdom of Narabia, he supposed he would have to return her at some point.

He tugged off the blanket covering his lap, then risked another rueful smile at the evidence of his arousal.

He'd been forced to rescue the woman when he'd spotted her stranded by her Jeep. But maybe having her here didn't have to be bad. These few days alone were supposed to be an escape from the burden of leadership, a chance to reconnect with the basics of his life before he had become Kholadi Chief well over a decade ago at the age of seventeen.

His role as Chief had become a great deal more complex and challenging five years ago, when the decision to mine the huge deposits of minerals had given his people vast riches. Riches that had to be managed and invested to give his tribe a more settled, secure existence. It had been his mission to use the wealth to alleviate the hardships of life in the desert and give the tribe's younger generation choices he had lacked. But dragging the Kholadi into the twenty-first century, while protecting the traditions that had shaped their lives for generations, was a juggling act, which had only become more difficult as his life abroad had dragged him away from the homeland that had defined and sustained him.

What better way to relax and escape those burdens than to lose himself in a woman, if she were willing? How long was it since he'd had the chance to enjoy such soft fragrant flesh, to explore the pleasures of an angel? Or a witch?

He rose to his feet, and made his way out of the tent. As he breathed in the dry desert air, and the sun burnished his skin, his usual vitality returned.

Once he had washed and eaten, he would wake the girl. And see if she was as open as he was to some harmless fun before he returned her to the palace.

* * *

Kasia woke slowly, then shot up so fast she had to breathe through the dizziness.

Where was the Prince?

The bed beside her was empty. Bright sunlight shone through the open flaps of the enormous tent.

She scrambled out of the bedding and raced to the entrance. Had he left her here? Gone for a stroll? How long had she slept?

Guilt assailed her all over again as she recalled bandaging the cut on his arm, listening to the rambling cries of his nightmare, and paying far too much attention to the impressive ridge in his pants.

She shielded her eyes against the bright sunlight, blinking furiously as she headed to the corral to search for her rescuer.

The stallion's head lifted and it whinnied, before returning its muzzle to the trough full of fresh water. At least he hadn't ridden away in disgust.

The sound of the spring water tumbling over the red rocks of the oasis beckoned. After giving the stallion's nose a pat, she edged through the grove of palm trees towards the blue pool created in the rock crevice.

She spotted the bandage first, lying unravelled on the ground, the flecks of dried blood making her stomach hurt. Then the black pants, hooked over a desert shrub. Standing at the edge of the trees, her bare feet sinking into the wet sand by the water's edge, she scanned the pool.

Heat raged to every one of her erogenous zones as she spotted her patient, standing under the waterfall.

Her nipples tightened, and her thighs weakened, the moisture pooling in her pants like the water gushing from the rock face.

Wow!

Thigh deep in water and with his back to her, Prince

Raif was every teenage fantasy she'd ever had made flesh. All strong lines and hard contours, the serpent tattoo coiling over his shoulder, the bruising from the cut on his arm just one of the many scars marring the smooth brown skin. Her gaze dropped to the tight orbs of his backside, which flexed as he scrubbed the water through thick dark hair.

Goodness, he was even more magnificent naked than he had been in full ceremonial wear at Zane and Cat's wedding.

Kasia stood transfixed, knowing she should move, to leave him to bathe in peace. Hadn't she already caused him enough trouble?

But instead she watched him, absorbing the beauty of his hard male body. She'd never seen a naked man before. Not one in the full prime of manhood. She'd been asked on dates during her years in Cambridge, but had always shied away from making any kind of commitment outside her studies. She hadn't partied much because she'd wanted to return to Narabia with an education that would make her an asset to Narabia's ongoing struggle to become self-sufficient.

Cat and Zane had invested a fortune in her education. Cat had always insisted the money was not important, that Kasia had earned the opportunity after her years at the palace. But she wanted to be worthy of that investment. She was the first native Narabian woman to get such an opportunity. And she intended to be the first of many. Her studiousness had never felt a burden, though, until this moment.

She had no experience of what to do with a physical attraction so intense it scared her a little.

She'd always been curious about sex and excited to explore it—when the time was right. But as she watched the Prince's butt muscles bunch and flex as he bent to scoop more water over his head, her breath clogged in her lungs and she wondered if it was possible to be too aroused. Too excited. Because the tightness in her nipples, the looseness in her thighs, and the gush of longing in her panties was becoming painful. And her heartbeat was so frantic she was concerned she might pass out.

She breathed, trying to ease the sensations besieging her body, but then the Prince turned and began to wade towards her.

Her gaze devoured his full-frontal male glory.

Oh, my...

Her thundering heartbeat crashed into her throat.

His chest was as broad and heavily muscled as it had appeared last night, but now his skin glowed with health and vitality. He had his head bent, to watch his step as he strode over the rocks in the pool, giving her precious seconds to absorb every inch of him unobserved.

And there were a lot of inches.

He had to be at least a foot taller than her. But as her thirsty gaze drank in the sight of mile-wide shoulders and the washboard ridges of his abdominal muscles, it was drawn downwards.

Even no longer erect, his penis did not disappoint, completing the mesmerising picture of strong, sensual masculinity.

She blinked, suddenly aware he was no longer moving.

She jerked her gaze to his face. Flaming heat blasted across her chest, flooded up her neck and exploded in her cheeks.

'Good afternoon, little witch,' he said, in perfect English—his deep chocolate gaze sparkling with mocking humour. 'Are you assessing the damage?'

'I...' The word came out on a squeak. She swallowed, folding her arms over her chest to control the ache in her nipples. It didn't help.

'I'm so sorry I shot you, Prince Raif.'

And I've just invaded your privacy by ogling you naked while you bathe.

She kept the last part of her apology to herself. He didn't seem bothered that she was seeing him naked. Arrogance and confidence issued from every perfect pore.

'Prince...*who*?' His lips quirked. Even with the beard covering the lower half of his face, the half-smile was devastating. '*What* did you call me?'

'Prince Raif,' she said, confused. Had she addressed him incorrectly? Wasn't that what he'd told her to call him?

From his amusement it was obvious she'd misunderstood. Perhaps she was supposed to kneel? As she once had before Zane, because he was a sheikh?

But as the man before her strolled the rest of the way out of the pool and stopped in front of her, she resisted the urge to drop to her knees.

He didn't seem particularly outraged by the breach of etiquette. And, anyway, if she knelt down she would be at eye level with his... She jerked her chin up.

Do not stare at his junk again. Haven't you been disrespectful enough already?

'Just Raif,' he corrected her. 'I am not a prince in Kholadi, only Chief.'

There was no *only* about it, she decided as he reached past her, his pectoral muscles rippling as he snagged the black pants off the shrub where he'd dumped them.

She inhaled the aroma of desert thyme alongside the salty aroma of his skin, gilded now by the sheen of fresh water instead of sweat. He used the cotton to mop the moisture drying on his magnificent chest and swept it through his hair, before finally putting the pants back on.

Her breath released, the muscles of her neck finally allowed to relax as he drew the loose pants up to his waist.

'My brother insisted on giving me the title of Prince Kasim when we reached an accord ten years ago,' he said, bending his head to tie the drawstring. 'But it means nothing in the desert.'

The comment sounded casual, but she detected the edge in his voice.

She knew the Kholadi and the Narabian kingdom had been at war for several years, before the old Sheikh, Tariq, had been incapacitated by a stroke. As soon as Zane had taken control of the throne, he had negotiated a truce with his half-brother and the two countries had lived in harmony ever since.

But it seemed their fraternal relationship wasn't entirely comfortable. Her heart stalled as she thought of the scars all over his body, and the nightmares that had chased him the night before. Like everyone else, she'd heard the stories of how he had been kicked out of the palace as a boy to make way for his legitimate brother, and left to die in the desert.

She had no idea how much of the myth was true. And she'd never given a lot of thought to the devastating effect a trauma like that might have, because the legend of Prince Kasim's survival and battles to lead the Kholadi had been just that, a legend. A fairy-tale. A myth.

But the myth now seemed as real and raw as this man's scars. Of course, his relationship with his brother would be strained, after being rejected so cruelly by their father.

He might seem strong and invincible, but he could be hurt, just like anyone else.

The wave of compassion washed over her as she took in the torn flesh on his upper arm from the injury she'd caused.

'I should re-bandage your arm,' she said, the guilt choking her. But as she went to touch him, his hand shot out and he grabbed her wrist.

'There is no need,' he said.

'But what if it starts to bleed again?' she said, tears of shame stinging her eyes.

Could he feel her pulse pummelling her wrist in staccato

punches? Did he know how aroused she was? Even though he was hurt? And she was the one responsible?

The half-smile returned and spread across his impossibly handsome features, and her pulse sped into overdrive.

He knows.

'It is barely a scratch,' he said, releasing her. 'I have survived much worse.'

'Not from me,' she said, appalled at the thought of all the other scars on his body. Was injury a regular occurrence for him? 'I feel awful that I shot you.'

'You did not shoot me, you missed. And you were scared. You were defending yourself. It is a natural reaction.'

'No, it's not,' she said. 'I've never shot at *anyone* before.' He appeared unmoved.

Because he must live in another world. A harsh, cruel world where people shoot first and ask questions later.

'Would you let me check the wound at least, Prince Kasim?' she said, trying to maintain at least a semblance of decorum. Although decorum was the last thing she felt. 'It would make me feel better.'

He stroked a thumb down the side of her face. 'You can check the wound if you wish, but only if you agree to call me Raif.' His hand dropped away, leaving a trail of goosebumps ricocheting down to her core. 'Given how much of me you have already seen, there is little point in standing on ceremony.'

She shook her head, mesmerised by the husky tenor of his voice and the effect it was having on her.

It was only five minutes later, as he sat on the edge of his bed and she knelt beside him to bandage the wound again, that she realised her error.

Because the memory of his body, wet and naked, only made being with him in his bedchamber, inhaling the intoxicating scent of man and desert, all the more overwhelming.

So much so, she wasn't even sure this was reality any more, because it felt like all her teenage fantasies come to vibrant, vivid life.

'What is your name?' Raif asked, needing a distraction as the girl's fingertips brushed his biceps while she wound the new—and entirely unnecessary—bandage around his arm.

She'd been tending him for two minutes—and controlling the surge of heat to his groin each time she touched him had become excruciating.

Did she know the effect she was having on him? Surely she must.

'Kasia. Kasia Salah,' she said, concentrating on the bandaging. But he noted the bloom of colour darkening her cheeks.

'You are Narabian?' Why did that seem important? He'd slept with women of many different nationalities. He didn't judge women by their geography but by how much he wanted them. And he wanted this woman, very much.

'Yes, I was brought up in the Golden Palace. My grandmother worked there as a cook. I was one of the domestic staff.'

Something unlocked inside his chest. So she was of humble birth. Not unlike him.

'Until I became Cat's assistant,' she added, the hint of pride unmistakeable.

'Cat? Who is Cat?'

'Catherine Smith, who is now Queen Catherine Ali Nawari Khan—you know, the Sheikh's wife,' she said, her chest puffing up. 'She is my best friend. It is because of her I have spent the last five years studying abroad.'

'Not because of yourself?' he asked, annoyed by her willingness to give someone else the credit for her achievements.

Zane's wife was beautiful and accomplished. But no

more so than this woman. The only difference was that Catherine Khan hadn't had to fight for her education, the way he would guess Kasia had.

The girl's gaze flashed to his—direct and irritated at his observation.

The heat in his groin surged. Her golden gaze sparkled enticingly when it wasn't shadowed with guilt or shame.

'Well, yes,' she said. 'But… Cat is the reason I sought an education. And she and Zane…' She sank back on her heels, finally having finished caressing his biceps. 'They made it possible for me to study abroad in a place called Cambridge University.'

A place called Cambridge University!

Did she think he had never heard of the British institution? What did she take him for? A savage?

His pride bristled—but he bit down on the urge to correct her.

She had been away from her homeland for five years, meaning all she would know of him was that he was the Sheikh's bastard son—a primitive warlord, an unprincipled womaniser.

The rumours had some truth behind them, especially when he'd been a younger man, and he'd been more than happy to foster them because they had always given him a power and mystique he could use to his advantage—in politics, in business and in his bed.

Being the Bad-Boy Sheikh had been an advantage with women, because they loved the allure of the forbidden, the wild.

Why not exploit Kasia's misconceptions about him? He had never been ashamed of that unloved child, who had been strong enough to survive thirst and starvation in the desert, or the angry teenager who had been savage enough to defeat the Kholadi's greatest warriors and become Chief. His past still lived inside him—and defined him in many ways. It always would. Wasn't it to reconnect with those parts of himself that he had returned to the desert?

Adrenaline raced through his bloodstream. This woman had seen him helpless, something that had made him uneasy. But being the womanising warlord would put the power back in his hands.

She took a tube of antiseptic cream out of the medical box. 'I noticed some scrapes on your back, where you fell off the horse,' she said as she unscrewed the cap. 'Turn around and I'll dab some of this on them.' She held up a finger covered in ointment. 'Before they get infected.'

'Enough.' Raif captured her wrist, satisfied when he felt her pulse pummel his thumb.

'But I should treat the scratches,' she said.

'It's not my back that hurts.' He interrupted her nonsense.

Taking the hint, her gaze dipped to his lap. The blood pounded into his groin. He was as aroused now as he'd been during the depths of his nightmares.

She lifted her head.

Her pupils dilated, obliterating the rich amber of her irises. She was as aroused as him.

'I… I see what you mean,' she stuttered, desire colouring her skin.

'We have had enough foreplay,' he said.

He preferred to be open and honest with women about his appetites. When it came to sex, he never played games.

'If you want me as much as I want you, we can take this ache away.' He touched her cheek, not able to keep his hands off any longer, the heat rising at the way her breath hitched. 'If you don't, I will escort you back to the palace.' He let his hand drop. He wasn't usually so abrupt with women, but something about her made it hard for him to be subtle about his needs. 'What is your choice?'

CHAPTER FIVE

I CHOOSE YOU.

'I... I...' Kasia stuttered, the heat in her cheeks nothing compared to the liquid tug in her sex.

Prince Kasim's bold offer seemed to be genuine. With no ands, ifs or buts, just like the man himself.

The tug turned into a yank.

Not Prince Kasim... Raif. She corrected herself. Because he was the furthest thing from a prince at the moment. Even a desert prince.

He had no airs or graces, no polite manners, no etiquette. His desire was basic and unashamed, and so much more compelling because of that. His need was arrogantly displayed by the tension in his jaw, the direct gaze and the thick erection.

'I don't know what to say,' she blurted out. Disconcerted by her own driving need.

She'd flirted with men before, even kissed a few. But she'd never been subjected to such a focused assault on her senses by a man like him—who was so bold and unambiguous.

Why did that seem refreshing, and yet disturbing?

'It is a simple question, Kasia.'

Was it simple? Maybe it was to him. Because he had so much more experience. But she could hardly tell him she had never slept with a man before. It felt too revealing.

His lips quirked beneath the beard. 'Let me make it

simpler. Do you want me, Kasia? For I dreamed of having you last night.'

The raw declaration tugged at her romantic heart.

He cupped her cheek, and her breath seized, the rasp of his callused skin sending heat spiralling into her tender sex.

His thumb traced her cheekbone, then slid down her neck into the well of her collarbone. The rabbit punches of her pulse echoed in the sweet spot between her thighs.

'I want to make you sob with pleasure.' His thumb circled her breast through her T-shirt and bra. 'To make your nipples ripen and swell beneath my tongue.'

Her nipples squeezed into peaks, as if already being subjected to the promised caress. She panted, unable to catch her breath under his intense gaze.

He chuckled, the sound arrogant, and so unbelievably hot she felt burned.

'Tell me you want me, Kasia, and we can feed this hunger.'

'Yes.' The word popped out before she could stop it. 'I want you.'

Surely this didn't have to be wrong? They'd survived a sandstorm. They were young and alive. Their worlds might be miles apart, but here and now she wanted to feed the hunger, too. A hunger that had tantalised her all through the night.

She would return to the palace today. Cat and Zane would be frantic with worry—she'd been lost for over twenty-four hours already. She would go back to Cambridge at the end of the month. She had no intention of venturing into the desert alone after this, so she would be unlikely to see him again.

Why couldn't she have this moment? When she wanted him so much? And what better person to initiate her than a man she had idolised? A man who was supposed to be an incredible lover? A man whose 'assets' she'd been assessing most of the night?

He nodded, accepting her surrender as if he had expected no less. Then he grunted something in his own dialect.

She didn't need a translation, though, when his nostrils flared, his gaze becoming so focused her flesh felt scalded.

Standing, he tugged her to her feet. Framing her face in his hands, he positioned her head, then licked the seam of her lips. She opened for him instinctively. The kiss was firm, coaxing. The hunger roared from her core. She had expected him to devour her, but his tongue danced with hers, allowing her to follow his lead in subtle licks.

But as the hunger built, the driving need became more urgent, and the kiss changed, his tongue exploring her mouth and capturing her sighs as he demanded more.

His hands skimmed up her back underneath her T-shirt. The hook of her bra was released. She gripped his shoulders, overwhelmed by sensation as he cupped her breasts, playing with the responsive nipples until she was sobbing into his mouth, the tight peaks yearning for more.

He lifted his head, his eyes dark and unfocused. 'I want you naked, Kasia.'

The gruff request shimmered across her skin, and the ache in her breasts intensified, the hot spot between her thighs throbbing.

She nodded, no longer capable of coherent speech.

Stepping back, he lifted the grubby T-shirt over her head, disposed of the bra.

She folded her arms over her chest, desperately self-conscious.

'No,' he said as he captured her wrists. 'Do not hide, you are so beautiful.'

She felt beautiful as she forced herself to relax, to let him pull her arms gently away from her body. The morning sunlight gilded his chest, making her aware of the bunch of muscle.

The huge erection stood proud under the loose cotton pants and her mouth watered as she imagined seeing him naked and fully erect. But to her surprise, he sank to his knees in front of her. Undoing the buttons on her shorts, he watched her as he drew the denim down with her panties. His rough hands slid down her legs, stripping her bare with exquisite tenderness.

She stepped out of her shorts at his direction, the need charging through her system as he blew across the triangle of curls, then pressed his face into her sex.

She gripped his shoulders—so broad, so solid—to steady herself as he opened her with his thumbs and licked.

She shuddered, her ragged panting filling the tent as he lapped at the very heart of her. He held her firmly for the shattering exploration. Licking, sucking, discovering the root of her pleasure and ruthlessly exploiting it.

At last he captured the swollen nub of her clitoris and suckled.

The climax broke over her, the waves battering her body. She collapsed over his shoulder, the afterglow like an impenetrable cloud of bliss.

'More,' he grunted, as he stood, lifting her.

Within seconds, she lay on the bed as he stood over her, blocking out the sunlight. He shucked his pants.

Her gaze devoured his nakedness, her tender sex melting at the sight of that massive erection—even larger and harder than she had imagined.

'I need to be inside you,' he said, as he covered her body with his.

'Yes,' she croaked.

She wanted that thick length inside her. Wanted to recapture the glorious oblivion.

Hooking her leg around his waist, to leave her open to him, he angled her hips.

The pinch of pain made her stiffen as he thrust deep. She choked off a cry, struggling to absorb the overwhelming feel of him, lodged so fully inside her.

He swore, every sinew of his body going deadly still. She couldn't read his features, cast into shadow by the dazzling sunlight, but she could feel his shock.

'You were untouched?' he said, the question coming out on a tortured rasp.

'I'm sorry,' she said. 'I should have told you.'

'Yes, but it is too late now,' he said.

She didn't know what he meant. Was he angry with her? But he didn't sound angry, just stunned.

He touched her cheek, cradled her face.

'Am I hurting you?'

It did hurt a little, he was so large and hard inside her. But she didn't want to lose the connection.

'No,' she said. 'I want to feel the pleasure again.'

He buried his face into her neck, pressed his lips to the sensitive skin under her ear, and circled her breast with his thumb. Teasing, tempting, until the tendrils of sensation returned.

'You must tell me if it hurts,' he said as he grasped her hips, anchoring her to him.

The arrows of sensation darted into her sex, devastating and demanding, echoing the same relentless rhythm as he drew out and sank back.

He rocked his hips, further, faster, nudging a place deep inside her, triggering a new tsunami of sensation.

Kasia sobbed. The storm was so much stronger and wilder this time, whipping at her skin, making every pulse point ache.

The pleasure overpowered her, battering her body and making her heart swell. She clung to him, the only solid object in the storm—just like before, her staggered mind cried, when he had cocooned her as the sandstorm had raged.

She screamed as he drove her over that final ledge and she plunged into the abyss, exquisite joy bursting everywhere.

She heard him shout as he collapsed on top of her, and his seed spurted into her womb.

CHAPTER SIX

WHAT HAVE YOU DONE?

Raif struggled to control the vicious punch of his heart-beat, and forced his fingers to release their death grip on Kasia's hips.

Shame and horror galloped on the heels of groggy afterglow as he withdrew from the tight clasp of her body and she flinched.

He had climaxed inside her, he had not intended to do so. But even as he grasped the humiliation of that, far worse was the knowledge that as soon as he had plunged into her to the hilt, and destroyed her virgin state, he had bound them both to a solemn covenant they could not break.

Why hadn't he taken the precautions he always took, to research a woman's background, to ask her the questions that would protect them both?

Because he had been desperate to have her, to claim her, something had been driving him as soon as he had stepped from the water this morning and seen her watching him, her eyes dazed with arousal. Maybe even before that. Had it been driving him as soon as he had spotted her, standing by her Jeep, her amber eyes sparkling with fear and defiance? Or as he had clawed his way back from the nightmare, coaxed by her soft voice and soothing fingers?

However, the beast had been awakened, and the destruction it had wrought—on his life, on hers—could not be undone.

Where he would have expected panic or even resentment, all he felt now was numb and strangely ambivalent about the inevitable repercussions.

Lying on his back, he stared at the ceiling of the tent, the rich fabrics, the dappled sunlight. Everything looked as it had when he had woken an hour ago, but now his whole life, and hers, would be different.

He had played with fate too many times before, he had known the risks always, had been so careful to guard against them, but with Kasia it had never even entered his head. Was that significant? Was there some comfort in knowing their fates had already been sealed?

'Is everything okay?'

He turned to find her watching him, her hands clasped against her breasts, the rings on her fingers glinting.

The surge of renewed yearning was unmistakeable even as his mind reeled with the implications of what had just transpired. He examined her artless expression, looking for signs of duplicity.

Had she planned this? To trap a prince? The broken-down Jeep, the gunshot, the long night as she'd helped him through the nightmare and then come to him at the waterside?

It seemed unlikely but plausible, until he remembered the storm.

No, she could not have planned that. Perhaps she had simply seen an opportunity and acted on it. Bitterness rose in his throat, but he swallowed it. Whatever her plots and schemes to get them here, he must take the lion's share of the blame. He was in charge of his own libido.

He was the one who had chosen to seduce her without knowing enough about her. And had lost control so spectacularly—as soon as he had pressed his face into the sweet seam of her sex and tasted her arousal.

Whatever her reasons, her motives, whichever one of

them was to blame, the consequences were stark and inescapable.

Shifting onto his side, he placed a hand on her cheek and hooked the riot of midnight hair behind her ear.

'I should not have taken you without protection,' he said, feeling humiliated all over again about his loss of control. 'There is no excuse. But a pregnancy hardly matters. Now we are to be wed.'

Her eyes popped wide. She scrambled into a sitting position, her brows shooting up her forehead.

'What?' she said, her tone raw with shock.

Interesting. Either she was the greatest actress he had ever seen, or she had not planned to trick him into marriage.

He took some solace from that. He had not been the only one to lose their head in the intense heat of their lovemaking.

He propped his head on his hand and studied her, convinced her shock was entirely genuine. And actually quite beguiling.

A delicious blush darkened her skin. She was exquisite. Perhaps this marriage would not be such a hardship.

'You were a virgin, Kasia,' he said, because she looked as if she was waiting for an explanation. Although he did not know why. However long she had been out of the kingdom, surely she must know of the sacred marriage laws of the Sheikhs, being Narabian. 'Even though I am a bastard, the blood of the royal house of Nawari flows in my veins,' he prompted, but still she looked clueless. 'So we must now be married.'

'But I can't marry you. I don't even know you. There won't be a baby, I'm right at the beginning of my cycle.'

He frowned. Okay, she looked more than shocked now, she looked panicked.

'A pregnancy is not the reason. Honour dictates it,' he continued, his throat closing on that one crucial word.

Honour. The one thing his father hadn't been able to steal from him. His honour had sustained him, through the loneliness, the pain, the starvation, the thirst, and the many other humiliations of being a boy without a people. Honour had ensured his survival. Had driven him to fight and fight until he had eventually triumphed. Not just finding a people, but becoming their Chief.

His honour meant everything to him and he could not compromise it. Not for anything. Or anyone. Not even himself.

'I have taken your maidenhead,' he added. 'To maintain my honour, I must make you my wife and my consort.'

'But that's…' Kasia pulled in a few precious breaths, trying to stop herself from hyperventilating, not easy when she was edging towards hysteria. 'You can't be serious.'

Raif stared at her, his frown only making him more handsome. But she was so over the ripples of awareness making her sex throb.

'I am absolutely serious,' he said. 'We have no choice now.'

'Don't be ridiculous. There's always a choice.'

'Kasia.' He pressed his palm to her cheek, making the traitorous ripples worse. 'You must calm down…you are breathing too fast.'

She jerked her head back. She couldn't do this. She couldn't have a sensible conversation with him, especially not when he was looking at her with that pragmatic intensity.

She'd heard of the Law of Marriage of the Sheikhs. The ancient, archaic law was written into the country's scrolls. Scrolls she had studied along with Cat, once upon a time. She had once whispered about the old law furtively with her school friends. How it was a dream come true, a way for nobodies like them to become queens.

But it wasn't a dream any more, it was a nightmare.

The old law hadn't even occurred to her when she'd neglected to mention her virginity to Raif. Because she'd been far too caught up in the moment to think about anything. Not even contraception!

Standing up, she grabbed her T-shirt and tugged it on. She couldn't stay here and have this conversation. It took a while for her to find the armholes because she was shaking so hard.

Why hadn't she given a lot more thought to the repercussions of sleeping with Raif? He was clearly autocratic and arrogant. But what had been so exciting and seductive before she'd slept with him seemed fraught with disaster now.

She didn't want to be married to a stranger. She was supposed to be returning to Cambridge. This trip was to do preliminary research for a PhD in the eco-systems of the Narabian desert she was hoping to get funding for.

The intimacy of what they had shared would be tarnished for ever by his callous demand that she succumb to his will. And for what? To maintain *his* honour? What about hers? She was a person, an individual, with her own free will. He couldn't ride roughshod over her future, her choices, because she'd been too caught up in the moment to warn him of her virginity.

She'd always promised herself that when she married, *if* she married, she would marry for love. She wanted the kind of fairy-tale romance Cat and Zane shared. She would never marry for duty or honour. And especially not to a man who didn't seem to know the difference between honour and duty and love.

She tugged on her shorts, suddenly desperate to escape the stifling tent, and the scene of her downfall, the lingering scent of sex only emphasising her stupidity.

If you slept with a man you didn't know, what the heck did you expect?

That had been her mistake. Not just trusting him, but trusting her own judgement. Because there was an element of what she'd done that made her remember her mother. The woman she hadn't seen since she was a girl.

'I can't be your mother any more, Kasia. Your grand-mother will take good care of you.'

Her mother had abandoned her—because she could no longer bear the shame of having a child out of wedlock. Of being ostracised, vilified, damned for her pregnancy when she was alone. But Kasia had paid a far greater price, forced to grow up without her mother and battle for years the insecurities her absence had wrought—and all because of customs that punished people for loving in the wrong place, at the wrong time.

She did up the buttons of her shorts with clumsy fingers.

But as she went to leave the tent, he grasped her elbow. 'Where are you going?' he demanded.

'I need some air, and some time to think. And to wash.'

He'd put on his pants, thank goodness, but even so desire echoed in her sex as her gaze connected with his broad chest. She could see the red marks etched into the tattoo covering his shoulder where she had held him in the throes of passion.

What had she been thinking? Giving herself to him, without a thought to any of the consequences?

'Kasia, you must not panic,' he said. 'This is frightening, I understand that. It is not a choice I would have made either,' he added, and she heard it then, the brittle note of judgement. Of accusation. Because she had been the one to keep her virginity a secret. 'But we are bound now.'

She could hear the steely determination in his voice.

But this was madness.

Why should they honour a code that had been set down hundreds of years before they were even born?

'I need to be alone for a bit,' she said. 'To consider all this. It's a lot to take in.'

He let his hand drop. Then he nodded. 'Okay, go to the pond and bathe, I will pack up here. We must travel to the Golden Palace before nightfall. Speak to your relatives.'

What? Panic clawed at her throat. 'But I don't have any relatives. Not since my grandmother died. Maybe if we just don't tell anyone about…'

'We cannot lie, that would be an even greater breach of honour,' he interrupted her, his frown deepening. 'If you have no relatives, then I will make the request for your hand to my brother. He is your employer, yes?'

He was moving too fast. She didn't want Zane and Cat to know what she'd done. She certainly didn't want to put them in the middle of this situation. They would, of course, support her decision. They weren't barbarians like Raif. But from the few times Prince Kasim had mentioned his half-brother it was obvious their relationship was problematic at best, and probably delicately balanced politically.

Good grief, her stupidity could start a new war.

The panic started to consume her.

Breathe—just breathe. And don't add any more drama than you absolutely have to.

She forced her lungs to function. Struggled to think. 'How far are we from the palace?' she asked, as a plan began to form in her head.

'A day's ride, to the north,' he said.

Oh, thank goodness.

'Okay,' she said as a strange calmness descended. 'I won't be too long.'

He grasped her arm. 'Do not despair, Kasia,' he said, his voice strained.

Her heart beat heavily against her ribs.

'We will find a way to make this work,' he said.

She nodded. Because she couldn't bring herself to speak.

Arguing with him was pointless. And she'd never been very good at disguising her feelings. If he knew how frantic she was, and how determined not to go through with this madness, he might not let her leave. But as she left, she couldn't resist glancing over her shoulder.

He stood, tall and proud and indomitable, trusting her to return.

She couldn't help hating herself a little as she headed towards the oasis, then doubled back through the trees. She didn't take any time to saddle his horse, simply used the corral's railings to mount the huge beast.

She hadn't ridden a horse for five years. But she had been an accomplished rider, as happy riding bareback as with a saddle. She prayed the ability hadn't left her as she kicked her bare heels into the horse's flanks. It snorted and reared, but she clung to its mane, her thigh muscles straining, the tenderness in her sex rubbing against the ridge of its spine.

She heard a shout and saw Raif run out of the tent, his face a mask of surprise and then fury as his stallion cleared the fence in one bound.

She dug her heels into the horse's sides, bent her head low over its neck and allowed the beast to have its head, managing to direct it towards the north as it flew over the rocks and towards the dunes.

Tears blurred her eyes, but she didn't look back this time. She couldn't.

CHAPTER SEVEN

'KASIA, IF SOMETHING happened to you, however traumatic, you know you can tell me, right?'

Kasia stopped folding her recently unpacked clothes back into her suitcase. Her best friend, Catherine Ali Nawari Khan, stood with her back pressed against the door of Kasia's chamber, her face a picture of concern and distress.

Kasia nodded, determined to keep her voice calm and even. Or as calm and even as she could while the shame threatening to choke her since she'd arrived back at the palace an hour ago—heck, the shame that had been choking her since she'd galloped over the dunes and away from Raif's encampment—expanded another few centimetres.

'I just... I need to return to Cambridge.' It was cowardly, but it was the decision she'd made as she'd ridden Raif's horse.

She'd made a terrible mistake, not just sleeping with Raif but not telling him about her virginity. She'd put them both in an impossible situation—a situation that could have constitutional implications for both countries if Raif continued his quest to marry her—and the only way to remedy the problem was to leave. And leave quickly, before he followed her to the palace.

She'd had a lucky break, spotting the column of SUVs that had been sent out to search for her only an hour after leaving his encampment. They'd driven her straight back to the palace, where Cat and Zane had been waiting. There had been hugs and kisses, tears of joy and relief, but then had come the questions. What had happened to her? How had she survived after her vehicle had been buried? Was she okay now? Did she need a doctor?

She'd devised a deliberately vague story. She'd been rescued by a tribesman who had taken her to his encampment and then loaned her his horse to return to the palace once the sandstorm had settled. But as soon as Zane had suggested they contact the man and thank him for his help, she had known her story wouldn't stand up to scrutiny for long. Not least because she suspected Zane knew she wasn't telling the whole truth. As soon as he'd tried to probe into the facts—why hadn't the man given her a saddle, where were her shoes, where did they return the horse as it was clearly a valuable thoroughbred—Cat had intervened, insisting Kasia be given time to bathe and eat and recover from her ordeal. But she'd known it was only a matter of time before Cat's concern got the better of her.

Tears welled in her eyes. And Cat rushed across the chamber.

'Kasia—oh, my God. I knew something was wrong.' Gathering Kasia in her arms, she pressed a kiss to her forehead. 'Did the man who rescued you assault you, is that it? Whatever happened, it's not your fault, okay? You don't have to leave. We'll figure this out.'

Kasia shook her head, scrubbing away the tears of self-pity. She didn't deserve Cat's concern, didn't deserve her friend's comfort. And she was going to have to explain herself. Admit the humiliating mistakes she'd made while at the same time protecting everyone—Raif included—from the consequences.

'It's not that, he didn't assault me. In fact, it was the other way around. I actually... I shot him.'

Cat's eyebrows rose, but her gaze remained supportive and direct. 'Is he dead?' she asked flatly.

'Goodness, no. He's okay, it was only a flesh wound.'

'All right,' Cat said. 'Well, that's good, I guess,' she added as if she weren't sure.

A raw chuckle burst out of Kasia's throat. 'How can it be good?' she said. 'I still shot him.'

'So what? If he was assaulting you, he got what he deserved,' Cat said, with complete pragmatism. And Kasia felt the tears scour her throat again.

'But he wasn't assaulting me,' she managed through the emotion thickening her throat. 'He was rescuing me from the sandstorm.'

'And you both survived, so it's all good,' Cat countered, gripping Kasia's arms. 'But something else happened, right? Something that's made you think you have to leave. And that's not—'

'I slept with him and now he's insisting we get married because I was a virgin.' The words burst out of Kasia's mouth in a flood, silencing Cat.

Her friend's eyebrows rose again. 'Okay,' she said. Her eyes narrowed as she stroked Kasia's arms in a gesture of solidarity Kasia wasn't sure she deserved.

'He definitely didn't coerce you into sleeping with him?' she asked.

'No, no, he didn't.'

If only he had, she might be able to let herself off the hook. But how could she, when she had been fully compliant, he'd given her a clear choice and she'd taken it. Heck, she hadn't just taken it, she'd jumped at it. 'It was absolutely, one hundred percent consensual.'

'Are you sure, Kaz?' Cat said gently. 'If he was your first, sometimes the issue of consent can be more complex.'

'Not this time. I wanted it to happen, very much,' she murmured in the interests of full disclosure, the humiliating truth making her cheeks burn. 'We'd spent the night together. He was exhausted and then he had this terrible nightmare… It was intimate and I totally objectified him. Because…' The flush climbed up to her hairline. 'He's really, really hot. And when we did it, I enjoyed it. A lot. In fact, I had two orgasms. I really couldn't have asked for a better experience for my first time. But afterwards…'

She sat down on the bed, scrubbed her hands over her face, trying to erase the brutal memory of his face, so indomitable, so proud, so unyielding—and yet so trusting. 'He was adamant that his honour means we have to get married.' She clasped her hands together in her lap, remembering the leap of her stupidly romantic heart when he'd suggested it.

For a moment she'd actually considered it. She'd been shocked, yes, but a tiny part of her had been flattered and excited. Because that teenager who had spun romantic dreams about Raif before she'd ever met him had leapt out of hiding. But that adrenaline hit had been quickly followed by the cruel, harsh jolt of reality as soon as he'd begun to talk about honour and duty.

Marrying Prince Kasim, marrying anyone in these circumstances, would be totally wrong. However hot he was, or however many orgasms he could give her. They'd been thrown together by chance and, yes, they had sexual chemistry. But that was all they had. They didn't know each other.

And one of the few things Raif *did* know about her he didn't seem to think was relevant. She had a life plan, a plan that had changed and evolved since she was a little girl trying to justify her mother's abandonment, or that starry-eyed and over-excitable teenager working as a servant in the palace and dreaming of marrying a prince. And that life plan did not include an arranged marriage to a man who thought his honour was more important than her future, or his own.

'He can't force you to marry him,' Cat said, covering

her clasped hands. 'Even if you went to him willingly and didn't tell him you were a virgin. If he follows you here and tries to insist, Zane will have his advisors explain the law to him. You don't even have to see him again if you don't want to. You certainly don't have to go back to England to avoid that confrontation.'

'I know,' she said. She turned her hands over and clutched Cat's.

Now would be the perfect time to tell Cat the whole truth, to reveal that the man she'd slept with was the ruler of the Kholadi and Zane's half-brother. And the reason he was demanding marriage was bound up in his bloodline and his legacy and the responsibilities he had to his position—it wasn't just a generic obsession with Narabia's more traditional and outdated customs.

But she couldn't tell Cat.

Not only was she hopelessly ashamed of her behaviour, she knew if she told Cat, and by extension Zane, they would still back her to the hilt. But it would put them in an impossible position. Especially given Zane's strained relationship with Raif.

She'd screwed up, and the only way she could see to fix it was to leave. If she returned to the UK, Raif wouldn't follow her there. It would let them both off the hook—erasing the problem and releasing him from an obligation he didn't want. He would no longer be bound by the ancient law if the woman he had compromised, or thought he had compromised, was thousands of miles away. Surely even *his* honour wouldn't dictate that he leave the desert, leave his people to venture out into a world he knew nothing about to track down a woman he'd had an ill-advised one-morning stand with?

'I'd rather just go back to the UK,' she said. 'And forget this ever happened.' Not that she ever would be able to forget Raif, she thought miserably, as the swelling in her throat was joined by the hot throb of reaction in her sex.

He was going to be a hard act to follow. But that's what happened when you chose to lose your virginity to the man of your dreams, and he lived up to every single one of them.

'Are you sure?' Cat said, her eyes shadowed with concern.

'Yes, I'm positive. If the man follows me here...' There was always the possibility that Raif wouldn't come to the Golden Palace, but from the furious frown on his face the last time she'd seen him, she wasn't taking that chance. If nothing else, she felt sure he would want to get his beautiful horse back. She ought to have at least a couple of days' grace as he only had the small pack pony to ride and would have to return to the Kholadi encampment first to get a new mount. 'It'll be easier for everyone concerned if you can explain I'm no longer here. I know it's cowardly but I—'

'Stop saying that, Kasia. There's not a cowardly bone in your body. I totally understand if you want to avoid this guy,' she added, patting Kasia's arm. 'I'll help you pack. Then I'll arrange a car to take you to the airport in Kallah—we can book you on the flight out tonight.'

'Thanks.' Kasia smiled at her friend, so pathetically grateful for Cat's stalwart support she had to swallow down another wave of tears. 'Will Zane be okay with that?'

'He'll have questions, I expect,' Cat said. 'But he trusts my judgement and he trusts you, too, Kasia. And no way would he make you face this guy if you don't want to, okay?'

Kasia nodded. 'Thanks.'

Cat smiled. 'At least it's good to know you got two orgasms out of him before he turned into a jerk.'

Kasia forced herself to smile back. 'And they were spectacular ones, to be fair.'

Cat laughed. 'There you go. Spectacular orgasms are never bad.'

But Kasia's heart shrank in her chest as Cat dashed off to make the travel arrangements and left her to finish packing.

Zane trusted Cat's judgement because he adored his queen. Theirs was the kind of relationship Kasia had always hoped to emulate. It was one of the other reasons she had never dated seriously in Cambridge. Because she'd wanted what Zane and Cat had—before she'd been hijacked by her own pheromones.

But it wasn't just her pheromones that were to blame for this disaster.

The bedrock of a relationship like Zane and Cat's was trust and honesty—something Kasia had failed at the very first time she was tested.

Somehow she doubted Zane would trust her once he found out to whom she'd given her virginity so thoughtlessly. In fact, he might well hate her a little if there was any political fallout from this mess. She may well have soured her relationship with the Sheikh—a man she had always admired a great deal and whose respect meant a lot.

But why did it hurt so much more to know the person who would probably hate her most was Raif?

CHAPTER EIGHT

'KASIA SALAH—I need to speak to her. Now.'

Raif controlled the fury that had been building for four days now, and held onto the curse word lodged in his throat as the woman standing at the gate of the Golden Palace's women's quarters trembled visibly but still refused to open the damn gate.

He didn't bully women. But this was intolerable. He'd arrived fifteen minutes ago and he still hadn't been able to locate Kasia.

Following a short ride and a very long walk to the nearest Kholadi encampment, he'd been forced to rest overnight to get his strength back after a bout of vomiting before he'd been able to make the two-day ride to Zafari.

A pain in his right side had developed during the journey. And he'd had to stop several times to recuperate—turning the two-day ride into three. Somehow in the midst of this titanic mess he'd managed to pick up a very persistent stomach bug as well.

He probably should have waited until he had completely recovered from it before making the journey. But the urge to find Kasia and confront her had been stronger than his common sense.

She'd run out on him. Stolen his horse. And all after promising to consider his proposal of marriage. He should have expected it. No one was ever as guileless as they appeared. He should never have trusted her.

'I'm sorry, Prince Kasim, but she is not here,' the girl said.

'Then where the hell is she?' The shout rang out as his smouldering temper burst into flames and the aching pain ground in his gut. The girl cowered.

'Kasim, I've only just been informed of your arrival. We hadn't expected you.'

Raif swung round to see his brother striding across the courtyard towards him, followed by two of his advisors.

Terrific. Just what I need—a political delegation to slow this process down even more.

His brother clasped his hand, giving him a jolt that seemed to knife into his gut. Raif struggled not to flinch.

'It's good to see you, as always, brother.' While Zane's smile was tight—he was probably wondering what Raif had been doing at the gates of the women's quarters, shouting at one of his staff—it looked genuine, which only annoyed Raif more.

He was far too irritable and out of sorts right now to make the effort to pretend a brotherly bonhomie he didn't feel.

He respected his half-brother, had been forced to acknowledge over the last ten years that Zane was a good Sheikh. But they were hardly friends. Even if Zane could overlook the difference in their upbringing—as the legitimate, wanted son of the old Sheikh and the son he had never acknowledged—Raif could not.

For some reason, Zane always acted as if their tainted past didn't exist, often going to extraordinary lengths to deny the strained nature of their sibling relationship.

The only time Raif had managed to get a rise out of Zane had been five years ago when Zane had arrived at the Kholadi camp with the academic he had hired to write a book about the kingdom. Raif had sensed the attraction between Zane and Catherine Smith and had decided to have some fun at his brother's expense, mercilessly flirting with the young woman during their evening meal and then assigning her the same tent as Zane, even though Zane had insisted they be accommodated separately. Raif had won that round. Zane had been furious with him, but unable to show it because he had been maintaining the fiction he wasn't sleeping with his beautiful biographer. But the last laugh had eventually been on Raif when the two of them had married a scant three weeks later and Catherine had become Zane's queen.

Since then, and for the sake of diplomacy, Raif had made an effort to be civil to his brother. But right now he just wanted to see Kasia, to talk to her, to find out why she'd run from him and to impress upon her again the reality of their situation. And to have this damn pain in his gut go away.

He did not have the time or the patience to deal with his brother.

'Come, Kasim, and have coffee with me.' Zane finally let go of Raif's hand and held out his arm, directing him away from the gates. 'We can catch up.'

'Okay,' he said, struggling to keep his voice low despite his rising temper. His tender stomach ached after the endless ride through the desert, his skin felt clammy, his head was pounding as if Zarak had kicked him in the temple. But he would have to humour his brother before he returned to discover where Kasia was. Because he had no desire to explain his situation with the girl.

Never show weakness, that was the motto he lived by. And especially not to the man who his father had decided mattered, when Raif did not.

He knew that the way he had been treated by their father was not Zane's fault—both of them had been pawns in Tariq's political manoeuvres—but still he couldn't shake the feeling that where Zane was concerned he always had to be better, stronger, and smarter to prove himself worthy.

Sweat trickled down his back beneath his robe, his mind fogging with frustration and exhaustion, the pain in his right side making it hard for him to walk. But as they approached the ornate silver doors to the Sheikh's private chambers, the pain sliced agonisingly into his gut.

He bent over, his grunt of agony echoing through the corridor.

'Kasim, what the…?'

He could hear Zane's voice through the wildfire spreading through his body.

He locked his knees.

Stay upright, dammit.

But his legs refused to obey him, dissolving beneath him like sand.

The dull thud reverberated through him as he went down hard on his knees.

Zane's arms wrapped around Raif's torso as he tried to catch him, but it was already too late and darkness rushed towards him.

'Malik, get the doctor for Prince Kasim. Now.'

'My name is Raif,' he corrected his brother. 'Not Kasim.' The words were expelled on a final tortured breath as he crashed head first into the abyss.

Raif blinked up at the luxurious velvet drapes, the scent of jasmine echoing in his groin.

My angel? Where is my angel?

The powerful sense of *déjà vu* overwhelmed him, but as he turned his head, he saw a middle-aged woman beside the bed in a white coat, who stood up and leaned over him. But as she spoke in a stream of Narabian—while checking his temperature and his vital signs—the deep sense of disappointment became a hollow ache.

She isn't here. Not this time. She ran away from you.

'Where am I?' he asked in English, his throat raw with thirst as he tried to dispel the miserable inadequacy that had plagued him as a child.

'You are in His Divine Majesty's private chambers, Prince Kasim,' the doctor replied. 'Nurse, tell the Sheikh that Prince Kasim is conscious.'

A young man seated at the end of the bed rushed from the room.

Damn. Damn. Damn.

He had collapsed, fainted like a fool, in front of his brother. Humiliation washed over him. He shifted, tried to lift himself, clenching his teeth against the dull pain in his stomach. And the pinch in his forearm as the movement tugged on the drip taped to his skin.

He needed to get the hell out of this bed. He was lying here naked and exposed, like an invalid.

But the doctor placed a hand on his sternum, finding it pathetically easy to press him into the sheets—he had no more strength than a newborn baby.

'You must not move, Prince Kasim,' she said, the pity in her voice increasing his humiliation. 'You have a lot more healing to do. We had to operate as there was an infection.'

Operate? Infection?

He noticed for the first time the stars in the dark sky glinting through the elegant carved wooden screens on the chamber's window. Hadn't he arrived here in the afternoon? How could it already be night-time? Had he been lying here for hours?

'How…?' he rasped, the effort to speak exhausting him. He cleared his throat. 'How long have I been here?' he managed.

'Two weeks, Your Highness,' she said.

Two weeks!

Horror replaced his humiliation as a flush of shame engulfed him.

He'd been helpless, laid out like a child, relying on his brother's charity for two whole weeks?

'Raif, you're finally awake.'

Zane strode into the chamber, the picture of health and vitality, the bastard.

Except he isn't the bastard—you are.

But why had Zane called him by his Kholadi name? Raif frowned, confusion adding to his growing misery. His tired mind struggled to grasp the implications. The new intimacy between them was almost as disturbing as knowing he'd been at his brother's mercy for two weeks.

'How is he?' Zane addressed the doctor.

She reeled off a string of jargon and he realised he had been operated on because of a burst appendix. That he had nearly died. Then she told his brother he was on the mend.

But he didn't feel on the mend, he felt broken. And it had nothing to do with the tenderness still lingering in his gut.

How could he have sunk this low? To have risked his life. To follow a woman. A woman who didn't want him. Who had run from him and had no respect for his honour or her own. And how could he still want her?

The burning shame in his chest began to change into something more fortifying. He was limp with exhaustion, yes, but that would pass, and when it did he would find Kasia Salah. And he would make her pay for bringing him to this.

After more admonitions for him to remain in bed and focused on his recovery, the doctor left the room, leaving him alone with his brother.

Zane sat in the chair the doctor had vacated and leaned forward. 'So, Kasim...' He paused. 'Sorry, I mean Raif.' He folded his fingers together, levelling Raif with a stare that brooked no argument. 'Why didn't you tell me years ago you prefer to use the name Raif? And why the hell did you ride all the way here in agony?'

CHAPTER NINE

Hey, Kaz,

I hope all's good with you, and you're over your hot night with the mystery tribesman. You'll be glad to know no one has turned up here to claim your hand in marriage, so I hope you'll consider coming back for a visit again very soon.

Why haven't you been in touch? Six texts saying precisely nothing in four weeks doesn't count btw—just in case you were wondering.

All's good on the home front.

Zane has bought Kaliah her own pony and begun teaching her to ride. Personally, I think five-going-on-fifteen is too young, but I've been overruled by both of them, as usual! I include photos of her on her horse for her Auntie Kaz, at her insistence.

William, meanwhile, continues to be an absolute terror. I can't believe he still isn't sleeping through the night and he's nearly two. Neither can Zane, who says he's going to get tough on his son, then doesn't...

His Divine Majesty is a complete push-over where his children are concerned, and unfortunately for us both they know it.

We got a surprise visit from Prince Kasim—over a month ago now—who promptly collapsed and had to be nursed back to health. He turned up unannounced

*and without the usual honour guard of tribesmen. He
left us last week.*

*He had a burst appendix and had to be operated
on. When he finally came round he steadfastly refused to talk about why he had come to visit us in
the first place and ridden for three days in agony
to get here.*

*I told him he was definitely taking the whole 'Bad-
Boy Sheikh' thing a bit too far. He did not see the
funny side—having apparently had a major sense of
humour failure. As it turns out, desert princes make
the worst possible patients! Who knew?*

*The doctor also noticed he had a fresh scar on his
arm from what she thought might be a bullet wound—
which made me think of your mystery tribesman. But
I'm guessing your guy couldn't possibly be Prince
Kasim—or Raif, as Zane now calls him, for no reason I can fathom—because you totally would not have
kept the juiciest piece of girl talk in a millennium a
secret from your BFF, now, would you?*

*Give me a call soon and let me know how every-
thing is going.*

I miss you.
All my love
C xox

KASIA RE-READ THE handwritten letter, which had arrived
that morning, for the sixth time in as many minutes. Tears
stung her eyes and dripped onto the photo Cat had sent of
her five-year-old daughter. Kaliah's wide grin showed off
her missing front tooth as she sat on her new pony.

Kasia wiped the moisture off her cheeks and stuffed the
letter back into its envelope. Then, with trembling fingers,
pinned the print of Kaliah and her pony onto the board
above her desk.

Raif had been seriously ill for three weeks because of her. He'd only just recovered. How would she ever forgive herself?

Guilt and nausea roiled in her stomach, making the fatigue that had been dragging her down for a week weigh on her shoulders like a slab of concrete.

Placing the letter in the top drawer of the desk, she fished out the cardboard box she'd bought from the chemist's yesterday.

She turned the pregnancy testing kit over in her hands and read the instructions. Again.

She couldn't put it off any longer. Cat's letter and the devastating news about Raif's illness and recovery was a sign. A sign she had to start taking responsibility for her actions. She was convinced her symptoms were psychosomatic—even though he hadn't pulled out during their lovemaking, she *had* been at the very beginning of her cycle. And her period was only two days overdue, which wasn't that unusual for her.

This obsession with her so-called symptoms—the mild nausea, the tender breasts, the emotional roller-coaster, the bone-deep fatigue that had hit every evening for a week— was some weird psychological hangover from her time in the desert, which she hadn't been able to get out of her head.

Every night she dreamed of him. Not just the vivid erotic dreams that woke her up sweaty and unfulfilled, her skin prickling with sensation, her heart thundering, her clitoris slick and swollen from the far-too-real memory of his tongue stroking her to orgasm. But also the much more unsettling visions of him when they had ridden together through the storm, when he'd cried out in his sleep and the harsh frown of disbelief on his face as she'd galloped away from him.

And now Cat's letter had made all those symptoms that much more pronounced.

Something had happened to her at the oasis, something profound and life-changing that went beyond the sex. Something she wasn't going to be able to come to terms with until she made absolutely sure, once and for all, that she wasn't pregnant with Raif Kasim Ali Kholadi Khan's child.

Emotion caused a lump to form in her throat as she walked into the small en suite bathroom of her room in the hall of residence.

After unwrapping the test stick, it took her several agonising minutes to manage to pee on it. She placed it on the vanity unit and washed her hands, then sat on the toilet seat and set the stopwatch on her smartphone to the required two minutes to get the result.

Which turned in to the longest two minutes of her entire life.

The questions she didn't want to answer that were roaring around in her head were almost as deafening as the sandstorm she and Raif had survived all those weeks ago.

She should have done this yesterday when she'd bought the test. Why hadn't she? Was it because she didn't want to have a pregnancy confirmed, or the much more disturbing thought that she did? Why would she want to be pregnant by a man she barely knew? A man who appeared to comprehensively lack the sensibilities she had always dreamed of finding in a life partner? Was she really that needy and lonely and insecure that she yearned to have a child, whatever the circumstances of its birth?

But the combination of anticipation and dread tangling with the nausea in her stomach didn't feel as if it was just a result of her long-held desire that one day she wanted to be a mother. No, these complex urges were not generic or anonymous, but intrinsically linked to Raif and the intense time they had shared together, every single moment of which she kept reliving.

Her phone buzzed and she shrieked.

Okay, it's official—you are actually going insane.

But when she looked at the stopwatch she realised her two minutes weren't up yet. Instead, a message had appeared on the phone screen from the sponsorship team at Devereaux College. She frowned as she read the message.

Ms Salah,

We've received a request that you attend a black-tie reception tonight in London at eight p.m.

The guest of honour Mr R Khan —a billionaire businessman from your home region, I understand—is thinking of funding a scholarship programme at Devereaux. We would very much appreciate it if you would agree to attend this event so that you can discuss your current research with him. We are hopeful that a scholarship programme of this nature, if agreed, will help fund your PhD.

A car will be made available to transport you to London.

Regards

Alice Evershot

Devereaux Scholarship Team

The request was not at all what she needed right now. But she would have to attend the event tonight and make a good impression—any chance of getting her PhD funded was not something she could afford to pass up.

But when the alarm on her phone buzzed again, making her jump, she realised Alice Evershot's request had managed to take her mind off Raif and that one seminal night in the desert for ten full seconds—a record for the last month.

Drawing a breath into her lungs, she reached for the test stick, finally ready to face what the rest of her life might hold.

The breath was released in a shattered gasp as she read the result.

CHAPTER TEN

KASIA RE-READ HER notes as the car drew into the forecourt of a landmark hotel on London's Strand.

She stuffed the creased pages into her clutch bag and stared up at the silver-plated sign on the hotel's Art Deco frontage.

She was no stranger to luxury, having lived in the Golden Palace for as long as she could remember before moving to the UK, but—as a uniformed doorman stepped forward to open the heavy glass doors with a flourish and the porter led her through the lobby area resplendent in Edwardian marble and gilt-edged antique furniture—the grandeur took her breath away.

But, then, she'd been struggling to catch her breath all day, ever since reading the results of the pregnancy test.

She pressed a hand to her stomach, her palm sliding over the sleek red silk of the cocktail dress she'd found at a second-hand boutique in Cambridge that afternoon.

She was going to have Prince Kasim's baby. Raif's baby.

Her breath seized all over again as it had so many times since that morning.

So many uncertainties and challenges awaited her in the weeks and months ahead—and most of them seemed insurmountable at the moment.

Somehow she would have to tell Cat and Zane that Raif was the mystery tribesman. That his burst appendix was her fault. And eventually she would have to tell the desert prince himself about her pregnancy. He had a right to know he was going to become a father.

But all the reasons she had run from him and her homeland a month ago still applied. In fact, this development would make them even tougher to negotiate.

Raif had obviously decided not to pursue marriage once he had recovered, but he might well insist on it again when he discovered she was going to have his child. And how could she expect Cat and Zane to protect her from such a union when they might be conflicted, too? Especially Zane. After all he had insisted on marriage with Cat when she had become pregnant with *his* child. And Raif was his brother. Where would his loyalties lie? With her—however close she was to the Royal household—or with his own blood?

Overwhelmed didn't even begin to describe how she had been feeling about her condition ever since she'd seen the fat red plus sign. But despite all the questions and uncertainties, and the impact her baby would have on her academic career, the one thing she did know was that she wanted this baby. Raif's baby. Very much.

She pushed the recurring questions to one side, or tried to, her clutch purse instinctively guarding her belly as the porter directed her through the inlaid silver doors of a lavish ballroom.

At least she had time to consider her options. Once she'd told Cat, she could talk the situation through with her best friend, figure out how best to break the news to Raif and when. Luckily, having Raif thousands of miles away gave her a buffer zone from having to confront anything before she was ready.

Right now, all she had to do was absorb the surreal joy at the prospect of becoming a mother in approximately eight months' time. Something she'd always dreamed of being. Maybe she wouldn't have planned for it to happen this way, but once she got over the shock—and worked out how and when to tell the father to avoid an all-out war on the Narabian peninsula—she could embrace the awe. Luckily, she'd always been a positive, self-sufficient person who knew how to think on her feet—or she would be, once she got over the feeling that the rug had just been pulled out from under said feet.

As she stepped into the crowd of elegantly dressed guests—the men in tuxedos and most of the women in ballgowns—she recited her speech again in her head while searching for the Devereaux College representative she had been told would be there to introduce her to the potential donor.

She walked through the room, faking confidence. With her wild hair tamed and curled after an hour spent with her trusty curling irons, the high heels she'd borrowed from another post-grad student and her newish dress, at least she knew she looked good.

She took a moment to calm her erratic heartbeat. She needed to remember the speech she'd worked on to charm the billionaire donor she wanted to impress. Securing funding for her PhD was very important now, or her future—and her baby's future—would be even more insecure.

French doors lined one side of the high-ceilinged hall, affording the guests a stunning vista of the Thames at twilight. Big Ben and the Houses of Parliament were spotlighted from the balcony at the far end, while the London Eye lit up the Georgian splendour of the old County Hall building across the water.

The clink of glasses and the hum of polite conversation covered the delicacy of a Brahms concerto being played by a string quartet in one corner while discreet wait staff passed around gold trays of canapés and vintage Champagne.

The scene really was breathtaking. Who knew there

was this much money—and glamour—in university funding initiatives?

'Miss Salah? You made it.' The familiar face of one of Alice Evershot's assistants popped up beside her.

'Yes. Hello, I—'

'Come this way.' The young man interrupted her attempt at polite introductions to direct her through the crowd. 'Mr Khan is impatient to meet you and I really don't want to keep him waiting any longer,' he said as he moved swiftly through the throng.

She had to speed up to keep pace with the young man. Her heartbeat became erratic again as they stepped out of the French doors. A man stood at the far end of the balcony alone, in an expertly tailored tuxedo, his tall muscular frame silhouetted against the Houses of Parliament. This was the donor? She'd expected someone much older. Even from behind this man looked young and fit.

And oddly familiar.

It's not Raif. Are you mad? You have to forget about him, at least for tonight.

Goosebumps ran riot over her skin. Which was strange. It was a warm late-summer evening and there was no breeze to speak of.

'Mr Khan,' the assistant called from behind her. 'I have located Ms Salah for you.'

The music and laughter and the hum of polite conversation was drowned out by the thud of her own heartbeat and the low rumble of the traffic along the Embankment as she walked towards the donor with the assistant at her side.

Her heels echoed in the night, but her heartbeat became deafening. Even his stance reminded her of Raif. So proud, so arrogant. His close-cropped black hair shone blue in the lights from the reception.

He hadn't turned, and she wondered if he was annoyed

she had arrived a little late as his stance seemed tense. Not a great start to this schmoozing initiative.

She swallowed down the strange feeling of unreality as she approached him, but the goosebumps continued to run riot over the bare skin of her arms. And a heavy weight sank low into her abdomen. Hadn't he heard the assistant?

'Mr Khan, I'm so sorry I'm late,' she said.

The man turned at last, bringing his face into the light. And dark chocolate eyes bored into her soul.

Recognition slammed into her and she staggered to a stop.

A giddy rush of desire followed as she devoured his rugged features, the thick brows drawn into a sharp line, the clean-shaven jaw revealing the tense muscle bunching in his cheek.

It can't be him. I'm hallucinating.

Her hand covered her stomach as if she could shield the child already growing inside her from the shock.

His shuttered gaze roamed over her, entitled, assured, alight with barely suppressed fury... And undisguised desire.

Her breath cut off, the weight plunging down to throb and ache in the sweet spot between her thighs. Her already tender breasts squeezed into hard peaks, her nipples thrusting against the satin.

'Raif?' Her mouth formed the word, while everything inside her rebelled.

The assistant began to make the introductions but she couldn't hear a word of what the eager young man was saying. And it seemed neither could Raif, his gaze fixed firmly on her burning face.

He's not real. He can't be. This isn't happening.

How could the Desert Prince be standing in front of her, handsome and indomitable and completely at home at an elite high-society reception in the heart of London, his pristine white shirt making his skin look even darker?

His lips lifted on one side in a sarcastic half-smile, both sensual and brittle. And the memories she had been holding so carefully at bay for four weeks bombarded her all at once.

'Hello, Kasia.' His rough, accented voice scraped over every one of her nerve endings.

The assistant stopped talking abruptly, then cleared his throat. 'Mr Khan, I had no idea you already knew Ms Salah.'

What are you doing here?

Her mind screamed. The painful breath left her lungs as she struggled to engage with the evidence of her eyes.

This was Raif, but not as she had known him. This man was still the Desert Prince, she could feel his strength, his authority, still pulsing under his skin, barely contained. But he looked as comfortable in the tailored suit as he had on an Arabian stallion.

'We have met before,' he said, stepping closer as he glanced at the assistant. 'I wish to speak to Ms Salah in private, if that is all right with her,' he said, his intense gaze challenging her to deny him this intimacy.

But how could she? He'd nearly died on her account. Racing across a desert to find her when he'd been gravely ill. And he was the father of her child.

'Ms Salah?' the assistant said, clearly confused now. 'Is that all right with you?'

'Yes,' she murmured, as sensation rippled over her skin and gathered in her sex, telling her, in case she had ever doubted it, that she still wanted him.

The assistant left swiftly, probably feeling like the fifth wheel he was, and closed the balcony doors behind him.

'Why are you here?' she asked, at last.

'I think you know,' he said, stepping closer, filling her

lungs with the intoxicating scent of him—man and musk and clean pine soap. 'I deserve answers. And I intend to get them.'

His chin lifted and she heard voices behind her. A couple had walked out onto the balcony. Her heart bounced into her throat as he swore under his breath at the interruption. 'It's like a train station here,' he said. 'Will you come with me to my suite?'

She should say no, she was still in shock from seeing him again, and going to his suite would hardly enhance her reputation. But her body refused to yield, the yearning to be with him again almost painful as she imagined him near death in Narabia.

She nodded.

'Good,' he murmured, then captured her hand and marched down the balcony. Entering the ballroom, he hauled her behind him. She had to lengthen her stride to keep up as he made his way through the crowd.

'Mr Khan, Ms Salah, how is the discussion going?' The young assistant rushed towards them, blocking their path to the exit.

'Very well,' Raif replied, impatience rippling through him as he was forced to stop. 'I am inclined to agree to fund the scholarship initiative,' he added to the assistant, disconcerting Kasia again.

Raif was the billionaire donor? *Really?* But how? And why? The Kholadi were a nomadic tribe, they had no wealth, no riches, their ancient lifestyle and customs based on barter and trade, not money. Or that's what she had always believed as a teenager.

'That's wonderful,' the assistant said, his cheeks flushing with pleasure. 'Can I get you both a drink?'

Raif tensed, and she could sense his frustration at the assistant's interruption almost choking him now, but instead of demanding the man get out of their way, he turned to Kasia. 'Your choice, Ms Salah,' he murmured. 'Would you like a drink?'

The words shot through her, reminding her of another choice he'd given her a month ago. A choice that had ended in the baby now growing inside her.

Despite his fury with her, his obvious sense of grievance, he was giving her a choice again. A choice she had accused him of denying her all those weeks ago.

A choice to escape his questions, or face up to this discussion—a discussion she had avoided the last time by running away.

Gathering her courage, she turned to the assistant. 'It's okay, Devon,' she said. 'We're going to go to Mr Khan's suite to discuss the proposals for the scholarship in more depth.'

Devon looked delighted. 'Wonderful. Don't let me stand in your way, then,' he said, stepping aside to let them pass. 'I'll let Ms Evershot know about your discussion,' he shouted after them as Raif led her through the crowd.

But Alice Evershot and the scholarship initiative flew out of Kasia's mind as Raif marched her out of the ballroom and up a sweeping staircase to the next level. Nodding at two bodyguards, he shoved open a door marked 'Royal Suite'.

She found herself in a luxury suite of rooms, the sitting room decorated in cream silk and dark mahogany. The panoramic view of the river from a large terrace beyond the suite was even more spectacular than the one from the ballroom below.

But as he let go of her wrist and slammed the door behind them, it wasn't the view that made her breathless.

Her whole body began to shake as she wrapped her arms around her waist.

He tugged his bow-tie loose and shrugged off his jacket, throwing it over the back of a three-seater sofa. Then he undid the top buttons of his shirt. She could see the edge

of the serpent tattoo on his collarbone, the red and black
ink coiling over his skin—and the forceful reminder of
the night they had spent together brought with it another
devastating truth.

He nearly died.

The information in Cat's letter that morning reverberated in her skull.

His pursuit of her had nearly killed him. No wonder he
wanted answers. But little did he know she had much more
to answer for now.

'I'm so sorry,' she blurted out, backing away from him
as he stalked towards her across the silk carpet.

'What for?' he asked.

'Cat wrote to me and told me how ill you were. That's
because of me. I never should have run away like that, but
I never meant—'

'Stop.' He pressed his hand to her mouth to silence her.
Then captured her waist and pressed her back against the
silk-papered wall of the suite. Instead of fury she saw the
same riot of emotions on his face that were churning in her
stomach—desire, confusion. But most of all need.

He took his hand away from her mouth.

'That's not because of you.' His forehead touched hers
as his fingers gripped the silk of her dress. Reaction shuddered through him and echoed through her. Powerful and
unstoppable. 'I should not have ridden through the pain
for three days to get to you,' he murmured, his lips touching her earlobe.

He had ridden for *three days* to follow her? Risking his
health in the process? Agony and ecstasy echoed through
her body. Why did his actions seem romantic, instead of
foolhardy or simply insane? Maybe because no man had
ever cared about her enough to do such a thing?

His lips closed over her earlobe. She arched against him,
instinctively encouraging the contact, her whole body rev-

elling in the response as he buried his face in her neck. The remembered ache became real and vivid again and a tortured moan escaped her lips.

'It was madness and I paid for it,' he said, his warm breath sending shivers down her back, his palms rubbing her waist, the silk feeling like sandpaper against too-sensitive skin. 'I'm not here for an apology.'

She pressed her palms to his jaw to draw his head up. His dark gaze was tortured, as tortured as she felt.

'Then why are you here, Raif?' she asked, around the knot of fear and joy in her throat.

'Because I still want you, dammit. And I can't make it stop.'

It wasn't what Raif had meant to say. Not even close. But once the words left his lips, he knew they were true.

He'd spent the last week—after finally managing to convince his brother and his brother's doctor and his brother's wife that he was fit enough to travel again—catching up on the million and one things that had been neglected during his illness while also planning this event.

He'd wanted to lure her to London. Had used the promise of funding a scholarship programme to control the interaction and had settled on a public meeting to ensure he didn't lose his temper with her. Where Kasia Salah was concerned, he already knew his ability to be rational had deserted him long ago. Why had he seduced her, why had he tried to bully her into marriage—a knee-jerk reaction that he had regretted after the week spent in his brother's home with far too much time to think—and why had he put his pride and dignity and his health in jeopardy by pursuing her to the Golden Palace like a lunatic?

But as soon as he'd seen her again, the fury, the desire for revenge had turned into something a great deal more volatile.

In a grubby T-shirt and shorts she had been exquisite; in the silky red dress, which clung to her slender body, accentuating her high, full breasts and subtle curves, she was irresistible. Her amber eyes, the lids smudged with glittery make-up, had met his and all he'd wanted to do was feast on her again, and make her moan. His tongue had thickened at the thought of licking the side of her neck. His fingertips had itched to find the pins holding the waterfall of curls on top of her head and pull them out until the vibrant mass fell into his palms. And the blood had surged straight to his groin, the desire to pump into her tight heat all but unbearable.

But more than that, and somehow worse, when she'd searched his face a moment ago, her eyes filled with shame and remorse, he had wanted to take her distress away. To protect her, to hold her, to take all the blame, when this situation was more her fault than his.

He'd made some stupid knee-jerk decisions, but she'd made more.

Her gaze widened with shock at his revelation, but the flare of desire told him all he needed to know.

Why was he complicating this? He had planned this meeting precisely to take this yearning, this longing away.

This was about sex—it had always been about sex. Maybe it had become complicated by her virginity and his illness. But now he was here, in London, and fully recovered, why should they be bound by an ancient ritual that meant nothing outside their homeland?

He'd tried to do the right thing, to honour his culture and to honour her—and to show her the respect due to her after some warped reading of what he had discovered about his mother's situation with his father several years ago.

But this situation was not the same as what had happened to the woman who had died giving birth to him. A woman who he had refused to think about, until Zane had insisted he read his father's journals.

Given his overreaction to Kasia's virginity, he wished he had never read the damn journals. Never discovered the truth. What did the circumstances of his birth have to do with who he had become anyway? He had never known the girl his father had exploited and his father had never acknowledged him, her child.

The truth had messed with his head, his sense of self, or he would not have made that stupid declaration about his honour, about having to marry Kasia. And even if an elemental part of who he was and had always been made him feel responsible for her virginity, and the loss of it, surely the point was that her virginity had no bearing on where they were now.

They were both a continent away from their culture, those rituals. The Law of Marriage of the Sheikhs did not apply in London, even if it ever had in that tent.

Kasia Salah had chosen to leave Narabia five years ago. After four years of living—and succeeding—in this world as well as his own, he knew how it worked, too. So why should he not treat her as he would any other woman he desired? She certainly looked the part in that provocative dress and her high heels.

She wasn't a virgin any more. And they weren't in the desert now.

He cradled her cheek, traced with his thumb the spot where her pulse fluttered against her collarbone and adjusted his stance so she could feel the thick erection and know exactly what she still did to him.

'The only question I need an answer to is do you still want me, Kasia? If not, you can leave now, and I will never seek you out again.'

It was a promise that it would kill him to keep, if he had read the flare of arousal, her passionate response to him wrong. But he *would* keep it. Because he wasn't the barbarian she had assumed he was. And he'd debased himself enough already to have her—not just travelling across a desert in his frenzy, and leaving himself at the mercy of his brother, but travelling across an ocean, across continents. He hadn't been able to get her out of his head for a whole month; his whole damn life had been thrown into turmoil because of his association with her.

But he didn't *need* Kasia, he just wanted her.

'Answer me,' he demanded. 'Do you still want me?'

Her breathing was ragged, her features tense, but he could already see the truth in her eyes, and the rush of arousal surged.

'I… I *do* still want you,' she said at last, her tone anxious but not unsure.

It was enough.

'Good,' he murmured in the Kholadi dialect as he bent to scoop her into his arms.

He marched through the suite's living area and into the palatial bedroom—the light from streetlamps outside flickering over her dark skin. He didn't turn on the bedroom light before stripping off her clothes then tearing off his own. He watched her watch him as he rolled a condom on the massive erection.

He would have her now and he would find a way to keep her, for as long as it took to feed this hunger and take this inexplicable yearning away.

And then they would part, and he would never have to feel so unsettled or desperate again.

He cupped her breasts, licked the areolas, then sucked the swollen peaks into his mouth as he tested her readiness with his fingers. She sobbed and arched into his hand, the feel of her slick folds, the swollen nub enough to drive him a little crazy as he grasped her thighs, positioned her hips. He sank to the hilt in one thrust. Her muscles contracted around him in spontaneous orgasm. He set up a deep driving rhythm, wanting her to come again, to come apart in his arms.

He wasn't that little boy any more, alone and afraid, marked and then discarded by his own father and made to feel he was nothing.

He was a man, a chief, a prince, a business tycoon and everything he wanted he could have—if he fought hard enough for it—until he didn't want it any more.

He picked up the pace, going deeper, taking more. He wanted all of her. All her pleasure, all her desire, all her passion. Her moans turned to frantic sobs as she clung to his shoulders. Her nails raked over the slight scar from the wound she'd caused, but he welcomed the sting as he held onto the edge and ruthlessly worked the spot he knew would drive her wild.

The madness—to own her, to possess her—overtook him as the climax gripped the base of his spine. She massaged his length, the spasms of her second orgasm forcing him over the edge. The titanic climax exploded along his nerve-endings as he buried himself deep one last time and let himself tumble.

But as he rolled off her, his body shaky, his mind dazed from the intensity of the orgasm, he could hear the cry of that forgotten child clearly inside his head begging…

Don't leave me.

Before he managed to smother it again.

CHAPTER ELEVEN

KASIA TREMBLED, feeling dazed and disorientated and exposed as she watched Raif stand up.

He didn't speak to her, didn't even look at her, as he strolled to the door of the bathroom then disappeared inside. She heard the toilet flush, could see his reflection in the wall of mirrors as he washed his hands, having discarded the condom.

The sudden rush of insecurity she'd thought she had conquered a lifetime ago made her shiver.

Maybe you are not as unlike your mother as you want to believe?

How could she have given in to the rampant desire—again—when so much between them was in turmoil?

Not so much. *Everything.* Everything between them was in turmoil.

He hadn't wanted her apology for the wound she had caused—and genuinely didn't appear to blame her for all the pain and suffering he had endured after his ride to follow her, even though she was finding it hard not to blame herself—and he hadn't repeated his demand that they marry.

But what would happen when she told him about the pregnancy?

He wasn't the same man he had been when she'd left Narabia five and a half years ago. In many ways this man was even more of a stranger than the man to whom she'd given her virginity.

Why hadn't he told her about the drastic change in his circumstances while they were in the desert? She sat up and wrapped the bed sheet around her naked body, taking in the luxury suite, the magnificent views of London's landmarks across the Thames.

She lifted her dress off the floor with shaking fingers. She really ought to leave. She needed more time to consider how she was going to break the news to Raif about his impending fatherhood and shore up her own defences.

'What are you doing?'

She whipped around, her dress slipping through her fingers. He stood silhouetted in the bathroom doorway, his broad shoulders cutting out the light, completely unconcerned by his nakedness. She noticed the livid scar above his right hip from the emergency operation he had required and shuddered.

'I thought I should go,' she said, wanting to sound adamant but strangely conflicted about her course of action.

'Don't.' His bare feet padded on the carpet as he crossed the room. He sat on the edge of the bed. 'I don't want you to,' he added, as he curled his fingers around her neck and tugged her closer.

Her choice wasn't about what he wanted. But when he placed a kiss on her temple, the tenderness of the gesture was so compelling her resolve faltered.

'Stay with me tonight,' he said, running his thumb over her cheekbone, his watchful gaze so intent on her reaction she felt it echo at her core.

His sensual lips quirked in an assured smile. 'We left a lot unfinished. I think you agree.'

The heat climbed from her core into her cheeks. How did he do that? How did he read her responses so easily? But before she had a chance to feel embarrassed or, worse, threatened by how gauche she must appear to him, his gaze drifted to her hair.

'Your hair is lopsided,' he said.

She pressed a hand to the up-do and discovered it had tumbled down on one side.

'I should… I should really go,' she said, but as she attempted to scoot backwards off the bed, he captured her wrist and halted her getaway.

'No, you shouldn't,' he said. 'Let me help. It must be uncomfortable,' he added. It wasn't really, but as he proceeded to locate the pins holding her hair aloft, pluck them out and throw them away, her heart began to pummel her ribcage.

She watched him as he concentrated on the task, the care he was taking making her heart melt.

'How did you tame it?' he asked with a frown—as if he preferred it wild.

'A curling iron,' she said, her breathing catching again.

'An iron! Does that not hurt?' he said, his frown becoming concerned.

Her heart rate jumped, but still she smiled. 'No.'

He sank his fingers into the mass of curls she'd spent an hour arranging that afternoon as she'd practised the speech she'd never had a chance to give him. A moan escaped as he massaged her scalp, lifting and dividing the heavy weight.

She shivered, the delicious sensation rippling through her and reawakening the heat at her core that she'd thought would be sated for ever only minutes before.

'It feels good?' he asked.

'Yes, very good.'

Too good.

She didn't want to go now, she wanted to stay. But could she risk it?

'Turn around,' he said, and she did as he'd commanded.

He tugged on the sheet she had wrapped around her torso and she tightened her grip, but he only chuckled. 'Let it go, you do not need it. I promise not to ravage you again until you ask.'

She let the sheet fall, but crossed her arms over her naked breasts, brutally aware of her reflection in the window.

She sat on the bed naked, his large silhouette behind her as his thumbs dug into the tight muscles of her neck. She had to bite off another groan as his fingers worked their magic, finding each knot and releasing it, melting her resistance as they went.

At last he reached her bottom and the moan escaped.

He gave her butt a playful slap. 'Stop that, or I will not be responsible for my actions.'

Her eyes flew open. She met his gaze in the glass. He was smiling, but his jaw was tense. And she could feel his erection against her back.

She swung around, not as wary as she had been.

She would tell him about the baby soon. But there was no reason to tell him tonight. Would it be so wrong to enjoy this time with him, while he was relaxed—or more relaxed than usual—and playful?

Reaching out, he ran his thumb under her nipple and made her gasp. She felt it squeeze and tighten, instantly responsive to his touch.

'It is strange, but they seem larger than I remember them,' he said.

Because they were.

She thanked God for the shadows in the room so he couldn't read the guilty look that crossed her face. He dipped his head, ready to take the aching peak into his mouth and build the hunger again, but she drew back.

'Is something wrong?' he asked, instantly alert to her hesitation.

Her heart pounded hard. How could this man be so aware of her needs, her wants?

'Could we…? Is it okay if we just talk for a minute?'

His eyebrows rose. 'This is not what a man in my state likes to hear,' he said boldly, but his lips had quirked in a strained half-smile and she knew he was joking. Or mostly joking.

Climbing off the bed, he found the boxer briefs he had discarded earlier and put them on, then walked to the bathroom and returned with a fluffy robe. 'You had better put this on.' He threw the robe to her and she stuffed her arms into it, wrapped the belt around and tied it.

He had picked up the phone next to the bedside. 'Are you hungry?'

She nodded. The truth was she was ravenous, and for much more than food. He looked ridiculously gorgeous standing there in his boxer shorts, but she wanted to speak to him and food felt like the perfect distraction. Also, she hadn't eaten since before she'd done the test that morning, thanks to her nerves.

'Is there anything you don't eat?' he asked.

'Sheep's eyeballs,' she said, knowing it was a delicacy of the Kholadi, and he laughed at her joke.

'You do not know what you are missing,' he said, then reeled a selection of delicious items off the room-service menu.

Her stomach rumbled as he sat on the bed, leaning against the headboard. Stretching out his legs, he beckoned her. 'Come.'

She crawled towards him, impossibly touched when he wrapped an arm around her. She went to rest against his right side, enjoying the moment of closeness, but remembered the appendectomy scar just in time.

'I'm sorry.'

'Stop apologising,' he said, tugging her back down again, until she was nestled under his arm. 'It doesn't hurt.'

She didn't entirely believe him, but he seemed unconcerned. He was clearly a man who had endured a lot of pain in his life—enough that a wound such as this was insignificant.

'What is it you wish to talk about?' he asked.

There were so, so many things she wanted to know about him, she realised, but she didn't have the right to ask them. Not until she had told him about her baby. Their baby. So she settled for something she did have the right to know.

'Why did you pretend you were still just the Kholadi Chief at the oasis...' *Just.* The qualifier echoed in her consciousness.

Whatever had happened to change his circumstances in the last five years, to turn him into a billionaire with considerable power and influence outside his desert kingdom, he had never been *just* a chieftain. He had always been charming, intelligent, a brilliant political strategist and a worthy diplomatic opponent, according to Zane. Hadn't Cat once mentioned that he spoke seven languages fluently?

The Bad-Boy Sheikh tag was one the girls in the palace's women's quarters had created for him, because it had added to the fantasies they'd all whispered about him. It had made him hotter. But he really didn't need to be any hotter than he already was. Maybe he had no formal education, unlike her, but he had risen to the task of leading his people as a teenager and she would guess that was the motive behind what he was doing here now.

She looked up at him. His brows quirked, the smile widening, and she wondered why her question amused him.

'I did not pretend to be something I am not.'

'But you could have told me about your other life. Your life in the West. As a businessman. Why didn't you?' She looked away, out into the night sky. Embarrassed at the memory of telling him about Cambridge University as if he would never have heard of the place.

Wow, she'd really messed up—in so many ways.

Strong fingers captured her chin and tugged her gaze to his. The sparkle of amusement had died, his eyes intent. 'You think because I have money now, because I know how to work the stock market, how to invest and diversify the riches of my people, my country, so they can have more options, that this makes me a better man than I was before?'

She shook her head furiously. 'No, no, not at all.' She had insulted him and it hadn't been her intention. 'But it does make you different from the man I believed you to be.'

'How?' he said. 'I am the same man underneath the suit as the robe. As you can see.' He spread his arm out, drawing her eyes to the many scars on his chest, illuminated by the light from the bathroom, the red marks where her nails had scored his skin during their lovemaking, and the faded ink of the tattoo. 'It is only your perception that is different.'

Was it? Perhaps he was right, and her impression of him was about her own prejudices—her own fantasies. And the truth was that so much of him was unchanged from their night in the desert. But, still, she couldn't quite give up her argument.

'Really? Would you have chosen to get that tattoo now?' she asked, seizing on the crude, pagan and unsettling design—which made him look even more wild than all the injuries he had suffered. He must have got it when he'd become Chief of the Kholadi, as a teenager, the serpent a well-known symbol of the tribe.

He glanced at his shoulder, almost as if he had forgotten the tattoo was there. Then stared back at her.

'This tattoo was not my choice. My father had me inked before he threw me out.'

'Sheikh Tariq forced you to have that tattoo?' Shock and sympathy hit her like a punch to the stomach. 'But... Why?'

'So everyone would know I was nothing more than a Kholadi whore's brat.'

She tried to absorb the horror of that, and the sadness at the casual way he made the remark. 'How old were you?'

He shrugged, making the snake writhe in the dim light. 'Ten.'

Ten? 'But that's… That's hideous.'

She'd heard the stories about Tariq's abuse of Zane. When she and Cat had gone to the marketplace together during the early days of her friend's employment, an old woman who had delivered fabric to the palace had told of how Zane had been beaten for trying to run away, after being kidnapped from his mother in LA.

Why was she even surprised that Tariq had treated his other son with equal brutality? The old Sheikh had become mad with bitterness after Zelda Mayhew, Zane's mother, had run away from him with her baby son. But this wasn't just cruel, it was twisted. To permanently mark a child, to treat him with such contempt, your own flesh and blood. How could Tariq have done such a thing? And how had Raif survived it?

'Do not be distressed.' He sent her a confused half-smile. 'I survived. Once you get used to the needle, it doesn't hurt. And I wear the tattoo with pride now as the Kholadi's Chief. He was crueller to my mother.'

The minute he had mentioned his mother, Raif knew he should not have done. Because Kasia shot upright, dislodging his arm, the curiosity in her gaze outstripped by the concern and compassion that had already turned her eyes into twin pools of amber. Pools he had lost himself in a moment ago.

Was that why he'd mentioned his mother, because he was basking in the compassion? Exactly how weak and pathetic did that make him?

'Your mother? You mean…' She paused and looked down, her fingers toying with the robe's belt. She didn't want to say the word, he realised—and was trying to think of a more polite way to describe her. At last she raised her chin, the honest sympathy turning the pang in his chest to an ache.

'I'm sorry, I only know the stories about your mother, that she was a…' He waited for her to say it, a word he had heard many times, a word he himself had used to describe his mother. A word he had always been determined to own. People had judged him because of her and he had hated her for it, but had refused to admit the shame he felt, persuading anyone who would listen, his brother included, that he was proud to be a whore's son.

Strange to realise that when he'd finally discovered the truth about her, two years ago, while reading his father's papers, the only real emotion he had felt, instead of anger or regret or sadness for the woman who had given birth to a sheikh's son and been destroyed in the process, had been a vague feeling of disappointment. That he had gone through his childhood, his whole adult life fighting to prove it didn't matter that his mother was something she had never really been.

'That she was Tariq's paid companion,' Kasia finally managed.

The ache in his chest became more pronounced when he realised how hard Kasia was trying to spare his feelings. Feelings that no longer existed. Or hadn't until he'd taken her virginity all those weeks ago and triggered a reaction he'd found hard to explain.

'A whore, you mean?' he said flatly.

'I wouldn't use that term,' Kasia replied fiercely.

'Why not, if it is the truth?' He was baiting her now, and he knew it, because the truth about his mother was more complex. But he couldn't help wondering how Kasia would have reacted to his heritage if his mother had been the whore everyone had convinced him she was? Would

Kasia have judged him, too? And his mother? Or was her sweetness, her innocence as real as it appeared?

'Because it's a cruel and derogatory term and it doesn't take into account why women are often forced to make those choices,' she said without hesitation, the passionate defence making the ache in his chest worse.

Apparently she was as sweet as she appeared.

He wondered how different his life might have been if he had met Kasia before the lies about his birth—and the degradation he had suffered because of them—had forced him to grow up far too soon and had hardened him into the cynic he was today? He rubbed his knuckles over his chest, determined to take the foolish ache away. They could not turn back the clock. Maybe he had become the man he was today—hard, cynical, immune to love—based on a lie, but he had no desire to change who he was.

'Perhaps it is good, then, she was not so much of a whore after all,' he said, deciding to tell Kasia the truth. 'Or not until after she became pregnant with me.'

'I don't... I don't understand,' she said. 'But I thought she died when you were born?'

'She did,' he said, then watched her make the connection. His mother had taken men into her bed for money while she had been with child.

A part of him wanted to let Kasia believe that was all there was to the story, the truth he had lived with his entire life. What difference did it really make *why* his mother had become a prostitute? And when?

But instead of looking shocked, or disgusted, Kasia's eyes brimmed with tears and the ache he was trying to numb started to pulse again.

'Why are you crying?' he said, as he watched her swipe the moisture away.

'She must have been so desperate. I can't even imagine it.'

No one had ever cried for his mother, no one had ever mourned her, not even him. But as he watched a single tear track down Kasia's cheek, something was released inside him and the prickle of guilt and shame—in himself, not his mother—that he had held at bay joined the brutal ache in his chest.

Why would she cry for his mother? Defend her? Lament the terrible choices his mother had been forced to make?

And if this girl could cry for her, who had never known her, and still only knew the worst about her, how much of a bastard did it make him that he could not?

'She *was* desperate,' he said, no longer able to deny the truth he had never confided in anyone, never wanted to acknowledge or confront, until now. 'She was a virgin, only sixteen years old when he took her to his bed. But he refused to marry her, and when she became pregnant he discarded her, had her branded a whore. She did not return to the Kholadi because of the shame, so she ended up in a brothel in Zafari,' he said, mentioning the city that had sprawled around the walls of the Golden Palace for generations.

'The madam there brought me to the palace after my mother died in childbirth. And the women took me in. My father was furious, of course, but even he could not order a baby cast out of the palace, especially one that carried his blood, however tainted. But he never acknowledged me and always refused to see me—until Zane arrived in the palace and Tariq wanted me gone. Everyone told me always that my mother was a whore, and I believed it, but I found out two years ago, when Zane gave me our father's journals, that it was not the whole truth.'

He had been furious with Zane for giving the journals to him and insisting he read them, especially when he had discovered the inconvenient truth contained within them. He had felt nothing for his mother's plight, his heart already hardened towards her, but he had been instantly suspicious of Zane's motives.

Why would Zane presume he would want to unearth ancient history? To revisit something about his birth that would rewrite the principles on which he had founded his life? Was Zane expecting him to be grateful? Expecting him to give Narabia political and economic concessions in their trade negotiations in gratitude for this interference in his private life? Or was it even simpler than that? Did Zane simply wish to weaken him?

Zane, of all people, had to know that the chaos, the struggles, the disadvantages of his childhood had ultimately given him strength—therefore he must have known that showing Raif that his mother had been a victim too might undermine that strength.

But as Raif watched Kasia struggle to hold back her tears, the sympathy and understanding in her eyes probed that place deep inside him that he had never wanted anyone to find—and the ache in his chest rose up to push against his larynx.

No. No. No.

Kasia pressed a hand to her belly, trying to contain the pain, not just at the hideous truths Raif had revealed about his childhood and his mother's mistreatment and exploitation but also at the guilt tying her stomach in tight knots. Because Raif's revelations about his mother put a whole new complexion on what had happened a month ago.

'Is that why…?' She paused, her throat dry as the guilt sharpened. 'Is that why you were so insistent we marry? Why you wanted to obey the Law of Marriage of the Sheikhs.'

Had he been trying to right the wrongs his father had done his mother, and him, by observing the same sacred law his father had broken so callously?

She had so easily dismissed his demand that they marry as a backward and autocratic request based on arrogance and a misguided honour system that had no place in modern society, but it had always been much more personal than that. How could it not be after what he had discovered about his mother's treatment? She had put him in an untenable position by not telling him about her virginity, then had compounded it by dismissing his attempt to solve the problem. She had used him for her own pleasure, and then underestimated him at every turn.

'I don't know.' He shrugged, the movement stiff. 'I'm not sure what I was thinking at the time. I was shocked by your untouched state. I had not expected it. Or the intensity of our lovemaking.'

Her skin flushed at the bald statement, and the knots in her abdomen heated. She wasn't sure whether she was moved or flattered or simply aroused by his honesty and the knowledge she wasn't the only one who had been blindsided by their intense physical connection.

'But afterwards…' He sighed. 'Especially as I lay for days in the Golden Palace with nothing to do, I kept recalling our last moments together. And questioning why I had been so inflexible, so belligerent, so determined to insist upon marriage.' He hesitated. 'And it occurred to me that maybe I was more affected by what I had learned about my parents' past than I had assumed.'

'I'm so sorry,' she said. 'For putting you in that position.' It wasn't the first time she had apologised for not telling him of her virginity, but it was the first time she had meant it without reservation.

Maybe she'd had no knowledge of his past, his priorities, when she had slept with him, but she had assumed he was a thoughtless man, and had never examined his motives properly. His honour was important to him, not because he was arrogant or overbearing but because he had been forced to fight for it every single day of his life.

He lifted her hand, stared at her fingers as he brushed his thumb across her knuckles.

The heat in her stomach warmed further and glowed, and seemed to wrap itself around her heart, making her ribs feel tight.

The guilt twisted, though, when he raised his head, his expression tense. And guarded.

'I think perhaps it is *I* who should apologise to *you*,' he said, his voice gruff but forceful.

'Why?' she asked.

He touched a finger to her cheek, drew a tendril of hair behind her ear. Then sent her a lopsided smile that made her heartbeat slow and thicken.

'For trying to bully you into marriage, perhaps?' he murmured, the rueful twist of his lips beguiling. 'And for scaring you away. If I had not reacted so recklessly, made such a ridiculous demand, we could have found a better way to end our time at the oasis, is this not so?'

She forced a smile to her lips, stifling the ripple of sadness that he now considered marriage a 'ridiculous demand'. Of course he did, because it *was* ridiculous, they didn't know each other. Not really.

Should she tell him now, about the baby? The question had the guilt tightening in her stomach, but she dismissed it. Why destroy this moment of closeness, of connection? She would tell him soon, just not yet.

At least now she knew she didn't have to be scared to tell him when the time came. He was a much more intelligent and thoughtful man than she had given him credit for, despite the harshness of his upbringing.

'Perhaps we both need to apologise?' she offered.

He chuckled, the sound helping to release the knot of guilt still lodged in her belly. 'An excellent compromise.'

Warmth flooded her system at the approval in his gaze.

She would tell him about the pregnancy soon, but for tonight she just wanted to enjoy his company.

He was the father of her child, and while this liaison was based on a sexual connection and would not last—because they were still such different people, with such different goals in life—he would always have a place in her life now. And her child's life. It was good to know that didn't scare her any more, it excited her. She hadn't given much thought to what kind of father he would make, had been too scared to consider it because of her assumptions about the kind of man he was—rough, uneducated, wild—but now she could see she didn't need to be scared about that either.

He cradled her face, pulled her close for a kiss, and the pheromones gathered—as they always did—to overwhelm her thoughts. But as his lips touched hers, the electric contact sending a familiar shiver down her spine, a loud knock sounded in the next room.

'Mr Khan, room service. We have your order.'

He swore against her lips in Kholadi—his frustration palpable—and she let out a strained laugh.

Shifting to kiss her forehead, he drew back. 'I think we had better let them in,' he said, not sounding at all pleased at the prospect.

'Must we?' she shot back, surprising herself. Was she actually pouting?

He let out a rough chuckle. 'Unfortunately, yes, my little witch.'

The hot promise in his eyes had the heat rushing straight to her core as he climbed off the bed.

'You need to build up your stamina for the night ahead,' he added, wiggling his brows as he teased her.

The flush exploded in her core as she watched him stride across the bedroom in his boxer briefs. Her gaze drifted down the line of his spine and snagged on the bunch of muscle in his taut backside.

She would tell him about the baby soon, but for tonight she wanted to indulge in the pleasure of having him all to herself. And make full use of the chance to get to know him better. A *lot* better.

She choked off a playful laugh.

In every possible sense of the word!

CHAPTER TWELVE

KASIA AWOKE THE next morning feeling warm and sated and a little overwhelmed by the feel of Raif's big body wrapped around hers. His arm was draped over her waist, his even breathing stroked her nape. His hard chest pressed against her back, his muscular thighs cradled her own legs and something long and firm nestled against her bottom.

She blinked, adjusting to the morning light flooding through the open curtains, and couldn't stop a grin from spreading across her face.

Who would have guessed the Bad-Boy Sheikh was a secret snuggler?

But, then, there were so many things she'd discovered about him last night. Information that she'd stored away carefully to take out and examine at a later date. Not just the devastating details about his childhood but also what she'd learned about his strength of character, his code of honour and his ability to admit when he was wrong.

The heat settled in her abdomen, loosening her thigh muscles and making her feel giddy at the memory of all the times he'd taken her during the night. That first time, fast and furious and frantic, and unbearably exciting.

And then later, as they'd sat eating together and he'd insisted on feeding her a bite of his steak, the succulent flavour had exploded on her tongue and she'd groaned. The food had been abandoned, and they'd ended up back in the bedroom—and this time the fire had built slowly, sensuously. He'd made her beg, using his tongue and teeth and touch to drive her insane. Around midnight, they'd bathed together in the whirlpool tub in the suite's bathroom and then started all over again, making the delicious discovery that she could drive him insane in return. She'd finally dropped into a deep, dreamless sleep with his arms around her.

She sighed, the surge of arousal nothing new, but in the stark light of morning came self-consciousness as well.

Shifting on the bed, she lifted his arm and scooted out from under it. Laying it down again, she heard him grunt. He had rolled over onto his back.

She had to cover her mouth to hold in her delighted laugh at the sight of his beautiful torso, all strong lines and sculpted contours, revealed by the sheet lying low on his hips and the tent formed by his morning erection.

Liquid heat throbbed at her core.

Yes, she would definitely have to take care of that erection soon, but first things first. She needed to wash her face, check her hair hadn't gone completely wild during the night, brush her teeth and work out the etiquette for the morning after a night such as the one they had just shared. She could feel delicious tenderness in her sex, the rub of beard burn on her nipples. Was that normal?

She tiptoed across the room, plucked the bathrobe off the floor where it had been flung during their mad dash back to bed after supper, and put it on. But as she walked passed the open door to the living area, a vague whiff of last night's dinner hit her nostrils.

Nausea rose from nowhere like a tidal wave. Slamming a hand over her mouth, she dashed into the bathroom, reaching the toilet just in time before her stomach and everything inside it heaved.

When the violent retching finally stopped, she flushed away the evidence of her first bout of morning sickness and slid into a sitting position on the floor. Exhausted.

The nausea still sat like a crouching tiger under her breastbone, ready to pounce, the subtle scent of rose perfume from the vanity offending her nostrils.

She gulped in air. But as she gripped the vanity unit, attempting to hold the new wave of nausea at bay, a deep voice—thick with concern—had her jerking round.

'Kasia, what's wrong? Have you just vomited?'

Panic gripped her already tender insides as Raif crossed the room. He wore only the boxer briefs, but the jolt of arousal that always accompanied the glorious sight of his nearly naked body was short-lived.

Her stomach rebelled.

He grabbed her, holding her upright on unsteady legs and sweeping the wild hair back from her face as she bent over the toilet.

'I've got you,' he said, stroking her back as she retched. The wave finally passed as her stomach emptied, leaving her exhausted and shaky. And terrified.

Tears leaked from her eyes, emotion and anxiety overwhelming her.

Why did the sickness have to hit for the first time this morning?

She'd felt vaguely queasy in the last week, but she'd hadn't been prepared for anything like this. And the last thing she wanted was for him to witness it.

'Has it passed?' he asked gently.

She nodded. 'Yes, I think so.'

Dropping the toilet seat, he directed her to sit on it, then filled a glass with water.

She had to leave. She needed more time to work out the best possible way to break the news of her pregnancy to him. And having to admit it while she was sitting on the toilet of his luxury bathroom, with her hair rioting around her head as if she'd been electrocuted and her nipples still sore from his lovemaking, definitely wasn't that moment.

The anxiety she'd taken a break from the night before bounced back.

She didn't feel sexy and empowered any more. She felt weak, inadequate and worn out.

'Sip this,' he said, handing her the glass. She did as she was told, but the cool, refreshing liquid soothing her raw throat did nothing to tame the anxiety still churning in her stomach as she watched him rip Cellophane off a new toothbrush then add toothpaste, and run it under the tap.

Taking the glass from her, he handed her the prepared toothbrush.

She brushed her teeth, aware of his watchful gaze.

'What do you think has caused this sickness?' he asked when she had finished rinsing out her mouth.

She concentrated on wiping her lips, deliberately avoiding eye contact as she spoke. 'It must have been something I ate.'

But even she could hear the tremble of dishonesty in her voice. She had always been a terrible liar.

'I should probably head home,' she said, more firmly. 'It might be a bug and I don't want you to catch it, too.'

He hadn't said anything, hadn't even moved.

She swallowed down the lump of shame at her deception. She couldn't deal with him now, not in this condition.

If she could just get out of here, she would be able to regroup, recharge, re-evaluate. At least her stomach had finally settled.

But as she dropped the towel on the vanity and turned to go, his fingers closed around her biceps. 'Not so fast. Look at me, Kasia.' He grasped her chin.

Their gazes connected and the guilt exploded in her chest like a nuclear bomb as he studied her face, the mushroom cloud billowing across her collarbone and rising into her cheeks.

'We ate the same thing, and I am not sick,' he said, but

she could hear it already in his voice—the edge of suspicion. And see it in the hooded look in his dark eyes. 'And if it was a stomach bug, I doubt it would have resolved itself so quickly.'

'Please, I have to go.' She tried to wrestle her arm free, the frantic urge to flee overcoming her, even though a part of her knew it was already too late.

Raif was not a stupid man, and he could read her far too easily.

His grip on her arm tightened, a muscle in his jaw flexing as his gaze dipped to take in the swell of her cleavage. And assess the size of her breasts again, which he had noticed the night before were larger than they had been. When his gaze returned to hers, the last of the warmth and concern had leached away, to be replaced by the brutal chill of anger.

Guilt and regret combined in the pit of her stomach to create a deep well of sadness.

The guarded, wary cynicism in his eyes, which had been banished the night before—as they'd eaten and talked and bathed together, as they had made love—had returned.

The closeness, the connection was gone so quickly she wondered if it had ever really existed in the first place, especially when he spoke again, the bite of contempt evident in every syllable:

'Answer me without lying this time, are you carrying my child?'

Raif could see the answer in her face before she replied.

'Yes,' she said, then ducked her head.

The slow-burning fury in his gut turned to white-hot rage but worse than that was the stabbing pain of her betrayal.

Kasia carried his child and she had not told him. Had she ever intended to tell him?

She had said nothing all through the night they had spent together. While he had taken her with fire, with passion more times than he could count. But also while they had talked, and communicated with more than words.

When he had woken up a few minutes ago, the first thing he had done was reach for her. The wave of panic when he had found her gone had been real and devastating and not just because of the painful erection he'd been sporting. He hadn't just wanted to take her again, he had wanted to hold her, to touch her, to capture her in his arms and keep her with him. He had never had that need for any other human being in his entire life. He had tried to dismiss it, forced himself to control it, but that instant visceral yearning had scared him on a fundamental level.

The sound of her in the bathroom had brought with it a wave of relief, which had only disturbed him more.

As he had stared at the ornate plasterwork on the ceiling, willing his erection to subside—not easy while her scent filled his nostrils—he had forced himself to assess all they had done the night before, and had tried to figure out what had happened to him.

Kasia had captivated and aroused him, intoxicated him with her passion, her wildfire responses, yes, but more than that he had found a closeness with her during the hours they had spent together. As they had talked, as they had teased each other.

He had spoken of things in his life he had never told another living soul. Not just the truth about his mother, but the truth about the tattoo—how his father had him branded like cattle. The more he'd thought about everything he had said and done, the weaker he'd felt.

Why had he trusted her? When he had never truly trusted anyone in his life? And after so short an acquaintance?

But then his hearing had tuned into the noise from the

bathroom and he'd realised she was being sick. All he'd wanted to do was help her.

She'd looked so fragile, seemed so shaky in his arms. He'd held her while she'd retched and felt wretched himself.

That, too, had been a brand-new sensation. If he had been in a similar situation before, not that he ever had, his inclination would have been to allow his lover her privacy. But with Kasia, as with everything else about them, he had been determined to intervene.

Had he sensed her condition the night before? Was that why he had felt this weird connection to her? Had revealed information that he had never trusted anyone to know before now?

It had to be, he thought, desperate to dismiss the hollow feeling that had started to seep into his bones.

She had betrayed him. Had hidden the truth from him. And that he could never forgive.

'Why did you not tell me?' he asked, struggling to control the rage, not just at her deception but at his own stupidity.

Her face lifted. The sheen of tears looked genuine, but he steeled himself against them.

She had deceived him, deliberately. The tears weren't real.

'I wanted to wait for the right time,' she said, her voice faltering. She dropped her chin, to stare at the fingers she was clutching. 'Last night was…' Her jaw clenched. 'Last night was special, I didn't want to ruin it.'

His heart swelled, but he pushed his fury to the fore.

She had deceived him and manipulated him into telling her things he should never have revealed. He would not make that mistake again.

He could not undo last night—but he could use it to his advantage, something he was more than prepared to do for the sake of his child.

His gaze dropped, to take in the swell of her breasts where the lapels of her robe drooped. The surge of heat was inevitable and familiar—and gloriously uncomplicated—the surge of possessiveness not so much. But still it made sense. His child grew inside her. He had always known he would have to become a father, that he would need to have heirs to ensure a peaceful transition of power within his tribe.

Yes, there was his honour to be considered too now. The urge to protect his honour at the oasis, which had made him demand marriage, an urge he had been determined to dismiss only last night as a knee-jerk reaction to the circumstances of his birth, had become stronger than ever.

He needed to start thinking clearly again. Thinking pragmatically. And make decisions based on the good of his people, his position, not based on weakness or want or the whims of a girl he couldn't even trust.

The child was the only thing that mattered now… His child and the child he had once been. He would give this child the legacy he had worked for twenty years to create, ever since a small band of Kholadi tribesman had discovered him abandoned and dying in the desert, his shoulder covered in scabs from the enforced tattoo, and had recognised him as one of their own.

He owed his tribe his loyalty and his life. He owed this girl neither.

Tucking a finger under her chin, he lifted her gaze back to his and forced himself to hold onto his fury. And ignored the shiver of sensation that always assailed him when he touched her. This indiscriminate desire would come in useful in the years ahead. But for now he had to ask the only question that mattered.

'Do you intend to keep the child?'

'Yes,' she said, covering her belly with her clasped hands

as if to instinctively protect the babe within from the suggestion of termination.

He nodded, resenting the leap in his chest.

It was not joy or gratitude he felt. Why should he be grateful or joyous when she had chosen to keep the very existence of this child from him?

'Then we must be married as soon as possible.'

'No!' She stepped back, her eyebrows shooting up as if she was surprised by his demand, panic sparking in her eyes. 'That's not… I can't marry you.'

He grasped her arm, the fear that she would run again churning in his gut, but he clung onto his fury, forced himself to loosen his grip. She still appeared fragile and shaky from the bout of nausea. And bullying her had not worked before. Which meant he would have to reason with her. Something that would be a great deal easier if her nearness didn't fire every one of his senses, and her refusal to accept their situation didn't make his temper ignite.

'There is no other option now,' he said, struggling to bite down not just on his fury but also his resentment. 'I will not have my child born a bastard, as I was.' He ground out the words, hating that he was being forced to reveal his feelings again, feelings he wished he had never shared. 'As the mother of my child, you will become my princess, you will have everything you could ever want, and our child will be heir to the Kholadi principality. Is that not enough?' He was offering her everything he had. How dared she refuse him?

'No.' She tugged her arm loose. 'Because I won't have the one thing I want most. A choice.'

It was the same argument she had used before, the argument that he had eventually agreed to last night, after much soul-searching. But the situation was very different now. They weren't independent people any more. They were parents and they must protect their child.

'There are no choices now,' he said. 'Not for either of us.'

'I refuse to believe that, there is *always* a choice,' she said, the tears spilling over her lids.

These tears were not fake, even he was forced to acknowledge as much despite his resentment.

Her wariness and her regret were replaced by pride and stubbornness in the upward tilt of her chin and the stiff set of her shoulders. She was prepared to fight him on this, and there was something about her bravery and determination that had a tiny kernel of respect blossoming inside him. But he refused to give in to it.

He had given way once before. He would not do so again.

'The only choice now is marriage,' he said.

'I can't marry without love,' she said, as she straightened. 'And I won't.'

'Love!' The enraged shout came out before he could think better of it. 'There is no such thing as love. It is romantic *nonsense*. If that is what you have learned from your fancy education, it is better you stop wasting my brother's money.'

He had gone too far, said too much, even though every word was true. Her body went rigid, the fierce compassion sparking in her eyes that had stirred him to make so many reckless, foolish decisions from the moment he'd met her.

'That you think love is nonsense is precisely why I would never choose to marry *you*.' She hurled the words at him, the fire and passion reverberating through her slender body, then turned and fled from the room.

He swore viciously in Kholadi, the ugly curses echoing off the marble surfaces like rifle shots.

He forced himself to breathe, waiting for the squeezing pain in his lungs to ease, and stayed rooted to the spot, even though his instinct was to storm after her. Not to let her get away.

He curled his fingers into fists, clenched his teeth so

tight he was surprised his jaw didn't crack, and waited for the storm of destructive, counter-productive emotions to pass. Or pass enough for him to think clearly.

He knew how to conduct a negotiation. But he had blown this one, by letting her see how much he wanted this marriage. He had shown his hand too early and then allowed his frustration, his need to distract him from his goals.

They *would* be married. That much was non-negotiable. But bullying her and shouting at her was not the answer. It was how his father had always behaved. And it made him less of a man.

He could hear her getting dressed in the bedroom. A part of him, a very large part of him, wanted to stalk in there and stop her from leaving. As he was sure she intended to do—because running away was her default.

But instead of doing so, he stalked to the sink and turned on the tap.

He washed his hands and face, threw cold water on his chest, to contain the anger—and the passion still rioting through his body and evident not just in the pounding pain in his head but the stiff column of flesh stretching his boxers.

When he had finally calmed himself enough to control the fury, the passion and the pain, he walked out of the bathroom.

The bedroom was empty, as he had suspected it might be. A scrawled note lay on the bed, propped on the unkempt sheets where they had devoured each other during the night. He picked it up. As he read the note, some of the writing smudged with what had to be her tears, the fury and frustration twisted his gut again.

I'm sorry I didn't tell you about the baby last night. That was wrong of me. And I apologise.

*But the reason I didn't was that I feared exactly
this reaction from you. We cannot be wed. Because
love means everything to me and nothing to you. I
want this child very much and I love it already. Rest
assured it will never be a bastard to me.*

Once it is born, we can speak again.

Until then, please don't contact me.

Kasia

He crushed the note in his fist. He would contact her again,
and soon. She could not run far this time, only to the college he already had the power to control with the funding
he had offered.

He refused to give up on the necessity of marriage, as
he had far too easily before, because much more than just
his honour was at stake now.

His child grew inside her. That gave him rights and responsibilities he could not shirk. Rights and responsibilities he *would* not shirk.

He could not allow his child to be born defenceless,
without his name, his wealth and the legacy he had fought
so hard to create. But neither would he turn into his father
to get what he wanted.

So he must figure out a strategy to force Kasia to see
what was right in front of her eyes.

No child deserved to be born without its father's name,
its father's protection.

Love was not enough. It couldn't feed you or clothe
you, it couldn't fight your enemies for you or shelter you
from a storm.

He could not change her fanciful, foolishly romantic
notions, but she was smart and intuitive and she wanted
him—as much as he wanted her—so he would find a way
to persuade her that marriage was the only option.

If that meant charming her, bribing her, seducing her,

blackmailing her or even kidnapping her, dammit. He would do it. He could not fail.

Because the one thing he would never do was abandon his child.

CHAPTER THIRTEEN

Ms Salah, please come to my office immediately.

Kasia stared at the text from Dean Walmsley. The dropping sensation in her already over-sensitive stomach exacerbated the tangle of anxiety.

She took a sip of her tea and a tentative nibble of the dry crackers she had been advised to snack on by her doctor, then gathered up her backpack and the textbooks she was returning to the library.

She would speak to Dean Walmsley on the way.

She had been expecting this confrontation for over a week, ever since she had returned from London. All she could do now was pray that he hadn't been informed of the full extent of her unprofessionalism at the funding event. He'd been furious when he'd called her to his office on the Monday morning to inform her that Alice Evershot had emailed him to say the funding had not been forthcoming from the donor she had met.

Given that the donor was Raif, she was not remotely surprised at the decision to withdraw the offer. That she would have to wait to hear if she would receive the funding she needed for her PhD seemed somehow fitting in the circumstances as payback for the mistakes she'd made. She could not accept the funding from Raif now anyway, because it would give him a hold over her that could cause massive complications given their personal relationship.

Not that they had a personal relationship, she thought

wearily as she made her way through the campus buildings towards Dean Walmsley's office. The only thing that connected them now was the baby.

She'd had no word from Raif in the last week, which she should have been glad about. He must have read her note, realised she would have made him a terrible consort and decided not to contact her again until after the baby was born.

So why was she so disappointed? She didn't want to have another confrontation with him on the question of marriage. But at the same time she couldn't ignore the deep well of sadness, the yearning in the last week every time she woke in her single bed after another night spent dreaming about him and missed that leaping joy when she had woken up on the Saturday morning to find his arms around her.

Perhaps it was simply that, despite their terrible row, she knew Raif, for all his cynicism about love, was not an insensitive man—*because* of the dreadful cruelties he had suffered as a child, not in spite of them.

Regret tightened her throat.

It's just the pregnancy hormones, Kaz, messing with you again. Even if you could have loved Raif, he could never have loved you back.

He had spent his whole life guarding against making himself vulnerable. And without vulnerability how could you have love? No matter how sensitive or intelligent he could be—the heat glowed in her stomach—or how attuned to he was to her sexual needs.

She trudged up the stairs of the red-brick building that housed the Dean's office.

It's a good thing he has seen reason—not a bad thing for you and your baby. Stop second-guessing yourself.

They would reach an accord together once the child was born, but to do that without enmity or anger, they needed a break now, which was precisely why she had asked that of him in her note. That he had respected her decision was a positive sign. He was not intractable, not averse to see-ing reason.

She wanted very much for her son or daughter to know its father, to have a relationship with him and for him to have a relationship with his child. For that to happen, they needed to be able to negotiate with each other in good faith without the spectre of past hurts, past wrongs rearing their heads. To take time out was a good thing. That Raif had seen reason—and hadn't stalked straight after her—was therefore all good, even if it didn't feel that good at the moment.

Of course she felt vulnerable, scared, lonely. She was going to have to bring up her child alone. And find out how to continue her academic career as a single parent. She still hadn't gained the courage to contact Cat and tell her what was going on.

She blew out a breath as she reached the top of the stairs and headed down the corridor to Walmsley's office and the bad news she was sure awaited her about her PhD.

If only she didn't feel so tired all the time—the bouts of nausea restricted themselves to the early morning, thank goodness—but the pregnancy, and the difficulty she'd had sleeping since she'd left Raif's bed, had also taken a heavy toll on her energy. Shifting the books in her arms, she tapped on the door to the Dean's office. 'Dean Walmsley, it's Kasia Salah.'

'Come in, Miss Salah,' came the curt response.

She straightened her spine, hearing the irritation in Walmsley's tone. Okay, that did not sound promising.

If the Dean was about to kick her out of the college, she would just have to find another way to get funding. The PhD she wanted to pursue was important to Narabia. And also important to her.

But the prickle of unease became an explosion as soon

as she stepped into the office, and saw the man sitting in front of Walmsley's desk.

Raif.

He stood, his tall frame clad in a designer business suit silhouetted against the sunshine flooding through Walmsley's window.

'Miss Salah, it's about time you arrived. Mr Khan and I have been waiting…' Walmsley began to talk, but his reprimand was drowned out by the pounding in Kasia's ears.

Her gaze devoured Raif, the brutal awareness, the painful longing she couldn't seem to curtail or control only becoming more disturbing as she took in the flare of desire in his dark chocolate eyes and the harsh, unyielding line of his jaw.

The books in her arms clattered to the floor. But she couldn't seem to hear that either. All she could hear were the questions in her head peppering her like bullets as she tried to fight her misguided burst of joy at seeing him again.

Had he come here to demand marriage again? To bully her? To blackmail her? He was an extremely wealthy man—the college depended on donors like him to fund its postgraduate programme—which gave him a power over her career that she hadn't acknowledged until this moment.

'Miss Salah! What on earth is the matter with you?' Walmsley's horrified exclamation didn't really register either as she stumbled back, unable to take her eyes off Raif as he stepped towards her and bent to scoop up the books she'd dropped.

'What are you doing here?' she whispered as he straightened, his gaze locked on her face. The clean, intoxicating aroma of man and soap suffocated her.

'Mr Khan has come to talk more about the funding initiative,' Walmsley butted in. 'I have a lecture to give, so I will leave you two alone,' the Dean added with a sniff. 'Make sure you make a better impression this time, Miss

Salah,' he finished, sending her a scathing look as he left the office.

But somehow she couldn't seem to engage with the Dean's censure as the door shut behind him, leaving her alone with Raif.

'Why are you really here?' she asked again, doubting the funding initiative had anything to do with Raif's presence in Cambridge.

'You know why, Kasia,' he said. 'Did you really believe I would abandon my child so easily?'

'I can't… I still can't marry you, Raif, my answer hasn't changed,' she said, feeling humiliated by the quiver in her voice.

He placed the books she had dropped on Walmsley's desk without replying. Then, to her astonishment, he nodded.

'You do not wish to marry me, because you do not love me? Is this correct?'

It was the very last thing she had expected him to say. Of course, it wasn't the only reason she couldn't marry him. And she wasn't even sure it was entirely true, because she suspected she was already halfway in love with him. Despite everything. How else could she explain the bone-deep yearning that had gripped her as soon as she had stepped into the office, the needs and wants that went way beyond simple physical desire, or all the dreams she'd had with him as the star player, not just in the last week but also the last month? Or her immediate decision to have this child, which she could now see with complete clarity was not just because she wanted a baby but because this baby was his.

No, the real stumbling block to a marriage between them wasn't her feelings, it was his. His refusal to accept that love even existed.

But as she watched the stark expression on his face, and realised the effort it was taking him to be reasonable, not to simply repeat the demands he had made a week ago, the foolish bubble of hope pressed against her larynx.

Surely no one's emotions were ever set in stone, even those of a man like Raif—who had spent years protecting himself from weakness, because of the appalling way he had been treated by his own father.

If she was already half in love with him, didn't she owe it to herself and their child to at least give him a chance, give them both a chance to find a compromise?

'Well, yes,' she said. 'That's part of the reason.'

'Then perhaps you could love me if you got to know me better. And we could be married, is this not also correct?'

But it's not just about me loving you, Raif.

The qualification screamed inside her head, but she could see the flicker of wariness he was trying to hide. And she couldn't bring herself to challenge his interpretation of the obstacles to their marriage. Not yet.

This was a man who had never known love, had persuaded himself he didn't need it or want it. That it didn't even exist. At least not for him. And because of the terrible things he had confided in her, she knew why he felt that way. But still he was here willing to talk about it to her. Willing to take her needs seriously.

Yes, she would have a mountain to climb to persuade him he did need love in his life. And she didn't want to put herself in the position of trying to make him love her, because that way could only lead to heartache. She knew how painful and pointless such an endeavour was because she had blamed herself for her mother's absence. She had finally grown up enough to realise her love could never have been enough to make her mother stay—that she couldn't hold herself responsible for her mother's choices.

But what choice had Raif ever had to understand and embrace the importance of love if no one had ever loved him unconditionally? Perhaps he would never have the ability to do that with her, but she wanted so much for him to be able to find that with their child. Surely as long as she protected her own heart, there was nothing to be afraid of, or not much.

She let the bubble of hope expand in her throat. 'Perhaps,' she said.

'Then I have a suggestion,' he said.

Anticipation leapt under her breastbone.

'I have important business to attend to in Paris and New York over the next three weeks,' he began as he planted his hands in his pockets and turned back towards the sunlight, breaking eye contact as he spoke. His devastatingly handsome profile made her heartbeat accelerate.

Not fair.

'Business I cannot ignore and that was neglected while I was recovering at the Golden Palace.' He mentioned his illness with pragmatism, making her sure he hadn't intended to make her feel guilty, but she felt the pang nonetheless. 'But there will be some free time between meetings when we can spend time together…' He turned, the desire in his eyes intensifying as his gaze fixed on her face, direct and dogmatic and as overwhelming as always.

She ought to be wary of his request. Spending three weeks with this man had the potential to seriously endanger her heart. But then his Adam's apple bobbed.

He was nervous, or at least apprehensive, about her answer and trying extremely hard not to show it.

It was the first time she'd ever been able to read him, the first time she'd seen a crack in the wall of confidence he presented to the world.

The bubble of hope swelled to the size of a hot-air balloon in her chest.

This was progress. Maybe it was only baby steps, but still it felt important and exhilarating in a way she would never have believed possible. And it felt like enough, for now.

'Will you come with me?' he asked, his tone curt. But the edge of uncertainty made the hot-air balloon bob under her breastbone.

'Yes,' she said, fighting her own fears to give them both a chance.

'Good.' He whipped his hands out of his pockets, cradled her cheeks between rough palms and captured her lips with his.

The kiss was deep, hungry and demanding. His tongue explored the recesses of her mouth, commanding her response—which rioted through her body on a wave of emotions she couldn't even begin to control.

But when they finally parted, the line of his jaw had softened, and along with the hunger, the satisfaction, the cast-iron confidence she could see the flicker of relief, and it was enough to steer the hot-air balloon full of hope towards her heart.

CHAPTER FOURTEEN

KASIA SIGHED AS she stepped onto the balcony of the Parisian hotel's penthouse suite. The Eiffel Tower seemed close enough to touch, its elegant steel beams lit by a million tiny lights in the sunset, while it watched over the warren of streets like a benevolent giant.

'Wow.' She spun round as Raif joined her on the terrace, having just tipped the battalion of porters who had brought up their luggage. 'This view is incredible.'

'I'm glad you approve.' He wrapped an arm around her waist to pull her back against his body. His lips found the rapidly beating pulse in her neck—the pulse that hadn't stopped fluttering since he'd arrived at her hall of residence in a chauffeur-driven car three hours ago. The pulse that had been going a little haywire ever since: when he'd escorted her aboard the Kholadi Corporation's private jet; when they'd been picked up by another chauffeur-driven car at Orly Airport; when he'd pointed out the cluster of iconic landmarks they'd passed on the drive through the Eighth Arrondissement to their hotel.

She had sighed over the elegance of the Élysée Palace, gawped at the splendour of the Grand Palais, fed her passion for people watching as they'd cruised down the Champs-Élysées and almost got a crick in her neck as they'd passed the Arc de Triomphe. She'd never been to Paris before, had never really been outside Cambridge during her five years in Europe, having been far too focused on her studies.

But her elevated pulse as she took in the magnificence

of the City of Light for the first time had more to do with
the man beside her and the thought of spending three whole
weeks in his company.

She had made a decision the day before, after they had
parted in Walmsley's office and he had contacted her later
that day with details of their trip, that she would embrace
the chance he was giving her to get to know him. He wanted
this trip to end in marriage, she understood that. And she
had no doubt at all that he would pull out all the stops to
make that happen.

But just because he wanted marriage for all the wrong
reasons—for honour, and duty and responsibility and because she was carrying his child—it didn't mean they
couldn't fall in love, or at least use this trip to find an accord that would stand them in good stead when they became parents.

She wasn't going to rule anything out. She wanted to
keep her heart and her mind open, to absorb every sight and
sound and sensation and to discover everything she could
about a man who had always fascinated her.

Raif trailed kisses up her neck, the teasing licks and nips
of his tongue and teeth sending the familiar shivers of anticipation darting down to her core. She softened against
him, the magnificent view nowhere near as awesome as
the feel of having his arms around her again. She tilted her
head to give him better access, and covered his hands with
hers as her breathing accelerated.

He hadn't touched her since the kiss they had shared to
seal the deal they'd made in Walmsley's office. And she'd
been looking forward to continuing their sexual relationship every moment since—because sex was the one thing
in their relationship that was uncomplicated and straight-
forward. And sex seemed like the perfect way to get closer
to him, to continue knocking down the wall he used to shut
people out.

Feeling his erection pressing against her back, she shifted in his arms, more than ready to take his tantalising kisses to the next level. But as she lifted her arms to draw him closer, his hands gripped her waist, keeping her at arm's length.

'Stop, my little witch,' he said, a tight smile on his face. 'We cannot.'

'Why not?' she asked, unable to hide her disappointment as she let her arms drop, suddenly hesitant and unsure of herself.

'There is not enough time,' he said, as he brushed a thumb across her cheek, setting off all the usual reactions at her core. 'I have an important meeting to attend this evening.'

'Really?' she said, perplexed now as well as disappointed. 'But it's almost dark.' And she'd been looking forward to some quality time alone with him ever since yesterday's kiss.

Why had he started something he couldn't finish? Her gaze darted down to the thick ridge in his pants that suggested she hadn't read the situation entirely wrongly.

'In Paris, they conduct business at all hours,' he said, giving a strained chuckle. 'I must shower and change before I go. And you should rest,' he added. 'It has been a long, tiring journey.'

No, it hadn't. He'd only picked her up a few hours ago, and being transported in a chauffeur-driven limousine and a private jet—and waited on hand and foot—was hardly stressful.

'I'm not tired,' she said. Then, getting up all her courage, she added, 'Perhaps I could join you in the shower?'

His pupils dilated to black and his jaw tensed, but the tight smile remained as he shook his head. 'It is going to be a cold shower—if you join me, the purpose of it will be defeated.'

'Oh, I see,' she said, unable to deny the little leap of excitement that she could affect him in that way.

But when he lifted her hand to graze a perfunctory kiss across her knuckles, then left her standing on the balcony alone, the disappointment—and confusion—returned. Especially when she discovered Raif had directed the porters to put her two suitcases in a bedroom on the other side of the suite's luxury living area from his own.

Had she misconstrued his intentions? Should she say something? She had thought that they would be together. Really together. And it wasn't just about the sex, she wanted to share the intimacy of waking up in his arms, and discovering all his annoying little habits. They only had three weeks so why would he want to spend them in separate bedrooms?

'Will you be okay on your own tonight?'

She swung round from the balcony of her bedroom to find him standing at the door in a newly pressed suit, his damp hair slicked back, his jaw clean shaven.

She swallowed her disappointment and tried to contain the inevitable leap of lust. She was being ridiculous, this was their first night, he was giving her space, being considerate. She must not overreact.

'Yes, of course,' she said.

He strode towards her, and clasped her face in his hands. 'Order something from room service, there is a Michelin-starred chef here, I believe.'

'You won't be back in time for dinner?'

'I'm not sure,' he said, but she could see the lie in his eyes—she wouldn't see him again tonight. 'But if I am delayed, I don't want you to go hungry.' He gave her a chaste kiss on the forehead. 'Get a good night's sleep.'

After the main door of the suite had closed behind him, she turned back to the romantic view, which seemed to be mocking her. The sun had almost disappeared behind the rooftops, making the lights on the iconic tower glow orange in the dusk. She let out a tortured breath.

Maybe a cold shower wouldn't be a bad idea for her, too, before she examined the room service menu.

She had three whole weeks to get to know the father of her child, and she had this beautiful city to explore over the next few days while he was busy in his meetings. Intimacy couldn't be rushed. And they were as hungry for each other as they had ever been—a slight delay would only make them more eager.

She was being paranoid and insecure, because she had no experience of how to conduct an intimate relationship, any more than she suspected Raif did.

She placed a warm palm on the waistband of her jeans, which had already started to get a little tight, and smiled.

She needed to slow down and enjoy the moment, and stop wishing for more, when she already had so much.

CHAPTER FIFTEEN

You need to stop messing about and seduce him—tonight.

Kasia smoothed shaky palms down the purple satin of the gown she had been fitted for that morning in an exclusive designer boutique just off the Champs-Élysées.

They'd been in Paris for four days now—and four nights—and despite two evening meals in the hotel's Michelin-starred rooftop restaurant, when their conversation had been stilted and polite, she'd barely seen Raif or spoken to him. Part of that had been her fault. Each morning, after surviving the now regular bout of morning sickness, she'd fallen back into bed exhausted and woken up hours later to find him gone.

But the nights she had spent alone, deposited back at the suite with a perfunctory kiss and an increasingly banal excuse, were entirely Raif's fault.

Why didn't he want to spend any quality time with her? Why didn't he even want to sleep with her? She knew desire was not the problem, from the way she'd caught him looking at her on several occasions before he could mask it.

Keeping herself busy and trying not to dwell on the progress they weren't making hadn't been too hard. He'd left a car and driver at her disposal and given her a platinum credit card that she'd used to buy a suitable wardrobe for the charity ball they were attending tonight.

There had been so many places to explore, so many sights and sounds to excite and entertain her, but underneath the excitement had always been the disappointment she wasn't seeing any of them with him. She hadn't pressed him, though, on the time they spent apart. She knew he was busy, and the principal reason for him being in Paris was his business interests in Europe. She'd been impressed with how hard he worked, had even been a little bit astonished to discover he spoke fluent German, French and Italian.

On the one morning she'd managed to wake up before he'd left for the day she'd heard him conversing in all three languages during a conference call.

But tonight was going to be different. They were attending a charity ball at the Petit Palais and she'd spent all day preparing her master plan—to finally turn the heated promise in his eyes into reality.

The gown's classic lines and sleek, simple cut hugged her curves and managed to look elegant despite accentuating her increasingly generous bosom. Having spent most of the afternoon since she'd returned from the dress fitting visiting the hotel's spa—being buffed and primped to within an inch of her life—and then the salon where her hair had been tamed and styled into an elaborate chignon, she finally felt like a queen, instead of a serving girl playing dress-up.

Tonight was the night.

She stepped into the suite's living area and spotted Raif adjusting the cuffs of his tuxedo as he stood on the suite's balcony.

The heat fired down to her core. She took a hitched breath as she absorbed the sight, making the bodice of the gown tighten like a corset. The suite's view of the Eiffel Tower was magnificent as always, but it was the man— dark and impossibly dashing in the designer tuxedo and white shirt—who took her breath away.

Clutching the jewelled evening bag that matched the gown, she cleared her throat.

His head lifted and his gaze roamed over her skin.

Walking towards her, his lips lifted in a strained smile. 'You look exquisite,' he murmured, lifting her fingers to his lips. 'I see you put the credit card to good use.'

'I only had to buy the shoes and the purse,' she said, pleased about the bargain she'd arranged. When he was working so hard to increase the Kholadi's investment profile in the West, what right did she have to spend his money on frivolous things? 'The boutique was happy to loan me the gown for the evening when I told them the event we were attending.'

His brow furrowed. 'Why did you do this? I do not wish you to wear borrowed clothing.'

'But it was very expensive, Raif. Thousands of euros. I would feel uncomfortable spending that amount of—'

'Thousands of euros is nothing,' he interrupted her. 'Kholadi Corporation made over fifteen million euros in an hour yesterday from our investments alone.'

She swallowed, suitably staggered by the amount. She'd known he was wealthy, but she hadn't been prepared for how wealthy.

'I think I can afford to buy the mother of my child a gown,' he added, cupping her cheek, his eyes flaring again. But instead of being warmed by the heat, this time she felt a little overwhelmed, the compulsion to stand her ground somehow more pronounced.

'Yes, but it's not my money. Of course when the baby's born I'd be more than happy for you to pay any support you feel is—'

'Stop.' He ran his thumb over her lips. Then pulled a small velvet box out of the pocket of his tuxedo. 'We are not strangers, Kasia,' he said as her gaze became fixated on the box. Was that what she thought it was? And how was she supposed to react? Because the sudden blip of panic was swiftly followed by an equally disturbing swell of emotion.

'I want you to be much more than just the mother of my

child.' He flicked open the box, tugged out an exquisite diamond-studded gold engagement ring and then dropped the box on the balcony table. 'Which is why I wish you to wear this.'

He lifted her trembling fingers and without waiting for her reply slid it onto her ring finger.

She stood stunned, emotion threatening to close off her air supply.

'But… I haven't agreed to marry you, Raif,' she said, feeling sad at the thought that they were no further along than they had been in Walmsley's office when she'd agreed to this trip. 'It's a beautiful ring, but I can't wear it.'

But when she went to drag the ring off, he clasped her fingers, preventing her.

'Wait, and hear me out,' he said, his thumbs stroking the backs of her hands in a gentle caress.

Forced to listen or start a wrestling match, she waited to see what he had to say, the ring heavy on her finger.

'An engagement ring is a symbol of intention, is it not?' he said, his eyes guarded but so intense she felt the burn right down to her soul.

'I suppose so,' she replied.

'I intend to marry you at the end of this trip, Kasia, and I want everyone to know it, which is why I wish you to wear my ring.' His gaze coasted over the gown she'd borrowed, making the exposed skin of her arms and cleavage burn. 'And why I wish you to purchase everything and anything you need with my money.'

The possessiveness in his tone was so compelling it made her feel scalded, but what he was talking about was still rights and responsibility and nothing more.

'But I haven't agreed to—'

'Shhh…' Tugging her close, he kissed her, his lips silencing hers, his tongue driving into her mouth until she was breathless. When he finally released her she was more than a little dazed.

'Wearing my ring does not take that choice away from you,' he said, the fierce determination on his face only stealing more of her breath. 'But I am a proud man, and until you have made your choice, while you are by my side I want everyone to know you—and your baby—are mine. Do you understand?'

Oddly, she did understand. This wasn't about taking her choices away from her, it was about him asserting his responsibilities to his child and her. And maybe she owed him this much, even if it was going to make it harder for her to make her choice. But then why should her choice be easy? He was right, a child was involved now. Not just her. So she nodded.

'You will wear the ring?' he said, finally asking instead of telling her.

And because he had, she nodded. 'Yes.' Her lips quirked in an unsteady smile. 'And thank you.'

'You are welcome.' Lifting her left hand, he kissed the ring, and the lump of emotion made it hard for her to breathe.

But it was only as he escorted her out of the hotel into the waiting limousine, a protective arm around her waist, that it occurred to her that wearing his ring didn't just make her feel as if she belonged to him. It made her feel owned.

CHAPTER SIXTEEN

How CAN I want her so much, all the time? Why can I not control it?

Raif's fingers firmed on Kasia's waist as she shifted away from him to talk to some minor royal, who had been flirting with his fiancée for the last twenty minutes. Kasia seemed oblivious to the young man's intentions, or that the bastard had conducted their conversation about her research into desert agriculture almost entirely at her cleavage. Her lush, beautiful bust pressed provocatively against the purple satin as she gesticulated to make a point about Narabia's need for greater yield and the research she was doing into how to achieve that.

Blood surged into his groin, and Raif tensed, annoyed all over again by the effect she had on him. He had tried to be considerate these last four days, had deliberately made himself scarce—especially at night. She'd been exhausted when he'd seen her in Walmsley's office, the bruised smudges under her eyes disturbing him. And each morning he could hear her retching violently as she had done on their morning together two weeks ago. He would have to bed her soon or risk exploding. But it was beginning to concern him, not just how little control he had over his own libido but also the toll the pregnancy seemed to be taking on her.

She was radiant tonight—and all the more intoxicating—but he did not want to hurt her, to over-tax her. However, the more he tried to give her space, the more difficult it became to control the hunger. At least he had managed to get her to wear his ring. But as his gaze caught the flicker of the diamond on her finger, he knew it was not enough.

He wanted to stake a legal claim. He needed to make her his wife.

'Your fiancée is extremely captivating, Mr Khan.'

Raif jerked his gaze from the valley of Kasia's breasts to find the renowned Swiss financier he had been chatting with observing him with a knowing, masculine smile.

Embarrassed heat scorched the back of Raif's neck.

The older man had caught him checking out his own fiancée while they were supposed to be having a discussion on... What had they been discussing?

'And intelligent,' the man added, as Raif tried to recall what exactly they had been talking about before he had been distracted—again—like a callow teenage boy. 'She speaks very knowledgably about your region's agricultural challenges. She will make you an excellent wife. When is the wedding?'

Good question.

'Soon,' he said, the frustration he was trying—and failing—to control, by avoiding his fiancée, suddenly making it hard for him to breathe.

A waiter passed them with a tray full of colourful cocktails. He rarely drank alcohol, it wasn't part of his culture and he preferred never to dull his senses, but he grabbed a Bloody Mary and knocked it back in one go. The salty fragrant flavour soothed his dry throat, but did nothing to sooth the hunger and impatience smouldering in his gut.

This was madness. What was he doing dressed up in a monkey suit making small talk he couldn't even follow and letting some over-privileged fool leer at Kasia's breasts when all he really wanted to do was strip her out of that provocative dress and feel those full nipples swell against his tongue?

Avoidance was not the answer.

'Would you excuse me, Stefano?' he said, dismissing the financier as he tightened his grip on Kasia's waist and pressed his face into the sensitive skin under her earlobe.

'Kasia, let's return to the hotel,' he murmured, as he kissed her neck and inhaled the intoxicating scent of jasmine and spice. The heat rose up his torso, but he'd had enough of caring about how primitive or uncivilised he appeared by mauling her in a public place.

Appearances were overrated. And he was not a civilised man. Especially where this woman was concerned. So why was he trying so hard to pretend he was? She was beautiful, captivating and wildly attractive, not just her body but also her mind—he'd caught enough of her conversation with a variety of people to realise that. Stefano was right, she would make him an excellent wife and an excellent princess. So why was he waiting to seduce her?

Kasia shuddered, her amber eyes darkening with surprise and arousal. The young aristocrat finally detached his gaze from her cleavage to frown at Raif. The superior, vaguely disgusted expression told Raif all he needed to know about the whelp's opinion of his behaviour.

He sent the pampered fool the caustic smile he had used to unnerve his opponents before the many brutal bareknuckle fights he had been forced to win to gain leadership of the Kholadi over a decade ago.

Back off. She belongs to me.

The young man got the message and disappeared into the crowd.

Satisfaction stirred, feeding the heat and the hunger.

Maybe he had masked the feral teenager he'd once been in designer clothing, and learned how to survive and prosper in the world of high finance, but the instincts of that wild boy still existed inside him and he had no desire to tame them.

'Okay, Raif,' Kasia said, the edge of desire in her voice

only adding to the pheromones now firing his blood. 'I'd like that.'

'Good.' Grasping her trembling fingers, the ring biting into his palm, he led her through the crowd of partygoers towards the domed entrance of the lavish Belle Époque ballroom.

His impatience heightened as they waited for the cloakroom attendant to find her stole and his coat. He slung the stole over his arm and wrapped his coat around Kasia's shoulders. He didn't need the garment himself, he was already burning up. His hunger surged when he caught a flash of something raw and needy in her eyes as he escorted her into the street and flagged down a cab along the wide boulevard. He couldn't wait for their car.

The cabbie weaved through the streets in the short drive to their hotel. He kept her fingers clasped in his, stroking her knuckles, trying to reassure her as much as himself. Despite appearances and the judgement of other, more pampered men, he wasn't an animal.

And he would be gentle if it killed him. He didn't want to endanger the babe or exhaust her. But he could not wait any longer.

'Is everything okay, Raif?' she whispered in the darkness, and while he could hear the tremble of uncertainty in her voice he could also hear the naked desire that she was making no effort to hide.

Pride surged. Despite her apprehension she was here, with him, ready to meet his needs with needs of her own.

'It soon will be,' he said, devouring the sight of her, silhouetted against the glittering lights of the city, as the cabbie drew up outside the hotel.

But as he escorted her through the lobby, dragged her into the penthouse elevator, and waited for the damn thing to finally reach their suite, he felt the tight leash he had kept on his hunger start to fray.

As they stepped into the suite, she let go of his hand to shrug off the coat and lay it on the back of one of the couches, revealing the seductive dress, and the lush curves he could no longer wait to caress.

Kasia's thigh muscles loosened and pleasure ached at her core as Raif's arms wrapped around her and his hands caressed the smooth satin covering her abdomen. His lips nuzzled her neck and her breathing became ragged, her heartbeat hammering her ribs.

At last.

The ring had thrown her and so had his presence by her side during the glittering event. She'd assumed he would leave her as he had so often in the last four days to attend to his business commitments. But instead he'd remained beside her, his arm banded around her waist, never letting her stray far from his side.

But what should have felt suffocating had been exhilarating. Feeling owned also made her feel cherished, and important. He'd introduced her as his fiancée and had never let her out of his sight. But then something had changed suddenly. She'd felt his irritation at the attention she was getting from the royal she was talking to and had assumed it was because the young man's conversation was so inane.

But when Raif had whispered in her ear, she'd heard the note of possessiveness, the note of arrogance and desire—and instead of feeling outraged or appalled she'd felt elated.

The journey to the hotel had been agony, her anticipation reaching fever pitch.

His large hands cupped her breasts, his thumbs stroking her nipples through the dress until she was panting.

'I need you naked,' he growled, his breathing as ragged as her own.

'I know,' she said.

He turned her in his arms, found the tab of the dress's

zipper under her arm. The sibilant hiss echoed in the shadowy room, the only light coming from the lamps outside. The evening breeze brushed over her skin, but that wasn't what made her shiver as he stripped the dress off her.

Seconds later he removed her bra. Bending, he scooped the swollen flesh into the palm of his hand and captured the stiff peak in his teeth.

He flicked his tongue over the engorged nipple, making the blood flow painfully to her core. She sobbed, the sensations unbearably wonderful as pleasure rolled and crested.

He lifted his head, his eyes dark with arousal. 'Are they more sensitive?'

'Yes,' she said on a broken sob.

He chuckled, then captured her other breast and continued the torture, sucking and nipping her into a frenzy as his seeking fingers slipped into her panties.

The heel of his palm pressed against her vulva. She rolled her hips, desperate to increase the delicious pressure, then moaned as his fingers delved, brushing and circling the stiff nub of her clitoris, forcing her to dance to his tune.

The vicious orgasm crested, her body bucking against his touch—so firm, so sure, so right. She cried out as she shattered, grasping his shoulders to stop herself from falling into the abyss.

As the last of the orgasm waned, her knees weakened, but as she threatened to dissolve into a puddle of passion on the carpet, he scooped her limp body into his arms and strode into the master bedroom.

He placed her gently on the four-poster bed. She lay there, feeling dazed and disorientated, her body alive with afterglow, as he stripped.

Her gaze consumed the planes of muscle and sinew, the scarred and inked skin, the scatter of dark hair and the large, thick shaft of his erection.

He knelt on the bed, but instead of thrusting that swollen shaft deep inside her, he cupped her bottom, draped her legs over his shoulders and blew across the slick folds of her sex. Then, holding her open with his thumbs, he licked across her clitoris.

Her body bowed back, the shocking pleasure so raw she could hardly bear it as he laved the swollen flesh, tasting every part of her. He held her bottom, anchoring her to his mouth as he finally found the hard nub and suckled. She clutched his head, scraping her nails across his scalp. Crying, begging, the pleasure too raw, too intense as she tumbled over again.

'Please, Raif, I need you inside me,' she moaned, as the waves of orgasm finally ebbed a second time.

She felt empty, she needed to feel the thick length inside her, wanted to see him shatter the way he had made her shatter—not once but twice.

As he rose over her, she could see the strain on his face, his eyes wild and unfocused, as he gripped her thighs, angled her hips and notched the wide head of his erection at her entrance.

But instead of burying himself deep, thrusting hard and fast, to ease the emptiness, he edged inside her so slowly her heart began to race, her body clutching and clawing at him.

The ecstasy turned to agony as he teased her, easing in so gently she wanted to scream. She was so frantic for the hard thrust she thought she might die if he didn't do it soon. 'Please, Raif, I need all of you.'

'Shhh… I must be gentle,' he said, the elemental groan full of the same raw desperation.

'Why must you?' she asked, the yearning so sharp, so primitive she could barely think, let alone speak. What was he waiting for?

'I don't want to hurt the babe.'

What?

The raw pledge came so far out of left field it took her

a moment to understand what he was saying. His sweat-slicked body was as tortured as hers.

'You are so tight, and I am not a small man.'

'You won't hurt the baby, Raif,' she said, even as her heart pummelled her chest wall at the taut desperation to hold back, to take care of her and their child, even if it drove them both insane. 'It's only the size of a peanut.'

'Are you sure?' he groaned.

'Yes!' She clutched his face, forced his gaze to hers. 'Please give us what we both need.'

She saw the moment the cast-iron control finally snapped. He grasped her hips and thrust hard, sinking right up to the hilt.

The brutal orgasm slammed into her and she heard him shout out as he rocked out, pumped back hard and fast—once, twice—then crashed over that final barrier behind her.

But as the pleasure exploded in her nerve-endings, shimmering through her body, her heart expanded in her chest.

As she drifted into an exhausted sleep, with his arms holding her securely, and the rapid rhythm of his heartbeat slowing in her ear, her own heart seemed to burst in her chest, the bone-deep yearning no longer contained.

CHAPTER SEVENTEEN

KASIA WOKE THE next morning to find the bed empty, but before she could let her crushing disappointment overtake her, she was scrambling out of bed and rushing into Raif's bathroom.

Ten minutes later, she was brushing her teeth with a spare toothbrush, her stomach finally having settled again, and making plans.

She must not get disheartened. They had made huge strides last night. Not just with the sex—which had, of course, been spectacular—but also with the engagement. Maybe Raif was uncomfortable with the intimacy of waking up together, but she would move her luggage into his room today, without asking for his permission. And make a suggestion for their two weeks in New York.

Her spirits lifted considerably when she walked out of the bedroom in her robe, ready to start fetching her things, to find Raif seated at the breakfast table on the balcony, reading a newspaper.

He put the paper aside and stood as she approached, his concerned frown making her heartbeat jump and jiggle—the memory of his words the night before, in the throes of passion, coming back full force.

'I don't want to hurt the babe.'

Was that why he had been avoiding sex? Not because of a fear of intimacy but because he was concerned about her health and the baby's? Why hadn't she considered the possibility before? This pregnancy had to be new and scary for him, too.

'Are you well enough to be out of bed?' he asked, his gaze searching her face as he assessed her condition.

'Yes, I'm fine,' she said, realising she had a lot more energy than usual after the morning bout of vomiting, and even the smell of his coffee had not unsettled her stomach.

Holding her elbow, he directed her to the chair opposite his and seated her. 'Are you sure? I do not wish you to tire yourself.'

She heard the unfamiliar note of uncertainty.

'Really, Raif, I'm well.'

'But the vomiting,' he said, as he sat opposite her, 'it is so severe.'

So he had heard her each morning. And worried about her. The thought made her heart go a little crazy.

'Are you sure our…?' He paused, and she saw the unfamiliar flush of colour darken his cheeks. 'Our activity last night has not made it worse?'

'Actually, I feel much stronger this morning—despite the nausea,' she said, finding his concern utterly adorable. 'Apparently multi-orgasmic sex is a cure for pregnancy fatigue—who knew?'

Her heart leapt at the slow smile that curved his lips and the sparkle of heat in his eyes.

'Then I suppose it is my job to make sure you are supplied with it,' he murmured.

His phone buzzed on the table, disturbing the moment. Picking it up, he frowned.

'Is everything okay?' she asked.

He nodded. 'Yes, but the series of meetings I am attending in New York have been moved forward. I will have to leave tonight.' He wiped his mouth with his napkin and placed it on the table, before getting up. 'If you would like to remain in Paris for the extra days, I can arrange it.'

'I would rather come with you,' she said, perplexed by his offer until she saw the fierce satisfaction in his gaze.

Good, they were still on the same page.

'I will have my staff make all the arrangements so you can join me on the company jet this evening.' Resting his hands on her shoulders, he leaned down to kiss her neck. 'I do not want you tiring yourself, is this understood?'

She nodded, her heartbeat galloping at the delightful domesticity of the moment. But as he shifted away from her, obviously ready to leave her for the rest of the day, she covered one of his hands with hers and swung round. 'Wait, Raif—can I make a suggestion?'

'Of course.'

'Could we…?' She swallowed, suddenly nervous. This really wasn't a big deal, but it meant a lot to her and she was scared he might refuse. 'Would it be okay if we stayed in an apartment while we're in New York instead of a luxury hotel?'

His brows lifted a fraction, and his forehead creased. He was obviously surprised and a little suspicious of the request.

She rushed to explain herself before he could object. 'It's just that I'd like to be able to cook my own meals.'

And I want to cook for you.

She heard the plea inside her head but didn't say it, because it made her feel suddenly vulnerable and exposed. Last night had been important to her, and not just because of the sex. It had deepened the intimacy between them and made her realise she was already more than halfway in love with this man. But she needed to tread carefully now, to make him see how much they could have together.

They would be in New York for over two weeks. While she'd loved sightseeing in Paris, and being treated like a queen, she'd much rather spend the time in New York making a home with Raif, however temporary.

'But there is no need for you to cook,' he said, clearly confused by her request.

'I know, but I enjoy it. My grandmother taught me how and it always reminds me of her.'

Her grandmother had shown her how to use spices, to judge flavours and juggle tastes, to create her own unique recipes, because she had considered it an important life skill for any woman.

'How can you keep your husband satisfied if you cannot fill his stomach?'

At the time Kasia had found her grandmother's thinking about marriage antiquated and silly, but she'd still loved learning the intricacies of Narabian cuisine at her side. It was something they had shared, her grandmother's way of showing her she approved of her, and she loved her. Unlike her mother. And it was a skill Kasia wanted to share with Raif, because she suspected, for all his wealth and status, both in Kholadi and in the outside world, he had never been nurtured in the way that only a meal cooked with love could nurture a soul.

She wanted to give him that, because he had already given her so much—she didn't have money or status, but she did know how to conjure magic in a kitchen.

His frown remained, but then he shrugged, and relief flooded through her.

'Okay, I will have my assistant rearrange our accommodation.'

She wanted to suggest she find the apartment herself, because she had visions of finding somewhere cosy and comfortable and intimate, and not too lavish, but she decided not to press him. The apartment wasn't important, it was what they could establish inside it—a new level of understanding, of intimacy and domesticity. Together.

An apartment represented a chance to make some semblance of a home with Raif—with no staff looking over their shoulders and cleaning up after them, and no restaurant or room service meals they hadn't created and cooked themselves. To just *be*, in their own space, together, however temporary, was more of a luxury to her than going on shopping sprees with his credit card, or seeing even the most amazing sights without him.

As Raif left, her heartbeat galloped into her throat. It was such a small thing, a small thing that Raif didn't understand the significance of, but that was okay, because it had huge significance to her.

Plus she'd never been to New York before.

The next two weeks would be an adventure, for both of them, that she could not wait to explore.

CHAPTER EIGHTEEN

'THAT SMELLS INCREDIBLE—what is it?'

Raif dumped his briefcase by the door and tugged at his tie. He was tired. The day of meetings with a Mexican retail consortium looking for investment had been conducted in both English and Spanish—a language he was not yet fluent in. But as he slipped off his shoes and walked into the loft apartment's generous open-plan living and dining space he spotted Kasia, her wild hair pushed back from her face by a colourful bandana, busy stirring something on the five-ring stove.

His heart did a giddy two-step. And the fatigue lifted, to be replaced by the familiar punch of lust. And longing.

She sent him a quick grin, making the longing wrap around his heart. And begin to choke him. It had become a familiar sight since they had arrived in New York a week ago and his assistant had found them this apartment.

Kasia's request had confused him when she had made it in Paris. He always stayed at the Plaza when he was in New York. Had never had any desire to stay anywhere else. And if truth be told, he hadn't been that happy about agreeing to this shift. He didn't like her having to cook for them. And he liked even the less the daily excursions she made to scour the local markets to find the spices and ingredients she needed for her latest creation. But he'd had to stifle his objections because it made her so happy.

And he liked to see her happy.

Plus, the food she managed to conjure up—an eclectic

mix of Middle Eastern, African and other ethnic flavours from her travels around the local neighbourhood shops—was quite simply the best he'd ever tasted. So much so he'd managed to regain nearly all the weight he'd lost while lying flat on his back at the Golden Palace.

'Sarma, moutabal and hummus to start,' she announced proudly. 'Then lamb tagine, whipped garlic mash and Armenian salad. I hope you're starving. The bread is from an amazing Lebanese bakery I found in Tribeca.'

After popping the pitta breads in the toaster, she produced a tray of colourful dishes from the fridge.

'Please tell me you didn't walk all the way to Tribeca.' He'd cautioned her before about not taking the car and driver.

'Then I won't tell you,' she said, the flirtatious wink making it hard for him to be annoyed with her. Even though she had been defying his express order.

Dammit.

'Kasia, you must not tire yourself,' he said, trying to be firm. The nausea still hit every morning like clockwork. And he knew how tired she became in the afternoons, because he'd come back between meetings only yesterday, hoping to surprise her, and had found her fast asleep. 'Especially not cooking for me.'

'But I *like* cooking for you,' she said, disarming him all over again. 'Tribeca is not that far. And I had a nap this afternoon. So I'm not tired. Plus, the bread is amazing.' She pointed to a delicious-looking concoction, made with chargrilled eggplant, on the tray of dishes, attempting to distract him. 'And it goes perfectly with the moutabal. A lovely Lebanese man at the farmers' market on Hudson told me how to make it.'

'I don't want you talking to strange men either,' he said, frowning, as she whisked the pitta out of the toaster, chopped them up with a few efficient strokes of a very large knife and sprinkled them with some aromatic spice.

'He was ninety if he was a day, Raif.' Her eyes flashed with the rebellious spirit he had become captivated by. Taking the dish off the tray, she presented it to him with the plate of prepared bread. 'Now, stop talking nonsense and taste it, so you can tell me what you think.'

It wasn't nonsense, he thought grumpily, but then he tasted the dish. The flavours exploded on his tongue, lemon and sesame and garlic perfectly combined with the savoury charcoal flavour of the charred aubergine. A moan came out before he could stop it.

'Good?' she said, the eager smile making his heartbeat thicken.

'Excellent,' he was forced to admit.

'Sit down and sample the other dishes while I finish the mash.'

He did as he was told, perching on the stool on the other side of the bar as he had become accustomed to doing for the past week. He would ask her about her latest research, and the progress of her PhD, which the Kholadi Corporation was helping to fund after setting up the scholarship programme at Devereaux College. She would often ask him about his work, what he had been doing, and tell him what else she'd done during her day—which usually involved making friends with people she didn't know. And walking miles after he had told her not to.

But it was hard to chastise her when she enjoyed it so much. Kasia, he had discovered, was a naturally sociable person, who thrived on meeting new people and exploring new places.

Her stories enchanted him. And disturbed him.

How could anyone be so trusting? So devoid of cynicism? The question had begun to haunt him and make him feel vaguely guilty. After all, he was planning to use her gullibility—her naivety—against her to get her to agree to their marriage.

She launched into a story about the Lebanese man she'd met at the farmers' market. Usually he loved listening to what she had been doing all day, because she was an entertaining storyteller, and he found himself fascinated by how open she was. It also gave him no small amount of pride, her instinctive abilities in social situations, yet more evidence of what an excellent princess she would make for the Kholadi people. She had a genuine openness and honesty and seemed to be able to fit in anywhere. People gravitated towards her naturally—even he was not immune.

But as she talked about the Lebanese great-grandfather and how he had reminded her of her own grandmother, while she was mashing the potatoes, and he tucked into the delicious tray of *hors d'oeuvres*, the question that had been sitting on the tip of his tongue for days popped out of his mouth.

'Kasia, how did you lose your parents?'

She stopped mashing abruptly and lifted her gaze. A shadow crossed her face, and he wished he could take the question back.

'I didn't lose them exactly.' A resigned smile curved her lips, intensifying his desire to take the sadness out of her eyes. 'They lost me.'

He knew he should not pursue this line of questioning, he couldn't afford to get too invested in Kasia's past because it had the potential to make him even more conflicted about using her artlessness against her to get what he wanted. For himself, for their child, for his country. But he couldn't seem to stop himself from asking the obvious next question.

'How did they lose you?'

Kasia's heart lifted into her throat at Raif's troubled expression. He'd never asked her about her past before. She could see he was uncomfortable about asking her now. But the fact he wanted to know more about her seemed like another huge step forward, adding to the progress they'd already made since arriving in New York. The apartment his assistant had rented in Gramercy was, of course, a lot grander than what she would have preferred—with four bedrooms, a roof garden and the sort of stark, modern style that wouldn't look out of place in a design magazine. But the kitchen was magnificent and it hadn't taken her long to turn the apartment into a home.

Even though it had only been a week, they'd already slipped into a routine, a routine that involved not just spectacular sex every evening but also private dinners during which Raif devoured her food and discussed his work while taking a genuine interest in hers. But he'd shied away from more intimate conversations—until now.

As happy as it made her to have him ask, it was also hard for her to revisit that time of her life. But she forced herself not to hold back. They needed to be able to share the truth about who they were and where they had come from. She knew the terrible degradation he'd suffered as a child, so why should she feel inhibited about talking about her own childhood?

'Well...' She concentrated on mashing the potatoes, not wanting to see his reaction. 'I never knew who my father was. My mother went with a group of other girls to the mining camps in Kallah to work and came back pregnant, she said by a French mine-worker.'

'So you are also illegitimate?' Raif murmured.

'Yes.' Panic twisted in her gut, which made no sense. Why would she be concerned about his reaction to her heritage when she hadn't agreed to marry him yet? 'Is that a problem?'

'How do you mean?' he asked.

'Maybe you don't want a bastard for your princess?' she said, forcing herself to voice her fears.

His brows launched up his forehead but then he laughed. 'The Kholadi have a bastard for their Chief. Do you take me for a hypocrite?'

She smiled, feeling stupidly shy under that intense gaze. 'No, I don't.'

He picked up a piece of pitta and dipped it into the moutabal, then directed her to continue. 'When did your mother die?'

She shook her head. This bit was tougher. 'She didn't die. As far as I know, she's still living, but she decided when I was four that she could no longer live with the shame of being the mother of a bastard. So she left me with my grandmother and never returned.'

He stared at her for the longest time, swallowing the food, then swore softly in Kholadi. Lifting his thumb, he traced it down the side of her face. The caress was light but very sensual, and the approval—and anger—in his eyes so vivid she felt as if he was stroking her heart. 'Your mother was a fool.'

She'd spent her whole life convincing herself she didn't need anyone else's validation, that her mother's choices were not her own, but why, then, did his support mean so much? She blinked, releasing the tears stinging her eyes. They rolled down her cheeks unchecked as a fear she hadn't even realised she had been holding inside her—that she might be as fickle and flawed as her own mother when it came to having a child—was defeated by the honest approval in his eyes.

'I am sorry. I have made you cry,' he said. But as he went to remove his thumb, she pressed her palm over his hand, holding it in place, and leaned into the caress.

'Don't be sorry,' she said. 'They're not sad tears.'

His lips lifted in a rueful smile. 'I am glad.'

Fierce joy pierced her heart—for all his wildness, for

all his arrogance and over-protectiveness, the father of her child was a good man.

'I wish to make love to you,' he said. 'Will the food wait?'

Her heart jumped at the intensity in his eyes and she nodded. The mashed potatoes would taste terrible cold, but she didn't care as he switched off the oven and lifted her into his arms.

As he carried her into their bedroom and stripped them both naked, she tried to persuade herself it was the pregnancy hormones making her feel so emotional. But as he made slow, sensual, tender love to her, bringing her to an earth-shattering climax with his tongue, before thrusting deep and rocking them both towards another orgasm, she clung to his shoulders, trying to hold the emotion in, to justify and control it.

But as he worked that spot inside her that he knew would make her shatter, the pleasure slammed into her… And as her body plunged over that high, wide ledge, for better or worse, her heart followed.

Much later, as they sat in bed together, he fed her the cold tagine with his fingers, then licked away the juices from her chin.

She giggled, her heart lighter than it had been for a long time.

But then he cradled her cheek and her spirits sobered. His eyes had lost the boyish twinkle she had become so attached to in the past week.

'I must return to Kholadi in four days' time—the tribe is setting up a new encampment and I need to be there. For a month, maybe longer.'

She nodded, suddenly bereft that this blissful time together would have to end sooner than planned.

'I don't want to leave you behind. I wish to take you with me as my princess, Kasia.'

Her heart expanded even as her head cried it was still too soon for such a leap. She had no guarantee her feelings were returned, or would ever be returned, and her love for him was still so new.

But when he asked: 'Will you marry me?' she was powerless to resist the matching hope in his gaze.

She didn't want to be without him for a whole month. He was the father of her child. How could it be wrong to give their love this chance?

So she said the only thing she could. 'Yes, I will.'

CHAPTER NINETEEN

THE WHIRLWIND OF activity over the next few days was so overwhelming, Kasia had no time at all to revisit any fears she had about her decision to accept Raif's proposal.

They agreed her PhD would have to be put on hold until after the baby was born, but Raif was eager to fund additional research while they were in Kholadi as her work could be of great benefit to his people… *Their* people.

As he finished the last of his business in Manhattan, Kasia spent her time reading as much as she could about the Kholadi. She didn't want to be as ignorant as she had been about their lifestyle when she'd first spent the night with Raif. A licence was arranged at City Hall two days before their departure and they were married the next day on the roof terrace of the Gramercy apartment with his assistant and the building's supervisor, who Kasia had made friends with, in attendance as witnesses.

She made a tearful call to Cat that evening to confess all, and her friend had been thrilled at the news. Although she did chastise Kasia for keeping her affair with Raif a secret for so long.

'I cannot believe you're pregnant and married and I didn't even get to be maid of honour. You're also going to have some serious explaining to do to my daughter, who has been dreaming about being your bridesmaid since she was about two. And my husband, who would have wanted to give you away and have a completely inappropriate conversation with your new husband about his responsibilities!'

The memory of the conversation still made Kasia smile. How silly she had been to wait to tell Cat everything until after the marriage had taken place. Her wobble over whether Cat and Zane would give the marriage their blessing was even more ridiculous. They were her friends, so why wouldn't they be overjoyed for her?

Because they know he's not in love with you.

She pushed the niggling doubt aside.

That was her insecurity talking. Cat had only asked her if *she* was in love with *Raif*, so she hadn't had to lie. And maybe Raif wasn't in love with her *yet*. But less than a day after their marriage he was already giving a very good impression of an over-protective husband, insisting they stop off in London en route to Narabia to see a Harley Street specialist about her continuing nausea.

She'd tried to explain to him that it was perfectly normal to be sick and tired. In fact, it was practically a cliché, and she'd also pointed out there were a network of state-of-the-art maternity clinics in Narabia where she could get all the antenatal care she needed. But he had refused to be swayed.

So here she was, sitting in the elegant Georgian office of one of London's best obstetricians with her husband, having been whisked from Heathrow in a chauffeur-driven limo and given a series of blood tests by the practice's nurse.

'So, Mrs Khan…' Ms Siddiqui, the consultant, smiled at Kasia, her expression both kind and fiercely competent.

Mrs Khan.

'I've reviewed the notes sent from your GP in Cambridge and your blood tests. Everything looks good, although you are a little anaemic, so I would suggest we increase your iron. I understand from my conversation with your husband that your morning sickness has been quite pronounced and you're often exhausted?'

Aware of Raif's eyes on her, Kasia replied, 'I'm sure it's nothing out of the ordin—'

'Kasia, you are violently ill every morning—surely this is not normal, Doctor?' Raif interrupted her, his concern palpable.

'Every pregnancy is different, Mr Khan,' the obstetrician replied in a soothing but also firm tone. Kasia's tension eased. While it was wonderful to have Raif worry about her, she really didn't want him to worry quite so much. 'But let's do an ultrasound to check everything and put everyone's mind at rest,' she finished.

Excitement stirred in Kasia's blood as they were led into the ultrasound room. Five minutes later she was lying on the bed, the cold jelly smeared on her abdomen and the obstetrician pressing the wand into the small baby bump.

The sound of a heartbeat beating in double time echoed around the room as Kasia watched the monitor, the indistinct shapes making her blink back tears. This was her and Raif's child. The lump in her throat grew and she gripped his fingers. He squeezed back, instinctively answering her sudden need for reassurance.

'Aha,' Ms Siddiqui said, as if she'd just made an important discovery. 'I think we have the source of your nausea and the exhaustion, Mrs Khan.'

'Please call me Kasia,' she said as the obstetrician circled two of the shapes on the screen with a wand.

'You're carrying twins, Kasia,' Ms Siddiqui replied with a benevolent smile.

Twins?

'There are *two* babies?' Raif released her fingers, his voice raw.

'Yes, Mr Khan.' She pointed to the two shapes she'd circled. 'Here and here. And can you hear that slight echo on the heartbeat? That's because there are actually two heartbeats but they're beating almost in unison.' The obstetrician continued to press the wand into Kasia's belly, moving it around to get a better view of their babies.

Their *two* babies.

Kasia's stomach leapt and jiggled along with her heartbeat. She'd always wanted to be a mother and now she was going to be a mother twice over. She couldn't think of anything more wonderful.

But as the doctor took a series of measurements and answered all her eager questions about the pregnancy, Raif remained silent and tense.

Ms Siddiqui was fantastic, both pragmatic and kind, reassuring them that while the babies were big for the dates and a twin pregnancy was always more of a hormonal shock to the mother's system—which probably explained the nausea and the tiredness—Kasia was strong and healthy and once her body adjusted, everything should settle down. Raif did not look convinced.

'Are you okay, Raif?' Kasia asked, after he had helped her into the waiting car, as if she were a hundred and two years old and made of spun glass and might fracture into a thousand pieces at any minute.

He didn't reply to her question, his body language still painfully tense as he stared out of the car window at the passing scenery, lost in his thoughts. They were staying in a hotel in Cambridge tonight, so she could supervise the packing of her belongings in the morning, then leave for Narabia tomorrow evening to visit Cat and Zane and their children before heading into the desert and the Kholadi encampment in a few days' time.

She knew arrangements were already under way for a royal wedding ceremony—their marriage wasn't legal in Kholadi, according to Raif, unless they said their vows in front of his people.

'Raif, is something wrong?' she repeated as the car turned onto Euston Road. 'You're not unhappy about it being twins, are you?'

He swung round, finally having heard her. 'No, of course

not,' he said, but the muscle in his jaw was twitching so violently she was surprised he hadn't got lockjaw, and the expression in his eyes—hooded and wary—reminded her of the man she had first met in the desert. The man who had suffered a gunshot wound without saying a word.

He'd opened up so much in the last three weeks, she'd seen a softer, more relaxed side to his personality. And she'd loved meeting that man, getting to know him. But why did it suddenly feel as if that man had disappeared?

Stop freaking out. You're still suffering from mild shock yourself.

Two babies *was* a lot to contemplate.

'How are you?' he asked, his eyes narrowing as he studied her face.

'I'm fine. I'm great,' she said, wanting to reassure him, even if she was feeling a little weary. And some of her own fears, about the burden of motherhood and how she was going to cope with bringing up two children instead of one, had resurfaced.

As excited as she was about this pregnancy, she also knew there would be struggles ahead. But she was determined to be positive. No matter what. One thing she knew for sure, nothing on earth would make her want to abandon these babies the way her own mother had abandoned her.

'Don't lie,' he said, reading her too easily. 'Come here.' Lifting his arm, he beckoned her towards him. 'Sit next to me,' he suggested. He unlocked her seatbelt and refastened her into the seat next to his. Then wrapped his arm around her.

She placed her head on his shoulder as directed, and listened to the comforting beat of his heart as her eyelids drooped.

'Get some sleep,' he murmured, placing a kiss on top of her hair.

She snuggled into his arms, the anxiety at his reaction—

and her own irrational fears—fading as she drifted into an exhausted sleep.

They arrived in Cambridge at nightfall. After a light meal in the living room of their suite, he insisted on carrying her into the bedroom, undressing her and feeding her one of the iron tablets the obstetrician had prescribed.

She was so tired she could barely lift her arms, let alone persuade him to join her in their bed. But as he kissed her forehead, she thought she heard him whisper, 'Sorry.'

Don't be ridiculous, Kaz.

He was her husband now, the father of her babies. Both of them.

A weary smile lifted her lips as her eyelids shut.

Tomorrow they would travel together to Narabia. She couldn't wait to see Cat to tell her the news about the twins.

And then she would meet his people as his princess. What could her husband possibly have to be sorry for?

CHAPTER TWENTY

Dear Kasia
I have returned to Kholadi. I think the desert is not
the best place for you, especially in your present con-
dition, so I have arranged for a property to be pur-
chased in Cambridge, where you will stay for the
foreseeable future.

Internet connectivity is not good in the kingdom,
but I will endeavour to contact you soon.

Dean Walmsley has been informed that your new
research as well as the PhD will be fully funded by
the Kholadi Grant to the faculty.
R

KASIA BIT HER lip so hard she could taste blood, desperately struggling to control the choking sobs lodged under
her breastbone ever since Raif's assistant had arrived five
minutes ago to deliver his letter.

Not letter, she thought as she tapped Cat's name into her
phone, Raif's instructions.

She had only just recovered from her regular bout of
morning sickness and was eating some dry toast and wondering where Raif could possibly have disappeared to when
the knock had come on the door of their suite. She hadn't
even noticed that Raif's luggage and all his toiletries were
gone until after she'd opened the cream envelope with her
name written across it in his bold script and had read the
devastating contents.

So businesslike, so polite, so unemotional.

Shock had come first. How could the man who had carried her to bed and undressed her so tenderly have written such a note? Had he been making plans even then to abandon her? He must have been.

Next had been all the furious questions. Why had he left her here? Why hadn't he spoken to her about his decision? Was she not entitled to a say in where or how she should live?

But beneath the questions was the devastating sense of déjà vu, propelling her back to a time in her life it had taken her many years to recover from. And all the fears she had kept so carefully at bay—on discovering her pregnancy, when agreeing to their hasty marriage, after realising she was having not one baby but two—leapt out of the darkness, too.

Suddenly she was that little girl again, small and defenceless, insignificant and unloved. That little girl who could never be enough, watching her mother leave without a backward glance as her grandmother squeezed her fingers.

'Do not fear, little one, your mother will return soon.'

But her mother hadn't returned. Kasia had waited and waited. And the only conclusion was that if her mother had ever loved her, she hadn't loved her enough.

The choking sob rose up her torso as the call connected.

Cat's voice came on the line—calm but concerned. 'Kasia, is everything okay?'

'I'm sorry I called so early,' Kasia said, the words scraping her throat as the sob pushed painfully against her larynx. It was before dawn in Narabia, she realised.

'Kasia, what's wrong? Has something happened?'

'He's left me. He doesn't want me, Cat. I knew he didn't love me, but I thought maybe…' The words spewed out, expelled on a wave of desperation, but were soon overrun by the choking sobs that racked her body in debilitating gut punches of anguish.

The crying came in waves, loud and raw and exhausting as she sank to the floor by the lavish four-poster bed and pressed her forehead to her knees, trying to hold in the pain, the devastation.

He's gone. He won't return. He's ashamed of me, as she was. Ashamed to have me meet his people. I did something wrong. But what did I do? How can I make it right? How can I be better so he'll love me? So he won't abandon me?

The questions that had tormented her endlessly as a child returned, like big black crows pecking at the scar tissue that had grown over the gaping wounds left by her mother's desertion.

She wrapped her arms around her knees and pressed the phone to her ear. But the choking sobs refused to stop, turning the anguish to agony.

'Shhh… Shhh… Kaz, you have to breathe… Try breathing.'

Her best friend's voice—soothing but firm—pushed through the fog of devastation. Chasing the crows back as the heaving sobs finally turned to ragged panting.

At last exhaustion settled over her, she simply didn't have the strength to cry any more, her body wretched.

'Kaz, are you still there?' Cat said, a light in the darkness threatening to engulf her.

'Yes,' she said, her voice broken and raw but still there. She hadn't dropped off the abyss. That had to count for something.

'Now you need to tell me exactly what's happened,' Cat said. 'Can you do that?'

Kasia nodded. Then realised that Cat couldn't hear a nod, but as she gathered the strength to form an audible reply she heard a groggy voice in the background, asking what was wrong.

She'd woken up the Sheikh now, too. But before she had a chance to apologise she heard Cat's whispered reply to her husband.

'Your brother has been a monumental ass and upset Kasia. She's distraught. Next time I see him, I may have to shoot him myself.'

And then Zane's mumbled—and utterly dry—response. 'If he's hurt Kasia, perhaps she should do the honours. But tell her not to kill him, he's got a baby to support.'

Kasia dropped her head back onto the bed, the exchange between her two best friends making the strangest thing happen. A bubble of hope swelled under her breastbone. She placed her palm over the slight curve of her belly where her babies slept. Her and Raif's babies.

The devastation receded, to be replaced by something else flowing through her veins. Something it had taken her years to acquire the first time she'd been abandoned. Resilience.

The pain and anguish were still there. What Raif had done had been callous and cruel, he hadn't considered her feelings, hadn't even bothered to discuss his decision with her.

Her scars were rawer and fresher now than they had been. The fears real and vivid. But she wasn't a little girl any more, she was a grown woman, about to have two babies of her own. Curling up in a ball and letting these feelings defeat her wasn't an option any more. And oddly it was the knowledge that she could recover from this blow, because she had before, that gave her the strength to read out Raif's note to Cat.

Cat's assessment was stark and unequivocal. 'Kasia, that's ridiculous, he can't just decide these things for himself without even talking to you. In a marriage there has to be communication. I know you've only just fallen in love but—'

'He doesn't love me, Cat.' She forced the words out. However humiliating, however debilitating she had to own them, she realised. Because she had made mistakes, too. In her optimism and excitement about the pregnancy, about the man she'd discovered in the past weeks, she'd let her heart rule her head, had pushed all her fears under the carpet and married Raif without having any real commitment from him that he could ever love her back. 'And I'm not sure he ever will,' she added.

Her friend's sigh was audible. 'How do you know that?'

'Because he made it clear to me he doesn't believe in love—that he thinks it's nonsense. He…' She sighed. 'He had a miserable childhood, Cat. You know most of the details, I'm sure, from Zane. I knew…' She heaved a breath through her constricted lungs, the tears now for Raif as much as for herself. 'I knew it had hardened him, had made him cynical and determined never to trust anyone, but I thought…' She pressed her palm to her forehead, where a headache was starting to form. 'I still thought we had a chance, which is why I agreed to marry him, but if he doesn't want to share every part of his life with me, what real chance do we have…?'

'Okay, Kaz, listen, maybe I'm being the starry-eyed romantic now. But the note you read to me doesn't sound as definite as that. He's a guy and a prince, he likes to be in control, so he's making decisions for you both, but he doesn't necessarily know what the right decisions are. Did you tell him you love him?'

Kasia swallowed heavily, the rawness in her throat returning. 'No.'

She'd never spoken to him about her feelings or his. How could she accuse him of not communicating properly when she'd failed to do so herself?

'I thought that once we shared a life together, love would grow,' she continued, trying to explain the unexplainable to her friend. 'In New York and Paris, the time we spent together made me so happy and I think it made him happy, too. I fell in love with him but I didn't want to put pressure on him by making a declaration that might not be returned straight away…'

'I think maybe now is the time to put pressure on him. How can you know where you stand otherwise? And how can he?'

'I'm not sure I have the courage.' Kasia's heart thudded painfully against her ribs, that broken child coming out of hiding again. 'I don't want to risk another rejection. What if it breaks me?'

'It won't,' Cat said, with complete certainty. 'You're a strong woman, Kasia, much stronger than you think. You survived your mother's abandonment when you were just four years old. And let's face it, you can't possibly stay in Cambridge for goodness knows how long, waiting for him to deign to contact you. That's madness. You need to know where you stand. And he needs to stop acting like a dictatorial ass.'

Kasia felt a small, sad smile split her lips at the fierce determination in Cat's tone. Cat was such a good friend. Strong and supportive, always.

She wished she had Cat's confidence and her courage.

But then she rubbed her hand over her abdomen and imagined the babies growing there. She wanted to give them the start in life both she and Raif had lacked, of being cherished in the bosom of a loving relationship.

If there was a chance for that, didn't she owe it to her children to fight for it?

She would find the courage to go to Raif in the desert, where he had decided she didn't belong. She would defy his orders and tell him how she truly felt about him—and what she wanted in return. She would reach for the stars and if she fell short, if *they* fell short, at least she would know she had tried.

But whatever happened, she would survive, because she had to.

For her children, as well as for herself.

CHAPTER TWENTY-ONE

'CHIEF KHAN, an outrider has arrived from the Golden Palace—the Sheikh's party is coming.'

Raif straightened from his position—knee deep in mud—and threw down the shovel he had been using to dig a well with a group of his tribesmen.

The hard physical labour of setting up a new encampment had helped get him through the last few days. Ever since he had been forced to leave his wife sleeping in a hotel bed thousands of miles away.

The boy's shout in Kholadi confused him, though. What was Zane doing, coming for an official visit to the new encampment without informing him first?

They had been in brief contact a week ago when Zane had sent a text to congratulate him on his marriage. And Kasia's pregnancy. But that had been before their visit to the obstetrician in London. Before the fear for her safety had become so huge that Raif had struggled to contain it.

The shame had consumed him every day since, and the agony of loss, which he did not understand. How could you lose what you had never truly possessed? Kasia did not belong to him. She had married him out of duty, and kindness, would bear his children for him—and in return he had put her life in danger.

Was he really any different from his father? A man who had used women for his own pleasure and then discarded them?

Because of his hunger, his need, he had planted two babies inside her slim, fragile body. The doctor had said they were too big. He was a foot taller than her, it stood to reason his children would be too large.

He had killed his own mother, and now his children would kill theirs.

Rinsing his hair and chest in the bucket of water they kept next to the well, he picked up his shirt, annoyed at his brother's unannounced visit. He'd be damned if he'd get dressed in anything more formal when he had not been given prior warning. Zane would just have to see him as he was.

But as he picked up the dirty shirt to put it on, a thought occurred to him—and panic tore at his insides.

What possible reason could Zane have to come all this way—unless there was something wrong?

With Kasia.

Did Zane have news of his wife? Had something happened to her, or the children he had planted inside her? Had they killed her already?

Dropping the shirt, he ran, his heart thundering, his ribs aching with the pain that had gripped him for days—and the longing that tangled in his stomach like a snake and would not let him sleep.

He'd left her in Cambridge so she would be safe. But how could she ever be safe when he had put her life in such grave danger?

At last he reached the front of the encampment, just in time to see the pack of about twenty horses gallop over the ridge.

He spotted Zane at the front of the party, sitting easily on his horse, Pegasus, but next to him was a woman, dressed in traditional Narabian style to protect her from the sun.

Catherine, it had to be. Zane had brought his queen with him. Kasia's best friend. To give him the terrible news.

His whole body began to shake as he sent up frantic prayers—to any god that might listen.

Please let her be safe. I will never touch her again, I swear.

The longing and the desperation seemed to tear at his soul as the horses approached, picking their way down the rocky dune. The female rider arrived first, her smaller horse stopping a few feet away. But then she tugged away the headdress masking her face and her wild hair appeared like a cloud of black silk.

Her darker skin registered. That exquisite shade that smelled of jasmine and spice. Not Catherine. Kasia. *His* wife. *His* woman.

The woman he dreamed about every night. Was he dreaming still? Hallucinating? Was she a ghost? How could she be here? He had left her in Cambridge, to protect her. How could she be in the desert? Riding a horse?

He stared, unable to move, the longing he had tried to dismiss, to live with washing through him on a wave of emotion so strong he could do nothing to stop it as his hungry gaze devoured her beautiful face, the guarded expression, the round amber eyes, the lush lips now pressed into a determined line. But behind the determination he could see the same longing, the same compassion that was making his own breathing ragged.

Was he going mad? Was this the penance he would have to pay? For his many sins against her? To see her one last time, with love in her eyes, and know it could never be real? That he didn't deserve it to be real?

'Kasia?' he whispered. 'Is it you?'

Her eyes widened. 'Yes, Raif, it's me. Now, could you help me down? It's been a long ride.'

The sound of her voice broke the spell holding him captive. And the longing, the yearning, the joy and the confusion suddenly crystallised into one unstoppable thought as he marched towards her and grasped her round the waist.

She rested her hands on his shoulders as he whisked her off the horse and cradled her against his naked chest.

'You are well? The babies are well?' he asked, the tremble of terror in his voice impossible to hide.

'Yes, Raif, I'm okay, just a little tired.'

She was real and solid, but he could barely comprehend the joy of that—or the inevitable tug of arousal that would never die—around the rising tide of his fury.

At his brother.

His wife had ridden for two days through the desert. Against his orders. Putting herself in grave danger. And his brother had allowed it. Had facilitated it.

He swung round with his wife in his arms to see Zane strolling towards him.

'Can you stand?' he asked Kasia, his voice vibrating with fury.

She nodded, her eyes wide with confusion. 'Yes.'

Putting her gently on her feet, he released her and marched to his brother.

'You son of a bitch,' he shouted in Kholadi, then heaved back his clenched fist and struck the Sheikh on the chin. The pain reverberated up his arm but he didn't care as he heard his brother's surprised grunt and watched him tumble backwards onto his rear end.

'You dare to put my wife's life in danger?' he said, in Narabian this time as he stood over him. 'She carries twin children.'

He heard the click of rifle firing mechanisms engaging, and the shouts as Zane's men and his own drew their weapons.

'Stand down,' Zane shouted to his men, lifting his arm as he levered himself off the ground, rubbing his chin.

Fury still flowed through Raif's veins. Until Kasia's cry from behind him.

'Raif, stop! What are you doing?'

Her fingers gripped his bare arm, the jolt of awareness drawing him back from the edge. He turned and gathered her into his arms. He cradled her cheeks in his palms, then pressed his face into that wild hair, inhaling the spicy scent of her, letting the longing flow through his veins.

'Raif, you have to tell your men to lower their rifles,' she whispered.

He lifted his head, nodded to his men. Who put away their weapons.

Zane's hand touched his shoulder. 'I have a message from my wife,' he said, as he pressed his fingers to his torn lip, the slow smile on his face confusing Raif.

If there was anything amusing about this situation, he could not imagine what it was.

'I'm so sorry, Zane. I should never have involved you in all this,' Kasia said from beside him.

'It's okay, Kaz, we've always got your back,' his brother said, with a familiarity that had Raif's temper spiking again.

But the Sheikh hadn't taken his gaze off Raif, and what Raif saw in his brother's blue eyes wasn't the anger or contempt he expected but something that looked strangely like affection and understanding.

'What is this message?' he snapped at his brother, hating it that he didn't understand what was going on—not just with his wife and his brother but also within himself.

He'd almost started a war between their two nations by punching the Sheikh, but as he flexed his fingers, he knew he would do it all over again to protect Kasia from harm.

'Cat said stop being an ass,' he said, the smile that split his face only confusing Raif more. 'And talk to your wife.' Clicking his fingers over his head, he summoned his men to mount up. 'Now, I must leave you two if we are to get back to our camp before nightfall.'

'Wait!' Raif grasped his brother's arm, fury rising again to disguise his confusion. 'You can't leave Kasia here, it is not safe for her, she needs to return with you to the Golden Palace.' Perhaps she would refuse to return to Cambridge, but at least she would be well cared for at the palace.

Zane covered Raif's fingers with his and eased his grip, the look he sent him almost pitying.

'That's not my choice, brother, or yours. It's your wife's.' He glanced past Raif to the woman standing beside him and nodded. The silent communication between the two of them had the anger rising into Raif's throat even further. 'She's a grown woman, and your princess,' his brother added. 'She makes her own choices. And for some reason, the person she wants to be with is you.' Speaking to Kasia, he added, 'Kasia, I will wait at the overnight camp for a day. Send a rider if you would like me to return for you.'

He watched Kasia nod and thank his brother. He remained silent, so furious and confused now he could not speak. Then Zane bade them both farewell and mounted Pegasus. He waved once, then shouted to his men, urging the stallion into a gallop as he led the party back over the ridge.

'Raif, we must talk,' Kasia said, her voice quivering with emotion. But the unwavering gaze and the defiant tilt of her chin told a different story.

He scooped her up and began marching towards his tent, set apart from the others at the back of the camp.

'We *will* talk,' he said, struggling to contain his temper at this turn of events, and all the emotions that had been churning in his gut for days now, maybe even weeks. 'And then I will escort you back to Zafari and the Golden Palace myself.'

She could not stay here. Already his hunger for her was

all but overwhelming him. He wanted her so much, but more than that he needed her.

He could not give in to that need. Because he could not risk destroying her, too, as he had once destroyed his mother.

'Raif, put me down, I can walk,' Kasia said, trying to sound firm and coherent.

Not easy when her emotions were in turmoil and had been from the moment she'd spotted him, standing strong and proud, his bare chest glistening with sweat, staring at her as if she were an apparition. She'd expected surprise, maybe shock, possibly irritation that she had defied his orders and come to the desert anyway, but what she had not been prepared for was the explosion of violence—and the raw emotions she had seen in his eyes. So much more than shock.

She'd seen the anguish in his face when he'd hit Zane and knew that there was much more going on here than she had realised.

'No,' he said. 'I will not put you down.' She clung to her husband's neck as he marched through the encampment, his people turning to stare at them both.

'Please, Raif.' She was squirming—his bare chest, the captivating scent of his sweat, the rough tattoo glistening on his skin, the scars she had become so accustomed to making her ache.

'Stop wriggling,' he said as he carried her into a large tent at the edge of a water hole. He shouted something in Kholadi to the older woman who was busy arranging his clothing. Kasia had been studying the language for over a week and followed the gist of it—there had been a mention of a doctor.

'Stop,' she said in Kholadi as the woman rushed to leave

the tent and obey his orders, then formed a basic sentence, telling her the doctor was not needed.

'You speak Kholadi?' he said as the woman left and he finally placed her on her feet.

'I've been studying the language.'

He nodded, obviously surprised by this development, and she felt a prickle of annoyance. What had he expected? That she wouldn't bother to learn the language of his people? But before she could question his assumptions, the furrow on his forehead deepened. 'You must see the doctor,' he said. 'Then you must return to the Golden Palace.'

'I don't need to see a doctor. I'm perfectly fine. During the last week since I've seen you the nausea has started to ease, just as Ms Siddiqui said it probably would.'

'You have been riding all day in the desert heat, how can you possibly be fine?' His voice rose to match the fury she could see he was having great difficulty containing. But rather than be cowed by his temper, she felt strangely empowered by it. 'You should not have come here,' he added. 'Why did you risk everything?'

Kasia drew a ragged breath at the raw tone, the deep anguish in his words.

She'd travelled thousands of miles to have this confrontation. But this was not at all what she had expected. She had assumed Raif would be cold towards her, unemotional, dismissive. She had been prepared for the worst, that he would tell her he didn't love her, could never love her and then he would discard her—as her mother once had.

But he wasn't cold, or unemotional. His dark eyes flashed with more than temper.

It was something she had never seen in his eyes before, something she had not believed he was even capable of feeling. After all, he was so strong, so indomitable, so commanding, what could he have to fear?

The heat in her core flared and sparked as she took

in his broad chest, the dark pants hanging loosely on his hips. He looked once again like the man she had first met, the Desert Prince, but now she knew that while this man could be wild and untamed, primitive in the best sense of the word, beneath that tough outer shell was a man who had cares and needs just as she did—who could be tender and gentle and kind.

Gathering the courage she had worked so hard to nurture all her life, she forced herself to tell him the truth she should have told him weeks ago.

'I came because I am your wife and I love you. And I want this to be a real marriage. If we are to be a couple, I want to share *every* part of your life with you, which includes living with you here in the desert, as well as living with you in Cambridge or New York or London, or anywhere else we need to be.'

He stepped back, the shock on his face as raw as the emotion. 'No, you cannot love me. I am not...' His voice drifted into silence.

She touched his arm. 'You're not what, Raif?' she said gently.

He gripped her arms and dragged her into his embrace, burying his face in her hair, his shallow breaths tortured as a shudder ran through his body.

'I am not a good man,' he said.

Emotion seized her own throat as she grasped his cheeks, forced his gaze to meet hers. 'What do you mean, Raif? Of course you are.'

'No, you do not understand,' he said, touching her cheek. 'I killed her and now I will kill you, too.'

Her? Who was he talking about? But as he continued, his voice breaking, suddenly she knew. He was talking about the mother he'd lost, the mother he'd never known, the mother he'd tried to honour by insisting on marriage all those months ago.

'I didn't pull out, I made you take my seed,' he said. 'When you were untouched. And now you are bearing two babies. *Two* babies that are too big for you.'

Her heart shattered in her chest. The tears eased over her lids at the pain in his voice. The raw, unguarded fear. She had thought this man couldn't love her, couldn't love their children, when he already loved them—maybe too much.

'I don't want to lose you,' he said, his voice weary as she noticed the dark shadows under his eyes. How much had he slept in the last week? How could she not have seen how tormented he was? 'If you truly love me, you must go back and stay safe.'

'Shhh...' she whispered, the tears falling freely now as he clung to her. She stroked his cheeks, felt the delicious rub of stubble against her palms. And pressed her lips to his. 'It's okay, Raif. Look at me,' she commanded, and his tired gaze finally met hers. 'I'm not going to die. I promise. I'm strong and healthy. You have doctors here and midwives and there is a clinic only a day's ride away. Women have babies safely here all the time, even twins.'

'But they are Kholadi women,' he said. 'They are accustomed to the desert life.'

She smiled, impossibly touched by his stupidity.

'But I'm a Kholadi woman now, too.'

This wasn't about the desert culture, though, not really. Or her ability to handle the nomadic lifestyle that was so much a part of who he was. He knew that to be the Kholadi Princess she would have to embrace that lifestyle, too.

No, his fear for her life, was much more personal than that.

What he really feared was his own feelings, the way she had feared hers. She understood that now, even if he did not. Of course this was harder for him to navigate because she doubted whether he had ever cared for anyone the way he cared for her.

So she would have to show him how.

She took his hand and pressed his palm to the bump beneath her robe. She couldn't feel the babies moving yet, but the bump had become quite pronounced already.

'Do you feel that, Raif? Our babies grow inside me and I will keep them safe always. And love them the way I love you. Love is a gift and, yes, it's terrifying at times because you mean so much to me now that I couldn't bear to lose you either. But the only way we can navigate that fear is to do it together.'

He stared at her belly, his large palm resting on her bump. When his gaze finally lifted to hers she could read every emotion in it. Fear, still, and heat, but most of all love. Raw and basic and untamed. And all the more powerful for it.

'I didn't want to lose you,' he said. 'I wanted to keep you safe.'

'I *am* safe,' she said, with complete certainty. 'As long as I am with you.'

At last he nodded, then he dropped to his knees in front of her. Bracketing her hips with his hands, he held her tight and pressed his cheek to her belly. Worshipping her in a way she had never expected any man to worship her.

She threaded her fingers through the short hair on his scalp, felt his shiver of reaction and the leap of desire arrowed down to her core.

He lifted his head at last, to peer up at her. 'You refuse to go back?' he asked.

'Yes, Raif. I refuse to go back.'

Nodding, he got to his feet then lifted her into his arms and carried her towards the lavish bed at the back of the tent. 'Then I suppose I will have to make good use of you,' he said. And for the first time in what felt like for ever she laughed.

He made slow, careful love to her—too slow, too

careful—as night fell over the desert, but as she reached one climax and then another and another, she felt herself soar into the stars, and knew that, however high she flew, her Desert Prince would never let her fall.

EPILOGUE

Nine months later

'CAN I HOLD one of the babies, too?'

Raif detached his gaze from his oldest daughter's wide dark eyes as she stared at him with complete and completely terrifying trust to find Zane's young son William tugging on his trouser leg. The toddler's eager expression had a shudder running through Raif.

No way, buddy.

'Perhaps when you are older,' he murmured, cradling his tiny baby a little tighter against his chest and rocking her gently.

The boy frowned. 'Why not now?' he demanded with the uncomplicated logic of a child. 'Auntie Kasia let Kaliah hold one, why can't I?'

'Because Jazmin and Amal are very precious to me. And I would not want you to drop them,' Raif replied bluntly, admiring the boy's audacity if nothing else. And deciding he would have to have another word with his wife. Seriously, was it safe to let a six-year-old with the temperament of a lion hold their daughters?

'But that's not fair!' His nephew pouted.

'I know,' Raif said, unable to hold in a rough chuckle as the boy stomped out of the ornate chamber they had been given for their stay in the Golden Palace, no doubt to tell tales to his father in the suite next door.

Good luck with that, buddy.

Zane would be on his side, because he was as protective of his children as Raif was of his. In truth, they had been having many surprisingly reassuring conversations in the months since the girls had been born—every time Raif freaked out over a bout of colic, or a sleepless night, like last night, when Jazmin had resolutely refused to settle. Every time Raif convinced himself he had to be the worst father in existence, Zane had been the one to reassure him.

'Cut yourself some slack, Raif. And wait till they're six and want to ride a horse faster than you do before you freak out too much.'

Raif let out another rough chuckle at the memory of that conversation. How times had changed in the space of a few months.

Strange to think he had found a friend as well as a brother while staying in the Golden Palace—waiting for his wife to recover from the excruciating twenty-two-hour labour that had brought his children into the world.

The terror of seeing his wife in such pain, and the responsibilities of parenthood had turned his old rivalry with his brother into something supportive and strong…rooted in the shared trauma of new fatherhood, no doubt.

It had been a steep learning curve.

Pressing his lips to Jazmin's downy soft skin, he inhaled the sweet scent, elated to see her eyes had finally closed. His heart expanded with love—and pride—as he returned his daughter to the adjoining bedroom.

His heart ricocheted into his throat as he spotted Kasia in the armchair beside their bed, nursing their younger daughter, Amal, at her breast, the bright morning sunshine gilding her skin.

She glanced up and smiled and his heart expanded another inch, all but gagging him.

God, how he loved this woman. Her smile, her sweetness, her support, her intelligence and her love.

He placed Jazmin in her crib as if she were the most precious thing in the world. Because she was. She and her sister and her mother. If anything ever happened to any one of them, he would go out of his mind with—

He cut the thought off.

Do not go there or it will drive you insane.

He patted Jazmin's tiny back until she stopped struggling against her exhaustion and settled into a deeper sleep.

'Well done, Papa,' Kasia murmured around a jaw-breaking yawn. 'You finally got her to sleep.'

'Of course,' he said with a confidence he didn't feel, but was determined to fake as he straightened and walked towards his wife. 'One down, one to go.'

Kasia smiled a sleepy smile, her wild hair rioting around her head, the amber eyes, which he hoped both of their daughters would inherit glimmering with amusement. 'Actually, I think Amal has gone, too,' she said, glancing at the baby fast asleep on her breast. 'So that's one for Mum, too.'

Slipping one finger under their younger daughter's lips, Kasia detached the small cupid's-bow mouth from her nipple.

The familiar jolt of arousal shuddered through Raif at the sight of his wife's exposed breast.

He flinched, shame making him tense as he ruthlessly controlled the insistent shaft of heat, which had only become more insistent in the last few weeks.

What kind of a bastard was he that he could lust after his wife when she was nursing their child? And had spent so many agonising hours in labour a scant three months ago?

'Let me put Amal down,' he said, needing to do something with his hands. He averted his eyes from the display of soft, tempting flesh as he lifted his daughter from his wife's arms.

After rubbing Amal's back until she gave a satisfying belch, he laid her gently in the crib beside her sister's—

amazed all over again at how small and defenceless his children were.

One day they would lead the Kholadi, because they were as smart and brave and strong as their mother—but as the pride rippled through him, so did the panic.

He forced his erratic heartbeat to slow down.

They were not ready to lead the Kholadi *yet*, or ride horses like his fearless niece Kaliah, thank goodness. He still had a few years at least before he had to worry about diplomatic incidents or broken necks.

'What time is it?' Kasia asked from behind him.

'Just after ten,' he said, keeping his eyes on his daughters until he could slow the blood flowing into his groin.

'Are you returning to the Kholadi camp today?' she asked.

'No, tomorrow,' he murmured, listening to the rustle of clothing. Was she undressing? The thought of her naked had a predictable effect, so he strode across the room to stare out of the window at his brother and sister-in-law's suite of rooms across the courtyard.

Lunch wouldn't be served for several hours. Perhaps he could interest his brother in a ride? Or maybe he would go alone. He needed to do something to take his mind off sex, and leave Kasia in peace to catch up on the sleep they'd both lost the night before.

'Wonderful,' she said. 'That gives us two whole hours to enjoy ourselves in the bath I had Ahmed draw for us.'

He swung round, shocked at the seductive tone of her voice. His eyebrows launched up his forehead, and his jaw went slack as a punch of lust hit him firmly in the crotch.

She stood virtually naked, her lush body covered only by a diaphanous robe. He could see the dark outline of her erect nipples through the fabric, the curls covering her sex. His shaft stiffened to iron.

'Kasia, what the hell are you doing?'

* * *

'Seducing my husband. What does it look like?' Kasia watched her husband's eyes darken with lust as power, excitement and passion surged through her.

'But you must sleep,' he said, his voice a croak of barely suppressed agony.

She knew how he felt. She had recovered from the twins' birth weeks ago, but he had not touched her since weeks before their birth.

She had acceded to his request that she have her children in the Golden Palace, instead of at their home on Kholadi land. She had even agreed—after much furious debate—to the compromise of staying in Zane and Cat's home until the twins were four months old, having finally managed to beat him down from six.

She wanted to return to her own home with her children and her husband. But she understood how much the birth had taken out of him. He had been beside himself when she had been in labour, the fear in his eyes tangible. But she refused to avoid this issue any longer.

If she couldn't return home for another month, she could at least have their sex life back. She was the one who had given birth—not him—and the doctor had given her the all clear a couple of weeks ago. But Raif was scared to touch her. She'd tried to give him time, tried to understand. They were both tired, two beautiful but demanding baby girls didn't leave much time for them. But surely that was why they needed to seize every moment they could.

She wasn't tired now, she was hungry. For Raif.

She untied the robe Cat had lent her for this seduction, and let the silky see-through material glide off her shoulders.

His nostrils flared, his eyes narrowing and his breathing ragged. The pounding length in his pants became all the more pronounced.

Holding her shoulders back, she allowed him to look his fill.

Her body had changed. Her stomach wasn't as flat, her breasts not quite as firm, her hips more rounded—but the shyness deserted her as his eyes met hers, the hunger she could see in the chocolate depths as raw and potent as her own.

'What's the matter, Raif? Don't you like what you see?' she asked, bold and unashamed.

'You know I do,' he said, his voice husky with need.

The passion built, weakening her knees but not her resolve.

'Then perhaps you would like to join me in the bath,' she said, turning and walking into the adjoining bathing chamber, being sure to sway her hips to give him the best possible view of her backside. She heard him swear in Kholadi and smiled.

Petals floated on the steaming water that filled the bathing pool. She stepped into the fragrant warmth, loving the feel of the heat and essential oils softening her skin and easing the tension in her muscles.

She'd been planning this seduction for over a week.

She heard him enter the room, and channelling Salome as best she could, she scooped up some water and ran it over her breasts.

A string of curses was accompanied by the sound of clothing being removed in a hurry.

A loud splash was followed by callused but gentle hands clasping her arms and pulling her round to face him.

His huge erection butted her belly and she ground against it instinctively.

'You little witch, you know I cannot resist you,' he said—but she could see the shadow of shame in his eyes, as well as the desperation.

Cradling his hard, stubbled jaw, she pulled him towards her. 'Then don't.'

But before she could claim the kiss she ached for, he drew back.

'I don't want to hurt you.'

'The only way you could hurt me,' she said, taking pity on him, 'is to deny us what we both need.'

'Are you sure?' he said, his desire finally outstripping the panic and caution.

Gripping his broad shoulders, she launched herself into his arms, laughing as he caught her hips and she wrapped her legs around his waist. The head of his erection butted against the wet folds of her sex.

'Absolutely,' she said, as she sank down, taking him in to the hilt.

They groaned in unison.

The glorious feeling of having him back where she needed him spread through her like wildfire. Her heart floated into the cosmos at the thought of all they had achieved together... And the glorious journey still to come.

'Now make love to me like you mean it,' she said. 'Before our daughters wake up.'

He buried his face in her hair, pressed her back against the mosaic tiles of the bath and proceeded to work her eager flesh in sure, solid, overwhelming strokes.

For once, he was doing exactly what he was told.

* * * * *

A SHOCKING
PROPOSAL
IN SICILY

RACHAEL THOMAS

For the fantastic group of adventurers I trekked across the Sahara Desert with in November 2018, raising funds for many charities. Especially 'The Desert Girls'—Sohere, Hanna, Rowena, Danni and Pippa—with whom I shared the most basic tent. The whole week was an awesome and unforgettable adventure!

PROLOGUE

SHE'D HAD HER FREEDOM. Freedom which now needed to be paid for. The last five years of resisting the urge to fulfil the archaic traditions of her country counted for nothing. Her duty to Ardu Safra could no longer be ignored. Or avoided.

Kaliana Benhamed stood outside her father's office. She knew exactly why he'd demanded she return from London. From the new life she'd carved for herself after the tragedy of five years ago. Why he'd insisted she leave a job she loved, as campaign manager for Charity Resources. It didn't concern him she'd have to say goodbye to Claire, a friend who knew everything about her but still treated her like an everyday girl. With that one command, her father had all but brought her world crashing down around her, leaving her no option but to return to her homeland and face him. Face her duty.

Kaliana stood taller, taking a deep breath, desperate to quell the churning of her stomach, her heart pounding hard and fast at the thought of the discussion to come. She swallowed down the nerves she couldn't allow her father to see. She was a different woman from the one who'd left Ardu Safra after the nightmare of losing the man she'd loved. Since then, she'd found her independence and happiness. She'd pushed aside her dreams of love and happy ever afters. Made a new life for herself. A life she wasn't about to relinquish easily.

Not even to her father, ruler of Ardu Safra, a small desert kingdom on the north-eastern edge of the African continent. He'd been a strict father, but fair. Would he really force her to do the one thing she didn't want to do? Would he force her to accept a man he'd selected, as her husband? After everything she'd endured?

She closed her eyes briefly, sending up one last prayer for the strength to do this, wishing her mother had a more modern outlook on life. Wishing she would stand up for her only child. But those wishes were futile. Her mother was kind and loving, but of a very different era.

Kaliana tried to shake the tension from her shoulders as she gave the command to the guards, always stationed around the palace, to admit her to her father's office.

The big doors swung wide and she walked across the vastness of the marble floor to the ornate desk at the far end of the room. Her father looked up from his work, watching her intently. Did he notice how different she was? How strong? How ready she was to do battle with him? To fight for her right to be a modern woman in a modern world?

She knew she had to marry and when that happened she wanted to drag the kingdom of Ardu Safra into the twenty-first century. For the people of the small kingdom as much as for herself. But she wasn't ready yet.

'Kaliana.' His voice was cool. Distant. As if he was addressing one of his aides, not his daughter. His only child. And that was the core of her problem. She was the only heir of Ardu Safra. 'At last you return to your country.'

The reproach in his voice bounced round the vastness of the ornate office, mirroring itself in his dark, watchful eyes. Warning her he wasn't in the mood for her wilfulness, as he often called it.

'You didn't leave me much choice.' Kaliana stopped a short distance from her father's desk, satisfaction racing through her as he took in, with annoyance, her shorter hair. She loved the long bob style she'd opted for as part of the new Kaliana. Already she could feel her hackles rise, her indignation at the injustice surging to the fore. She battled to keep it contained. Keep it from her father. 'You made it clear that my coming was not a request, Father, but a demand.'

The shock of receiving the curt email directly from her father still hadn't subsided. Neither had the knowledge that the life she'd built herself was in serious danger. She was expected to marry and, at twenty-five, she was acutely aware he considered that duty well overdue.

She'd stepped outside the life of Kaliana Benhamed, Princess of Ardu Safra, for five years and now it was time to go back to the life her title demanded. It was time to do the duty she'd hoped she'd never have to do. Live the life she'd tried to be free of.

'What are you wearing?' His gaze took in her fitted navy skirt and white blouse, teamed with heeled shoes. Her chosen clothes for her new work life. He wouldn't approve of them, just as her traditionally brought-up mother didn't. Kaliana was a big disappointment to her parents in many ways.

'This is who I am now, Father.' She lifted her chin defiantly as he stared at her, his annoyance that she'd turned her back so blatantly on her country vividly clear on his face. Once again it was clear she was a total disappointment to him. The daughter who'd brought shame to him. To the country. 'Whatever it is you want of me, this is who I am now.'

He stood up quickly, his heavy chair scraping noisily on the marble floor. Anger burned in his eyes as he leant on the desk. 'What I want is for you to do your duty.'

Kaliana wanted to step back from his fury. 'My duty, Father?' she asked, in a voice so light it didn't even sound like her own. But to show her fear to him, her fear of what he now expected her to do, would be to hand him the ace card. Give him all the power.

And it was a power she'd slowly and bit by bit taken from him over the last five years as her new life had proved she could succeed without the title of Princess Kaliana of Ardu Safra. She'd got herself a managerial job, a place to live and friends she could count on without disclosing her royal title. Only Claire knew the truth. To her employer, her colleagues and friends, she was simply Kaliana Benhamed. And the fact she'd achieved all that irritated her father far more than he let on.

'Marriage.' He hurled the word she least wanted to hear at her. 'Marriage is your duty, Kaliana. Your duty as Princess to the kingdom of Ardu Safra. Your duty as my daughter and only heir.'

She clenched her hands tightly, her nails digging into the sweaty palms. 'Not in the life I now lead, Father.'

'The life you now lead?' Her father's voice lowered with disappointment, the scowl on his face full of annoyance and frustration. She was only making this worse. Making it harder for herself. Making him angrier. 'I've allowed you to indulge in that fancy long enough.'

She stepped forward, her own frustration making her reckless. 'It's not a fancy, Father, it's my life now. One I needed to make for myself.'

He sighed slowly and looked at her, his expression softening very slightly, making her think of the father he'd been when she was younger. The father who'd loved her even though she hadn't been born a son. The father who had been more relaxed—until the burden of inheriting and ruling a financially struggling and small kingdom had snatched that man away. 'I understand why you needed to go. That's why I said nothing when you turned your back on the lifestyle your title could have brought you.'

'Then you will understand why I can't marry. Not ever.'

'It's not that simple, Kaliana. Our kingdom is in jeopardy. Our people too. The only way out of it is for you to marry.' The resignation in his voice shocked her. The angry ruler of moments ago had gone. The man she'd loved as a carefree child had returned. It was that man who tugged on her conscience.

'And who will I marry, Father? Alif, the man I loved, the man you were perfectly happy for me to marry, died—remember?' A stab of pain shot through her as she recalled being told her fiancé had been killed in a tragic helicopter crash just weeks before their wedding.

'Nassif has asked for your hand in marriage.' Her father's words cut savagely through that memory.

'Nassif?' Kaliana couldn't believe she was hearing right. How could he do this to her? How could her father even think she would marry anyone? But Nassif?

'Alif's uncle? Alif's cruel and spiteful uncle? You can't mean that?' Her voice was a strangled cry of pain and despair. Her throat had gone dry, as if she'd walked all day in the heat of the desert and not taken one sip of water. Her head spun and she dragged in rapid deep breaths, desperate to regain control of herself and this conversation. 'I can't. I. Can't.'

'Marriage to Nassif will unite our countries, just as they should have been five years ago, if you'd married Alif.' Her father sat once again behind his desk, the formidable ruler he'd become slipping back into place. The glimpse of the father she'd known long ago, gone. Or was it just her wishful thinking? She'd foolishly been hoping her father would be pleased to see her after five years. How wrong could she be?

Kaliana's knees weakened and she wished she could slump to the floor as past hurt, past pain and heartache collided with the panic of what her father had planned. What he expected her to do without question. 'But Nassif is so much older than me.'

'That is true,' he said slowly, his response to her objection so obviously rehearsed. 'Now that his wife has passed away, he wants to make you his wife.'

Kaliana backed away, needing the roar of panic in her head to stop, needing the wild spinning of her mind to cease. 'No. I will not marry him.'

Sweat prickled on her forehead. Nausea rose and the need to turn and run became almost irresistible. But she couldn't run. Somewhere deep inside her, the duty her mother had implanted so innocuously into her from a young age resurfaced. Took over.

She wanted to run. But she couldn't. She had a duty to do. Duty to her family. Her kingdom.

Deep down, she'd always known her father had allowed her time away, allowed her time to heal the pain of her broken heart. But now that reprieve was over. It was time for her to do the right thing. Do the duty she'd been born to.

But marriage to Nassif? She shivered with sickening revulsion. Marriage to anyone would be bad enough, but to her late fiancé's vile uncle? Unthinkable.

Her father watched her without saying anything. He didn't even flinch when, with a great shuddering breath that could lead to tears if she let it, she looked at him. Imploring him to understand. Imploring him to tell her he'd find someone else.

Someone else. The words wandered around her mind like mist on an autumn morning in London, shrouding all other thoughts. What if she did marry someone else?

Spurred on by the idea, the desperate thought that this was the solution, she moved back towards him. 'I can't marry Nassif, Father.'

'Ardu Safra is facing financial ruin. Whilst you have been in London things have become very bad here.'

'Why didn't you tell me?'

'It is for me to deal with. I was counting on your marriage to Alif to make things right.' The sharpness of his words only just hid his panic, the seriousness of the situation.

'There were problems even then?' she asked, saddened to think she'd been happy and free in London, while her mother and father had carried this burden.

'Yes. And now I must ask that you make a marriage with Nassif.' His voice had hardened. Was that to hide his shame that things had got so bad in the country he ruled? Guilt raced through her, forming a potent cocktail, mixing with her fear. A cocktail that made her almost physically sick.

'Father, no. Not Nassif.'

'He is a very wealthy man.' Her father looked at her, no longer the strong ruler but a man who looked broken and defeated. A man who was depending on her. Her heart wrenched. 'And he is willing to invest in Ardu Safra.'

She shook her head in protest, but the straight line of her father's mouth warned her it was in vain.

'Your marriage will bring the finances you should have brought with your marriage five years ago.' She knew that gritty determination in his voice. He would get what he wanted. One way or another. And he wanted to save Ardu Safra by marrying her off to a wealthy man.

But did that man have to be Nassif?

A solution barged into her mind, making any further words almost impossible. Her heart thudded loudly. Dare she risk telling him? Risk his anger? And, worst of all, his disapproval of her. 'No. I can't do it.'

'Imagine the shame your mother will face.' He believed he held the ace cards, but she wouldn't allow him to emotionally blackmail her. He wouldn't use the close relationship she and her mother had always shared. He wouldn't do that to her any more.

'This isn't about Mother,' she said flatly, glaring at him, that wilful streak of hers beginning to take over as the solution to her problem grew in possibility. Like the sun as it rose over the mountains of the desert. Becoming bigger and stronger with each passing minute.

'And the people of Ardu Safra? Will you stand by and allow them to wallow in poverty and hunger because you won't do your duty? Because you won't make a marriage to bring wealth back to our kingdom?'

Damn it, he did hold the ace cards. All of them. And he played them well. Too well.

'Don't, Father,' she snapped.

'How will your charities view you when they know who you really are? That you turned your back on the country of your birth? Its people?' He stood once more, realising she was retreating, on the verge of accepting defeat. His threat to reveal her true identity, even though he'd helped her keep it secret, all he needed to use.

'That's not fair.' How had she thought he was a fair man?

'You will *have* to marry someone, Kaliana. A man with great wealth. A man able to rule by your side when the time comes.' He paused, letting the image of her future permeate her mind. 'This is your country. Your people.'

Marry someone. That was what he'd said. Again, the other less hideous option rushed into her mind. That was it. She would find her own husband.

'Then I will find someone else.' The words tumbled out in a panic and she knew she was in danger of losing the control she was fighting to keep on her emotions. 'I will find a man to marry who can bring the finances needed to Ardu Safra.'

Her father looked at her, scowling, but before he could shut down her idea she spoke again. 'I cannot and will not marry Nassif.'

She expected him to be angry. Braced herself for his wrath, but it didn't come. He looked as stunned as she felt.

He shook his head in disbelief. 'You really think you

can find a man, one wealthier than Nassif, willing to marry you and take on the demands of being husband to a princess?'

'Yes, Father, I do.' Now her panic changed direction. How could she ever achieve that?

'Very well, I will prepare for a wedding.'

'What?'

'On the day of your twenty-sixth birthday you will be married.'

'But that's…' She paused to calculate, her mind too numb to function. 'October. The beginning of October. Only four months away.'

He nodded solemnly. She wanted to rail against him, but he'd changed. There was something different about him. Something that tugged mercilessly at her heartstrings. Something that once again hinted that the father she'd loved as a child, the man she wished he could be, lingered beneath his tough exterior.

But she wasn't about to let go of the chance he'd given her. 'And if I haven't found a husband by then?' Inside she was a wild rush of panic. She could do this. She *had* to do this.

'You have until September,' her father solemnly said. 'Find a suitable husband by then or marry Nassif on your twenty-sixth birthday.'

CHAPTER ONE

Early June

RAFFAELE CASELLA COULD hardly control his frustration. Even as he'd flown back from Sicily to London, he hadn't been able to halt the flow of anger. The irritation. His father, alarmingly calm after his cancer diagnosis, had hammered home the stark reality of the situation the family was now in.

The Casella name could end. And with it the possession of land and wealth which had been handed from one Casella generation to the next. With appalling timing, his twin brother, Enzo, had chosen that very day to admit his marriage to Emma was in jeopardy, after a fertility test had proved he was unable to father children—Casella heirs. His father had panicked, turning immediately to Rafe, putting the duty of providing the next generation squarely on his shoulders. Now he was the only one who could ensure the Casella land and wealth stayed exactly that.

Rafe had fought to control his anger, his shock, throughout the discussion with his father and Enzo. Reminding himself the old man was ill, holding it all in, thinking instead of the father he'd spent his life trying to please, but failing at every turn. Enzo, the first-born twin, was the son who had always achieved that honour, even when he'd betrayed Rafe in the most heartless way, tearing apart a family already living under the cloud of tragedy.

The Casella name would end if he, the second-born twin, the spare heir, didn't marry and have children. The biggest crisis the Casella family had faced for three generations now loomed over them.

Rafe was in the spotlight, its brightness harsh and unyielding. Inescapable. He was the only one who could save the Casella name, and with it the family fortune. Pressure bore down on him. His future was mapped out, demanding he take a route that involved a marriage he'd never intended to make. Children—or, more precisely, a son to continue the Casella name—something he'd never wanted.

He had no choice. Either that or stand by and watch their cousin Serafina and her greedy husband, Giovanni Romano, take everything, ending the Casella dynasty.

Rafe couldn't allow that. Not when part of that dynasty was the one piece of land which meant more to him than anything else. His mother's land. The place he and Enzo, along with childhood friend Franco, had once played happily. It was a place full of memories of his mother. Memories he'd treasured since her death when he and Enzo had been only teenagers. For those olive groves alone, Rafe would do anything. Even marry. Even become a father. It was far more than ensuring nobody else, other than a Casella, owned Pietra Bianca. For Rafe it was about keeping his mother's memory alive.

The thought of Giovanni at the ancient olive grove

slammed into Rafe as he ordered a second whisky. A surge of anger raced through him, almost blocking out the subtle tones of the gentle piano music weaving through the bar of the exclusive London hotel.

There was no way Giovanni Romano was having anything to do with Pietra Bianca.

Rafe swigged the fiery liquid back and banged the empty glass down on the bar. During the last heated words he and his brother had shared, Enzo had made it clear that, despite everything that had gone on between them, he expected Rafe to step up. Expected him to save the Casella fortune. Proving his twin was as mercenary, as motivated by wealth, as their father.

'Damn you, Father,' Rafe muttered as he glared at the offensively empty glass. 'And damn you, Enzo.'

Rafe pushed his hands through his hair as he thought of Serafina and Giovanni claiming the Casella fortune. No. That could never happen. Irritation tipped over to anger and Rafe called over the bartender, watching him with narrowed eyes, his thoughts elsewhere, as another glass of whisky was poured.

Picking up the glass, Rafe raised it to his reflection in the mirrors behind the bar. To his future. Marriage. Fatherhood. The things he'd never wanted, now his only option.

Rafe looked down into the amber liquid in the crystal tumbler, still questioning the wisdom of marriage. The ice-cold shock which had hit him as his father had made his expectations clear was still frozen inside him, the whisky unable to thaw it.

His father had always considered Enzo the true heir, expecting his first-born son to marry, produce the new generation and claim it all. Rafe was, as always, merely the back-up plan. An extra card in his hand.

A card he was now forced to play after Enzo's marriage was crashing on the rocks so spectacularly. Divorce seemed the only option. Poor Emma. Rafe tried to push the sympathy away. She might have been his first love, but she was now Enzo's wife. Enzo and Emma's betrayal had gone far deeper than just killing his love for her.

Rafe swirled the whisky in the glass, brooding into it as if it held the answers to the nightmare he now lived. He had no wish for marriage. No need for emotional complications. How was he to find himself a wife? And one that would bring the kind of prestigious advantages to the marriage he required and the son the Casella family required? Did he really have such little choice that he had to accept a marriage deal arranged by his father?

Anger chased the whisky through his body. Was he to parade himself like a stud horse? That stung his male pride as much as being the standby heir.

'Champagne.' The husky voice of the woman joining him at the bar caught his attention, dragging him from his despair, her accent intriguing him as she made her demand to the bartender. Despite the weight of his problems, he was captivated in a way he hadn't been for a long time.

Rafe studied her in the mirrors behind the bar and, despite the rows of optics, saw the woman was as attractive as her voice. There was an air of sophistication about her. She radiated confidence, drew him ever closer. Making him want more than a curious glance in the mirror. Making him want to get to know her. Effectively sealing his fate.

Attraction surged through him and he reluctantly admitted he'd go as far as to say she was the sexiest woman he'd seen in a long time. She was tall and slender, wearing a tight-fitting pale gold silk blouse, sleeves folded up past her elbows and open low at the front. Her dark shoulder-length hair was pulled back away from her face, accentuating her vivid brown eyes, her brown eye make-up making them appear as black as coal. Her full lips were pressed together into a sulky but sexy pout.

She was utterly gorgeous.

Watching her shouldn't have turned him on, but it did. A lick of hot lust, reminding him just how long it had been since he'd lost himself in the oblivion of a beautiful woman, fired through him. It would also be something he'd never be able to do again once he married. His marriage might not be for love, or any kind of sentiment, but his morals wouldn't allow for such betrayal as infidelity.

He knew how that felt. All too well.

Rafe nodded to the bartender, who swiftly brought over two glasses and a bottle of champagne, placing them on the bar between him and the woman. With a quick glance at the label, Rafe satisfied himself his usual standards had been catered for with nothing but the best and moved closer to the sexy woman.

'I don't recall inviting you to join me.' She turned, leaning one slender arm on the bar, cutting off any polite introductions he could have made as she glared up at him. That lick of lust just became a savage kick.

He conjured up an image of the kind of woman his father might suggest as a suitable wife and knew she'd never be a match to this sassy, sophisticated woman before him. He took in the brunette's long bronzed legs, the tight-fitting skirt skimming above her knees and the sexy gold sandals on delicate feet with red painted nails.

This woman oozed confidence. She was strong. Independent. And, with a body like that, she would fill his nights with hot pleasure. There was no way a woman like her would agree to a marriage purely for convenience.

This was a woman who undoubtedly played as hard as she worked. Exactly the kind of woman he was drawn to. He knew instinctively this woman would match him in every way.

'I think you will find it is you who is being invited to join me,' he taunted. Sparks of sexy annoyance shot out at him from her eyes, sending that savage lust roaring straight to his groin. He clenched his jaw against the kind of need he hadn't felt for a long time. The kind of need that right now would chase away the shock of all he'd discovered. All he must do.

'And how do you come to that conclusion? You were very clearly drinking whisky when I arrived,' she goaded him, leaning her head to one side, her diamond earrings sparkling and winking at him.

He smiled. She'd noticed. Noticed him. 'That is true.'

'I was the one who ordered champagne.' Her accent deepened. He'd never met a woman like this. For the last six years he'd consciously avoided complicating his life with female company. He'd used the alternative energy business he'd worked hard to set up, instead of joining his father and Enzo in the family business, to keep him from his homeland. Sicily held too many bad memories. The kind that wrote over any good times.

Here in London, or at his other base in New York, he didn't have to remember.

He didn't have to face the past. It didn't have to shape who he was.

Then all that had changed with his father's illness. He'd been forced to return to Sicily. Forced back into his brother's life. The twin who'd destroyed Rafe's planned future as though it was nothing more than paper. The only two women he'd got close to had been lost. His mother and then Emma. Damn it, he'd lost Emma to his own brother. And now the final insult was that Rafe had no choice but to step up to the mark and do his duty, to help his father and his brother keep the Casella fortune.

Rafe pushed his troubles aside. This wasn't the time for them. Not when this woman was exactly what he needed right now. A distraction he wanted to lose himself in—completely.

'You didn't order champagne. You demanded it.' The stunned look on her face at being reprimanded made him smile. This was going to be a very entertaining evening. Precisely what he needed.

Tonight, he wanted to lose himself. Completely and with this woman. From the way she was looking at him, eyes swirling with desire as much as annoyance, he knew it was only a matter of time until he did just that. A sizzling sexual attraction drew them inexplicably to one another and he had no intention of severing it. Instead, he would meet it head-on.

'I did no such thing.'

'I didn't hear a please,' he taunted her, watching the gold flecks in her dark brown eyes shine brighter with fury. 'And I am yet to hear a thank you.'

Beneath her dark complexion he noticed she had the

good grace to blush. She sighed, her breasts rising with the deep breath in, snagging his attention, ratcheting up his lust, tightening the binds of attraction.

Silence fell between them as the bartender poured two glasses of champagne, placing the bottle back in the cooler, before attending to other guests. She took hers and, still without a word of thanks, turned her attention away from him.

'Sorry. It's been a bad day,' she said quickly. 'A bad week. Two weeks, in fact.'

He watched her once more in the mirror as she sipped her drink, before putting the glass on the bar and tracing one long slender finger around the rim absently. Her thoughts far away from him. From this bar.

'That's both of us then.'

Her gaze met his in the mirror. They remained like that, gazes locked, drawing them together, keeping them linked. It was powerful. Hard to resist. But he had no intention of doing that. This beauty who'd exploded into his world was exactly the antidote he needed after this morning's meeting with his father.

'It might have just got a little better.' She tilted her head on one side, still watching him in the mirror. Again, the sparkle of diamonds hanging from her ears caught his attention as she openly flirted with him. Teased him.

Champagne. Diamonds. Who was this enigma of a woman who'd gate-crashed his private moment?

'Shall we agree to dismiss today? To live for now? This moment and nothing else?' He spoke to her reflection, not sure where his questions had come from.

He was the last person who would condone shirking duty for personal needs. But this woman's demeanour, her confident sexiness and charm, sparkling brighter than her diamonds, must be affecting him more than he knew.

She picked up her glass, raising it up to his reflection in the mirrors, her gaze intently holding his. In that hypnotic way a woman could seduce a man with just one look, he knew he was lost.

Tonight, he was hers.

'I will drink to that,' Kaliana said as she tried once again not to notice how incredibly sexy she found this man. Her friend and flatmate, Claire, had told her she needed to let go of the past. Get out there and have fun. Be the woman she really wanted to be.

So she'd thrown caution to the wind and headed out to do just that, planning to meet up with her friends as soon as they all finished work. But she'd never expected this. Not just the man himself, but an undeniable need to be with a man she didn't even know. And in a way she'd never experienced.

He was just the distraction she needed after today's call from her father, reminding her that two weeks had passed since she'd agreed to find a man wealthy enough to save her kingdom. And save herself from a marriage to a brutal bully.

Maybe Claire was right. Maybe she needed to find herself before she could find a husband. Had fate brought her this man for that exact reason? She focused on the stranger. His white shirt was open at the neck and, if she was brave enough to look lower, more than hinted at his bronzed and well-defined chest, dusted with dark hair.

That same call of hungry need which had first zipped

through her when she'd looked at his handsome face, into his intensely black eyes, unfurled once more. It wasn't like her at all. She'd always avoided men like him. Dangerously sexy men. Men who could make her want the impossible. Men who could make her forget. Because she didn't want to forget Alif and their innocent young love.

But tonight she needed this. She had no intention of avoiding anything or anyone. She wanted to take whatever the evening offered. When she'd seen the handsome stranger, glaring into his drink, she'd known with an unnerving certainty that he was what she wanted. What she needed.

Tonight, she wanted to be a different woman. She wanted a distraction. She needed the rebellion against the hand fate had dealt her. That need burned brighter than ever. Pushing her on. Making her want to taste what could have been.

You want him. A voice echoed in her mind, chanting and triumphant. The little miss prim and proper virgin she'd always been wanted this sex god of a man. And why shouldn't she have some fun? Rebellion rippled through her again, stronger than ever. Nobody would ever know if she had a little bit of fun. Indulged in a bit of flirting. Not here in London. Not so far away from Ardu Safra. In London she was simply Kaliana. Nobody knew her here and she could hide from her weighty royal title.

Excitement zipped through her. Maybe it was time to taste even more than that. Maybe it was time to finally let go of the past, of who she'd been, and discover what physically being with a man was like. But not just any man. This man.

She looked up into the stranger's face to see a slow sexy smile spread across his lips. Heat infused her cheeks. She knew he couldn't possibly read her mind, but she wondered if he had. If he knew just how much she wanted him.

He picked up his glass and raised it to her. 'A toast. To this moment.'

Her tongue slicked over suddenly parched lips, her breath seeming harder to come by. Less natural. Her heart thumped. Her body heated. She liked the way he made her feel. Liked the sensation of freedom and power this surge of sexual chemistry between them gave her. Freedom she might never know again if she did her duty by her family and made a marriage to financially save the kingdom of Ardu Safra.

The thought of the man she'd be forced to marry if she didn't make a deal with a man of her choice almost squashed her bravado. No, she inwardly berated herself. She wouldn't think of Nassif now or of how her life would be if they married. All she wanted to think about was this moment. *This* man.

'To the moment,' she said boldly, hoping she didn't sound as gauche and inexperienced as she really was.

She'd never chatted up a man like this before. Never given out such a clear message of wanting far more than idle chat to any man other than the man she'd once been engaged to. Yet here she was. Alone. In a bar. With a sinfully sexy man. Not wanting the moment to end.

She sipped her champagne. All the while his inky black eyes watched her, his brow slightly furrowed. His stubble-covered jaw was stern and set. He looked powerful. Commanding. And sexy.

He called to her on a level she'd never known existed.

Made her want the impossible. Made her want to be
someone else—for tonight at least. Something no other
man had made her feel since Alif's death.

'Allow me to introduce myself,' he said, his grav-
elly voice sending spirals of heat through her, nudging at the need, the attraction he raised. Demanding
the kind of satisfaction she knew instinctively only he
could give her.

'Just first names,' she said quickly, watching his
brows raise before a smile of conspiracy slid slowly over
his lips. Sinfully sexy didn't come anywhere near it.

'As you wish.' He lifted his glass of champagne to
her, his eyes darkening with wild desire, making her
head spin more than the champagne she wasn't really
used to. 'Rafe.'

'Ana,' she said quickly, unable to quell the shimmer
of excitement rushing through her.

The feeling was so powerful she drank the remainder of her champagne in one go, not missing his amusement, which set off sparks in his eyes as well as inside
her. He pulled the bottle of champagne from the cooler,
ice rattling as it was disturbed and, without a word, re-
plenished her glass.

When he looked at her again his expression was
speculative, but thankfully he didn't say anything,
didn't ask further questions. Instead he replaced the
bottle in the ice with the kind of familiarity that made
her think he must be a waiter. Maybe he worked here?
Maybe he'd just finished for the night?

'Are you a waiter here?' she asked as he took a sip
of his champagne.

His eyes widened and for a moment she thought the
champagne he'd sipped would be fired all over her.

She'd clearly shocked him. Offended him even. She'd been so taken in by him she hadn't paid that much attention to his clothes—just him. But now she looked more closely, she could see his shirt wasn't just any shirt. It was quality, fitting him to perfection, and had probably been made for him.

'No. I am a guest. As are you, I presume.'

'I am,' she said with renewed determination. She knew that whatever happened next—and the fact that something would was as certain as the full moon which would rise over London—she wanted this night.

She was a woman with needs. A woman with desires. A woman this man had set alight with one sexy smile.

She was more than entitled to this one night. She'd lost the love of her life and soon she would be forced into a marriage she didn't want. This moment was hers. And she intended to take it. All of it.

'Then I am honoured to be able to share this evening with you.' He glanced at her, pouring himself another glass of champagne. She watched, mesmerised by his olive hands, long regal fingers, wrapping around the bottle so eloquently.

What would it feel like to have those hands touch her? To have those fingers bring pleasure to her body?

He looked directly at her, a mysterious intensity in his eyes as they slowly travelled down her body, lingering on her breasts, the soft silk of her pale gold blouse offering no protection against the heat of his eyes. His attention lowered, down over the skirt of the same silk, fitting snugly to her hips. Then finally, when Kaliana thought she couldn't take it any more, his attention shifted to her high-heeled sandals and red painted toenails.

She shivered with pleasure. Anticipation.

He hadn't touched her, but he'd just undressed her. Right here. In the bar of an exclusive hotel. She felt totally and gloriously naked even though the cool silk against her skin told her otherwise.

Did he know her thoughts? Did he know how he made her feel? Did he know what she wanted? Right now.

'I think all night would be better.' Emboldened by the heat of her body, she pushed aside embarrassment. Pushed aside the last remnants of her reservations and made her intentions, her needs, clear. Before she married to save her family from the shame of financial ruin, she wanted to know the pleasure of being desired by a man. The pleasure of desiring *this* man.

His brows flicked up in surprise but instantly he schooled his chiselled features, the cool charm of moments ago back in play. 'You wish to spend the entire night in my company?'

No man had ever come close to making her feel the kind of desire Alif had made her feel. If only she hadn't been so insistent on going to her marriage bed a virgin, she would have known what it was to desire and be desired before he'd been tragically taken from her. Regret rushed through her.

No other man had ever made her feel that way.

Until she'd seen this man. Within seconds of her eyes meeting his she'd known she wanted him. Known he was the only man who could cleanse her body of its innocence.

She wasn't about to allow this moment, this feeling, this need, to slip away again. She wanted this night. Wanted this man. 'I do.' She held his gaze, challenging him to pull back, to call a halt to the dangerous game of passion she was on the brink of playing. 'I want to be with you all night.'

Kaliana wanted to indulge in the game, dangerous or not. What better way to forget about the future and move on from the past than in this man's arms?

His gaze narrowed. Was he thinking of a wife he'd left at home? Children even? 'You are playing a dangerous game, Ana.'

The silky softness of his voice was like a caress. It soothed. It excited. If his voice could do that, what would his kiss be like?

Her gaze flew to his lips; instantly a slow and very sexy smile spread over them.

'A game I want to play.' She looked up at him from lowered lashes, flirting coming surprisingly naturally to her. 'But if you don't want to. Or can't…' She allowed the words to trail off, seductively moving closer to him in a way she'd never, ever imagined herself doing. But tonight she wasn't herself. She looked boldly up at him. 'I will go.'

Instantly he put one arm around her waist, slowly but very purposefully drawing her closer. All the while his eyes remained fixed on hers. She moved willingly towards him, her body alive with a sensation she'd never experienced before. The pressure of his hand, his arm holding her, burning her skin.

'We will play the game your way.' His eyes darkened as he drew her a fraction closer, the narrowing gap between their bodies alive with sparks. 'For now.'

'Good.' She smiled up at him, feeling out of her depth and very much in control all at the same time. She moved closer still, inhaling the exotic scent of his cologne, the tang of citrus blending with cedarwood pushing her on, taking her higher. This was exactly the game she wanted to play.

Tonight, she wasn't Princess Kaliana of Ardu Safra. Tonight, she was simply Ana and it felt right. Tonight, she wanted this man. He was exactly what she needed. What she wanted. And she wanted him all night.

CHAPTER TWO

RAFE WATCHED ANA'S eyes darken. Desire thundered through him. Harder. Faster. Like the call of a war drum of old. He was losing the mask of the composed businessman who'd a short while ago been drinking whisky alone. Hell, he was losing himself. And he hadn't even kissed her.

Yet.

With this woman's body pressed so alluringly against his, he knew he was in danger of completely losing his grasp on reality. Losing everything. His whole body ached for her and the satisfaction he knew only she could give. He'd never been so hard. So ready.

She moved closer, her smoky eyes filling with need, exploding with desire. Shimmying her hips provocatively, pressing against his erection. And he thought he'd never been so hard.

He tightened his hold on her, keeping her delicious body against him. 'See what you do to me?' He barely recognised the coarse rasp of his voice.

She smiled. Moved her hips again, forcing him to bite down hard on the growl of desire threatening to rip from him.

'I feel,' she purred. Damn, but she was a merciless tease. 'But I don't see.'

He couldn't hold back any longer. He had to taste her. Had to feel her lips beneath his. Feel the passion that burnt in her eyes, taste it on her tongue as it danced with his.

But if he gave into that need here?

It wasn't worth imagining. Or was it? Erotic images swept through his mind, faster than lightning. Their bodies entwined in the erotic dance of desire.

Rafe inhaled deeply as she pressed her body even harder against his. Making those images so hot they became X-rated.

'I think we should retire to my suite.' His voice was hoarse and ragged with desire. He hadn't known anything like it. Ever. It was like a wild fire bearing down on him at an alarming pace, offering no escape. Not that he wanted any escape.

There was a slight pause as she looked up at him. A hint of uncertainty and hesitation. The fire cooled briefly, stilled, as if waiting to see which way the wind would take it. As he watched her, she looked innocent. Vulnerable. Then it was gone. The sex siren, the seductress, was back in play and the fire raged on relentlessly.

'And I was enjoying this moment.' She raised her brows, looking up at him, bringing her lips tantalisingly close to his. 'I was enjoying my power over you.'

'If you carry on with this power game, I am going to have to kiss you. Right here. Right now.' His voice was more of a feral growl, the like of which he'd never heard before. How could one woman, a woman he'd only just met, have such an effect on him?

'Then kiss me. Right here and right now.' Her bold

and brazen reply excited him further. There would be no backing out now. This would be taken to the inevitable conclusion—in the privacy of his suite.

She moved closer still, her breath feathering his lips. 'Kiss me.'

Hell, he couldn't wait any longer. He had to taste her. She moved her lips closer, a spark of sexy mischief in her eyes. He placed his champagne glass on the bar, not taking his eyes from hers, and spread his palm over her shoulder blades, at the same time crushing her lips beneath his.

She gasped into his mouth, her eyes wide, and again that aura of innocence briefly shone through. A woman playing with fire. The fire of desire. Desire he could no longer control. She closed her eyes, long lashes sweeping down over her cheeks as she began to kiss him back. As hard and demanding as his kiss, sweeping away any doubts.

This woman was far from innocent. This was a woman in control of her sexuality. A woman who knew exactly what she wanted. And right now he was in no doubt. She wanted him.

Her tongue entwined with his and her arms wound round his neck, her fingers sliding into his hair, long nails scratching his scalp. He delved his tongue deeper into her mouth, tasting champagne. Tasting her.

He had to get them out of here. He was in danger of ripping her sexy tight blouse and skirt from her body right here in the bar.

He lifted his lips away from hers reluctantly, dragging in a deep breath of sanity.

'Your suite,' she whispered, opening her eyes and looking up at him. Already she looked deliciously tousled.

Lust pounded through him. He barely had any control left. Virtually no restraint. His need for this woman, this moment, was so intense. He wanted to revel in her power. Be tamed by her. It either stopped here and now or…

'This is what you want?' He tried to steady his voice, needing to calm the heated desire thundering through him like a sudden eruption from Mount Etna. Despite this desire, despite the way her body begged him for more than just a kiss, he needed to hear her say it.

Did he really have to ask?

'It is,' Kaliana said softly, her voice husky, her breathing rapid and uneven. He was giving her the chance to back out, proving he wanted her as much as she wanted him. Giving her the power. Power which made her feel alive.

She brushed her lips over his lightly, wanting to kiss away the control he'd suddenly found. She wanted him at her mercy. Her at his. She breathed against his lips, driven by a need too powerful to resist. 'It is. Take me to your suite.'

He held her gaze, looking deep into her eyes, as if satisfying himself she spoke the truth and for a moment she wondered if he knew. If he'd guessed she was a virgin. As if he'd guessed her act of bold bravado was exactly that. Was this man of undeniable experience about to turn her down? Leaving her aching for him, for satisfaction? Leaving her not knowing what it would be like to be sexually fulfilled?

She wanted this night of pleasure, this night of unknown desires. She needed it. To prove she was alive.

Locked within her was the woman Alif had gently coaxed into the first flush of womanhood with his love.

She held her breath.

Pain rushed through her at the thought of Alif and the love they'd shared. The passion they should have known together. Was it wrong she felt such desire with another man?

She looked up at Rafe, felt the pull of attraction, the spark of desire, the heat of passion. It wasn't wrong. Something this powerful couldn't be. Unexpected, but not wrong.

'I want you,' she whispered, drawing again on the elation of being free to indulge in this desire. Free to be a woman who knew what she wanted and took it.

And she wanted this night and this man. Nobody except Rafe could stop it now. Tonight, she would finally bloom into the woman she could be.

'And I want you.' His accent suddenly deepened, the intensity in those dark eyes mirroring every need and emotion inside her.

'I want you to make love to me.' Her breath was ragged, her words slipping out, firm and decisive. Elation at her freedom, her power of abandonment to be exactly what she wanted, rose ever higher. She wanted to feel his kisses all over her body. His strong hands caressing her, pleasuring her in ways she could only imagine. For too long she'd locked herself behind a barrier of grief, but she couldn't do it any more. Not if she had to give up on everything she'd ever dared to hope for and sacrifice her secret dreams of one day finding the kind of love she'd shared with Alif. If love a second time even existed. 'I want you to make love to me. Tonight.'

'Tonight?' The hoarseness of his voice left her in

no doubt he was fighting a losing battle as much as she was.

'Tonight,' she teased. 'All night.'

He inhaled deeply, his eyes piercing into hers. Taking her hand, he silently led her through the serene calmness of the hotel bar, some guests casting them curious but knowing glances.

Together they stepped into the lift. The air crackled with tension. Neither moved. Towards each other or away. The only contact was her hand in his. Silence enveloped them as the lift moved swiftly upwards. She didn't dare look at him. Something wild was about to explode between them and if they even so much as looked at one another it would happen before they reached the privacy of his suite.

She drew in a deep breath, his scent stirring her desire ever higher, and she willed the lift to stop. Willed the doors to open. Beside her, he was rigid, his body motionless with control as he stared straight ahead. She didn't need to look at him to know it. She sensed it. Sensed the power of his control.

At last the lift doors swished almost silently open, directly into his suite, so vast she was sure it must occupy the entire floor. So, he was immensely wealthy. Not the waiter she'd mistaken him to be.

She smiled at the memory of his reaction to her question as she walked into the suite, past the sprawling pale grey sofa, covered with cushions. Past the vast desk where papers and a closed laptop confirmed he was a businessman. Towards the wall of windows which looked out over London, now twinkling with many lights, competing with the moon.

She closed her eyes, inhaling deeply. Here, tonight,

she could be a different woman than the one who'd handed over her future to the family duty she'd always secretly hoped to be free of, wishing instead for love and happiness. Here, tonight, none of that mattered.

Awareness prickled over her skin as he came to stand behind her, his hands gently holding her upper arms, subtly caressing them, pulling her slowly closer to him.

She looked at the window, their reflection, just as erotic as it had been in the bar. She watched him lower his head to kiss her neck, anticipating his lips on her skin seconds before it happened. She closed her eyes to the pleasure, her pulse racing wildly.

She sighed softly as his lips trailed over her skin, burning it. Setting her alight. But it wasn't enough. Nowhere near enough.

Kaliana angled her head, inviting more, needing more. She leant her head back against him as he drew her closer. Rafe's fingertips joined the torture his lips were inflicting on her skin. She shuddered with pleasure as the warmth of his fingers traced downwards, inside her blouse. Inside her bra.

She pressed her eyes tightly shut, desire wildly uncoiling deep inside her. Deep in the hidden femininity she'd locked away after losing Alif.

Rafe murmured against her neck, his fingers grazing over her increasingly hard nipples. It was exquisite. She trembled with need as he continued his torture, heated desire burning between her legs. She sighed softly as she turned her head to face him. He moved closer, the torture on her nipple continuing as he slicked his tongue over her lips. He moved slowly back and she licked her lips, tasting champagne and whisky along with something stronger. Desire.

He slid his hand away from her breast, trailing a blaze of heat up her neck. Every part of her was on high alert. Every part of her wanted him. Needed him.

She turned in his arms, clutched at his shirt and pulled, wanting to feel his body, needing to see it. Buttons popped to the floor as she dragged the shirt out from his black trousers, pushing it aside, pressing her lips to his bare chest. Tasting him. Inhaling his powerful masculinity.

She had no idea where the wanton woman she'd become had come from, but he tasted so good. His skin felt delicious on her tongue. He held the tops of her arms tightly as he spoke in another language and somewhere in the back of her mind she knew it was Italian. Then the carnal heat of desire took over, consuming her as it exploded into life.

'See what you do to me.' He spoke English with a harsh whisper. Had she imagined his words in Italian?

'No,' she said, spreading her palms on his chest. Pushing them through the silky soft hair that covered his well-defined chest muscles, smiling at the game she was playing once more with him. 'No, I don't see. Not at all.'

He laughed, a soft sexy laugh, unwinding the coil of desire inside her even more. 'Maybe I should remove my clothes?'

She smiled, heat and power rampaging through her, making her bolder and braver than ever. There was no way she could stop now. 'Maybe you should.'

'In that case, my sweet, sexy nymph…' He took his arms from around her, pulling off his shirt and stepping back a pace. He tossed the ruined shirt aside, his eyes never leaving hers, the hungry sparks of passion in them making her breathless. She looked at his chest, his shoulders, his strong arms, her attention lingering on a tattoo on his upper right arm.

The Italian words, *Vivi con passione*, inked on his skin fired through her, making this moment more intense. *Live with passion*—that was exactly what she intended to do. Tonight. With this man.

'I still don't see,' she teased him further, determined not to be side-tracked by the bold dark words inked against his beautiful olive skin.

With a wicked smile he slowly, deliberately and very tantalisingly removed the remainder of his clothes. His body toned and perfect. His erection large and proud. 'Now do you see?'

She should be shocked, embarrassed even. But she wasn't. How could she be when this was precisely what she wanted? To see him in all his masculine glory. To revel in the power she had over his body—over him.

She didn't answer his question but began to roughly pull at her blouse, desperate to take off every last barrier between them. To be as free as he was. Liberated from her lifelong prison as Princess of the ancient kingdom of Ardu Safra. Even if it was only for one night.

'Allow me, *cara*.' He moved back towards her, reaching out with steady hands to unfasten her blouse, button by button. Then he pushed the silk off her shoulders and it slithered to the floor as he unfastened the belt of her skirt before reaching behind her to the zip fastening. The action brought him close, so very close. She was painfully aware of his naked, aroused body, but he didn't touch her—only her clothes.

He pulled the zip of the skirt lower until the pale

gold fabric slithered down over her hips, watching her as she stepped out of it and towards him. His gaze raked down over her skimpy bra and panties, down her legs to her gold heels. She wanted to be as naked as him. Be his equal.

Without taking her eyes from him she slipped off first one sandal, kicking it aside. Then the other. The thud it made on the floor almost as loud as her pounding heart. Reaching behind her, she unclasped her bra, acutely aware of his eyes devouring her, waiting. She let the bra fall to the floor.

She lowered her hands to her panties, her gaze still fixed on his, unable to believe the wild desire she saw burning in them.

'No,' he said, his hand covering hers. He was so close she could feel the heat coming off him. Feel the need in his body for her.

'No?' she questioned.

'No.' Rafe looked into Ana's eyes, the thud of desire so loud in his veins, surely the whole of London must hear it. 'Not yet.'

She moved closer, reaching up, pressing her lips against his, her breasts brushing his chest. His control snapped and in one swift move he wrapped her in his embrace, claiming her lips in a hungry kiss. Her hungry need matching his. Demand for demand. Passion for passion. Their breathing hard and loud as desire threatened to totally consume them.

He needed to slow things down. Needed to take this night of unexpected pleasure more slowly. It would be the last he ever had because, even though his bride would be one brokered in a boardroom, he would remain faithful. He would never know a night like this again. Never know this carnal need for a woman after he was married.

He pushed those dark thoughts from his mind. They were for tomorrow. This almost naked, sexy vision of desire was tonight.

Her hand slid down his chest as she moved her body slightly away from his. Instinctively he tensed as her touch slid over his abs, then lower. Her palm pressed against him, then her fingers wrapped around him, exploring him.

The thought excited him more. Making him harder.

'So beautiful,' she whispered, looking down, as if she'd never seen a naked man before. She moved her hand upwards, then down and he bit back a groan of passionate despair. He had to stop her. Had to regain control. He wanted to pleasure her before she literally brought him to his knees at the altar of desire.

'Now you have seen—and felt,' he said, taking her hand in his. 'It's my turn.'

Her eyes widened a little and a faint blush spread over her cheeks, but desire pushed him on and, lowering his head, he took one hardened nipple in his mouth.

She gasped, her fingers delving into his hair as he slicked his tongue around her nipple, enjoying the shudder of pleasure which ran over her again and again. Then he stood up, pressing himself to her, feeling the heat of her body, her naked pert breasts against his chest. He kissed her—until she clung to him, her body begging his for release.

The loss of control threatened him again and he lowered his head, smiling as her fingers pushed into his hair, gently guiding him to where she wanted to be kissed next. He obliged, lavishing the same attention on her other breast.

'Don't stop,' she gasped, and satisfaction rushed through him. The little spitfire who'd walked into the bar demanding champagne had been tamed by desire. But he wasn't done with her yet. Nowhere near it. He wanted her to cry out with passion.

He murmured soft words of Italian as he kissed down her stomach, pressing his lips against the lacy cream panties, feeling her body arch towards him.

In one effortless move he pulled the lace down to her ankles, returning to the intimate dark hair. Holding her buttocks, he knelt before her, kissing into the silky soft hair. She placed her hands on his head, parting her legs slightly. He looked up at her and moved one hand to caress the soft skin inside her thigh, before trailing his finger intimately over her.

He stifled a groan of pleasure as he felt her eagerness, lust firing through him. Lust he had to ignore. He wanted to pleasure her, make this moment last.

'I never knew,' she gasped as he leaned forward and tasted her.

Never knew what? His question came and went, obliterated by a need to really taste her. To totally and completely possess her.

'Oh,' she cried out as waves of ecstasy racked her body, leaving her gasping, clinging to him as he continued his torment.

Instead of calming his need, giving him more control, hearing her cries of pleasure with such abandon only increased it. He wanted to be inside her. Deep inside her.

* * *

Kaliana shuddered as the intense pleasure of her first orgasm subsided. She'd been so lost in it, so swept away in delirium that only now was she aware he'd stood up, taken her hand and was drawing her towards the sofa.

He sat down, and she watched in fascination as he rolled on the condom he must have had in readiness for this moment.

The moment she gave herself to him.

Should she tell him she'd never had sex before? That he was the first man who had brought her to such a shuddering orgasm? Would he even know after what he'd just done to her?

He leant forward, taking her hand, drawing her closer. 'Come here.'

Before she had time to wonder where she should go, how she should sit with him, he pulled her onto his lap, her legs astride his. She was completely out of her depth, but it was wild and reckless and right now exactly what she needed. What she wanted.

'You are so beautiful,' he said softly, his eyes swirling with desire as his hand slid between her legs, touching her where, after her orgasm, she felt sensitive, so in need of more. He leant forward, taking her nipple in his mouth while his fingers slid into her.

It was too much. Too nice. Surely, he couldn't take her to that dizzy place of oblivion again? So soon?

She lifted herself up, his torturous touch stopping as his hands moved to grasp her buttocks, his mouth leaving her nipple as he looked up at her.

'Cara mia.' He spoke quietly, his tone firm and commanding, the Italian words so enticing, so sexy. Confidence filled her, pushing her on in her quest to find herself, to discover just who she really was.

She dragged in a shuddering breath as his expert touch took her higher. It was so much more than she'd ever anticipated. So powerful. So... Words failed her. She was close to the edge again. Close to being lost in pleasure. She closed her eyes, her head falling forwards, her hair cascading around her, shielding her from the scrutiny of those dark eyes as she enjoyed the moment.

'Look at me, *cara*,' he demanded, more firmly this time.

Fighting the waves of passion and lifting her head, she looked at him. His eyes were dark and glittering like diamonds. Had he guessed she was a virgin? Did the ease with which he could push her to another orgasm give away her inexperience? Her innocence?

'I want to see you.' His voice was husky and incredibly sexy. 'I want to watch your face as you take me inside you.'

She drew in a breath at his boldness, shocked by how wild and wanton it made her. She wanted to feel him inside her. Deep inside her. It all seemed so right. How could she not want this man to possess her in the most intimate way?

Her gaze locked with his. She lifted her hips, lifted herself over him, hoping her boldness, her attempt to control, to dominate, would hide the nerves she couldn't help but feel. No matter how much she wanted this.

His fingers bit into her buttocks as he encouraged her to move lower. The tip of his heated hardness forced instinct to take over and she moved slowly. With her arms around him, she moved her body up then lowered herself back to him, controlling the moment. Teasing him. Tormenting herself. Each movement making her bolder.

He gripped her buttocks tighter as she lowered herself again, a feral growl coming from him as he lifted himself up, sliding into her in one hard move. She cried out as a burning pain snatched her from the moment. He stilled. Deep inside her, he didn't move. Those dark eyes were full of questions. Full of doubt.

She didn't want that. Not now. Not until they'd both lost themselves in the oblivion of passion. She wanted that abandonment. Needed it. She wanted that ultimate climax to this moment. Questions could wait. Everything could wait.

She forced herself to move, lifting herself up, then lowering herself again, stoking the desire back up. He watched her intently as she controlled the moment. Controlled him.

His desire returned instantly. She could see it in his eyes. Feel it inside her as she continued to move up and down. The sensation of having him inside her was so much more intense than she'd anticipated. She continued to move until he swore savagely as he lost control, as he gave into what her body wanted and began moving with her. Each movement faster and more furious than the last. Each movement pushing her ever closer to the edge.

'Mia bella!' he cried out, his release coming fast, dragging her with him into oblivion.

Her body shook with pleasure as she found her release, her total fulfilment. Her moment of complete abandon. Waves of ecstasy held her in their grip, tossing her in the sea of passion until she was sure she would drown.

* * *

Rafe's breathing calmed, his racing heart eased. Ana's body limply clung to his and he tried to make sense of what had just happened.

He'd taken her virginity. A gift so precious it should never have been his to take. He didn't deserve that. He couldn't give a woman like this any more than tonight, even if he wanted to. He looked at her—head bent, hair cascading around her face, hiding her from him, from his scrutiny. His questions. Those moments of hesitation in the bar, that aura of innocence, had been real. That woman had been a virgin—until she'd accompanied him to his suite.

She lifted her head, still sitting astride him, looking down at him anxiously. He saw it then so clearly. The confidence of her actions earlier had deceived him. Her bravado. Her wild wantonness. Her complete power of seduction. It had all been an act. Had that innocence been there all along in her eyes? Had he been so blinded by desire he hadn't seen it or—worse—ignored it?

He should have seen it. Should have stopped. Should have been in control. But what they'd just shared, from the very moment she'd first looked at him, had been unlike anything he'd ever known.

'You should have told me.' His voice was firm, steady and steely controlled. Which, considering a very naked woman still sat astride his lap, was no mean feat.

'Losing my virginity to you—tonight—was my decision to make.' The bold, confident woman who'd walked into the bar earlier and demanded champagne was back.

She agilely moved herself away from him and stood up, proudly naked in front of him as if to prove her point. Daring him to deny her claim. She was right. Of course she was right. Yet he couldn't shake the nagging sensation that he'd taken something he shouldn't have.

'It was also my decision to take it—or not.' He reached forward, snatching up his hastily discarded trousers, pulling them on.

How the hell had this happened? He'd claimed this alluring woman's virginity in an unplanned night of passion when he'd just relented, just accepted that marriage, purely for convenience, was something he had to do.

He looked at her. Would she now cling to him? Cling to this moment, believing there was something more between them? Something he couldn't ever give any woman.

'You can rest assured that I have no intention of demanding anything other than tonight from you. I am not looking for long-term commitment and I certainly don't crave the elusive happy-ever-after of marriage. Not from you. Not from any man.'

She stood defiantly before him, dark hair loose and wild about her shoulders, gloriously naked. The first fresh stirrings of desire began to wind themselves through his body. He fought to ignore that primal call. This night of uncomplicated sex had suddenly become as complicated as his life.

'Why tonight? Why me?' he asked, needing to know more, even though it would be a mistake. A mistake because that would make him think of her after tonight.

She looked at him, an air of defiance in her gaze. 'Five years ago I was engaged—to a man I loved. A man I wanted to marry—as a virgin.'

Rafe frowned as he digested this piece of information. 'What happened?' As the question found voice, he instinctively knew that, whatever had happened, it was more than a falling-out-of-love issue.

Ana bit her lower lip, the first sign of nervousness he'd seen her display. Something inside him shifted.

'One month before the wedding, he was killed in an accident.'

The mood in the room changed, the tension increasing. 'I'm sorry.'

She moved closer to him, reminding him, if he needed it, that she was naked. 'What is your story?'

Her question took him off guard, his mind partly occupied by her admission and partly by the slow burn of desire striking up once more.

'My story?' He didn't want to do this. Didn't want to spoil the passion of all they'd just shared with emotional issues.

'Why tonight and why me?' she said, echoing his question.

He laughed, desperate to calm the tension building higher than the desire of moments ago. 'When a beautiful woman crosses my path, I'm not going to walk the other way.'

She looked hurt by his humour, his attempt to derail the conversation. His attempt to keep his secrets safe. Hell, she'd been honest with him, shared her pain, even if only briefly. It wasn't as if they were in a relationship. They'd never see one another again. Didn't he owe it to her?

Guilt forced his words out. 'I have to get married.'

The room suddenly filled with a heavy silence as Ana looked at him, her eyes narrowing slightly in disbelief.

'Have to?' Then her frown disappeared as she drew her own conclusion. 'You are going to be a father?'

'No, not that.' Rafe sighed. 'Although that would be a lot less complicated.'

Ana hugged her arms around herself, looking chilled. He turned to pick up his discarded shirt, then placed it gently over her shoulders, his hands lingering longingly. She looked too sexy in his shirt.

'I don't understand.' She turned to look up at him. Her expression, so serious, as if it really mattered to her. As if she understood.

'My brother, Enzo, and I are twins. Our family has much wealth and property to hand onto the next generation. My father is terminally ill, and my brother has chosen this moment to inform him that he is unable to father a child, that his marriage is in trouble because of it. My father cannot see past the fact that the family name will not continue unless I marry and have a son.'

He'd never talked so openly, always guarded himself, but Ana had set something free within him. Frustration. It tore through him. Frustration for all he must do and because this moment was lost to such a discussion. Annoyance that the duty he had to prepare to undertake could snatch away even this night from him.

He looked down into Ana's eyes, the gold flecks in them so bright, so full of desire that it took his breath away. 'No more talking,' she whispered, reaching up to kiss him.

'No more talking,' he said huskily, desire pounding through him once more. He wanted her again. Right now.

'Then what are we going to do?' she teased, as if

sensing his need to change the subject, to revive the passion between them.

She giggled seductively as he scooped her up, carrying her across the apartment to the bedroom. He felt free. Alive. And it couldn't end. Not yet.

'Make love all night.' He lowered her onto his bed before covering her body with his. 'That is what you want, isn't it?'

'So very much,' she said as she kissed him, setting fire to the embers of desire again. Whatever this was between them, it was far from over.

CHAPTER THREE

August—Palermo, Sicily

'THIS EVENING IS going to be a great success. Pure Seas and Oceans is really getting noticed now,' the coordinator of events informed Rafe as he scanned his speech for the final time. 'We even have someone from Charity Resources' London headquarters in attendance.'

'Really? How did you pull that one off?' Rafe asked, intrigued enough to look up.

'I have been working with Kaliana for the last month on this event, so when she said she wanted to attend tonight, how could I say no?' The triumphant look on the young man's face made Rafe smile. 'And she's requested a meeting with you afterwards.'

'Then who am I to disappoint someone who has helped our cause? After all, the charity needs all the exposure and promotion it can get.' Cleaning up the seas around the globe was something Rafe was as passionate about as he was his own renewable energy business. He'd agreed to be patron of the charity, hoping to help the cause. Judging by the expected turnout for this evening's event, having Charity Resources behind them must be having a good impact. The whole evening looked as though it would far exceed his expectations.

All the preparation for tonight had been better than dwelling on the ever-pressing need for him to find a wife. His father's health was not good and now Enzo had taken on the role of protector of their family's future. He'd even had the audacity to call Rafe and remind him time was not on their side, pushing him towards marriage, worried about the family fortune. Where was Enzo's remorse for all he'd done? Rafe had long ago let go of his love for Emma, but this threatened to permanently destroy the tense relationship between him and his twin for good.

His father's diagnosis made that family duty impossible to ignore. The noose around Rafe's neck was tightening. He didn't want marriage. Or a family. How could Enzo do this and expect him to step in where he had failed?

Rafe shook his head in annoyance. He was allowing his problems to infiltrate his commitments. He wasn't here to find a way out of this situation; instead, he had to keep his focus where it needed to be. Once this event was over, then he would give serious consideration to just how he was going to find a woman to marry—without bringing emotion and sentiment into it. He needed a marriage deal.

Annoyed with himself for letting those thoughts in now, he left the hall as the guests began to arrive and headed backstage. Rafe needed to try and shake off the anger induced by just thinking about Enzo and what he'd done.

Instead, he allowed his mind to drift back to that night in London. To the one and only time he'd ever had a real connection with a woman. Something that might have gone beyond pure sexual attraction had she not run out on him, slipping from his bed in the early hours while he'd slept.

He pushed that memory away, refusing to care. Refusing to be affected by the emotional intimacy he and Ana had shared so briefly that night. Refusing to think what could have come of that night if he didn't have duty hanging over him. If he and Ana had taken longer to explore that powerful sexual chemistry between them.

Emotions threatened to cascade over him—emotions he would never allow. Still the image of Ana wouldn't leave his mind. Why hadn't he found out who she really was? Two months on, she still had a hold on his imagination. His body. Why did he crave her still?

He'd tried to tell himself it was for the best, that she'd left without asking for more than just that night, without even leaving her full name or number. But it had jarred his ego. She'd had her fill of him, but he had been left wanting more. Not a situation he was used to at all.

Rafe shut his mind to those thoughts. Tonight was important. He had to make an impact on the audience, the many influential businessmen and women who could help. And especially the visitor from Charity Resources. If she wanted a private meeting with him, he was going to ensure he got her backing for the cause.

The spotlight was well and truly on Rafe as he made his speech. He kept his focus on several influential business owners in the audience but he could feel intense scrutiny from the front row. From where the visitor from Charity Resources had been assigned a seat. The lighting was too bright, he couldn't see the faces of anyone in the front row and it wasn't until he'd finished and the audience applauded that the lights burning on him dimmed. Finally, he could see who had been watching his every move for the last half an hour.

His breath turned to fire in his lungs. His heartbeat thudded to a halt.

It was her.

Ana.

The hot, sexy siren who'd filled his dreams since that night in London sat in the front row where the visitor from Charity Resources should be sitting. The slim-fitting black dress offset with a pearl necklace couldn't disguise her. There was no mistake. It was Ana. His body kick-started into life again, his heart thumping, his breath shallow and rapid.

Ana. Or, as he'd been informed, Kaliana. His mystery woman of passion. The woman who'd given him her virginity, creating a connection between them he hadn't been able to sever. He bit back the harsh obscenity, wishing he'd kept himself up-to-date with the event's organisation while he'd been away from Sicily. But that was what he paid his event organiser for.

Shock mixed with the heady, heated need flowing in his veins. Unbidden, the spirited beauty of that night in London flashed into his mind, overriding the elegant vision who sat in the front row.

He saw the woman of that night again, her naked body so perfectly formed. He felt the telltale scorch of the heat of desire which had erupted in him like the volcano of his homeland.

Enough. He gritted his teeth against the slow slug of lust which echoed in his body, his limbs, his mind, even now. The persistent and unsatisfied ache of need.

The annoyance that she'd walked away, keeping his lust very much alive.

The air in the room became heavy as those gold-flecked dark eyes met his, alive with sparks of mischief and laughter. Did she think this was amusing? He couldn't look away. All he wanted to do was drink in this vision. Savour the sexy body that had filled his restless nights all too often.

She smiled, cracking the veneer of control she wore so well. *Dio mio*, why had fate seen fit to tempt him once again with this woman?

The audience began to leave, chatting among themselves as they went. Rafe made his way towards the woman who'd got completely under his skin. A woman he'd never expected to see again. The woman, damn it—who'd given him her virginity then walked out of his life as if it was nothing.

The sensation of being a stallion at stud reared up again. But wasn't that exactly what his father wanted him to be? Needed him to be?

Ana moved to him and offered her hand. By some miracle Rafe maintained his composure. 'Ana,' he said, his voice harder than he'd heard it for a long time. 'Or is it Kaliana?' What kind of fool had he been to allow himself to be so utterly seduced by her charm? Her sexiness.

No questions.

The voice of reproach careered around in his head. But *she* had seduced him then left without a word. Why? Questions raged through him as he looked at her. The expression on her face was calm and devoid of emotion. Was it possible he had been fooled? That she hadn't just happened to be in the bar that night and found him irresistible. But, instead, had she set out to seduce him—

and he had willingly allowed it to happen? Why had he believed her story about the loss of her fiancé?

Because you wanted her. At any price.

Her brows rose in haughty indignation. Was that amusement dancing in the gold flecks of her eyes, behind the superiority which radiated off her in waves? 'Is there somewhere we can talk privately?'

The audacity of the woman. To boldly stand before him, so regal and elegant on the surface, while he knew, with every nerve cell in his body, the sex siren he'd first met simmered beneath her refined exterior.

'Talk?' Talking was not something she'd been much interested in last time.

'I have a proposition to put to you.' The firmness of her voice couldn't quite disguise the huskiness and he couldn't resist the urge to tease her.

'I think, *Ana…*' he deliberately used the name she'd given him that night, satisfied when her cheeks flushed '…that you may have already done that.'

Annoyance sparked in her eyes. 'I have a deal to put to you. A business deal that will be of benefit to both of us.'

Rafe laughed softly as she glared up at him. She was challenging him, not just with her words, her request, but with her body. Yes, that sex siren was still there—and fighting for release.

'A deal?'

'Yes, a deal.' Her voice was sharp as she looked around her, suddenly seeming uncertain. Nervous. 'Is there somewhere private we can talk?'

What was she doing? Why had she thought this was a good idea? That it would work?

Kaliana followed Rafe into the small office and waited until the door had closed tightly behind them. She didn't want anyone else to be a witness to what she had to say to Raffaele Casella, the man she'd given herself to with complete abandon.

Ever since that night she had dreamed of seeing him again. Dreamed that he would find her and tell her that night had been more than just passion. More than just lust. That he would tell her he loved her. Each one a fanciful dream which had faded once the light of day dispelled the magic.

That night she'd glimpsed the possibility that love could happen for her again. That out there, somewhere, was a man who could make her happy again. A man who could love her as much as Alif had. Ever since that realisation she'd been torn apart by guilt. Did the fact that she yearned for love make what she and Alif had shared any less real?

Never in her wildest dreams had she thought she would see Rafe again—or that she would be seeking him out so boldly. She could still hear Claire's advice now as her friend had made one last-ditch attempt to stop her.

'So what if he is the man who gave you the most pleasurable night of your life? You can't go to Sicily and ask him to marry you.' Panic had been in every word Claire had spoken, as well as in her expression.

'He is wealthy. He needs to not only marry, but to have a son. He is everything I need to escape marriage to Nassif.'

'But marriage, Kal,' Claire had pleaded.

But Kaliana had no choice. Not any more. It was barely two months until her twenty-sixth birthday—

and her wedding day. There was no way the man waiting for her at the altar was going to be Nassif. No way
at all. Even Claire understood that.

'And how may I assist you?' There was an aloofness
in Rafe's voice as he looked at her, his back to the door,
his face as impassive as stone. He hadn't looked at her
like that the last time she'd seen him. Then his eyes had
burned with passion, sparked with wild desire. For her.

She gathered her composure. Fought the urge to turn
and leave. To run. But she couldn't. She needed a husband. And she'd made her choice. 'I have a deal to put
to you, Signor Casella. One that will be of benefit to
both of us.'

His brows flicked up. 'I'm sure we can dispense with
such formalities, Ana. I'd much prefer Rafe.' This time
his voice held a hint of the man she'd met in London.
A hint of the man who'd shown her what real passion
could be like.

She relaxed a little. 'And I'd prefer Kaliana.'

'So, Kaliana, how can we benefit one another?' He
walked towards her and the air seemed to have been
sucked from the small office. Her heart was thudding
as her body betrayed her, reacting to his nearness as if
the last two months hadn't elapsed. As if only hours had
passed since he'd taken her on such a wondrous journey of discovery. To a place where she'd discovered the
sensual woman deep within her.

She pushed that image, that memory aside. The man
before her now was different. Detached. Was it possible the man she'd given herself to in London was just
part of her imagination, her wishful thinking? That her
memory was tricking her? Did he even exist?

'In London, you told me you needed to marry.' She

forced the words out over a tongue so dry it was almost impossible to sound in control, in charge.

Rafe stiffened, his expression impassive. Emotionless. She'd touched a nerve. A raw one. 'That is what I said, yes.'

This was harder than she'd imagined. His scrutiny, those dark piercing eyes, made her nervous. She swallowed down her nerves and gathered herself. Pushed on, before her courage failed her.

He narrowed his eyes suspiciously, watching her steadily, the tension in the room—in her body—increasing. 'What is this deal, exactly?'

'You also said that providing the next generation of your family fell to you.' Her words sounded calm. Cool and collected. Yet her heart was thumping. She clenched her hands, digging her red painted nails into her palms.

She could still feel the shock when she'd seen the photo of the patron of Pure Seas and Oceans while researching her new client. The image of the man she'd lost her virginity to in London smiling back at her. Not at all the waiter she'd first mistaken him for—or even the everyday businessman she'd later decided he was—but a man whose family and personal wealth was astounding.

A man who needed a wife and a son to continue the family name.

She'd stared at the image, her mind resisting the urge to revisit memories of that night as the realisation sank in that he could be the man to solve her problems, while she solved his. A mutually beneficial marriage arrangement. A marriage that could offer more still—the desire and intimacy her heart craved—if she was brave enough.

It had all seemed so simple. So clear-cut and easy to follow through on. Even on the flight here, it had seemed that way. But everything had changed as she'd sat watching him talk so passionately. He hadn't recognised her, even though she'd sat in the front row. Doubt had filed in.

Then he'd looked at her, his dark eyes locking with hers. He *had* recognised her.

Now, standing before his intense scrutiny, what she'd come here for was anything but simple.

'I understood you were here to represent Charity Resources. What does my personal life have to do with tonight's event?' There was a coldness in his voice. She could see his mind working, see the questions, the deep suspicion and mistrust flashing across his handsome face. A face she'd kissed. A face she'd pressed hers against as her body had been taken over by the pleasure of an orgasm.

'I know how it feels...' she paused, wishing she'd kept to her rehearsed script '...to be forced to marry.'

He frowned. 'I find that very hard to believe.'

She braced herself. If he didn't believe her, didn't feel something for her plight then she'd lost. She'd have to marry Nassif. 'It's true. My father is insisting I marry. He has even selected a husband.'

'That sounds like something from a movie, or a fairy tale.' He smiled at her and her heart flipped over as he moved closer, the atmosphere in the room changing instantly. Heating up. As if it were still that night. 'And are you going to marry this man?'

'No. I will do anything to avoid that.' Her response was instant. Full of indignation.

Rafe laughed again, his lips staying in a sexy smile,

reminding her of their night together. 'So, Ana… Kaliana…have you come to share some kind of plan with me? One I can also use to find a wife?'

She smiled bravely at him, crossing her fingers. 'Actually, that is exactly what I am here for.'

He came so close to her that she could reach up and brush her lips over his. 'Then tell me, sweet Ana. What is this plan of yours?'

His eyes searched hers, dragging her mind and body back to the passion they'd shared. She couldn't think of that now. She had to remain focused. Had to put her deal to him in a strong and confident way. She had to be the Princess she was, not the woman he'd awakened. 'I will be your wife.'

'My wife?' He stepped back, his dark eyes thunderous as he looked at her, taking in every detail, scanning down over her body with suspicion. 'Are you pregnant?'

'No.' The response was instant, but she was ready for it. Claire had warned her he might think that and Kaliana sent up a silent prayer of thanks for her friend. For having at least one person on her side, willing to fight her battles with her. 'No, I'm not pregnant.'

'Then what the hell? *Dio mio*, Ana. Marriage!' He flung his hands up in a wild gesture of disbelief, his use of her name snagging at the remorse she'd felt walking out on him that morning. But her need to flee had been driven by guilt. Guilt that she'd enjoyed such a night with him. Sadness that she'd never known it with Alif, the man she'd loved. She'd been so torn she'd had to leave. Had to walk away whilst he slept.

'We both need to marry. Wouldn't it be better to marry one another than marry strangers?' She held her breath as he looked at her then walked past her, across the room to the window. He looked out at the view of Sicily's rugged coastline. She stood still, rooted to the spot. 'Or to accept partners arranged by our families?'

Rafe's silence did little to instil any kind of hope in her. The tension in the room was explosive as she watched him. His broad shoulders were rigid and square. He couldn't even look at her.

'Why do you need to marry, Ana?' He paused, continuing to glare out of the window, and for a moment she floundered, unable to find an answer. At least one that wouldn't give away just how much she'd wanted him. Wanted that night. Needed it. To know she was desirable for herself, not her title.

She sighed. She owed him this truth at least. 'I am Princess Kaliana Benhamed of Ardu Safra and, as such, am expected to marry for the good of my country, my people.'

The room sparked, tension exploding. He looked at her as if seeing her for the first time. Never again would she be Ana to him. She could see it in his eyes, see the shock, the accusation. Her *normal* life was over. Whatever happened next, she could never go back to being a managerial assistant at Charity Resources. She could never have nights out with her friends again, never enjoy the quiet evenings at home with Claire when they'd talked about all sorts of things.

This was the moment her life changed—beyond recognition—for ever. It didn't matter what Rafe's answer was. Her life would change—had already changed.

'You were a virgin that night, no?' he demanded as he moved closer, his dark eyes hard and piercing. *'Dio mio*, Ana, a virgin *and* a princess.'

'Yes, I was,' she snapped indignantly. He would never understand what was at stake for her right now.

'You never intended to see me again, did you?' There was a hint of feral anger in his voice now. 'Yet here you are. A princess. Offering me, the man who claimed your virginity, a marriage deal.'

The memory of that night became sourer with each word he spoke, each accusing statement. She wanted to turn and leave but her feet wouldn't move, her limbs were frozen. She had to do this, had to finish what she'd started, if she stood any chance of saving the people of Ardu Safra from poverty—saving her father from the shame of financial ruin. If she wanted to avoid a fate worse than death, by marrying Nassif, then she had to make Rafe see this was the best way. For both of them.

'We both need to get married and we know…' She paused as embarrassment rushed over her, obliterating the cool, controlled Princess she was trying to be.

'That we can ignite intense passion between us?' he finished for her, moving closer still, his tall broad shoulders blocking out the light. Her head began to ache. Pressure mounted around her, making her nauseous.

'It's not just that I need to make a marriage for the good of my country. Or even to produce a much-needed heir,' she hastily added, wishing she could step away from him, wishing her body didn't long for his touch, his caress. Wishing she wasn't giving away all that with every breath.

'What else?'

'My family are on the brink of financial ruin. I need a husband. A wealthy man. One who can clear all debts, reinstate stability into our economy.' The truth rushed out and she looked up at him. Waiting.

His eyes scanned her face. Searching for lies. Searching for truth. 'And the Casella fortune that I stand to inherit is your way out?'

She blushed as the shame of it fell over her like the shadow of a storm cloud about to break.

Rafe's eyes darkened, reminding her even more of that night as he moved closer to her. So close she could almost taste him. 'Give me one good reason why I should marry you.'

'If you don't, I will have to marry a man chosen by my father.' She gulped down the panic just thinking about it induced. 'My wedding is set for October, my twenty-sixth birthday. If I haven't secured a husband by the beginning of September, I must marry Nassif.'

'Nassif?'

'A cruel man, older than me. Widowed.' She looked at Rafe, at the shock on his face. Should she tell him more? 'Uncle of the man I should have married.'

'Why not just say no?'

Her eyes widened in shock. 'I'm a princess. Marriage is my duty.'

'And you think my need to do my family duty will be as strong as your desire to avoid marriage with this Nassif?' The darkness of his eyes had hardened, his expression becoming sterner by the second. His handsome features, which had so captured her imagination that night in London, were hard and angry, showing the true man, she reminded herself, not the man of her wistful dreams.

Panic tore through her. If he didn't want to marry her…? She couldn't bear the thought of having Nassif as her husband. Of sharing with him the kind of intimacies she'd shared with Rafe. She shuddered at the thought.

With a deep breath, she touched the large pearls at her neck, wanting to be free of the clothes she'd chosen for this moment. Wanting to be in London, in her flat, in the life she could no longer have. Her panic increased. If Rafe didn't want to marry her she didn't know what she was going to do.

'And why me?' He moved another step closer, questioning her softly, sending her pulse rate into freefall.

'Because we can offer each other everything needed.' She looked up into his eyes, imploring him to understand. Willing him to accept her deal.

'And our night in London has nothing to do with this?' Suspicion laced through his words like mist in the winter.

'Nothing whatsoever. Although I am certain I'm not the first woman you have taken to your suite within hours of meeting.' The truth of that statement cut like broken glass, shattering the fairy tale of that night for evermore.

Rafe scanned Kaliana's face once more as he tried to push away the image of an older man touching her, when he'd been the first man to show her pleasure. Doubt clouded her eyes, but poise and elegance shone through. He didn't doubt her claim of being a princess. This was a woman in control. She wasn't going to stand by and be dictated to.

He respected that. Still his suspicions persisted. Why him? Why now?

'And if I don't wish to marry you?' Why had he said that when the answer to his dilemma stood deliciously in front of him, offering herself to him, reigniting that flame of desire? That powerful sexual chemistry. How could he be turning down more nights like the one they had shared?

But…marriage?

Her lips parted as his question hit home. The inviting softness of them reminded him of their lusciousness, of the way they'd tasted of champagne as he'd claimed them in that first demanding kiss at the bar.

'You said you needed to marry.' Her eyes widened, and a smile spread over his lips. She hadn't thought he would refuse. She'd been so sure of herself. A wave of satisfaction at disrupting her plans, her obviously well-prepared speech, surged through him even as he knew he would accept her deal. She was the key to keeping the only thing that mattered to him: Pietra Bianca.

She was the only key.

'Maybe I no longer care what happens to the family name—or the fortune.' He paused as he watched her beautiful face, fighting hard against the urge to reach out and brush his fingers across the softness of her cheeks.

'It would be a marriage we'd both benefit from.'

'I suppose there is the fact that we know we are more than compatible in the bedroom.' He couldn't help taunting her again. Reminding her of what they'd shared.

She flushed, her icy composure knocked once more, the woman he'd met that night shining through like the brightest star.

'That has nothing to do with my proposition.' The star dimmed, sliding behind the clouds of propriety. The aloof Princess who mourned her true love was back in play.

'Are you sure?' He moved forward, reaching out to

push back stray strands of hair, wanting to coax out the sex siren.

'Of course it hasn't.' She snapped out the denial, the frosty Princess façade truly on display. 'This is a deal which would benefit us both.'

'That is true.' He paused, his mind lost in another time, another night—another woman. He shut down those thoughts. 'But it will give us the opportunity to explore what still sparks between us.' Again, he taunted her, even knowing what she said made sense. Marriage was the one thing he didn't want. It was also the one thing he would do. For his family. For his mother.

But this woman? She'd already threatened to break through his defences. How was he going to share the intimacies of marriage with her when he already knew he could want her—if he allowed himself to?

'It will be a business deal, Rafe, nothing more.'

No, he couldn't do it. But if he didn't he'd lose the last chance of gaining his father's respect, along with the one thing that held precious memories of his mother. 'And if I don't want such a business deal?'

CHAPTER FOUR

KALIANA PANICKED. SHE hadn't expected the man she'd spent a passionate night with to throw her deal back at her. To virtually be telling her she was mad for even suggesting it. Stupidly, she'd expected him to be grateful to her for offering him a solution to the problem he'd confided to her that night.

She hadn't expected any of this. Hadn't expected the smouldering intensity in his eyes. The heat that just the brush of his fingers on her face could ignite—or the blatant reminder of what they had shared in London that night.

She hadn't thought this through properly. Maybe he'd already found a bride. The thought sent a spike of fear piercing through her. There was so little time left and she'd been so sure he would agree. But it seemed she'd got it all wrong. The thought of marrying Nassif looked like a scary reality.

'I can see I have misjudged things,' she said, stepping away from him as much as the small room would allow. Suddenly she couldn't bear to be close to him. Couldn't bear to be reminded of that night, of how he'd made her feel and think. 'It was wrong of me to assume. I'm sorry I have wasted your time.'

Kaliana turned, reaching out almost blindly to open the door, her heart hammering with hope. Hope that he would tell her to stay. Silence slammed into that futile hope. If he let her go now, she would have to walk away from not only the chance of being free of Nassif, but she would also be walking away from the man who still infused her body with desire. If she had to marry anyone, she would rather it was this man.

The thought of giving herself to any other man was now repulsive to her, but her marriage needed to create children—an heir for Ardu Safra. How could she even contemplate Nassif touching her? How could she endure it, knowing what real passion and desire were?

She closed her eyes against the pain of her situation. The humiliation of what she'd just done. She'd told him something nobody knew, other than Claire. She'd told him who she really was and in doing so had effectively ended the escape of that new life. Her father had made such anonymity possible and if word got out he would revoke that favour. He would insist she return to her life in the country she loved. But it was a country so stuck in the past, in old traditions, she couldn't face living there. Couldn't face being its Princess. She'd always vowed she'd change things, bring everything up to date when she became the Queen, but with Nassif at her side it would be almost impossible.

Time was running out. Fast. She needed a husband. A wealthy husband.

With a sensation of lead in her stomach she opened the door, the voices of the remaining members of the audience sounding loud and harsh. Rafe wasn't going to stop her. He was going to allow her to walk away.

After everything they had shared—or was it because of everything they'd shared?

Kaliana stifled her cry of distress, stepping out of the small office, her head high. The sensation that she was walking into a bleak future was suddenly so real. But she wouldn't look back. Wouldn't give him the satisfaction of seeing her distress, damn him.

'Ana.' He took hold of her hand, bringing her escape to an abrupt halt. Turning, she looked up at him. He was suddenly very close. Too close. Her body responded, the memory of his all too clear in her mind.

'You have made yourself clear. There will be no deal.' She wouldn't let him see her pain, her disappointment. Her panic. 'I hope you find the solution you need.'

His dark eyes held hers, the heaviness in her stomach lightening, becoming a flutter of butterflies. He moved closer still, the intensity in his eyes increasing. He was going to kiss her. She could see it in the darkening of desire in his eyes. She shouldn't let him. Shouldn't want him to.

So why did she? Why did she tilt her chin up? Why did her breath raggedly slip out and her pulse race? Why did she part her lips so expectantly?

She wanted him to kiss her. Wanted to taste him again—and more. Her body was remembering, the woman she'd been that night resurfacing, even as she tried to keep her cool façade, the demeanour of a princess. It was a futile battle. The Princess she was supposed to be faded fast as that spark, that intense sexual chemistry, swirled round them.

He moved closer still, until they were almost touching and, lowering his head, he brushed his lips over hers. She sighed, pressing herself to him, unwittingly begging for more. Rafe obliged, wrapping her in an embrace so tight her body was fused with his. The slumbering remains of the fire he'd ignited inside her that night in London burst back into life, the flame of desire leaping high, catching her unawares, dragging out the woman he'd awakened.

Kaliana closed her eyes, leaning against him, giving herself up to what she'd been wanting since the moment she'd walked away from him that morning. His touch. His kiss. She slid her hands around his neck, her fingers delving into his hair, passion beginning to consume them. Sweeping them away, making her oblivious to anything around them.

This was what she'd wanted for the last two months. This was what she'd fought so very hard against. This passion. This desire. This man. She kissed him harder as the flames of passion rose up, engulfing her completely. He responded, the intensity of his kiss matching hers.

Rafe moved backwards, still kissing her, his arms wrapped tight around her. She had no option but to move with him back into the room. He kept his arms around her, his body fused to hers, his lips demanding everything from hers. Reaching out, he pushed the door shut. The sudden intimate silence made her gasp against his lips.

They were alone again.

'We haven't finished yet, Ana.' He let go of her, walking away to stand once more in front of the window. Her body felt limp, weakened by his kiss, by being pressed against his body. Weakened by him.

'But I thought…' She struggled to find the words as her heart thumped wildly, the heavy pulse of desire heating her from within.

He turned to face her, anger sparking in his eyes, his jaw tight. 'That you could breeze back into my life, this time as the Princess you really are and not refer to all we shared that night?'

'You need a wife, Rafe.' Kaliana clung to the facts, desperate not to explore the way he made her feel, the excitement of being kissed by him again. Practicalities. That was what she needed to concentrate on. 'And I need a husband.'

'I don't want marriage, Ana, but I *have* to marry, choose a bride. That's why I was drowning my sorrows in whisky that night.' Rafe looked down at her, the war of emotions on his face, in his eyes, all too clear. All too familiar. 'Why should that bride be you, when we know so little of one another?'

'What do you want to know?' She kept her focus even though she couldn't help but smile at him, sensing she'd found a way through his armour. Found a way to make him see this was what they both needed.

'I want to know everything about you, Princess Kaliana, but, more than that, I want to know all about the woman I met in London.'

Rafe saw the smile slip from Kaliana's lips, saw her face pale. The throb of desire from their kiss, a kiss that had been witnessed by many before he'd pushed the door shut, still hummed in his veins. Demanding more. Demanding satisfaction.

'Like what?' The defensive Princess was back in play and he smiled at her prickly demeanour. Now he knew why she'd all but demanded champagne at the bar that night. She was used to the good things in life. Was that why she wanted to make a marriage that would bring wealth to her country? Or was it really her concern for her people? But he had other, far more pressing questions.

'Why did you leave that morning in London? Why did you sneak away before I woke?'

The moment he'd woken to find her gone had totally knocked him. In the previous hours he'd given so much more of himself to her than he had to any woman. He'd stupidly believed he'd finally met *the woman* but had pushed that aside as his predicament, his duty to his family, had swamped such ideas totally. That and the fact that any woman he'd got close to had slipped out of his life, leaving a void he had never been able to fill.

The coldness of the sheets in the bed had told him she'd long since gone. Had she waited until he'd slept? Waited until the exhaustion of such mind-blowingly hot sex had claimed him?

'Isn't that the protocol for a one-night stand?' Her chin lifted defensively and sparks of irritation verging on anger shone in her eyes, making their dark brown depths a deep gold. She tilted her head coyly to one side, her thick dark hair falling over her shoulder. 'I have never done anything like that before, so if I got it wrong I apologise.'

'*Sì*, sometimes that's the protocol,' he acknowledged, acutely aware that never had a woman slipped from his bed and left him before. He'd always dictated the longevity of an affair, be it hours or weeks. 'But I would like to know—would you have given your virginity to any man that night?'

She blushed and looked down and something crushed him. Hard. Wrapping tight binds around his chest. Standing there in that moment, she looked vulnerable.

Alone. Then she looked up, her eyes bright with unshed tears. He became aware of the clock ticking on the wall, marking loudly each passing second as he waited for her answer. He needed to know. Needed to hear that she'd been as drawn to him as he'd been to her. That their night of passion had been fate throwing them together. That it hadn't been contrived. That she had wanted it as much as she'd led him to believe.

'I never set out to spend the night with anyone. A bit of harmless flirting, yes, but not that.' Her whisper was soft. Her face pale. Vulnerability radiated from her so strongly now it was difficult to resist the urge to wrap her up in his life and protect her. 'But something changed...'

Her words trailed off as if she couldn't tell him. Didn't want to admit to anything.

'What changed, Kaliana?' He'd used her full name and it felt good. Right. Slowly he moved closer, unable to help himself. Wanting to be near her, wanting to touch her. Wanting even a hint of evidence that she'd been as consumed by him as he'd been by her.

She shook her head slowly. 'I don't know. It just felt right. Whatever was between us that night, whatever it was that drew us to one another so strongly, was right.'

She blinked hard and he replayed the moments before she'd all but seduced him once more. She'd thought he was a waiter, that he worked in the bar. The truth of that question was as obvious as her innocence had been as he'd claimed it—claimed her. The knowledge satisfied him that her so-called deal was indeed born out of a need to help her country, her people. After all, she could simply refuse to marry this Nassif but, just like him, she couldn't walk away from family duty.

He sighed impatiently, wishing his friend Franco were here right now to help him. To listen to his torrent of questions. But this decision was entirely his to make and he knew Franco would stand by his original advice. A romantic at heart, Franco would be sure to say that if there was an attraction, chemistry, what could go wrong? Was he looking for problems that weren't there? Things he didn't need to worry over? No, he was doing what he usually did when his emotions were threatened. When his defensive barriers were almost breached, as she had subtly begun doing after they'd first made love, asking him for his story, he built them higher. Stronger.

'Is it the Casella fortune or that night which makes me the ideal candidate to be Princess Kaliana's husband?' He couldn't keep the serious tone from his voice, even though he wanted to tease her playfully.

The more he thought about the idea of marriage to her, the more it seemed right. He and Kaliana had shared something amazing that night in London. She'd given him her virginity—a gift he hadn't realised he'd taken until it was too late—so didn't that mean he was the ideal candidate, even without his wealth?

'There is much for us both to gain with this marriage deal.' She moved away from him, calmer now. In control once more. 'In return for your financial support, my family name will, I'm sure, be of use to you in business. Renewable energy is a market ripe for expansion in Ardu Safra and beyond. Our marriage will also be built on the attraction we have for one another. Love isn't required to make it a success.'

'I can't ever promise anything like love,' he said firmly, needing the boundaries around him. Another thought, one more worrying, barged into his mind.

'What if you need more? What if one day you find more with someone else?'

She looked at him firmly. The cool and sophisticated Princess was back in play. The woman he'd met in London had slipped beneath the aloof exterior. 'I have had my chance at love. It hurts to lose it, and I don't need or want that kind of pain in my life. Love is not on the agenda, Rafe. Purely convenience.'

He folded his arms, hating this discussion. This topic. He'd never discussed such a thing with a woman so openly. 'And what we had that night, the spark of attraction, the sexual chemistry, proves this deal—our marriage—has a chance of working without love?'

'It proves exactly that,' Kaliana said, flushing once more, reminding him of the innocent virgin she'd been as she'd looked at him as he'd claimed her. Made her his.

'And what about children?' He asked the question, hating the answer, hating that his father was pushing him to do just that. He couldn't envisage himself holding a child of his own.

'You have already told me you need a son to continue the Casella name. Don't forget, Rafe, I am a princess. An heir will be expected of our marriage, but...' her voice trailed off and mischief sparkled in her eyes '... if you object to that, I understand.'

Object? To another night like that night in London? Was she serious? 'I have no objection,' he said far more calmly than he felt. He certainly didn't object to more hot sex with Kaliana, but he did object to the idea of fathering a child. Fear of being as cold and unloving as his father had cemented that idea in his mind long ago and now duty to his father, his family, meant he had to find a way to get past that.

'Then you accept my deal?'

He didn't know what to say, didn't know how to answer. All he knew was that if he allowed her to walk away again he'd regret it. Whatever it was between them wasn't over yet. Wasn't finished. And if it meant entering into a marriage deal, one that would enable him to keep Pietra Bianca safe and maybe even please his father, be the better son, then he would do it.

After all, marriages could be broken. Ended.

'Very well. I accept your deal.'

The relief on her face made him smile. She was as desperate to make this marriage as he was. But he wasn't done yet. She'd made her terms very clear, but he had some of his own to bring to the table.

'I do, however, have terms of my own.' Rafe's words left Kaliana speechless for a few seconds, tension filling her. He couldn't do this to her. Couldn't make demands now. Not after kissing her like that. Making such a scene as he'd all but dragged her back into the room, passion gripping them both. She blushed at the thought of how it must have looked. Like lovers who needed to get a room. Like they must have looked at the bar in London. She blushed at the memory.

Finally, she found her voice, but it was more of a stutter as uncertainty gripped her. 'What conditions?'

'I am a Sicilian. And we are a proud lot.' Humour weaved into his voice, lifting the tension. He looked so handsome, so irresistible. His dark eyes sparkled, his lips curving into that sexy smile.

She almost laughed as the mood lightened, becoming more like the time they'd spent together in London. 'I had worked that much out.'

His eyes fixed to hers, questioning if she was making fun of him. Seriousness took over once again, making Kaliana feel dizzy from the seesawing emotions. 'And I will not have anyone think I am marrying as part of a deal.'

'Is that why you just kissed me? In front of those people out there?' The questions rushed from her before she could stop them. 'To make it look like we are lovers?'

'No, Kaliana.' He smiled, that sinfully sexy smile he'd used in the bar of the hotel in London making her heart flutter as the zap of attraction rushed over her once more. What would it be like if he'd kissed her because he wanted to? She held her breath as he moved a little closer, his expression dark and serious. 'I kissed you because I wanted to.'

Kaliana's tummy flipped over. He had wanted to kiss her. Just as she had wanted him to. And she'd kissed him back with as much fervour as he'd kissed her. 'What are your conditions?'

'I do need to marry, yes, that is very true. I can also relieve the financial pressures your country faces. But I will not have it said we married out of necessity. I don't want anyone to know this is a deal brokered between us. After our little floor show just now, I'm sure the tongues are already wagging.'

'That's what I'm afraid of.' If word got out just who she was, any chance of living quietly until her wedding day would be over. She'd be forced to take on the role of a princess, might even be forced to return to Ardu Safra, where she would have guards assigned and be unable to be herself. To be free. She didn't want her children growing up locked away from reality as she had been.

'It's exactly what we need.' Rafe's words brought her

hurtling back to the reality of this moment. The reality of brokering a marriage deal with Raffaele Casella.

'Why, Rafe? Why do we need that?'

'If we are to marry, I want everyone to think it is because we want to do so. I want people to believe it's real. Believe we are in love. A whirlwind romance, no?' Kaliana's heart pounded as he said those last words. Love was what she still secretly desired but she was scared in case it couldn't happen twice in a lifetime. Mentally she shook herself. Whatever this was between her and Rafe, it was more like lust.

'Why would you want to do that?' Nerves made her voice quiver.

'I have spent all my adult life avoiding the state of matrimony. I told myself I never wanted to succumb to the dangerous emotion of love. My family and friends know this, so we need to convince them otherwise.'

'And you are a man who doesn't want to let love into his life?' They were more suited than he knew, but the look on his face told her she'd spoken the truth. For whatever reason, Rafe refused to let love into his heart or his life.

'How well you already know me. But what about you? Do you seek love in your life?' He walked away from her, back towards the window, giving her much-needed breathing space. At least she could think more clearly now without her heart pounding so loudly.

'No.' The word snapped from her. Was she trying to convince herself? Or Rafe? She was already dangerously drawn to him. Already he was making her forget Alif. Forget all they'd had. But what would happen if he crept into her heart? If she began to feel something for him? She pushed the questions aside. 'I have known love once and that is enough. I don't seek it any more.'

'*Bene.* Then I suggest we go out there and show everyone how we feel about each other.'

'How we feel?' The mischief in his eyes did terrible things to her. Made clear and concise thought impossible.

'That we are mad for one another.' He smiled at her and her stomach flipped over, tingles of pleasure rushing through her.

CHAPTER FIVE

LATER THAT EVENING, Rafe had stood at her side as she'd called her father, his official request for her hand in marriage met with unexpected enthusiasm.

'Kaliana and I are both duty-bound to make a marriage that will benefit our families and I would like to ask you for your daughter's hand in marriage.' Rafe's strong and determined voice had filled her with confidence. Everything was going to be all right.

'It's not the woman,' her father had said, the ruler he'd become booming loudly down the phone. 'You also marry the kingdom. Are you man enough for that?'

'I most certainly am.' Rafe's confident reply had made her smile and now, over a week later, as they sat having lunch outside a small restaurant, she couldn't help but smile at the memory of it.

His brows flicked upwards as he saw her smiling. 'You have a beautiful smile.'

'I was thinking about the way you all but told Father we were getting married.' She hid her confused embarrassment at the compliment. 'I just hope your father is as pleased when I meet him this afternoon.'

'He will be.' Rafe glanced at the other couples having lunch, all of them more interested in them than their food. 'It seems our news has travelled fast.'

'Sadly, yes. My cover has been blown and now I have to be Princess Kaliana.' She sighed. 'Which means I have to give up the life I'd made in London.'

'It had to happen. Whoever you married, that life could never be part of it. Even I know that.' Rafe genuinely sounded remorseful and she smiled as he settled the bill. 'Before we see my father, I'd like to take you somewhere quiet. Somewhere that will give us time and space to get to know one another a little better.'

Kaliana looked across at him. Time to be alone with Rafe was what she'd hoped for all week. What she'd yearned for like a lovestruck teenager. 'I'd like that.'

When they returned to his car, a soft laugh escaped her, one born of nerves. 'It's not easy getting to know the man I'm going to marry when we are always acting the romantic couple just because we are being watched. I'd like to get to know you better. The real you.'

He looked at her, seriousness filling his eyes, his dark, demanding gaze holding hers. The ever-present tension ramped up around them, the interior of his sleek car becoming far too confining.

'You want to get to know me?' Surprise filled his voice and a delicious sense of anticipation slipped over her. It didn't last long. 'Do you not know all you need to know?'

Kaliana swallowed back her surprise. He was reminding her that this was just a deal. This wasn't real. And whatever foolish sentiments were in her mind she'd do well to keep them to herself because she was in danger of reading too much into every smile, every caress, every kiss.

'Of course.' She kept her voice light, her smile disguising her shock. Her disappointment. She focused her attention in front of her, willing him to start driving. To stop looking at her. She needed to get her wayward thoughts in order, back into the mindset that this was just a deal and could never be anything else.

Each date they'd been on last week had proved to her she'd done the right thing. That together they made a good team. That they could both fulfil the requirements of their families with their marriage. And maybe she could have part of her secret wish and at least they could be happy together. Something she couldn't envisage happening with Nassif.

Not once had she and Rafe talked intimately. Not once had they shared who they really were. Kaliana knew she was guilty of hiding behind barriers and defensive walls. So, was it the same for Rafe? Was he using their role play of romance and his family duty as a barrier?

'Then I know the perfect place,' he said, turning his attention to manoeuvring the car into the traffic.

Within seconds they were in the flow of traffic, heading out of Palermo. She glanced across at him; his eyes were rigidly fixed on the road ahead. As if he didn't dare look at her. As if he could sense her gradually changing feelings towards him.

'Somewhere peaceful we can talk sounds perfect.' She couldn't help the small sigh of satisfaction at the thought. 'Just talk and get to know one another.'

'Better than we got to know one another in London?' This time he did glance across at her and that teasing sparkle filled his eyes. She never knew where she stood with him. Was that his way of keeping this arrangement purely that? His way of preventing it from ever coming anywhere near something more meaningful?

Kaliana's breath shuddered from her. She wanted to look away, wanted to hide herself from him, but she couldn't.

Instead she laughed. 'Raffaele Casella, you are incorrigible.' Then she turned to look out of the window, hiding the flush spreading over her cheeks. What was the matter with her?

She watched the view of the sparkling sea as they drove along the coast road. Anything other than look at him and give into the fizz of attraction which hummed through her. It sizzled in the air around them. Waiting to explode.

Rafe's silence continued as they turned off the coast road and began driving along narrow twisting lanes. It all looked so beautiful, but Kaliana couldn't speak. Her throat was dry, her nerves on edge. Was this what being alone with him would be like?

'Am I really incorrigible?' he asked, teasing her from her silence as he pulled the car off the road.

She turned to look at him, trying to beat down the intensity of her feelings. Sensations she couldn't put a name to. 'Yes, you are.' She smiled, unable to help herself be anything but charmed by him. By his sexy smile. She arched a brow upwards, feeling as flirtatious as she had that night in the bar.

He looked at her, the silence heavy, and she lowered her gaze, then looked up from beneath her lashes. 'I like that about you.'

Her gaze locked with his, her heart thudding wildly in her chest. So much so that when he glanced lower she was sure he must be able to see her pulse thumping at the base of her throat. 'Why are we here, Rafe?' she asked, needing to change the subject.

She had to get out of the confines of the car. Away from the scent of the man she'd given herself to with complete abandon, believing it would be her only chance at finding such pleasure.

Now she was about to marry him.

Except this version of Rafe wasn't the man she'd met that night. That man was as much of an enigma as she had been. They'd lost themselves with such abandon that night, and she certainly hadn't expected to see him again. Much less be preparing to marry him.

'We are here to learn more about each other,' he said, his voice husky as he looked into her eyes, making her pulse thump ever harder. 'This is what you want, is it not, *cara mia*?'

'Here?' Kaliana teased him with a smile and Rafe gritted his teeth against the hot spark of lust hurtling straight to his groin. How could this woman make him feel like this? How could his desire for her still be so strong? Unquenched?

Because you still want her. The voice of reason slammed into him. *You couldn't get enough of her that night, weren't ready to end the encounter, but she walked out on you.*

He smiled, trying to lighten the mood. Trying to push away those damning thoughts. He had to get out of the car. Had to get away from her before he did something stupid like kiss her. Again. There was no way he was going to allow her to know she had any kind of power over him. At least not sexual power.

'This is Pietra Bianca. It was my mother's land,' he

said, turning the engine off, the silence suddenly heavy around them.

'I can tell it's very special to you.' Kaliana looked across at him, unnerving him with her ability to see what he didn't want her to see.

'It's a place full of memories. Happy memories of a childhood with Enzo.' She was doing it again. Slipping under that defensive barrier he'd built around himself. Dragging him out. Exposing his innermost emotions.

'Are you sure you want to be here today?' she questioned slowly. Tentatively.

'*Sì.*' He grappled with English briefly as the urge to reach across the car and stroke his fingers down her cheek almost took over. Instead he opened the door, the August heat rushing into the air-conditioned interior. A heat that nowhere near matched the hot desire as he'd answered the primal call Kaliana's body had made to his in the hotel bar that night. Heat and desire that was still very much alive. That kiss at the charity event had proved that. A week of very public dates hadn't lessened it. The inability to touch her, hold her, kiss her, as he had done that first night, only intensifying his need. His desire.

All week he'd played the role he'd dictated. Courted the press. Showed off their romance. And it had worked. His father and even Enzo were on board with his choice of wife and mother of the heir they all needed.

He and Kaliana had crossed the first hurdle—gained family acceptance on both sides and created a buzz about their relationship. The next step was to get to know one another better. Which was why he'd brought her here. To the peace and quiet of the place that meant the most to him.

It was the one piece of land belonging to the Casella family which he needed to keep. The reason he'd bowed to pressure from his father and agreed to marry. Pietra Bianca had to remain in Casella hands.

'It's a pretty place,' she said, opening her door, stepping out, giving him a view of her long, lean denim-clad legs, which had wrapped around him so perfectly. Rafe refused to remember. Refused to be drawn by the desire she obviously could still evoke.

He hadn't been able to keep his eyes off Kaliana when she'd stepped out of her house that morning in jeans which hugged her hips to perfection and a navy loose-fitting blouse which she wore deliciously low, reminding him, if he'd needed it, just how perfect her breasts were. *Dio mio*, she still looked as sexy as hell. Still as hard to resist.

'There is a special place I would like you to see, and I thought a picnic in the olive groves would be the perfect spot to talk.' He paused and looked at the woman who was to be his bride. 'In private, before we make our romance, our engagement, official.'

He'd had the idea of bringing Kaliana out here when he'd decided to visit the olive and lemon groves his mother had loved so much. He wasn't sure why, but for some reason he needed Kaliana to see the place that was so special to him.

'Are you trying to be romantic with me, Rafe Casella?' Again that flirtatious and teasing voice lured him back towards desire, away from the pain of the past, away from the agony of losing his mother.

'Romance is not something I usually indulge in,' he said sternly, trying to control the rush of desire just being with her evoked. Too sternly if the look of shock on Kaliana's pretty face was anything to go by. 'I simply thought we could get to know one another better. It will make our *love affair* more convincing.'

'What do you want to know?' Caution sounded in her voice and he sensed her reservations.

'Things that will convince anyone we are in love,' he said, moving towards her, her eyes full of the same swirling desire he'd seen in the bar as she'd seduced him. Whatever it was between them, it was still vibrantly alive.

'I need to know more than where you like to be kissed, Kaliana.'

He couldn't help adding that taunt, his voice rising on the last few words, making it obvious he was teasing her again. He watched her eyes darkening, reminding him of when she'd looked at him in the bar just moments before she'd kissed him that first time.

That kick of lust threatened to unleash itself again and he stepped back, his feet crunching the gravel as he did so. Hell, if he didn't control himself he'd want to make her his again. Right here and now.

'Maybe I don't like to be kissed,' she said in a brisk but husky voice as she put much-needed distance between them by walking towards the olive trees. Towards the place that was so special to him—a place he'd never told any woman about, let alone shown, but Kaliana deserved to see it. After all, their marriage would keep it in the Casella family. Keep it for his children.

Rafe took the basket his housekeeper had prepared from the car and, with a carefree smile which didn't match the way he felt, looked at Kaliana. 'This way.'

At first she seemed uncertain, then she followed him, her flat shoes at least suitable for the gravel path which led towards the place he'd enjoyed so much before his world had been turned upside down by his mother's death.

Slowly they walked down through the gnarled old olive trees; as a young boy he'd found interesting things buried in the dusty earth beneath them. As a man, in a desperate attempt to keep the land from being developed by his father, he had set about making such finds known. For now, Pietra Bianca was safe—but only if he married Kaliana. Only then could he keep the memories of his mother alive.

'I'm surprised this hasn't been developed into one of those luxury complexes the Casellas are so famous for,' Kaliana said, looking about her as she walked at his side. She'd obviously done further research on him and his family since the charity event.

'My business interests do not include developing places like this. I am not of the same mind as my father or, indeed, my brother.' Rafe's tone was clipped and short as he recalled his father's fury when he'd refused to agree to be part of the impressive Casella business after university. Instead he'd told his father he wanted to forge his own way, create his own empire. Something his mother had backed him on, but sadly she hadn't lived to see it being fulfilled.

'Renewable energy, isn't it?' Kaliana asked as they reached a small stone house. He stopped, looking at her. She smiled, her eyes alive with triumph. 'You didn't think I'd marry you without learning something more about you, did you?'

'I assume that was to ensure I was wealthy enough in my own right to enable you to solve your country's financial problems.' The truth and reality of why he was even standing here with her now hit home. It was all about money for her and, for him, possessions.

'If you are so annoyed with that, why did you agree to marry me?' Annoyance sparked in each word, like flint on a stone.

'I have no other option. Like you, I am bound by family tradition. Honour.' He couldn't keep the bitterness from his voice. Enzo's misfortune had become his too. 'Your deal was the solution to my problem. As you so rightly said, we both stand to gain from the arrangement.'

'Duty is what drives us both, Rafe. Duty and honour.' Anger simmered in her sharp retort, stoking his own annoyance at the situation.

'More so in your case. Your country is at stake.' His words rushed out before he could filter them, strip them of the raw emotion just talking about this evoked. 'You are a princess. I'm an ordinary man.'

She turned to look at him as he stated the obvious, her hair swinging as she did so, brushing her shoulders. Even now, in the depths of the real reason they were marrying, she tempted him.

'I still feel there is another motive,' she said carefully, watching him suspiciously as they stood in the shade of the stone house. 'Another reason for agreeing to my deal.'

He drove his fingers into his hair, dragging his hand back over his scalp. She was right, and if he wanted to learn more about her, then didn't he need to give away details of his personal history?

'In my grandfather's time the Casella name nearly ended.' How could he explain all the complications of his family? 'My father is terminally ill and will not rest until he knows I am married and a father—to a son. He even insisted I undertook fertility tests to ensure Enzo's fate wasn't also mine. Not for me, but for the Casella name.'

'He made you do that?' The angry tension slipped back a notch, leaving him more relaxed. More open to such a discussion. To sharing secrets.

'Yes.' Just thinking how much his life had altered in the last few months brought anger rushing back to the surface.

Rafe could still feel the shock as his father had told him of Enzo's predicament—a problem that radiated far further than just Enzo and Emma's marriage. Rafe had been too blinded by the pain he knew Emma would be feeling to even worry what sort of implications the revelation had on him. On his life. His future.

A future which he should have shared with Emma. He would have, if Enzo hadn't competed for her so determinedly, taking away the only woman Rafe had loved. He'd stood back as they had married. Allowed his love for her to wilt and die and now, as their marriage threatened to fall apart, all he could feel was sympathy for Emma, who'd wanted children so much. After all, when they had been together, even for that short time, she'd made it clear that being a mother was something she really wanted.

It wasn't until their father had all but demanded Rafe have a fertility test to ensure that at least one of the twins would be able to father the next Casella generation that Rafe realised the implications for him.

'That's terrible.' Kaliana finally found a voice, pressing her fingertips to her lips and right there, at that moment, he wished he was kissing her, tasting her lips, instead of having this conversation. It was safer.

'Naturally, my father was more concerned about the continuation of the Casella name than Enzo's floundering marriage, or even the fact that Enzo had married the woman I once loved. So you can rest assured that our marriage will produce the children that both our families expect of us.'

Kaliana's eyes had widened, filling with disbelief at Rafe's confession of his father's actions. Not that it mattered now. His father was mercenary, and love meant nothing to him. Why else would he have made his own wife's life so unhappy? Even as she'd been seriously ill, Rafe's mother had tried to defend the man she loved. Tried to convince Rafe it was just his father's way. That, deep down, he loved her and his twins. Both of them—equally.

No, Rafe would never believe that.

'You don't want children, do you? Given the choice, that is.' The words were a whisper. A shocked whisper.

He couldn't lie to her. But he couldn't tell her how he feared being the same as his father had been to him. Cold and indifferent. 'No, given the choice, I don't. I don't want to be married either but, like you, having lost someone I loved, I'm doing so.'

'At least I know where I stand.' Kaliana's voice struggled beneath the heaviness of his honesty. Had he done the right thing being so brutal? So honest? Yes. He couldn't allow her to form any attachment to him. Not when he was so unworthy of love. When every person he'd ever loved had rejected him—or worse.

'This marriage, our marriage, is one we are making because of duty to our families. Not a marriage made with the promise of love and happy ever after. It is a marriage for financial gain—for both of us.' He forced home his point, reminding her of the real reason they were doing this. Reminding himself.

If he pushed her too hard, might she walk away? Might she free him of this deal, his duty? Was that why he was being so mercenary? So like his damn father? Because, deep down, he wanted to be free?

'You sound very bitter about love, Rafe, and happy-ever-afters. What happened?' Kaliana walked slowly towards him, her hands clasping her arms, hugging herself, as if she too felt the change in the atmosphere around them.

'I'm just being practical. And honest.' Rafe needed to redirect the conversation. In such a short time she had dug deep into his soul, opening old wounds, the kind of wounds he'd refused to deal with any more.

She shook her head in silent agreement, one hand rubbing the top of her arm in a gesture of comfort he so wished he could give her. But right now the past had been painfully exhumed and spread out before him and all he wanted to do was run from it.

'As practical as your father was when he insisted you have that test?' In one sharp sentence she'd ploughed deep into his insecurities. Passing that test had been the one thing he'd done right as far as his father was concerned.

'Si,' he said, distracted by memories. 'And what of your father? Is he happy with the marriage deal you have brokered? Will he be happy when he meets me?' He took it back to basics. Away from anything resembling emotion, even though he knew from his own father that Kaliana's was more than happy.

'Very much so.' She lifted her chin a little, the sunlight dancing in her hair. 'Wedding preparations are already underway.' She narrowed her eyes. 'Your father is not opposed to our marriage, I take it? Even though I am not Sicilian?'

'He too is happy,' Rafe said, recalling the conversation he'd had with his father about the marriage deal. His reaction to his son marrying a princess had been nothing short of overjoyed. Not only would the Casella name continue, but it would do so with royal blood in its veins. Rafe had excelled himself. Earnt his respect. 'You will see that for yourself very soon. All we need to do is continue with the pretence of a whirlwind romance.'

She nodded, walking slowly away from him, pretending to look around her, pretending none of this bothered her. 'I guess it is.' She turned, smiling. 'Did you say something about a picnic earlier?' Her voice was so light and carefree it was hard to believe they'd just been discussing something so difficult for both of them.

He smiled, enjoying her sensitivity. Marriage to Kaliana wasn't going to be a hardship, but then it wasn't the marriage he'd once envisaged as a young man. When he'd fallen in love for the first time.

'I did and I know just the spot.' He took her hand, forcing his smile to brighten. 'This way.'

Kaliana's mind filled with worry and she struggled to disguise it. The fact that Rafe needed her as his wife should have made her feel less anxious, less worried he might back out. But she could sense his hesitation, his reluctance. This was a man who went out of his way to avoid emotional commitment His admission of losing the woman he'd loved to his brother had proved that.

Maybe that was the best way. She'd had her chance at real romance, real love and happy ever after. A marriage based on sexual chemistry, one which solved the issues her country faced, was safer emotionally.

'This is where I used to picnic with my mother,' Rafe said as they reached a gentle downward slope dotted with ancient gnarled olive trees. A low stone wall, old and crumbling, stood in the middle of the small clearing, the afternoon sun streaming between the leaves creating a totally magical scene.

The beauty of the spot was overshadowed by his words. This was the first time Rafe had mentioned his mother and she wasn't going to allow the chance to pass, knowing from her recent research on him that he'd lost his mother when he was in his late teens. 'Do you miss her?'

'I was seventeen when she died. Almost a man, but still too young to lose a mother. I hope my child never has to experience such pain, such loss.' It was as if he'd forgotten himself. As if she wasn't there. Or at least not Kaliana, his bride-to-be.

'It must have been awful,' she said, instinctively reaching out to touch his arm.

Rafe looked at her, but she knew he was lost in the heartache of all he'd endured. 'Nothing was as bad as losing my mother, not even being the second-best son in my father's eyes.'

He paused, caught between the past and the present. He slipped backwards. 'My mother suddenly became very ill and when she died I lost my ally in life.' From the look on his face, she guessed this wasn't something he talked much about, was something he guarded well.

'Your father must have been beside himself.'

'My father never showed emotion. I don't know what he felt, but after my mother's death he became even harder to please.' His eyes became dark and thunderous. 'The only thing I ever did right since that day was pass that damned fertility test.'

Kaliana didn't know what to say, instinctively reaching out to touch his arm. He looked down at her hand on his shirt sleeve then up to her face. 'Oh, Rafe.' Her heart ached for the teenager who'd lost his mother so tragically. 'You did your best.'

'But it wasn't enough.' He shook his head, pressing his lips together as he reined in the anger sparking in his eyes. 'That's when I knew I didn't want to be a father.'

'But now? You need a child, an heir. We both do.' The words slipped from her lips so fast she couldn't check them, couldn't keep the thought to herself.

Rafe looked at her and for a moment, in the dappled light of the olive groves, he looked like the man she'd met in London. But then the sun slipped behind a cloud and the moment was gone. Now he was Raffaele Casella. The man who'd calmly agreed to her deal for a marriage of convenience.

'I know my duty, Kaliana. I can assure you our child will want for nothing.'

'What about love?' She could manage without love in her life, but she wanted her child to be loved—by both parents. If he couldn't do that, it was almost a deal-breaker. Almost because she had little choice now. The wheels of their deal had been put in motion. Time was running out. 'Can you love your children?'

Rafe's eyes narrowed in that way he did when he didn't believe her, didn't trust her. 'Love is the one thing I can no longer give. Not to anyone.'

The starkness of that statement, the total indifference in it, set off alarms in her mind, made questions race.

'Children?' Rafe spoke again before she could form her response to his declaration. 'You want more than one?'

Kaliana looked at Rafe, insecurities from her own childhood surfacing. She should have been a son, the one thing her mother had never truly got over. Her father's adoration for her hadn't been enough to ease her mother's worry that no further babies blessed their marriage. 'Yes, Rafe, children. I am a princess. An only child. I need to have children. My country needs heirs.'

'Hell, Kaliana, if that doesn't make us sound like pawns in their games, I don't know what does.' His angry outburst shocked her. Shocked him too. He looked at her as he sat on the picnic blanket, the innocence of the setting making the context of their conversation even more powerful. Even more scary.

'Our first child may be a boy,' she said flatly, trying to remember this was a deal. Not a real marriage. They were not like a normal couple talking through how many children they wanted. They would never be a normal couple. 'An heir to continue the Casella name and an heir for Ardu Safra.'

He moved closer. Very close. The mood of the moment had changed as quickly as the desert wind. 'I'm looking forward to creating that baby.' His voice was soft, every syllable caressing her. Stoking the desire she'd been suppressing since that kiss at the charity event.

Birds chattered in the trees around them, cicadas chirped and Kaliana's mind whirled, her body shimmering with heat which had nothing to do with the hot sunshine. Rafe reached out to touch her face and Kaliana held her breath as he gently brushed her windswept hair from her face. 'Making that obligatory heir will not be a hardship, no?'

'Don't,' she whispered, wanting to get away, wanting to move back from his touch. 'Everything is so complicated.'

'*Dio mio*, complicated isn't the right description. But this can save us.' He caressed her cheek with the backs of his fingers. 'This passion, this desire, can distract us.'

'Can it?'

'It's still there, Kaliana, that connection. That chemistry. You can feel it too, can't you?' His voice was husky, the caress of his thumb against her cheek hard to ignore. So hard to resist. But she had to; she couldn't allow herself to dream. To hope.

'It's just lust,' she said quickly, horrified at how husky her voice had become.

'You want me, no?' How could she admit that when it would give him all the power?

'No.' The indignant word shot from her lips.

'If I kiss you now, your heart rate won't speed up? Your breath won't catch in your throat? And your eyes won't darken until they look like the midnight sky? Just as they did when you kissed me in London.'

'Stop it.'

He laughed. 'I don't think you really want me to, do you, Kaliana?'

She lifted her chin defiantly. 'Then kiss me so I can prove you wrong.'

His lips lifted into a slow sexy smile, his pupils enlarging, darkening his eyes as his fingers brushed back and forth on her cheek. Just as he'd claimed, her pulse raced. Her breath caught audibly in her throat and she was sure her eyes were giving away everything.

'Very well, *cara*, I will kiss you.'

She smelt the delicious citrus tang of his aftershave as he brushed his lips over hers, forcing her eyes closed as the onslaught of desire stampeded over her. She dragged in a long ragged breath, waiting for his arms to hold her, waiting to feel his body against hers. She wanted all that and more.

He drew back. 'I think that proves my point.'

She blinked rapidly in shock, unable to stand the smug satisfaction on his face. Anger raged through her, mixing with the heady pulse of desire that light touch of his lips had ignited once more. 'That proves nothing.'

'It proves you want me. It proves what we had in London is still very much alive.'

'But that's not what our deal, our marriage, is about.'

'We can make it about whatever we like.' The suggestion in those dark and sexy eyes was all too clear.

Kaliana wanted to believe him. Wanted more nights like that night which seemed so long ago now. Like a dream which had dimmed over time. The weight of the afternoon's discussion lifted as he smiled at her, taking her right back to that moment in the bar in London. The moment she'd known he would be the man she'd give herself to.

'How can I say no?'

'You can't,' he said, gently bringing her against him. She lifted herself onto her tiptoes, brushing her lips over his, the fight she'd been trying to keep alive in her body slipping away as the need to kiss him took over. 'I don't want to either.'

Rafe squeezed Kaliana's hand as they entered Villa Casella later that afternoon. The potent kiss they'd shared had broken the tension between them, but he still sensed her apprehension at meeting his father. 'It will be fine.'

She looked up at him and he could almost forget this was an arrangement. For that moment it was as if something real drew and held them together. Something more than just convenience. More than sexual chemistry.

'Okay,' she said, pressing her lips together. 'Let's do this.'

The sensation of reality evaporated.

'Father, this is Kaliana,' Rafe said as his father met them on the terrace.

'*Sì*, the Princess. *Benvenuto*.' He embraced Kaliana warmly and Rafe saw the relief on her face. It really mattered that he accepted her. His father let Kaliana go and looked at him. 'You will, of course, have the engagement party here. I cannot yet travel.'

'It will be here,' Kaliana said without even glancing at him for approval. 'Especially as the wedding will have to be in Ardu Safra.'

'And what of your preparations for the big day?' he asked and Rafe watched, bemused, as his father took an interest. Had he finally done something that pleased his father? Earnt his respect?

'It's going well, thank you,' Kaliana said with a smile.

'And Franco?' His father turned his attention to Rafe. 'Is he to be your best man?'

'He is,' Rafe said and looked at Kaliana. 'In fact, we will be flying to Rome for a few days to meet him and his wife, Francesca.'

'We are?' Kaliana asked, looking up at him with astonishment.

'Franco is looking forward to meeting you, as is his wife.' Rafe had little choice. After all the support Franco had given since he'd first met Kaliana, getting his bride and friend together was something he needed to do.

'Then I guess we are,' Kaliana said, laughing conspiratorially with his father, and Rafe found himself looking forward to a few days—and nights—in Kaliana's company.

CHAPTER SIX

THEIR ARRIVAL IN Rome had created a fresh flurry of
interest from the world's press but Rafe's luxury apartment gave him and Kaliana the peace they sought.
Rafe had watched as Kaliana marvelled at the ornate
painted ceilings and the vastness of the three-storey
apartment.

'This place is amazing.' Kaliana turned, smiling at
him, looking more relaxed than he'd ever seen her.

'It is pretty special,' Rafe said, amused at her pleasure at the classical Italian architecture. 'And perfect
to enjoy some peace. An escape from all those curious eyes.'

Kaliana frowned, a serious expression slipping over
her face. 'Where will we live once we are married?'

Rafe had barely given a thought to the logistics of
their marriage. He'd been so focused on achieving all
he and the Casella family needed from their union that
their future as a married couple hadn't demanded any
of his attention.

'I am often in London on business. I see no reason
why we cannot spend some time there. We are making a marriage that is more convenient to our families
than us.'

Kaliana flinched at his words. Had he been too honest? Too brutal?

'Would that really work?' she asked firmly, then smiled as if trying to return to the teasing lightness of moments ago. 'Between each of our commitments in our homelands, it will be difficult for us to be together much.'

Had she read his mind? Or was that what she wanted?

'Something else we will have to work out. But first we need to continue the show of our whirlwind romance and to do that you need an engagement ring before we meet Franco and Francesca this evening.' Rafe spoke his thoughts aloud as he watched the woman who would soon be his wife walk across their suite to look out over Rome.

Her shoulder-length hair bobbing jauntily reminded him of the time it had fallen in a curtain around her face as he'd made her his that first night. A night he hoped would be repeated. He'd never experienced such a strong attraction to a woman. Not even Emma had fired such an intense desire through his veins. At least that part of his deal with Kaliana was right.

Kaliana turned from surveying the view of the city. She didn't speak, but the arch of her brow left him in no doubt she was still annoyed at him for insisting they put on such an act as part of their deal. Her silence had hummed with annoyance as he'd watched her, her sexy figure highlighted in the late-summer sunshine lighting the room.

That annoyance was still palpable as she looked at him, that haughty air he couldn't help but find sexy radiating from her. 'A ring that is also part of the act?' Her quick reply fired back at him.

He walked towards her, determined to thaw her increasingly icy mood. 'A ring that will seal our deal, *mia cara.*'

She lifted her chin, looking up at him, challenge clearly in her eyes.

'And there I was thinking we were in Rome for a romantic week together. That you wanted to rekindle the passion between us.' Her flippant reply, laced with seductive teasing, made it almost impossible to suppress his laughter. He couldn't yet understand why just being with Kaliana, even when she challenged him, made him want to laugh.

She made him feel carefree in a way he hadn't felt since he'd lost Emma to his brother. Just as she had that first night, Kaliana made him believe he could have more. That he was worthy of love. That if he could let go of the past, she was the one who would unlock his heart. He could almost believe something meaningful could grow between them—if only he opened himself to the possibility.

But could he trust that instinct, that elusive sensation, when he'd got it so wrong once before?

Whatever it was, Kaliana was the perfect antidote to Enzo's betrayal and the situation he now faced. The standby heir forced to perform like a stud horse. Forced to step up to his duty.

'Those were the terms of our arrangement, Kaliana. It is what we agreed.' Mentioning the word arrangement pushed those far-fetched ideas from his mind. Romance was the last thing he needed. And love was the one thing he didn't want. Such emotions destroyed you. Left you vulnerable to pain. Disappointment.

At least he and Kaliana were on the same page. She

wasn't harbouring notions of love and those non-existent happy-ever-afters. He could still recall her now, full of confidence, as she'd claimed she'd had her chance at love. That she didn't want to find it again.

'Naturally I wish to show off my fiancée. I want the world to see the beautiful woman I am to marry.'

'Then we had better get the biggest ring possible,' she taunted him, that wicked glint of mischief in her eyes sending fire hurtling through him. 'Make sure it's flashy and bold enough to leave no one in doubt.'

'If that's what you want, then so be it.' He entered into her game, the memory of the outcome of that seductive game she'd first played with him so fresh it was as if it had just happened. As if time had been turned back.

Rafe laughed. 'I can see our marriage will be entertaining at the very least.'

He kept that thought with him as he sat in one of Rome's most exclusive jewellers, an array of glittering rings before them. The staff were falling over themselves to get what Kaliana wanted and she was certainly doing as she'd threatened, demandingly ensuring she got the biggest and flashiest ring.

His mind raced back to the night she'd arrived in the bar, demanding champagne. How could he have been so stupid not to have realised she was a woman of such high calibre? Such breeding. A woman who demanded her exacting standards to be met. Did the version of Kaliana he'd walked among the olive groves with last weekend really exist? The woman whose lips he'd brushed with his. Tasting passion and desire as well as her fight to conceal it.

This sexy, spirited vision of confidence was the real Kaliana. Not at all the kind of woman he'd envisioned would one day become his wife once he'd accepted marriage was something he couldn't avoid. He'd always thought that woman would be soft, gentle and kind. Like his mother. A woman who would be able to heal his wounds and show him how to love. Give him the confidence to set his heart free from its prison.

Was that Kaliana? Sometimes. But right now she was exactly what he needed if he was to keep Pietra Bianca and prevent his cousin and her greedy husband from taking the Casella fortune and adding it permanently to the Romano name. No matter what else happened, he wanted that.

'What about this one?' Kaliana held her hand out, showcasing a small subtle ring on her long slender finger.

'An excellent choice,' the assistant said. 'The vintage raspberry tourmaline and diamond is quite stunning and so delicate.'

'It's not what I expected you to select.' Her earlier threat of buying the biggest ring possible rang in his ears. She'd been toying with him. Like a cat who had just brought in a mouse.

She smiled at him, softness lighting her eyes like the first rays of sun at dawn. 'This one would be my choice.'

'I thought you wanted a statement ring.' Rafe watched her with mock suspicion.

She laughed. 'That's not me, Rafe.' She looked down at the ring on her finger. 'But this is.'

'Then that is the one.' Her smile, her genuine pleasure at the dainty ring dragged him back to the place where he could almost wish it was real. Wish they were getting engaged for love.

He leaned forward, brushing his lips lingeringly over

hers. He felt her hesitation, her initial resistance, then she placed her palm against his cheek and kissed him back, unleashing the powerful attraction he had for her. Attraction that was merely lust. Merely the need to make her his once more.

As Kaliana prepared for a night at the opera with Rafe she tried to maintain the demanding Princess act. She'd only been able to hide behind it for a while whilst trying on big bright diamonds which glittered like stars. Then she'd seen her ring. It had caught her attention. Teasing Rafe had been fun, but a large flashy ring wasn't her at all. She smiled at his stunned silence as she'd showed him the ring she wanted.

When she'd kissed him as part of the act, the shock which had zipped round her body made her realise how much she wanted him. She wanted him as much, if not more, than she had that first night. As if they really were already lovers. She was in danger of falling for him, becoming seduced by the passionate desire. Worse than that, she was in danger of handing over something equally as precious as her virginity. If she allowed herself to, she could easily hand this man her heart.

She was falling for him—not just the man she'd shared that amazing night with in London, but this man. She knew she shouldn't, but she couldn't help it.

She pushed back those traitorous thoughts, emerging from her room wearing a sapphire-blue full-length gown befitting the Princess she was. A zing of satisfaction rushed through her as Rafe looked up from his paperwork briefly, only to look back up a second time, his work forgotten. The plunging sweetheart neckline and diamanté-encrusted shoulder straps had got the reaction she wanted.

'You look…' He stood up from his desk, walking towards her, seeming to choose his words carefully. She'd never seen him lost for words.

'Good enough to convince your friend our engagement is real?' she finished for him, giving him a slow twirl to ensure he noticed the criss-cross diamanté straps across her bare back due to the low cut of the gown. She had no idea why, but she wanted to torment him, tease the desire they'd once shared back out into the open.

Slowly she turned, feeling his gaze on her. Feeling the burning of her skin as he watched her. Feeling the crackle in the air as the tension increased. Feeling in control. Just as she had been in the bar the first time they'd met. But had she really been in control?

The question made her pause briefly, but when she looked back up at him her breath nearly left her. The heavy desire in his eyes was too much, taking her back to the moment she'd looked into his eyes for the first time, knowing even then there was no going back. She'd known that her spontaneous rebellion to lose her virginity was going to happen. She'd wanted him then and she wanted him now with a carnal need she'd never known. Never believed possible.

That night in London she hadn't been in control; her desire had. Just as it was now.

She fought it. She couldn't allow it to take over.

'Beautiful,' he whispered. The air crackled as if fireworks were sparking around them. Kaliana held her breath. She couldn't move. Her heart was thudding.

Rafe moved towards her, that intoxicating darkness

in his desire-laden eyes. 'Very beautiful.' His voice was thick and heavy. Her heart pounded with anticipation. Anticipation of his kiss. Only this time she didn't think she could turn it off, deny it, as she had done in the olive groves.

This time she wanted to stay. To taste his kiss and so much more.

'I have a role to play, that of a loving and willing fiancée.' Kaliana fought the sensation he'd set off inside her as he moved closer, but her words only intensified the desire in Rafe's eyes. She didn't think she could take such a hot sultry look from him for much longer and not act on it.

'A loving and willing fiancée?' Rafe repeated her words, following her lead.

She couldn't keep the sadness from her voice. 'Those were your terms to our deal, were they not? A deal born of duty.'

Once she and Rafe were married, all her father's problems would be over. She'd been so relieved to hear the worry had gone from her father's voice last week as they'd talked wedding details she'd almost forgotten the terms of the marriage she'd been forced to make. Terms Rafe had dictated after kissing her so passionately in front of everyone.

She'd made a deal to marry a man so very dangerous to her naive and innocent heart. He could make her heart light, her tummy flutter with just a smile. Worse than that, he made her want to believe in something she'd thought impossible to find again. Love.

'Only duty?' Rafe's words cut through her like an unexpected bolt of thunder. 'What about desire? The powerful pull of attraction?'

She smiled brightly, trying not to read anything into his words. 'That is, of course, an added advantage.'

'*Sì, cara mia,* an added advantage, although this evening we need to portray romance and attraction. The desire can be saved for when we are alone, no?' He paused, looking down at her left hand, at the ring she'd chosen this afternoon. A small delicate stone she'd fallen in love with, but now that ring felt heavy. Like a lead weight dragging her down to the seabed as he continued to speak. 'Romance is something Franco and Francesca really believe in.'

'Is that a problem?' she asked tentatively. 'That the powerful businessman you are might believe in love?'

'On the contrary. Franco and Francesca believe we are in love, thanks to the press coverage of our whirlwind romance. It is something I wish them to continue believing.'

Kaliana's heart constricted, any faint hope that she might find a happy ever after with Rafe instantly slashed away. This man didn't want love. Didn't believe in it. For whatever reason, he had barricaded his heart away. It was all about his family wealth. His business. At least she was marrying to make the lives of her people better and not for her own personal gain.

'But you don't believe in love?' She knew he didn't. Knew the losses life had dealt him made that belief impossible, but for her own sanity she needed to hear him say it.

'No, I don't.'

'But you have loved once, Rafe?' As always, she couldn't help but probe deeper, needing to know more about this man. He'd already hinted at having lost his love and now she was unable to keep her curiosity under control.

'Once.' The answer was firm. It didn't invite further conversation, but she wasn't going to let this moment pass—a chance to find out more about him.

'Was it very long ago?'

'Almost ten years.' Rafe's expression changed, as if he was examining the past again. Guilt that she'd jolted obviously painful memories rushed through her. He looked at her. 'You know what it is like when you think you have found the person you want to spend the rest of your life with. You know how it hurts when that doesn't happen.'

She gasped, pressing her fingers to her lips. He'd lost his love to tragedy too?

'I'm sorry.' She walked to the large windows which gave an unrivalled view of the Trevi Fountain bathed in glorious sunshine and crowded by tourists all waiting to throw in a coin and make a wish.

'There is no need for sympathy. She simply decided her future wasn't with me.'

'It doesn't matter how you lose your first love; it still hurts,' she said softly, wanting to offer him some comfort but sensing that even a sympathetic tone would be unwelcome right now. He still loved her—his first love.

'We have both been burned by love.' The admission lanced through the atmosphere in the room, robbing her of the ability to think. She couldn't even turn to face him.

'So it would seem,' she said softly, thinking of Alif, realising she had given little thought to him or their love affair since spending time with Rafe. Not that she'd allow Rafe to know that, when the relationship between them was based purely on lust.

She turned to face him, wanting to end this conversation. It was too intimate. Made her question too many things, not least how she felt about Rafe. She shouldn't have pushed him to reveal his hidden emotions, not when she was in danger of wanting to be part of them too.

Her fleeting and fanciful dreams of Rafe being the man she could discover love with were getting to her. All she'd ever wanted was love and happiness—the same kind her parents had once shared. Could a man as closed-off as Rafe, so obviously damaged by past emotions, ever love?

No. She had to remember that. Guard her stirring heart. And, more importantly, she would harden her heart. Lock it away. Freeze it. Anything to stop it from falling for this man.

She would be strong. As impenetrable as Rafe. Showcase her acting ability to the full tonight. Because, with a clarity she'd only felt once before—that first night in London—she knew she was in grave danger of losing everything to this man. In danger of loving him.

The evening had been a great success. Kaliana had played her part well over their evening meal, talking weddings and romance with Franco and Francesca. She'd been so convincing, Rafe himself had almost believed it. Almost believed she wanted to marry him for no other reason than she loved him.

She'd looked so beautiful, shining vibrantly as they'd chatted with the other couple over dinner. He had hardly been able to keep his eyes from her all night. The softness of her skin had tempted him as she'd sat watching the opera performance, totally caught up in the magic of the moment. She'd been so enraptured by it all, by the emotion of the story being told, he wondered if she really was as cold and emotionless as he was. As she'd claimed.

Right now, he wasn't sure if he was that devoid of emotion. He was all over the place. Kaliana was making him feel things he didn't want to. Things that brought back memories of the past, of a time when he'd been happy. All this was swirling through his mind as he guided Kaliana, with his hand gently in the small of her back, from the Teatro Valle to his waiting car.

As they left the building the night sky around them lit up with flashes. Kaliana moved closer to him. Instantly he turned protector, wrapping his arm around her, drawing her closer still. His body reacted to the contact and instantly he realised his mistake.

Kaliana tensed against him, but the Princess she was took over. She smiled for the cameras, flirted with them, and with him. Posing for the photographs he knew would make headlines in tomorrow's papers.

'Now there will be no peace from them. Soon everyone will want to know about the desert Princess you are marrying.' The heated remark pierced through the cool interior of the chauffeur-driven car as they left the pack of photographers behind and headed back to his apartment. She blamed him for the press interest. Anger glittered in her eyes, making them spark with gold, but he couldn't be swayed by it. Couldn't allow it to affect him. Allow *her* to affect him.

'But nobody will be in any doubt our engagement is real.' He tried to control the rollercoaster of emotions he was suddenly on. A rollercoaster that was beginning to reveal the things he'd long since locked away. 'Or that we are in love.'

'You could have warned me,' she snapped and looked out of the window as the city's streets passed by.

He shrugged when she looked back at him. 'Why? You handled it like a pro. It's part of our deal, is it not? And, more than anyone else, I want my brother, Enzo, to believe our marriage is real.'

'Well, he won't miss that when it hits the headlines tomorrow.' She frowned at him. 'Why is it so important he knows?'

He didn't want to tell her, but something inside him snapped. The barrier of resistance broke and the pain of losing his twin, slowly but surely, since his mother's death, flowed freely. Along with the need to talk about him. To confide in Kaliana.

'I haven't spoken to my brother for several years. At least not properly. Not as a brother.'

He could see again his brother's angry face as they'd stood beneath the shade of a line of tall slender cypress trees at Villa Casella. He'd accused Rafe of gloating over his possible marriage break-up, of wishing it would happen. They had slipped so far apart. Torn by their love for the same woman. But now Rafe didn't want that bad feeling to continue, didn't want to force guilt on his brother. He wanted Enzo to believe he was happy, especially with their father so ill.

His father's diagnosis had made him want to reach out to his twin, to mend the bridge which was in complete danger of collapse. Emma would want that too and he wanted to make Emma happy.

'What was the argument between you about?' The

sharpness in Kaliana's voice had lessened, luring him into opening up—just a little.

It was as if Enzo was standing there with him right now. The words he'd said that day, the day his world had fallen apart, had been so cold. He could still hear them.

'Emma loves *me,* Rafe. And I love her. We are getting married.'

Rafe had retaliated and the argument which had followed had been loud and heated. Since then they had avoided one another, which meant Rafe hadn't had to see Emma with Enzo, but if she was happy then he was too. And Enzo and Emma had been happy—until the devastating news that Enzo couldn't father children. Children Emma had wanted. Children the Casella family had needed.

It had also put the spotlight on Rafe. The spare heir. Losing Emma had nearly killed him, and he certainly didn't want the dubious honour of producing the next Casella generation. Another reason why Enzo probably hated him even more.

Rafe looked at Kaliana. She was an only child. Would she understand sibling rivalry? Understand what being a twin meant? 'We compete for everything. Always have done and Emma was no exception.'

'Everything?' she asked quietly, unlocking more memories. Moments from his and Enzo's past that had become the foundation for the cold indifference between them when they were apart and the heated exchanges whenever they came together.

The car hummed along the streets of Rome, the evening lights dancing around the interior. Being in the sanctuary of the car, surrounded by Kaliana's concern and interest, pushed Rafe further away from his defensive wall. Taking her with him. Allowing her in.

The danger of allowing Kaliana in outweighed the pain of those memories. The realisation that it shouldn't have been like that. He and Enzo were twins, but that had never meant anything to Enzo. 'At school it was grades. At home it was the attention or approval of our parents.' The echo of that constant need to please his father, to gain his respect, lingered painfully. Respect that Enzo had received so easily. Maybe that was why their mother had favoured Rafe. Or at least that was what Enzo had always claimed, always jealously taunted him with.

Rafe continued, lost in the past, 'Then as we grew older it was women, business deals.'

'It doesn't have to be that way, Rafe. You should send him an invitation to the engagement party—and the wedding.' He could see Kaliana's mind working. Could see the rush of questions going through her mind. If only she knew the truth. 'You could mend it. Get your brother back. Your twin.'

As they exited the car, Rafe inwardly flinched. Kaliana had hit the target. He did want his brother back. The brother who'd played as a young boy at Pietra Bianca with him. The brother who'd had his back when they started school. But not the brother who'd turned against him, taking from him the woman he'd loved.

'I really think you should.' Kaliana pushed home her point, seeing the uncertainty in his expression as they entered the apartment. 'Our marriage is about securing our families and surely your brother won't want the

Casella wealth to pass to a more distant relation. One who doesn't bear the Casella name.'

Target achieved. She felt the dart of her words strike its centre.

Rafe looked at her, as if seeing her for the first time. Or at least seeing her as an ally in the path they had both chosen together.

He moved closer to her. She held her breath as he stood looking down at her, so close now she only had to move forwards a little to step into his arms. To reach up and kiss him.

Gently, he brushed her hair back, using that sexy smile he must know she couldn't help but react to. 'You are right.'

'I know I am.' She smiled, flicking her brows up in the way she had the first time they'd met. The bold woman she'd been that evening, the woman he'd made her, had pushed back all pretence of being a princess making a marriage of convenience. She was now a woman who knew what she wanted—Rafe.

He laughed, that soft sexy sound which melted her core, shattered her defensive barrier, allowing him in. Allowing him emotionally close. 'You are also quite the seductress.'

'But that's what you like about me, isn't it, Rafe?' she teased him, leaning closer, pressing her lips together, inviting his kiss. Challenging him to refuse.

She couldn't help herself. He did something to her. Changed her with just a smile. All she wanted now was a repeat of the last time they had been alone. The difference this time was that Rafe was the one trying to shut himself away, be someone he wasn't.

'Rafe?' she questioned gently, knowing what would

happen when he kissed her. Knowing the explosive chemistry between them would be too much to ignore. Knowing the desire which hummed through the very essence of her body was sparking between them. Knowing once she kissed him back, allowed the desire to take over, she would be lost. She was mad. Insane. But she wanted that madness. It made her feel alive. Real.

She wanted them both to feel the desire, to forget everything, lose themselves in the passion.

Rafe wrapped his arms around her, pulling her against him, the evidence of just how much he wanted her unmistakable. His dark eyes bored into hers and her heart pounded, echoing the beat of desire deep within her.

She brushed her lips over his then stepped back from him. Testing him. Teasing him. Slowly she reached out, taking his hand, gently pulling him away from the window. She didn't want to say anything. Didn't want to break the spell.

'Don't do this, Kaliana,' he said, his voice rough and deep. Wild and feral. 'Not unless you want a repeat of London.'

'I want that, Rafe. Tonight, I want that.'

His kiss, hard and demanding, told her all she needed to know. He wanted it too. He wanted her. Right now, it didn't matter what outside influences had brought them together; all that mattered was this passion. This desire. This need for one another.

She kissed him back, allowing the passion she'd held back to flow freely. With a feral growl full of hungry desire, he swept her from her feet, carrying her to the bed. He laid her on it, standing over her as he pulled his bow tie undone, his eyes never leaving hers.

'*Dio mio*, I can't help myself.' He tossed the tie aside, hastily opening his shirt buttons.

She smiled up at him, loving the power of this moment. The power she had over him. She sat up, grabbed at his open shirt, pulling him closer, forcing his body onto her as she lay back on the bed. She was going to take this moment, this night, and lose herself in it. Lose herself in the lovers' game. 'Then don't.'

CHAPTER SEVEN

THE EARLY SEPTEMBER heat in Sicily did little to calm the scorching memories of the week Kaliana had just spent with Rafe in Rome. For one whole week they'd spent every night together and, much as she'd tried not to, Kaliana knew that each time they'd made love she'd become a little closer to Rafe. By day they had held hands as they'd explored the city and it had felt so much more than just an act. At night the explosive passion had backed that up and Kaliana had begun to open her heart to him.

She looked at Rafe as he joined her in the large open-plan living room of Villa Casella after having talked with his father. He took her breath away. His tall, athletic body she knew so well, dressed in a dark suit which emphasised his masculinity to perfection. His sex appeal. As he crossed the room and poured them both a glass of red wine, she couldn't take her eyes off him. She was falling harder for him every day.

How had she let that happen? How had he slipped beneath the barriers she'd erected around her heart to keep Alif in and other men out? She hadn't wanted to feel anything for another man, believing it would be almost as bad as adultery. Why wasn't she doing anything to stop herself falling in love with Rafe?

Her love for Alif was dimming, and it felt both liberating and sad.

Would Alif really have denied her love and happiness? He'd been such a kind and caring man. So eager to please her that he'd agreed to not having sex until they were married. She'd saved herself for Alif, but fate had changed that. Changed her.

Rafe handed her the glass of wine, drawing her from her melancholy thoughts, a sexy smile on his lips, that desire-laden darkness in his eyes. She knew that Alif would never have begrudged her happiness. Even if that meant loving another man. He would have been the first person to tell her to go out there and live her life. Find love again.

So why couldn't she? Even when it was so tantalisingly close to her.

You're scared of the pain. Pain that will come when the heat of attraction cools.

'You look beautiful tonight.' Rafe's eyes devoured her, making her body tingle with need. Heat unfurled within her as she recalled how often they'd made love in Rome. The first night had been so hot. So wild. She'd slept entwined in his arms, blissfully happy. That slumber had been invaded by yet more desire and in a sleepy haze he'd made love to her again, but that time it had felt so different, so intimate. She'd felt the heat of him as he'd entered her, skin against skin, and the freedom of that had pushed her over the edge, instantly dragging him with her, blocking out the reality of what was happening. The consequences which could follow. Something she now increasingly worried about.

'Thank you,' she said softly, taking a sip of the velvety red wine. She pushed that worry aside. After all, they would soon be married. She lowered her lashes as the hot memory of that moment of pure, unadulterated freedom fired desire through her once more.

'If you continue to look at me like that, I'll be forced to take you to my room—right now.' He moved a little closer, the spark of sexual energy jumping wildly between them.

She raised her brows at him, feeling like the woman who'd walked into that bar the first night she'd met him. The woman who'd wanted to cast off all her inhibitions along with her past, and be his for that night. She loved the freedom that memory gave her.

'That would be wholly inappropriate, Raffaele Casella,' she taunted, looking at him as she tasted the berries and the sunshine that had made the wine. 'Your father has allocated us separate rooms, for propriety. And it's something my father will also expect to see in place when he and my mother arrive.'

'Maybe.' He smiled and sipped his wine.

'How is your father today? Will he be well enough to attend the party tomorrow?' Kaliana needed to change the subject, needed to keep herself focused on what was really going on. She couldn't allow the passion, the ever-deepening emotions she felt for Rafe, to cloud the reality of the situation. The cold, practical deal they'd made to marry and have children.

Whatever she did, she had to tell herself that the desire between them was just lust. No matter how much she now secretly yearned for it, that lust could never be love. She had to remember what he'd told her. Like her, he'd loved and lost.

'He is responding well to his treatment, although it is taking it out of him physically.' Rafe stepped back from her. From the spark of sexual energy. 'Our engagement party has given him a new surge of life. He is determined to be well enough to celebrate with everyone.'

The reminder of what tomorrow would bring made her tense. A high society party here, at Villa Casella, to seal the deal she'd made with Rafe. The marriage deal made purely for convenience. Tomorrow, she and Rafe would officially be engaged.

Photographers from *Vive*, Italy's top celebrity magazine, were due to arrive in the morning. The fact that her engagement photos would be seen around the world was daunting enough. But, worse than that, tonight, among the many guests due to arrive, from Franco to Claire, was Enzo.

Kaliana had hoped he would come, hoped that this would be the beginning of the brothers—the twins—creating a new friendship. Rebuilding their relationship. 'It will be nice for him to see Enzo, to have both his sons together.'

'Enzo and I have agreed to put our differences aside,' Rafe said, his shoulders tensing. 'We've agreed to do that because our father is ill. Because he needs to believe we are now united. That together we will ensure the Casella inheritance remains just that. It doesn't mean I have forgiven him for anything.'

'Sometimes you have to let go of things from the past and move on, even if you don't feel good about it.' The words rushed from her and, looking at Rafe, she wondered why she'd said that. Was she trying to help heal wounds between him and Enzo? Trying to make him move on from the loss of his first love? Or was it because she was beginning to feel ready to do just that herself? That she was looking for her own approval.

Rafe looked at her, the hardness of his gaze leaving her in no doubt that her outburst had doused the flames of desire which had been whipping around them just moments ago. Maybe that was for the best.

'Enzo and I have...' he paused as if searching for the right words '...a very complicated past. One that can't just be put aside.'

'You can act like my lover, act as if we are in the middle of a whirlwind romance, for the sake of your family, so maybe, for the sake of your father, you and Enzo can not only portray the image of twins who have forgiven and forgotten, but actually do that. Actually forgive one another.'

Rafe looked away, as if ashamed of his thoughts. 'I'm not sure I can ever forgive or forget what Enzo did. He took Emma from me.'

'And you loved her?' Kaliana stepped forward, sensing Rafe's pain, wanting to help him heal as she was beginning to heal.

He looked up at her, questions and doubt in his eyes where desire had only recently been. 'I can't do this now, Kaliana. I know you mean well, that you think we should mend the broken bridges between us, but it takes two to do that.'

'If Enzo comes tonight?' She asked the question softly.

'Then maybe we can start to rebuild those bridges. But it will take time. And trust. On both sides.'

Had the argument between the twin brothers blown up because Enzo, the eldest, had discovered he was unable to father children? Because he couldn't do the one thing his father expected of him? Or did it go back much further? To Emma? All sorts of questions rushed through Kaliana's mind and she wished Rafe didn't shut her out so much. Wished he'd let her in.

But that would be more like being real lovers. And they weren't. They were acting the roles of lovers. For their own gains. Why did just being with Rafe cloud that sentiment? Make her wish for more?

'Franco and Claire are due to arrive soon.' Rafe's words interrupted her thoughts, bringing her back to reality at a startling speed. He'd clearly put their conversation to one side, focusing instead on what they needed to do as a couple. She wondered if Franco knew the truth of the arrangement, as Claire did. Somehow the idea of Rafe confiding in anyone, even his lifelong friend, didn't seem possible.

'I'm looking forward to seeing Claire,' she said, attempting to put some distance between the feelings deep inside her and the reality in front of her. 'It will be good to catch up.'

'It will be nice to dine with Franco and Francesca as well as Claire, no?' His voice now held that seductive amusement she found so hard to resist.

She loved the way he added no to the end of his questions. As if he doubted she could ever agree with him. It was just one of the many things about Rafe she'd grown fond of during their time in Rome.

'It will be really nice for Claire and Franco to meet and get to know one another.' Kaliana smiled up at him, revelling in the gentle closeness surrounding them— as if he cared, even though he'd actively shut her out emotionally once more. 'After all, they will be best man and bridesmaid.'

'*Sì,* it will be a good thing. And Franco tells me Francesca is excited to see you again,' Rafe said, that hint of amusement lingering in his voice.

'I don't think she believes it's possible the most untameable bachelor is getting married,' Kaliana teased him. She couldn't help herself.

'Is that what I am?' He moved closer to her again, the coldness of their discussion about Enzo seemingly forgotten.

'Didn't you know that?' She laughed. 'The headlines after our night out in Rome said that a mysterious princess had tamed the world's most untameable bachelor.'

'Mysterious.' He moved closer. 'I like that.'

'And being tamed?' she teased him again, unable to help herself. Especially when she knew that next he would brush his lips over hers in a sexy and very teasing kiss.

As if he read her thoughts, he smiled then lowered his head, brushing his lips over hers. 'It's a pity we are to be apart tonight, no?' he whispered against her lips. She laughed softly, like a teenager who'd finally got to go out with her crush.

'So the rumours are true.' A new voice broke into the sensuality of the moment. Kaliana sprang back from Rafe, turning to see a man who could only be Enzo. Inwardly she sighed with relief. He'd come. There was hope of making things right. That had to happen. Deep down she knew that whatever was going on between these two was linked to Rafe's impenetrable barriers.

She watched him as he walked into the room, as tall and as powerfully commanding as Rafe, but there was a hard edge to his expression. The hope that Rafe and his twin could mend things faded slightly.

'By that, I assume you mean that my fiancée and I are very much in love?' Rafe's voice bristled with irritation. And something else. Warning.

'And there I was thinking you'd finally decided to do your family duty and marry for the good of the Casella name. To have the heir we all need.' Enzo's voice was cautious as he came to stand in front of them, looking at her.

She could hear his unspoken questions. This was the one person Rafe had wanted to believe the whirlwind romance story. But from the look on Enzo's face, Kaliana suspected he wasn't fooled. He knew it was a marriage deal to keep the family fortune. Something he was unable to do himself. She couldn't tell Rafe now, that maybe she already carried the heir they all required. It would have to wait until they were married. Until Rafe and Enzo had rebuilt their relationship.

'So, tell me…' Enzo directed the question at her, smiling, the same curve to his lips as Rafe. She forced her thoughts back. Focused on the moment. 'How did my brother persuade a princess to become entangled in the Casella family?'

'Enzo…' Rafe growled, moving closer to Kaliana, putting his arm around her, drawing her against him. Staking his claim on her.

That possessive action was because Enzo had stolen his first love, Kaliana reminded herself, nestling even closer to Rafe as the need to stand up for him—for them and what they were doing—surged forwards. 'It was one of those instant attraction moments,' she said quickly, trying to deflect the tension which was weaving around them. Tightening its grip. 'And we haven't looked back since, have we, Rafe?'

Rafe's arm tensed around her and her heart began to race. 'No, we haven't.'

Enzo turned his full attention onto her. That expression of doubt she'd seen so many times before tugged at her guilty heart. He had the same seductive and very sexy smile that Rafe had. It made her pulse leap. Not with attraction, as with Rafe that very first night in London, but with her own loss and fear. She shouldn't allow it, but the worry of consequences from that night in Rome was seeping ever deeper.

Shock was the motivator for that pounding in her head. Shock that right now, right here, in front of his twin, the brother he'd already lured a woman away from, Enzo was once again turning on the charm. Was he really trying to seduce her away from Rafe—his own brother? Or was it to make a point? To prove that he knew the love between them wasn't real. Was he testing her?

Enzo must know they were acting. That it was all role play. He was trying to seduce the truth from her.

'That's very convenient,' Enzo said, his brows flicking upwards suggestively.

'Enough.' Rafe's voice was steady. Hard. Enzo turned his attention to his brother as Rafe continued. 'Kaliana is my fiancée, the woman I will be making my wife, and you will show her some respect.'

The hot sultry evening air froze around them. The crackle of ice hardening, filling the air, was laden with gut-wrenching tension.

Enzo turned to Kaliana. 'My sincere apologies.'

Before she could see what was coming, Enzo moved towards her, the customary kiss on each cheek planted on her. It was like being in a tug-of-war—Rafe rigidly holding her close, keeping his arm around her, Enzo following the expected protocol. Kaliana knew for sure he was exploiting it to goad Rafe.

'Apologies accepted.' She pulled back.

Voices in the hallway alerted Kaliana to Claire's arrival and when her friend walked in, accompanied by the tall and distinguished Franco, with Francesca looking so elegant that Kaliana wanted to rush off and change her emerald-green dress, she breathed a sigh of relief.

'Claire, thank goodness you are here.' She all but dragged her friend into the room, relief bursting through her. Finally, she could talk to someone about the confusion of emotions pounding through her.

'Problems?' Claire whispered as she glanced at Rafe and Enzo, now greeting Franco and Francesca.

'It's probably just me. I'm really nervous,' Kaliana said quietly, keeping the smile pinned to her lips as she felt Enzo's scrutiny on her once again. She couldn't say anything here. Not yet. 'Who wouldn't be nervous? I'm engaged. And very soon I'll be married.'

Claire took her hand, squeezing it reassuringly, and Kaliana relaxed. Claire understood and, more importantly, she was here for her. A friend she could rely on. A friend she could trust. Even with her worst fear.

'I think I may be pregnant,' she whispered.

Claire laughed softly, rubbing Kaliana's arm. 'Does it really matter now if you are?'

Rafe watched Kaliana as she spoke to Claire, the women's friendship and support clear. Guilt rushed through him. He should have backed Kaliana up. Should have told Enzo he and Kaliana were in love. Instead he'd remained silent while she'd stood up to Enzo. He'd allowed the past to rear its head again. He turned his attention to Enzo and Franco, the flurry of Italian now flowing between them as Francesca listened intently. He needed to get Enzo alone, needed to discuss things privately with him.

'Marriage will suit you,' Franco said to Rafe, drawing him from his thoughts. His friend smiled warmly at Francesca as he wrapped her close to him, the love between the couple as clear as the sparkling sea surrounding Sicily. The kind of love he'd thought he'd had with Emma, before Enzo had taken her from him. Could he have got that so wrong?

'Kaliana is very beautiful.' Francesca smiled, looking across the room to where Claire and Kaliana were deep in conversation. With her emerald-green dress hugging her slender figure, she looked the picture of elegance. Regal elegance. Every inch the Princess.

'She is, yes,' Rafe agreed. 'She is beautiful—inside and out.'

Watching Kaliana, he realised she was exactly that. But more startling was the realisation that she was so like his mother—a woman with strength and compassion in equal measures. The kind of woman his mother had urged him to find. The kind of woman who didn't deserve to be trapped in a loveless marriage. A woman who deserved to be loved.

Kaliana was everything he needed to put the hurt behind him without tarnishing the memories of happier days by dragging the past into the present.

So why couldn't he let her in?

Why did he want to push her as far away as possible emotionally?

'I see she's already got to you,' Franco said, his voice full of amusement. Then his expression turned more serious as Enzo was greeted by another guest, becoming embroiled in conversation. 'Don't shut her out, Rafe. It may be a marriage of convenience, but she is just what you need.'

Instantly Rafe was on his guard. 'I don't understand what you're talking about.'

Franco knew. He knew their romance wasn't real. Rafe couldn't have this conversation. He couldn't have this manly heart-to-heart right here, right now. He glanced at Kaliana, at the way the soft evening light glowed in her hair as she stood by the windows opening onto the terrace, her face filled with pleasure and happiness as she and Claire talked and laughed.

Last night, and every other night in Rome, her face had shone with pleasure and desire—desire they'd shared. But could he give her what she really deserved? Could he give happiness? Love?

Kaliana deserved happiness. She was giving up so much to save her small kingdom from financial shame, prevent her people living in poverty. Just like his mother, she had a loving and giving heart. Exactly the kind of woman he should love. But he couldn't. Not until he'd drawn a line under the past. A big bold line.

Yet still he was drawn to Kaliana. She was taking him back to a place he'd never wanted to go again. A place where his emotions would be exposed. A place where those emotions would be so very vulnerable. He couldn't allow that. He couldn't go there again.

'I've seen the way you look at her.' Franco said. Rafe snapped his attention back to his lifelong friend. The only person outside his family who knew everything, who knew all the pain he'd endured. He was the only man who knew why he'd barricaded his heart.

'You have seen through our façade. And yes, I do like for her, but convenience is the only reason we are marrying,' Rafe said after ensuring Enzo was out of earshot. 'What you think you see is just the charade of being lovers.'

'And you, my friend, forget I know you as well as you do. Maybe even better than you know yourself.' Franco placed his hand on his shoulder, a knowing smile on his face.

'Now you are talking nonsense,' Rafe said, unnerved by the way Franco went straight to the core of his fears. The reason why Rafe had to ensure that the sizzling attraction between him and Kaliana remained at the forefront of the relationship. That attraction, that sexual chemistry, had to remain his reason for agreeing to their deal as much as fulfilling his duty. Nothing else could ever become the reason.

'Hi.'

Kaliana's voice, as she and Claire joined them, jolted Rafe from his traitorous thoughts.

'This is Kaliana's friend Claire, and this is Franco and his lovely wife, Francesca.' Rafe made the introductions, aware of Claire watching him. He could feel her disapproval. Her doubt. Was he to be cross-examined by both Franco and Claire?

Francesca moved towards Kaliana, kissing her warmly on both cheeks. 'It's so lovely to see you again and be here to celebrate your engagement.' She then embraced Claire in the same way, with the same warm welcome. 'And to meet you, Claire.'

Kaliana had found it difficult to relax as the formal meal started. The small group had enjoyed lively conversation but, by unspoken agreement, nobody had mentioned their engagement, or the impending wedding.

That, together with her ever-increasing worry, had been so overwhelming that she hadn't able to face going into her room alone after everyone else had retired for the night. Instead she slipped out into the peace and quiet offered by the villa's terraces. The velvety black sky cloaking everything in softness, soothing the ache in her heart.

She inhaled a deep breath of the warm scented air, hugging her arms about her. The sounds of the night calmed her. She rubbed her hands up and down her arms, slowly beginning to relax.

The time she'd spent in Rome with Rafe had been like living in a bubble. A bubble of passion and happiness. A bubble where she'd begun to dream, begun to wish and want for more. Now the reality of what their engagement would mean, and their wedding, began to banish that relaxed state she'd managed to find.

'Couldn't sleep without me?' Rafe's teasing words startled her and she whirled round to face him. He'd discarded his jacket and the white of his shirt was stark and bright in the darkness of the terrace. The array of foliage growing up the trellis as shade against the sun shrouded him in darkness, making him seem more unreachable than ever.

'Something like that,' she said softly, the warm breeze feeling like a caress on her face, reminding her of Rafe's touch. How it felt. How it made her dare to hope. 'It's hard to believe this is really going to happen. That we are going to be married.'

He walked towards her, coming out of the shadows,

and she could see the concern on his handsome face. Feel it with every nerve in her body. It made her breath hitch, her heart race. It was as if he cared. Really cared. Like a lover would.

'It is what you want?' Rafe touched her arms, gently turning her to face him, the concern in his expression so clear, despite his face still being partially shrouded in darkness.

'It's what I have to do, Rafe.' She spoke softly, reservations coursing through her. Regret even. 'Marriage is what I have to do. If not to you, then to Nassif.'

A look of regret crossed Rafe's face that even the darkness of the terrace couldn't hide. Was he wishing he hadn't agreed to their marriage deal?

'You are doing a very honourable thing.' Rafe reached out, brushing her hair from her face. 'Giving up your chance of happiness and love for the sake of your country, your people.'

'It is expected of me, Rafe.' A horrendous thought rushed through her mind. What was he trying to tell her? 'You are having second thoughts, aren't you? You don't want this any more?'

All sorts of scenarios assailed her. Her father's disappointment. The shame she would bring to her family—to the country—if she didn't marry. Because how could she if she carried Rafe's child? The people of Ardu Safra would be forced to live under strict austerity if the country financially collapsed. Or, worse, if her father was forced to step down, unable to solve the issues he'd kept hidden from her for the last five years. What would happen to the country then? To her people? Her family?

It was unthinkable. As unthinkable as the possibility

that she might be pregnant. Because if Rafe was having second thoughts…

'No, I am not having second thoughts.' His soft words dragged her back from the fearful thoughts. 'Like you, this is something I have to do. Marriage is my duty.'

His answer hurt, his honesty cutting to the core. But what would she have done if he'd said something else? If he'd told her he wanted to marry her because he loved and wanted her? It was unsettling to even think of acknowledging this was what she'd secretly hoped for.

'It's always been that way, Rafe.' She couldn't allow him to derail her now. This marriage had to go ahead. For her country's sake—and for hers. Even if she wasn't pregnant, she could not, would not, marry Nassif. 'And once all the requirements of the marriage have been met, we can go our separate ways, live our own lives.'

He smiled at her. Like a lover might. Like he'd done in London that first night and all those nights in Rome. 'It will take some time to meet all the requirements, no?'

She pressed her eyes closed, hoping he couldn't see her face in the dark. Hoping he wouldn't notice her despair.

'Is it so bad, *cara*?' He spoke softly, gently lifting her chin, giving her little choice but to look up at him. She opened her eyes. Saw that all too familiar desire in his. 'When we have something so good?'

'No,' she whispered, feeling herself drawn to him, being lured closer, like a bee to a newly opened flower. She wanted him. Wanted him to want her. 'No, it isn't.'

He pressed his lips to her forehead and, closing her eyes, she inhaled deeply, trembling with need. And something more. Something far more dangerous to her heart.

'Rafe…' she whispered. Unable to understand the emotion filling her right now. One she couldn't bear to name.

She opened her eyes, pulling back to look up at him. Desire filled his eyes.

'I don't want to let you go tonight,' he whispered, the soft evening breeze turning those words into a caress. Or was that her wishful thinking?

'We have to be apart,' she said, desperate to prevent her words becoming a husky whisper. 'Here, and again when we are in Ardu Safra, before the marriage ceremony.'

'Are you saying I cannot make love to you until our wedding night?'

She smiled up at him, revelling in the knowledge that he wanted her. It gave hope. Stirred those emotions she couldn't admit to. 'Yes,' she whispered.

'But you don't want that, do you, *cara mia*?' He was teasing her again.

'No, I don't.' Boldly she made her claim, looking at him from beneath lowered lashes. 'But it's what we must do. We are marrying for tradition and we must uphold that tradition.'

'That is Princess Kaliana talking,' he said firmly, his eyes sparking with desire and laughter.

'Kaliana will have to wait her turn.' She laughed.

'Then I will say goodnight.' He gently drew her closer and Kaliana moved willingly against him, feeling every hard contour of his body. A body she knew and loved so much.

'She will be back,' she whispered against his lips, unable to help herself, as he lowered his head to kiss her. 'But not until we are married.'

The light teasing touch of his lips became hard. Demanding. Instantly her body was alight. Needing his. His hands splayed out across her back, keeping her body close against his, leaving her in no doubt as to how much he wanted her. His other palm skimmed down her side, his fingers brushing briefly against her breasts, making her sigh into his kiss.

'Can she wait that long?' he whispered, his forehead pressed against hers.

Her body was pounding with need. Screaming with desire. She couldn't give into either. If she did, she'd be opening the doors to the feelings she hadn't wanted. Emotions she'd thought she'd never feel again. Emotions she knew he wouldn't—couldn't—ever feel.

'She can.' She almost gasped out loud as he kissed her neck. Damn him, he already knew just where to kiss her. And how. 'And she will.'

'Spoilsport,' he said as he stepped back from her, his breathing deep and as uncontrolled as hers.

'Our deal has to come first, Rafe.' She dragged the Princess to the fore. Hauling out all the reasons they were marrying as defence against the one thing she didn't want to feel again.

He nodded slowly, seeming back in control of himself. 'You are right.' He held out his hand to her. 'Shall we retire to our very separate rooms?'

Kaliana took his hand. Princess Kaliana would have flounced past him, but she couldn't. He was offering her one tiny bit of romance, one small gesture of caring. And she, Kaliana, needed that almost as much as she needed him.

CHAPTER EIGHT

RAFE HAD ENDURED a restless night after he had escorted Kaliana to her room. He'd lain awake for hours, his body craving hers, but it was the expression on her face, the softness in her eyes hinting at so much more, which haunted him.

As that softness, the same loving glow Emma had once had in her eyes for him, had burned brighter, he'd inwardly panicked. Was it possible that Kaliana felt something for him? That she could be falling in love with him? He didn't want or deserve her love.

The startling revelation had rocketed through him and he'd watched her slam down the shutters on her emotions. He'd seen the moment she stopped being Kaliana, the woman he'd met that first night in London, and become Princess Kaliana, the woman he was marrying. A marriage for duty and tradition. For both of them.

Now, on the evening of their engagement party, he waited at the bottom of the grand staircase in Villa Casella. As of this evening they were officially engaged, their wedding just weeks away. For both of them, their lives would change once they were married.

He waited, his heart thudding. Who would come

and stand at the top of the stairs and look down at him? The woman he'd first met? The fiery passionate woman whose virginity he'd taken? Or the cool and aloof Princess, bound by duty to do what was necessary? He wanted—no, needed—the emotionless and practical Princess. He didn't want to have to look into the eyes of the woman who'd strode into the bar that night in London. The night he'd been drowning his sorrows over the marriage he had been forced to make. The night she had been looking for something—someone—to take her mind off her problems.

Above him a door clicked open, and then shut. He clenched his teeth, biting down hard. She had to be the Princess. If he saw any softness on her face, any hint of what he'd seen so briefly last night, he wouldn't be able to go through with this at all. He looked upwards, the intricate wrought iron balustrades allowing him to see who was on the landing.

Red silk of a long dress was all he could see at first as she moved to the top of the stairs. Rafe slowly lifted his eyes, looking up to the figure of the woman who'd ignited such passion in him he was in danger of forgetting himself. Forgetting what he needed to do.

As he looked into her eyes, she remained still, looking down at him. He could feel those gold-flecked eyes of hers taking in every detail. Was she too fighting the urge to turn her back on her duty, her family?

His gaze met hers. Showering over him like the first flurry of snow in winter. Soft, yet bitterly cold. The eyes of Princess Kaliana. She stood defiantly at the top of the stairs, dressed in the most stunning red strapless ball gown. She looked…amazing. Every inch the Princess that she was. The Princess he needed her to be.

Behind him he heard gasps, then Franco's soft chiding as he guided his wife away. 'Let's leave the lovers in peace.'

Rafe smiled at his friend's far from subtle comment. He and Kaliana might well be lovers, passionate lovers, but they were not *in love*.

Or at least that was what he'd thought—until last night.

Rafe moved to the bottom step, holding out his hands as Kaliana came down. Regal elegance shone from her like the brightest star.

'So, this is it,' she whispered to him. 'The moment everything becomes official.'

Rafe smiled. 'Very official. Especially when you wear these.'

He'd been holding the box containing the priceless Casella necklace, earrings and bracelet so tightly he almost couldn't move his arm, couldn't show her the box. His movement was far from fluid as he opened the box, holding it out to her.

'I wasn't expecting this.' Her gorgeous eyes were wide with shock and beneath her polished exterior he'd glimpsed the Kaliana he really wanted. The Kaliana he couldn't have. Didn't deserve.

'The Casella jewels.' He forced the words out, pushing back those useless sentiments. 'And as the next Casella bride you will be expected to wear them tonight.'

Once he'd dreamt of giving them to Emma. Then she'd left him for Enzo. They had run away to marry in guilty secret, shunning that tradition.

'I can't wear these.' She reached out to touch them, proving that, like most women, she could be won over by the sparkle of a diamond or two.

'They are yours to wear today, our official engage-ment, and on our wedding day.'

He could see the question in her eyes. Hear her ask-ing if Enzo had given them to his bride too. 'My mother was the last Casella bride to wear them. Enzo chose to marry in secret, so deprived his bride of that honour.'

As the explanation surged forward, Rafe realised he was happy it had happened that way. And that at least Enzo had had the decency to be guilty about all he'd done, running away with the woman his twin brother loved. In a rush of something he'd never taken the time to consider before, Rafe realised that Enzo had taken Emma away and married her because he was ashamed of what he'd done to his own brother.

'I see,' she said, her voice stern. 'In that case, can you...?' She gestured to the box in his hand, the unfin-ished question hanging between them.

He looked at her. At the bright gold flecks in her eyes now sparkling like angry fireworks. '*Sì, cara*, I can.'

He turned, laying the box on the hall table, taking out the heavy diamond necklace. He opened the clasp and looked at her, his eyes holding her gaze. Deep in those gold-flecked depths he saw fear. As if she was sacrificing herself.

Without a word she turned her back to him and waited. He allowed himself the guilty luxury of study-ing her naked shoulders before moving forward, encir-cling her body with his arms and the necklace, so that he could place it at her throat. She tensed as he fastened it. As his fingers brushed her skin her head bowed and she placed her palm over the gems.

Her breathing had become deeper and he fought the urge to turn her in his arms, to tell her it didn't have to be this way. To tell her it didn't have to be all about duty. That together they could both move forward. Slowly they could both regain their shattered belief in love.

What the hell was he thinking?

'Very beautiful,' she whispered as she turned to him, removing one of her small diamond studs in readiness to replace it with the matching earrings from the set. 'I had better wear it all, enter fully into the tradition, yes?'

'It will be expected of you.' He reached out, picking up one earring, its weight immense. And he was handing that weight of duty to Kaliana. The woman he could love, if only he had time to heal. If only she too could heal.

He watched as she put the earring in place then passed the second one, the weight of it more noticeable—the weight of his duty. His family duty.

She fastened the earring and picked up the bracelet, her arm brushing against him as she leant forward. 'Last one.' She smiled up at him. A smile which didn't quite reach her eyes. Did she sense the weight of those jewels, sparkling against her skin?

Kaliana could scarcely breathe. Rafe's fingers lingered on her skin, sending a flurry of hot desire-filled sparks through her. But, beneath her fingertips, the coldness of the jewels sealed their deal.

She would be a Casella bride. A deal to secure the future of the ancient Sicilian name with an heir. He was to be her husband, the man who saved her kingdom from financial ruin and her from a cruel loveless marriage.

She should be pleased. Relieved. It was going to happen. So why did she feel so disappointed? Why did she want more than that?

'They are very beautiful. I'm honoured to wear them.' The lie slipped with ease from the mouth of a princess trained from an early age how to be cool and calm. Unaffected. The Princess she now had to be if she stood any chance of holding onto her sanity in front of her parents and every other guest.

'As are you, *cara mia*.' Rafe's words were like a caress, the hungry look in his eyes as he looked at her real. She had to remember he performed the act of being in love almost to perfection. She couldn't forget what he'd told her. That love didn't have a place in his life.

She couldn't allow herself to weaken. Her heart was in danger of really falling in love with him.

He brushed her cheek with the backs of his fingers. 'Don't look so worried. Everything is going well. Even Enzo believes we are in love.'

'Enzo?' she questioned, the weight of those jewels increasing as all he'd told her about his mother being the last bride to wear them raced through her mind once more. Wouldn't her wearing them cause more upset between the two brothers? Discord she wanted to end.

'Will my wearing these cause more problems between you and your twin?' She couldn't hold the question back. Couldn't help but try to mend things. 'You should find a way to make it right between you and Enzo. I'm sure your father wouldn't want it, and your mother...'

She couldn't stem the flow of words. Couldn't stop herself from trying to help him. If she'd had a brother or sister, she wouldn't want animosity between them, simmering away.

'He may not be pleased, but he and his wife chose to

slip away and marry in secret—his bride had no right to wear these jewels.' Rafe cut across her.

'I'm sorry, Rafe.' She moved closer, placing her hand on his chest, feeling the soft material of his tuxedo. 'It must be hard to lose your brother like that, especially now the problems he's had in his marriage have affected your life.' If she kept these things at the forefront of her mind, she'd remember why he was doing this. Why he was marrying her. She had to remember that.

'Hard doesn't come close.' He sighed, then smiled. 'But none of this is about Enzo—or his wife. This is about us and right now we have guests to showcase our romance to.'

'Then let's go,' she said, pasting a bright smile on her face.

He took her hand. 'We make a great team, Kaliana.'

Her heart broke. The heart that loved Rafe.

His hand, wrapped around hers, was warm. Safe. Secure. She looked up at him as he walked just a pace ahead of her, taking her into the crowd of friends and family. As she followed, the truth hit her. Hard.

She was in love with him.

For her, this engagement, this impending marriage deal, had now become very real. It was now so much more than a deal. So much more than a fake romance to be acted out in front of their friends. Whatever the outcome of their nights in Rome, she was in love with him.

Rafe spoke first in Italian to those around them and she listened to his sexy voice, keeping a smile on her face when all she wanted to do was run and hide from the turmoil of her emotions. When he spoke again in English, talking to her parents, the realisation that she'd fallen in love with another man, putting Alif in the past, surged forwards. It was nothing compared to the future she would now face, married to a man who couldn't love her as she loved him.

'*Congratulazioni.*' The cheers went up from the crowd and glasses were raised at them. She kept her mask of happiness on her face. Kept hold of Rafe's hand.

His fingers were clasped around hers firmly, the warmth on her skin a reminder of the heat of the passion they'd shared. But was that passion enough? Again, doubts surfaced, threatening to manifest themselves into something bigger. Something she wouldn't be able to ignore.

She had to remember their deal. Remember the real reason she'd come to Rafe, a man she'd shared just one night of passion with. It was because she couldn't face life as Nassif's wife—married to a man as cruel and cold as Alif had been gentle and warm.

That is why you are here now. She forced those words into her mind, looking up at Rafe as romantic music began to filter through the warm evening air, refusing to give more thought to her increasing worry.

Rafe smiled at her, his eyes alive with amusement. Had he sensed her turmoil? Somehow heard her inner reasoning? 'We will be expected to start the dancing, *cara.*'

His voice was warm. Deep and sexy. It helped her to remember why she'd asked him to marry her. Why she'd thought she could spend the rest of her life as this man's wife.

Passion. Hot, sultry passion.

'Then we had better dance.' She glanced at her father as the array of emotions rushing through her for this man, and this situation they were in, made her voice husky, almost a whisper.

Rafe looked at her, his expression questioning. Did he see her doubts? Sense her fears? She looked away at the gathered guests, all expectantly watching them.

He took her hand and led her onto the terrace, now a dance floor, lit by a multitude of twinkling fairy lights. It was far too romantic for the kind of deal they'd struck. Something more suited to a fairy tale romance.

He stopped in the middle of the dance floor, looking so handsome in his black tuxedo, freshly shaved and oozing sex appeal, that her heart stopped before thudding wildly.

If only this was real. If only the complete romantic aura of this moment was real. She wanted to be able to allow herself to love this man. Be loved by him.

He inhaled deeply as he gently held her, bringing her body against his. She closed her eyes, unable to resist melting against him. Unable to resist falling in love with him further.

'You smell so good,' he whispered against her ear. She squeezed her eyes tight shut, a ripple of pleasure slipping over her, like the gentlest wave on a summer day. 'Too good. I don't know if I can hold you close and not kiss you.'

She opened her eyes, a smile coming readily to her lips as she leant back a little, looking up at him. She wanted him to kiss her. Wanted to lose herself in the illusion of love.

'I want you to kiss me,' she whispered as she moved towards him, bringing her lips so close to his.

'Then how can I say no?'

His lips met hers. Gentle and coaxing. Everything

she was struggling to hide rushed forward as she kissed him back.

His palm against the small of her back pressed her against him, but she didn't need that encouragement as her body melted into his. Like wax around a flickering flame, she lost herself to him. To the romance of the moment. To the love for him intensifying with every smile, every caress and kiss.

His tongue invited hers to dance and she sighed with pleasure, accepting that invitation, kissing him deeper, harder. The rush of love hurtling through her made it impossible to remember they were in the middle of a dance floor, being watched by friends and family.

He broke the kiss, tenderly brushing her face with his fingers. 'Very convincing,' he whispered, his eyes as black as the velvety sky at midnight. 'Almost too real.'

'Would real be so bad?' she asked tentatively, her mind, her resolve softened by the moment.

'It's not what we agreed, Kaliana.' His voice became sterner, although still a whisper, even though his fingers continued to caress her face. 'It's not what either of us wanted—or needed.'

'Things can change.' She smiled up at him, then quickly looked down, a blush spreading over her face. She was lost in the romance, still warmed by the love flowing through her. Love for this man. A man who'd actively banished love from his life. His heart. More than anything she wanted to tell him she'd fallen in love with him.

His hold on her slipped. His hand dropped from her face and when she looked back up at him his gaze, his attention, wasn't on her.

Kaliana turned in his loosened hold to look in the direction his attention had been taken. He was watching a woman who'd just walked in and was now mingling with the crowd. Her pale blonde hair stood out amongst the other guests, making her appear lost. Alone.

'Emma…' Rafe breathed the name of the woman he'd once loved and as she looked up at Rafe, then to the blonde, Kaliana knew anything she felt for him was futile. The way he'd said her name told its own story. He still loved Emma. And she was here. To see him?

As all she'd just witnessed, all she'd just realised, sank in, Rafe let her go, moving away from her far more than just physically. Stretching her emotions so taut that at any moment they'd snap with a painful sting.

'Excuse me.' He moved away, leaving her adrift on a sea of emotions she'd never wanted to sail again. Emotions which held pain as much as pleasure.

'Of course.' She stepped away from him. Hating the sensation of total abandonment. She blinked back the threat of tears, annoyed with herself. Annoyed she'd allowed emotion to influence her, to make her want more than she should have.

She turned her back on the image of Rafe striding towards the pretty blonde—the woman who'd held his heart all this time. Had she come to reclaim Rafe? To tell him she'd made a mistake? That she loved him?

Unable to help herself, she watched Rafe as he reached Emma. She didn't need to hear his voice to know his concern for the other woman.

'What's going on?' Claire's voice dragged her from her self-pity, the conclusions she couldn't help but jump to.

She watched as Rafe touched Emma's arm in that same caring gesture he'd used on her. 'She is the woman

Rafe loves. The woman who broke his heart…' She didn't care who overheard. Hurt and rejection cascaded through her like water over the highest falls.

'What?' Claire asked and Kaliana sensed the protective anger in her friend's voice. 'He can't back out now. You'll have to…'

'Marry Nassif,' Kaliana finished for her, then frowned as Enzo joined Rafe and Emma. Kaliana wished she could hear what was being said. She could see Enzo's annoyance in the square set of his shoulders. Emma looked from one to the other, appeal in her expression. Then Rafe hugged Emma. A hug that held so much emotion it broke Kaliana's heart. The heart which had only just accepted it was full of love for the man she was to marry. The man who loved another woman.

'It looks like Enzo and Emma are getting back together.' Franco's accented tones made Kaliana blink. She turned to Rafe's friend as questions fired through her, followed by the tiniest glimmer of hope.

'Back together? Enzo and Emma?'

Franco frowned. 'They are married—separated, but…' He paused as if searching for the right word. Kaliana's mind raced wildly as she watched him. Waiting. 'Circumstances pushed them apart. Rafe has been working hard to engineer this meeting over the last few weeks, sure he can help mend their marriage.'

'Rafe has?' She could feel herself stuttering. Hated herself for it. No wonder there was so much tension between the two brothers. She looked at Franco again. But Rafe had engineered this meeting. What did that mean?

She turned her attention back to Rafe as he moved away from Emma, still looking lovingly down at her. Their gazes were locked, then he turned to Enzo, clasping him in a manly hug before turning and walking away from them both.

'You have to go to him,' Claire said, touching Kaliana's shoulder, pulling her from her stunned and frozen state of shock.

'I can't.' How could she go to him when she'd just seen the truth of the love he still had for Emma? His brother's wife. How could her newly fledged love ever mean more than that?

'Go to him,' Claire urged softly, compassion in her voice. 'Go to him, Kaliana. Tell him.'

Kaliana turned to her friend. 'Tell him what?' She couldn't say anything about the possibility that she might be pregnant. Not now. How could Claire expect her to?

'That you love him.'

Kaliana gasped.

'I know you don't want to admit it, but you have to, Kal. You have to grasp this chance of happiness. Forget your stupid deal. Forget everything else. Even what you told me earlier. Tell him how you feel.'

Claire's impassioned plea made Kaliana's head spin. Were her feelings, the love she'd only just recognised herself, so obvious to others?

'She's right,' Franco said firmly, confirming her suspicion. 'You and Rafe have something. You both need to let go of the past. Embrace it.'

Kaliana looked at Rafe's retreating back as he left the party—their engagement party—heading for the sanctuary and privacy of the villa. Could she do this? Put her heart on the line? Admit she loved him when he clearly still loved another woman?

As the questions whirled in her mind, making her shiver with cold dread, she turned to see Emma and

Enzo embrace. And then Enzo kissed her tenderly on the forehead. He loved his wife. Emma, the woman Rafe also loved.

'No,' Kaliana said, not caring what Franco knew. 'No, I don't love Rafe. We don't have anything. There is nothing between us other than a mutually beneficial marriage deal.'

Rafe stood in the darkness of his office. He'd wanted time. Space. He needed to think. His emotions were running riot inside him. As he'd held Kaliana, as he'd kissed her, he'd felt the overwhelming burn of love. The one thing he didn't want to feel.

Whenever he'd allowed that emotion into his life, his heart, it had always let him down. Always left him in pain.

First his mother. Then Emma. Even his father and brother, damn it. He'd loved them all. And each one of them had caused him pain. It was a story that had repeated itself too many times. Made him question who he was.

'Why didn't you tell me how much Emma still means to you?' Kaliana's gentle question roused him from his self-pity. He turned to see her standing in the doorway, illuminated by the light from the party beyond the darkness of the office he'd retreated to.

The halo of light gave her an unearthly appeal, but he ignored it, focusing instead on her question. 'Even you've got to agree that it's a messy love triangle.' He laughed, realising for the first time just how silly he'd been to try and hang onto Emma, to hang onto the hope that she still loved him.

What kind of fool was he?

'About as messy as the marriage triangle I'm hoping to avoid if I marry you.' Kaliana's voice was harder now. Full of power. Determination. The voice of a princess.

'If?' He remained in the shadow of darkness, while she stood in the glow of light. If he dared to open up to her, dared to tell her that what he'd begun to feel for her far surpassed anything he'd ever felt for Emma, then he could move into that warm light. Step out of the shadows of a life without love. But he couldn't. 'We have a deal.'

'Exactly,' she said seriously. 'We have a deal. A deal the Casella family needs. A deal my country needs. And our feelings are irrelevant.'

He pressed his lips together, inhaling deeply. 'Yes, we have a deal and, whatever happens, I won't back out, Kaliana. I'm a man of honour. A man of my word. A man who will do his duty.'

And that duty was to marry the woman who'd turned his life upside down that first night in London, opening his heart even then.

'Then we should go back out there and undo any damage your moment with Enzo's wife, followed by your disappearing act, has done to our act of a whirlwind romance.' Her sharp words cut him, forcing anything he felt for her into hiding. The Kaliana he'd met, the Kaliana he'd made love to with such passion had already left him.

'That is precisely what we should do, but...' He paused, on the verge of asking her what she really wanted out of the marriage. From him.

'But what, Rafe?' The slap of her question was as stinging as her palm would be across his face.

The way he felt about Emma had never come close to what he felt for this woman. Kaliana made him hopeful for impossible emotions, but the Princess before him was so cold. So distant. Why the hell did he think a woman who'd agreed to have his children in order to save her country from financial ruin could ever have any kind of feelings for him? What kind of fool had he been?

Could he really go through with it? Could he marry simply for convenience when he knew all his mother had wanted was for him to find love and be happy?

'Do you want this deal? This marriage?' The question snapped from him. 'Because I can find a way out.'

'You know I do,' she implored as she moved forward a step. Forward into the darkness. His darkness.

'Why?' He had to hear her say it. Had to hear her cold words.

'Because I can't…' She walked closer, stumbling over her words, darkness enveloping them both. 'I can't marry Nassif. Not because he is older than me. Or cruel. But because I loved Alif, his nephew, the man I should have married.'

Did she still love Alif?

He still loved Emma.

Not in the way he'd once done. Not with passion and desire. He loved her as a friend. Nothing more. And he wanted Emma to be happy; that was why he'd set up the meeting with her and Enzo. He needed to let go of Emma and heal the long-standing coldness between him and his twin.

He looked at Kaliana, at the shadows hiding the expressions on her face. She still mourned and loved her fiancé. Could he ever compete with that? Was he worthy of trying to claim her love? Could he ever forget the past and love her?

He shook his head in answer to that last question. 'If that is what you want, we should get back out there and continue this show of romance.' He held his hand out to her. She looked at it and for a moment he thought she wasn't going to take it.

'It won't be for much longer,' she said as her hand fitted loosely into his. 'Once we are married, we can live separate lives.'

'We can indeed.' Why was he saying that? He didn't want a life separate from Kaliana. She was his life. A life he couldn't have. Her icy-cold words had already made that clear.

'I am returning to Ardu Safra in the morning with my parents.' Her words were so casual, so light and free of any painful emotion that Rafe stopped to look at her, bringing her to a stop too. She looked into his eyes, the gold flecks of hers almost dimming to nothing. He'd done that to her.

'That isn't what we planned, and I have meetings tomorrow. I can't go with you.'

'I know,' she said, her chin lifting defiantly. 'You can follow me there once you are finished—if marriage to me is what you want.'

She was leaving him. The moment his heart had opened up, the moment he'd begun to think he could love again, and she was leaving him. 'Marriage is what I need, Kaliana. What my family needs. I am the only male heir able to create the next generation. I have to marry and have children. If there was any other way, I'd take it.'

She sighed softly. 'You just said you want a way out,

so I only want you to come to Ardu Safra if you want me.' She looked down. 'If you want me to be your wife. The mother of your children.'

'What about your duty? Your country?' He couldn't believe she was doing this. It was almost as if she was saying goodbye.

'I will get married on my twenty-sixth birthday. My father has already seen to that.'

'You'll marry Nassif?'

She nodded, swallowing hard, as if unable to bring herself to agree to that. She pulled her hand free of his, stepping back away from him. 'An arranged marriage is bad enough, but to a man who is in love with another woman? I can't.' She shook her head. 'I'm sorry, Rafe, I have to go.'

Before he could answer. Before he could process everything she'd said, Kaliana turned and walked away. He watched the red silk of her dress as she disappeared upstairs. He should go to her. Tell her he wanted her. Needed her. So why the hell couldn't he?

CHAPTER NINE

THE HEAT OF Ardu Safra was suffocating. Kaliana stood by the open window, breathing in the warm air coming in off the golden dunes of the desert she loved so much, in a futile attempt to ease her discomfort.

For five days she'd relived that last conversation with Rafe. Her heart ached and her body was numb. She felt sick and each day Rafe's silence intensified those feelings. He'd allowed her to walk away the night of their engagement. He hadn't even tried to stop her She'd changed from her red gown, leaving it and the Casella jewels in her room, her heart breaking into so many pieces as she'd prepared to leave.

She hadn't said a word to her father or mother about breaking off the engagement, hoping that Rafe would come, that he'd honour their deal. They'd believed her claim that she wanted time to prepare for the wedding, but each day she'd woken with that heavy dread in her stomach. Deep down, she knew it was more than just dread. Knew it was because she carried Rafe's baby.

Claire's arrival earlier today had at least offered her some comfort, someone to talk to and confide in. She now faced the prospect of admitting to her father not only that the man she'd agreed to marry no longer wanted her, but that because of the baby she couldn't now marry Nassif. Or anyone.

An admission she couldn't make. Didn't want to make. Just as she couldn't yet face finding out for sure if she was pregnant.

Kaliana sighed, turning from the window. For the last hour she'd stood there, barely seeing the golden landscape of her homeland. Once the ability to do just that would have given her so much pleasure. She'd always loved the way the dunes changed as shadow or sunlight fell over them, making them seem alive. Leaving her birthplace to make a new life in London had been hard. Just as hard as finding her dreams shattered after Alif's death. But Rafe's silence was even harder to endure.

She should be about to start her life again in Ardu Safra, with her new dreams. Tender dreams—but they'd been shattered too. Obliterated. And along with them her chance to help her country, her people.

'That sounds like a sigh of defeat,' Claire said from behind her. She heard her friend put down the book she'd been lost in and cross the marble floor, joining her at the window.

'I guess I have to accept Rafe doesn't want to marry me any more,' she said as she listlessly walked into the room, her soft slippers scuffing on the marble floor. How could it hurt so much? How could she feel this rejected when all they'd ever had was an agreement to marry for no other reason than their families demanded it of them?

'Kaliana?' Claire questioned, a worried expression on her face. Kaliana didn't like the question in her friend's voice, or the way she was watching her. 'Before you do anything, before you give up on Rafe, you have to do a pregnancy test. You have to know for sure.'

Kaliana frowned. 'I can't. Even if I happened to have one to hand.'

For a moment Claire hesitated and Kaliana looked at her, sensing the worry, seeing the fear on her friend's face. They'd known each other for five years, since Kaliana had moved to London, but they knew so much about each other it felt like a lifetime. More than anything Kaliana trusted her. Thought of her as her sister.

'I do.' Claire got up and walked quickly to the chair in the corner of the room and grabbed her bag, producing a slim blue and white box, holding it out to Kaliana. 'I got one, knowing you wouldn't be able to easily get hold of one.'

With a sickening lurch of her stomach Kaliana looked at Claire, panic making any words impossible. Could it really be possible? She and Rafe had made love many times whilst they'd been in Rome. Each time he'd used the protection of a condom. He'd never failed to protect either of them—except that one time in the early hours of the morning.

That one time when they'd made love as sleep had tried to hang onto their exhausted bodies. The time when she'd finally accepted she felt something more than just lust for him.

She shook her head in denial. 'I can't be pregnant. We used contraception.' She thought of the way her stomach turned over each morning as she got out of bed, of the waves of nausea which washed over her during the day. Every day since she'd arrived in Ardu Safra. No. She couldn't be pregnant. She couldn't. 'It's just nerves. Worry.'

'Kaliana,' Claire almost snapped. 'You have to do this test.'

'It's just the worry of everything.' Kaliana hotly denied what Claire was saying, even though deep down she knew it was almost certainly true. And where did that leave her?

'Then do this test. Prove me wrong. Prove yourself wrong,' Claire challenged.

'Very well.' There was only one way to find out. Kaliana took the box from Claire with a weak smile.

Kaliana's hands shook as she opened the box. What if she was pregnant? The father a man who didn't want her any more. A man she'd stupidly fallen in love with despite his warnings. *His* warnings that he couldn't love her—or anyone.

'I can't look,' Kaliana said as she opened the bathroom door, returning to her room a short time later, the look of concern and compassion on Claire's face bringing a fresh wave of nausea over her. 'Whatever it says, it won't make any difference. Whatever it was Rafe and I had is over. Finished.'

'Oh, Kal,' Claire soothed as she took the test from her. Kaliana watched her friend's face as Claire looked down at the test, her heart pounding with anticipation. With fear.

The sound of an approaching helicopter above the palace snatched Kaliana's attention from Claire, from the test. She hated those machines now. Hated that they'd taken away the man she'd loved. The man she should have married. Had her father sent for Nassif? Had he sensed there were problems? Had Rafe officially called it all off?

There was no way she could marry Nassif now. Not

just because of the possibility that she carried Rafe's child, but because she loved him. Every limb ached with need for him. For his touch, his kiss. For his love.

Claire's silence suddenly seemed deafening, snatching her back from the thoughts of what love really felt like. She looked at Claire, her head lowered as she held the test in front of her.

'Am I...?' she asked, unable to finish the question. Because, if she was pregnant, she'd just driven away the baby's father with her selfish need for love—as well as destroying the future of her country.

Claire nodded.

The room spun and Kaliana couldn't focus on anything. Blackness, darker than the night sky, swirled around her, making standing up almost impossible. She wanted to give into it. Wanted the darkness to sweep her away. Take her somewhere she didn't have to think. Somewhere she could be alone with the knowledge that she carried Rafe's baby inside her. Somewhere she could be free of the pain of loving a man who would never love her.

Rafe strode into the room he'd been shown to. He hadn't even wanted to see Kaliana's father first. All he'd wanted was her. The doors closed behind him but Kaliana wasn't in the room. Only Claire.

'Where is she?' he demanded as Claire stood up to greet him, thankful that Kaliana's friend had been just that, with her parting advice to him as she'd left Villa Casella only hours after Kaliana.

'Don't give up on love, Rafe—or Kaliana.'

He could still hear her saying those words as the quiet of the house had shrouded them after the guests had gone. He had no idea what Claire had meant and had pushed that sentimental bit of advice to the back of his mind as he'd dealt with his business matters.

But he'd kept hearing it. Over and over. And then he'd known with such absolute certainty it was like standing under an icy shower. He loved Kaliana and if he loved her he needed to set her free from their deal. Give her the freedom to choose who she married. Who she loved. Then hope it would be him.

His business deals had quickly taken second place to negotiations with her father as the two men reached an agreement which financially secured the kingdom of Ardu Safra but meant Kaliana didn't have to marry— him or Nassif—to do that. Just as that had fallen into place Enzo had come to him, telling him about his rec- onciliation with Emma after news from his lawyer re- garding the Casella inheritance. News that freed both Kaliana and himself from their deal in a way he'd never envisaged possible. Once all that was secured, Rafe had left Sicily for Ardu Safra. For Kaliana.

One final meeting with legal teams last night had secured the deal Kaliana's father and he had agreed on. Her father hadn't asked why, but Rafe suspected he knew. Damn it. It seemed everyone knew that he loved Kaliana.

Except Kaliana herself. Something he intended to put right.

'What do you want, Rafe?' Kaliana's voice seemed to tremble even though her expression was firm and strong, but she looked so pale as she came into the room and sat down. Was she ill?

Rafe frowned, moving closer to the woman he loved, but she didn't look up at him. That welcome smile he'd imagined would be on her face wasn't there. She couldn't look at him.

'What's wrong?' When Kaliana didn't answer he looked to Claire.

'I'll leave you both to talk,' Claire said, walking away. Rafe watched her leave the room, even though he suspected she knew what was wrong. He turned his attention back to Kaliana. To her pale cheeks and the tell-tale darkness beneath her eyes. She'd had as little sleep as he'd had. Did she regret walking away? Was there one last ray of hope for him, for them? He'd come here hoping to find it—and the strength to admit what he felt for her. To admit he loved her.

Rafe waited as Claire's retreating footsteps quietened to nothing, the silence in the cool marble room almost screaming at him. Its heaviness filled with uncertainty.

Kaliana stood up, moving towards him slowly, her face so very pale. Her eyes full of sadness. 'Why are you here, Rafe?'

Her question confused him, but he couldn't help his gaze slipping down over her. He'd never seen her dressed in anything so beautiful as the pale blue silk which wound its way around her body, accentuating and yet concealing it. She looked regal. Elegant in the dress of her country. It was as if he was truly seeing her for the first time as a princess. Which made what he'd come here to do, to say, even more important.

'We need to talk.' He saw her lips pressing together, as if she was fighting to hold back her words. 'We need to talk about our deal. Our marriage deal.'

She looked down, becoming even paler. 'Yes, Rafe, we do.' There was resignation in her voice. He didn't want her to resign herself to marriage to him. If they married, it had to be for one reason only. But where did he begin? He couldn't just blurt out that he loved her. After that staunch denial about his ability to love anyone. She'd think it was the deal, his need to marry and produce an heir which drove him.

'When you left Villa Casella, I was sure it was over. Certain you didn't want to marry anyone. Not Nassif. And not me.' He injected firm determination into his voice. The revelations of the last few days, days which had kept him from coming to Ardu Safra, had fuelled that determination. He wasn't about to allow her to walk away from him yet. Not until she knew everything.

Kaliana's breath was dragged in on a ragged inhale, her nervousness all too clear. 'Want isn't part of it, Rafe. We both know that.' She moved away from him, sitting in the seat set beneath the windows, the view of her country spreading out behind her reminding him of who she was. Her eyes were full of sadness as she looked up at him. 'I made a deal, Rafe. A deal I have to keep—for my country's sake, my people's sake, I have to keep that deal. I have to marry.'

'I am here to free you of that deal, that marriage.' He stood firm against the shock rushing over her face. The same shock he'd felt surge through him when he'd realised there was a way out—for both of them. A way for them to be free to explore their love.

Her brows furrowed in confusion. 'How?' She breathed the word as if grasping onto a lifeline, confirming everything she'd led him to believe before she'd left Villa Casella. She didn't want marriage. Because she was still in love with Alif, the man fate had snatched away from her.

'I have put a deal to your father, one that will help

the country's finances and give you the time you need.' Her father had needed little persuading. It seemed he knew, even accepted, that deep down his daughter had no wish for marriage.

She blinked rapidly, sitting up quickly, dragging in a breath and pressing her fingers to her forehead, her face paling. He moved towards her, unable to help himself. Crouching down in front of her, he looked into those gorgeous brown eyes. 'Are you unwell?'

'No.' The word shot from her and she pulled back. 'I just don't understand. Why would you do that? Why would my father even accept it?' She looked up at him. 'Why didn't he say anything to me?'

'I asked him not to.' That got her attention. 'I wanted to tell you myself. Face to face.'

'Then you had better tell me. Everything.' She trembled, looking even paler, and again he worried that she was ill. 'Tell me, Rafe.'

'Your father and I have struck a deal, on the understanding that you do not have to marry at all. The finances of the country are now settled and the pressure off.'

'How?' Her delicate brows furrowed into a frown of disbelief. 'How are they settled?'

'I'm financing the deal.' He didn't want to go into details now. Not when he needed other details. Emotional details.

'Why would you do that?'

'I know you loved Alif. I know you believe you will never find that love again.'

He paused as she looked at him, her head tilting to one side, pain in her eyes, in every line of her frown.

'I did love him,' she whispered as she looked down at her hands, tightly knotted in her lap.

'I know,' he said, lifting her chin up, needing to see her face, her eyes. 'Now you are free to find real love. To marry for love.'

'What about the baby?' The words shuddered from her on a sob. One that was racked with pain.

'The baby?' For a moment everything stopped. The baby he'd needed but hadn't wanted. Now, just like his feelings for this woman, all that had changed. He did want to be a father. But only if this woman agreed to be his wife. And only when she could love him. However long that took.

'You are the only male Casella able to continue the family. You *need* a baby. A son.' There was a hint of hysteria in her voice and he sat next to her, taking her clasped hands between his.

'So much has changed since that night at Villa Casella. Emma…' he began but Kaliana pulled her hands back so quickly the words dried up. Even now, he couldn't believe what he'd learnt about his brother's marriage, or that his father was happy with it.

'You are in love with Emma, I know.' Ice slipped into her words. Her eyes.

Rafe looked down. Damn it, he should have been more honest with Kaliana. More open. Maybe then she'd have seen that the pain of Emma's rejection was keeping him from falling in love with her.

He took a deep breath, looking at her, willing her to understand. 'I was in love with Emma, but not any more. Now I love her as a friend. A sister-in-law. My brother's wife. The woman who, with her husband, my twin brother, is planning to adopt.'

* * *

A wave of nausea rushed over Kaliana and she placed her palm over her stomach. Over the baby she and Rafe had created with such passion. The baby he no longer wanted—or needed. The baby he'd done a deal with her father to avoid having. Panic rushed through her and she grasped at anything.

'What about the Casella heir? The next generation.'

He smiled at her, breaking her heart with the kindness she saw in his eyes. 'Enzo's lawyers have found one small loophole in the inheritance terms. So long as Enzo and Emma officially adopt, that child will be able to inherit. My father is more than happy with that news. As am I.'

He still crouched in front of her, looking at her with concern on his face, as if he knew she was worried about something. She looked into the darkness of his eyes and a smile slipped, weakly and involuntarily, to her lips. 'You'll be an uncle.'

He looked at her, his gaze steady and firm, holding her prisoner. '*Sì*, I will be an uncle. And, thanks to you, to the effort you went to, encouraging me to reach out to Enzo, I now have my brother back.'

'I wish you'd introduced me properly to Emma.' The words lurched from her as she searched his face.

'I should have,' he said, looking down briefly before looking back up into her eyes. The barriers he'd always locked himself behind were down. She could see beyond them. Could she reach the man she loved if she tried? 'I don't know why I didn't.'

But if she didn't reach him… The thought of rejection kept her silent.

'Maybe because our relationship was just pretence.

Because our emotions weren't involved.' He shrugged as if it didn't matter. But it did. It mattered because she loved him.

'What happens now you've made this deal with my father and the Casella heir is secured?' She shocked herself at how businesslike her voice sounded. How calm.

'We are both free of the obligations of our deal. We no longer need to marry.' His jaw was pressed firmly together, and his eyes hardened. He was waiting for her to agree. Waiting for her to free him.

'Then there will be no wedding,' she said, more to herself than Rafe, her mind drifting off with the secret of the baby she carried. Rafe's baby. She didn't want to be set free, but if she told him now? He'd think she wanted him just because of the baby. She looked at him, trying to read his mind. Trying to guess what he wanted. 'And no need to have a baby.'

'No. The deal is off. And one day, when you find love again, you will look back on this moment and thank me.' He stood up. That was it? He was walking out on her.

She dragged in a breath and the words almost tumbled out, but she stopped them. How could she tell him she loved him now? That she'd already found that love? A deep and meaningful love she'd never felt for Alif. How could she say that it didn't matter what deal was on—or off—she *wanted* to be his wife?

Because she loved him.

She pushed her fingers into her hair. She couldn't tell him that, couldn't open her heart to more pain. But she had to tell him about the baby. Whatever else happened, he had a right to know.

'It's really good that everything is sorted, that you

and Enzo are friends again, and that everyone lives happily ever after.' She dragged her hands down through her hair, clutching at the ends of it as if it were her lifeline, looking at him, hating how what she had to say would change everything. 'But there is one problem.'

'Problem?' His eyes narrowed in suspicion.

She lifted her chin determinedly, looking into his eyes, into the darkness that had so often been filled with desire for her. Now they were clouded with something which broke her heart. Fear. Already it seemed he was drawing away from her. He'd made a deal with her father simply to enable him to walk away from her, their engagement. Would he walk away from their child too?

'What problem, Kaliana?' Rafe asked firmly.

She just had to say it. There was no easy way. She took a deep breath, letting it go, looking directly into his eyes. 'I'm pregnant.'

The floor dropped from beneath Rafe's feet. Or at least that was how it felt. Kaliana was pregnant. With his child.

He'd thought he'd got it all sorted. Thought he was doing the right thing—for Kaliana—the woman he loved. He'd thought he was setting her free. She still loved Alif and he couldn't compete with a man who wasn't able to stand there and face him. Not that he'd been able to compete with Enzo, but this was different. This was real. His love for Kaliana was real and he couldn't compete with the memory of Alif. For her love. He had to let her go. Set her free to make her own choices. If what they'd shared since that first night in London meant something to her, there was a chance she might choose him.

He'd intended to stand back and wait, allow her time to adjust to her freedom from the need to marry anyone. But now? Everything had changed. All he'd sorted with Enzo and Emma, with his father and Kaliana's father, had all been in vain.

Kaliana was having his child. A child he didn't even know if he could be a good father to. His doubts crept in like a dark shadow. He'd done it all wrong, let Kaliana down.

'Rafe?' Kaliana questioned, dragging him brutally from his thoughts, pain and fear in her voice. Damn it, he wouldn't let her down. He wouldn't.

'Pregnant?' It was all he could say. He couldn't move to her, couldn't take her in his arms and tell her it would all be okay even though he wanted to. Because he didn't know if he could make this okay. He wanted to tell her he loved her, wanted her to tell him the same.

She was carrying his child. He had to marry her now. He couldn't live with himself if he turned his back on her—on his baby. After a fleeting glimpse of freedom, they were now back where they'd started.

'There was that one night,' she said in a whisper. 'We woke and made love…' She left the rest of the explanation unsaid and memories of that night rushed back at him, of how it had felt to make her his without anything between them. For that short time, he'd been certain there hadn't been any emotional barriers and neither had there been any physical ones.

'Without any protection.' He inhaled deeply. Damn it. This was his fault. He should have protected her, protected them both. Whatever the mood of the moment, he should have protected her. Once again, he'd failed.

She closed her eyes. 'Yes.' Her pained whisper slashed at his heart.

He walked towards her, wanting to reach for her, wanting to hold her, to inhale the scent of her hair as he pressed a kiss onto her head, but her rigid regal stance warned him off. 'This changes things.'

She sighed, a look of resignation sweeping into her eyes, taking the sparkle from them. The sparkle he loved so much. 'I thought it might.'

He searched her face, desperate for a hint of something more than resignation. But nothing. Cool, regal indifference shone back at him from her eyes. He knew, just as she did, that as Princess of Ardu Safra she couldn't be an unmarried mother.

'You can't expect me to turn my back on my child and I'm certain that your father will not tolerate you raising his heir alone. Unmarried. There is only one thing we can do and that is to marry as arranged.'

She looked up at him slowly, as if she couldn't believe what he was saying. 'What about the deal with my father?'

Was that all she could think of? Pain slashed at him like a whip to his flesh. If she had any feelings for him, if she had even the smallest bit of love for him, wouldn't she say it? 'I will honour my deal with your father, just as I will honour my duty to you—and my baby.'

His annoyance at himself, at falling in love—again— with a woman who didn't love him back drove him on, made his words sharp and brittle.

'No.' She backed away from him. 'No, Rafe. I can't marry you.'

'Can't or won't?' The question snapped from him like a firecracker.

'Both.'

He looked at her, seeing the pain in her eyes, in the furrows of her forehead, in the single tear which had slipped from her eye to run down her pale cheek. His heart wrenched. His gut clenched.

'Kaliana, the baby.' He could scarcely breathe. He was losing Kaliana—losing the woman he loved—and he didn't know how to stop it happening.

'When I saw you with Emma…' Kaliana looked down as if afraid to speak, then she looked back up, full of confidence, full of fire '… I knew we couldn't marry. I knew I'd have to return to Ardu Safra and marry Nassif. The deal you've made with my father will save me from that and I appreciate it, but the baby makes no difference. I can't marry you.'

'You appreciate what I have done?' What the hell was going on? Where was the woman who'd loved with passionate abandon in Rome? The woman who'd brought him slowly but surely from the darkness he'd been in since losing Emma? He'd been too stubborn to hold onto Kaliana at the party, to tell her then what he felt, and that stubbornness had given her the chance to walk away from him.

She reached out, placing her hand on his arm. 'Yes, Rafe. For that I am so grateful, but I can't marry you. Now more than ever.'

He drew in a sharp breath, turning from her, striding to the other window, looking out at a landscape that was so alien to him. As alien as the love which filled his heart—for a woman who didn't want him. Didn't love him.

He clenched his jaw as her words replayed in his mind, finally able to form his own words. 'Why not?

You are carrying my baby! You are a princess. You can't have a baby alone.'

'I can have this baby alone and I will. I want to marry for love, Rafe.' Her voice was like a strangled cry and he turned to face her, the distance between them small but insurmountable. 'Not because of a deal. Or the baby. I want to marry for love.'

'Love?'

'Yes. I want the man I marry to love me. I want to marry him for no other reason than he loves me.'

'You don't want to be loved, Kaliana. You've had your love. Isn't that what you told me?' Anger surged through Rafe. Anger for a man who'd made it impossible to reach the woman he loved. Or had that man been him? He had to put his heart on the line, tell her he'd fallen in love with her, deeper, harder than he'd ever loved any woman. But how could he when she was still in love with Alif?

'We are good together. We had something special.' Desperation and frustration fuelled his words like nothing he'd ever known. 'You can't walk away from that, just as I can't walk away from the duty to my child.'

CHAPTER TEN

KALIANA COULDN'T UNDERSTAND what Rafe was saying. First, he'd told her she was free of their deal. That he'd made arrangements with her father, a deal which meant she didn't have to marry anyone. The pain of realising he'd done that because he didn't want to go through with their marriage slashed at her face like tiny grains of sand in a cruel desert wind.

He'd made that deal because he didn't want to marry her. Didn't want to have children. Now that she'd told him she was carrying his child, he was telling her she couldn't walk away. She dragged in a sharp breath of despair. How could he say she didn't want love after everything they'd shared, all those passionate nights in Rome?

Because, for him, each time they'd made love had been nothing more than lust and desire. He hadn't felt love growing for her as she had for him.

She pressed her fingertips to her forehead, inhaling deeply, nausea battling with confusion and heartbreak. 'I do want love, Rafe. I want to be loved, but for me, because of who I am, not anything I can give a man.'

She turned her back on him. This was pointless and she couldn't bear the anger in his eyes. Her heart was breaking, and he'd done little to heal it since he'd arrived. If anything, he'd made it worse. It was duty which forced him to tell her she couldn't walk away from him. Duty to his unborn baby. The child he didn't want.

'You've shut love out of your life, and I get that.' She spoke more calmly now, but she couldn't look at him. Couldn't bear to see the annoyance on his face.

'But, unlike you, I'm beginning to realise I can't shut it out. That I want to be loved. That I want to love.' The admission was torn from her in a tortured whisper.

She could feel him moving closer. Feel it with every nerve in her body, but she still couldn't look at him. Silence lingered, tense and full of expectation. Her breathing was rapid and shallow as she waited for him to speak. Waited for him to tell her again that he couldn't love anyone.

'Then don't walk away from me, Kaliana. Don't shut me out.' His voice had become a hoarse whisper, full of pleading. She frowned, unable to turn to him, unable to allow the small glimmer of hope to spark into something bigger. Something that would let her down. Break her heart. 'Look at me, Kaliana. Look at me.'

She took a deep breath, turning to face him. In just a few minutes his expression had changed. Gone from that of a man totally sure of himself to a man walking into territory he'd never explored. An expression of uncertainty.

That glimmer of hope inside her flickered, rising a little higher.

'You are the one who has only just arrived here, Rafe. You are the one who has been absent, without even a message, for the last five days.' She couldn't allow herself to hope. Couldn't allow herself to read more into this. 'What else am I supposed to think after our conversation, other than you don't want our deal? Don't want me.'

'I couldn't come to you.'

'Or even send a message? Call me?'

'That is what lovers would do.' There was a trace of shame in his voice. 'And we are not lovers.'

Anger surged forward, making her thoughts irrational. 'We were portraying lovers.'

Rafe drew in a long deep breath. 'I was setting the deal up with your father so that you didn't have to marry me—or Nassif. I had nothing to tell you. But it seems you had plenty to tell me.'

'It was only this morning I knew for certain about the baby,' she defended herself hotly. How dare he turn this on her? 'You could have told me what you were doing, Rafe. I could have spoken with my father.'

'I wanted to present you with a done deal.' He moved a little closer and her heart hammered in her chest. 'I wanted to set you free.'

The flicker of hope dimmed. 'I could never marry Nassif,' she whispered.

He moved, the light from the sun streaming in behind him, leaving him in the shadow of the thick palace walls, reminding her of their last conversation in Villa Casella. 'I know.' His expression hardened slightly. Or was it the shadows? 'Just as I know you can't marry me, but we have made a baby together, Kaliana. A child. A child that changes everything. Even the deal you put to me in Palermo. The baby changes everything.'

'Yes,' she breathed. 'The baby changes everything.'

'So, what is the problem, *cara mia*?' Why did he have to call her that? Why did he have to soften her now?

When she was trying to be so strong. What would he do if she told him the truth? Told him she loved him.

'I loved Alif,' she said, suddenly needing to explain it all. Tell him everything which she'd kept hidden—even from herself. 'I loved him so much.'

He nodded. 'I know. And you lost him and believe love will never be yours again, that you don't deserve it.' The impassioned words rushed from him and she frowned. He'd never been this emotional before. Practical. Strong and resilient. But never emotional. The barriers around his emotions had never lifted like this. She could see it in his eyes. Hear it in his voice. He was letting her in, so shouldn't she allow him past her barriers?

'I did believe that,' she said softly, unable to help herself from walking to him, the need to be closer to him, to see if she could cross through that barrier around him too great. 'Until a few weeks ago.'

He looked into her eyes, the darkness of his filled with concern. Confusion. 'What happened a few weeks ago?'

He had no idea. No idea she'd fallen in love with him. That every caress, every kiss they'd shared in Rome had come from her heart. That every time they'd made love she'd fallen a little more in love with him. But then, she hadn't even seen it herself. She'd tried valiantly to deny it.

Could she tell him? She looked into his eyes, seeing them bare of that barrier. If she didn't tell him now she would have to walk away and never look back. Never wonder *What if?*

'I fell in love.'

The air stilled around them, as if the soft wind of the desert had eased, waiting to see what would happen.

The heat became even more oppressive as his eyes held hers, going deep into her soul. Her heart.

'Fell in love?' The deep and husky whisper reminded her of how his voice sounded after they made love. When he held her in his arms, making her feel as if she was the most precious thing in the world.

'With you, Rafe,' she whispered, holding that electrifying connection between them, not daring to let it break. If she did, she might never get this chance again. Never be able to slip beyond those barriers and barricades. 'I fell in love with you.'

For the second time in as many minutes the floor dropped away from beneath Rafe's feet. The world lurched and spun. Kaliana loved him? The woman he loved, the woman for whom he'd changed everything to enable her to have the freedom to live and love as she wanted, loved him? The woman who was carrying his child.

But could he believe it? Could he allow himself to hope, when she'd just told him she was expecting his child? He hated himself for doubting her, but what if she was just saying it because of the baby?

'Why did you walk away from me the night of our engagement party?' The hurt from that night, the pain of believing that he didn't deserve her love, rushed forward, making every word he spoke sound bitter.

'I saw the way you looked at Emma.' Kaliana's voice was as brittle as ice, her eyes full of fear, pain. 'I saw the way you touched her, Rafe, and I guess I made my own deductions.'

Kaliana looked down, a blush rushing prettily over her face, and he smiled. He shouldn't be happy with that explanation, with that reaction, but he was. It proved she felt something for him. Proved it was deep enough for her to be put out, even jealous, of the friendship he and Emma had carved out of the mess that was their brief love affair.

'I loved Emma once,' he said, his heart flooding with hope as she looked up at him, pain in her eyes, her expression. 'But now only as a friend. A sister. I'm happy for her—and for Enzo. Happy they are making a go of their marriage, that they are adopting a child. Emma always wanted to be a mother. Enzo felt he'd failed Emma, so did everything he could to push her away. But their love was too strong.'

It was a trait he shared, he acknowledged, looking at Kaliana, her expression changing as she processed all he'd told her. All he should have told her long ago.

'And the child they adopt will be enough to save the Casella inheritance? Save the family name?' She moved a little closer, as if she couldn't help herself. As if she too was hanging onto a fragile thread of hope.

He took her hands in his, keeping her close. 'Yes, their child will become the next Casella to inherit the family fortune.'

'So you really don't need to marry me?' Her voice wobbled, her eyes filled with unshed tears and his heart broke. The heart that loved her so much. 'Or have a child?'

'No, I don't.' Her shoulders dropped and her hands felt limp within his. 'But I want to. I want to marry you.'

She shook her head, the denial confusing him, knocking down the confidence to say those three words aloud. To tell her he loved her. 'Just because I'm pregnant? I can't, Rafe.' She pulled her hands free of his, pain in her voice. He had to tell her, had to knock that final barrier down before he lost her for good.

'Kaliana, stop,' he said, gently holding her face between his hands, looking deep into her eyes.

She closed her eyes. Shut him out. Damn it, he wasn't going to be beaten. She couldn't keep him locked out like this—when he'd dismantled almost every barricade he'd ever erected. But there was one more remaining. The one which kept him from saying he loved her. The one he intended to obliterate right now.

'Kaliana, look at me.' He breathed her name in a whisper, waiting until she opened her eyes, needing her to see the love for her in his. 'I love you, Kaliana. I want you to be my wife. I want you to be the mother of my children.'

Kaliana looked at Rafe, unable to think, to speak—or even breathe. He loved her? He'd spent the last five days ensuring she could be free of the need to marry anyone. Because he loved her.

She placed her hands either side of his face, mirroring his need to hold her, make her look at him, see deep into his eyes. Beneath her fingers she felt the uncustomary hardness of his stubble. She smiled and took a deep breath, inhaling the evocative scent that was Rafe. The man she loved. The man who had just admitted to loving her.

'You set me free? Because you love me?' she whispered, moving so close she could almost press her lips to his. Almost kiss him. And she wanted to, so much.

'*Sì*…' He stumbled from Italian to English. 'Yes, I love you, but I want you to be happy—even if that isn't with me.'

'The only way I can ever be happy is with you, Rafe.' She looked into his eyes, saw the questions slip away, saw the sparks of happiness brushing them aside. Slowly she pressed her lips to his, closing her eyes as that contact sparked the usual fireworks in her body.

When he kissed her back a tear sprang from beneath her eyelid, rushing down her cheek, wetting his. He moved back, looking intently at her.

'You are crying.'

'Tears of happiness,' she said as another tear tumbled down her cheek. 'I have everything I could ever want. A man who loves me, a man I love with all my heart, and his baby.'

He kissed her cheek, catching the next tear. 'I love you, Kaliana. So very much. Will you make me the happiest man alive and marry me?'

She laughed as another tear tumbled down her cheek. 'I will, but you don't have to do it here, in Ardu Safra, or so soon.'

'I'm not waiting any longer than I need to wait to make you my wife.' He gave her that suggestive flick of his brows, sending heat spiralling through her. She pressed herself closer to him, sliding her hands around his neck. She loved him so much and if she could marry him right now, right this minute, she would.

'The wedding preparations are all made. Everything is in place for us to marry. Is two weeks too long?' she teased as her fingers slid into the thickness of his hair.

'Far too long.' He kissed her gently, holding her closer still to him, so that she could feel every contour of his body. Feel the need he had for her right now. 'But waiting two weeks to spend the rest of my life with you will be worth it.'

'I love you, Rafe.' She breathed the words she'd longed to say since the night in Rome when their baby had been conceived.

'And I love you, Kaliana, and I intend to spend the rest of my life showing you just how much. Each and every single day.' He kissed her, deeper and harder than he'd ever kissed her, and Kaliana knew they had both broken down the barriers which had entrapped them since their first unlucky encounters with love. They'd both left the shadows of darkness, coming out into the brightness of love.

EPILOGUE

THE EARLY SUMMER sunshine bathed the gardens of Villa Casella in a golden glow as the sun began to set. The garden was filled with friends and family who'd come to welcome the arrival of the next Casella generation. Rafe's father took every opportunity to spend time with his ever-expanding family. Even Kaliana's mother and father had travelled from Ardu Safra for the party and from the smile on her mother's face Kaliana was certain she enjoyed being a grandmother. Her father, of course, tried very hard to remain serious, but to no avail. Little Paulo had quite literally got him dancing to his tune.

'Paulo is utterly gorgeous,' Kaliana said as she sat watching the toddler Emma and Enzo had adopted, their adoration and love for each other and the little boy obvious for all to see. Their happiness at finally being a family filled Kaliana with joy whenever she thought of where they'd all been this time last year.

Rafe leant forwards, kissing her cheek softly. 'It's hard to believe that a year ago there were no future Casella heirs. Now there's a whole new generation.'

Kaliana glanced at the baby monitor on the table next to her iced lemonade, still unable to believe she was a mother. The mother of a beautiful baby girl and a handsome baby boy. 'I'm looking forward to Lorenzo and Layla being able to toddle around the garden like Paulo.'

Rafe laughed softly, love shining from his eyes as he looked at her. 'Be prepared for them to be a real handful.' He sat back next to her, his long legs stretching out before him, unfurling that ever-constant need she had for him. 'My mother always said that's exactly what Enzo and I were. A handful.'

Kaliana laughed. 'You still are, both of you.'

'That is not fair.' His voice was mockingly stern, the sparkle of love brighter than ever in his eyes.

'Maybe a boy and a girl will be different.' The love she felt for Rafe, for her babies, filled every word as she looked at him, always ready to tease him a little.

Baby snuffling noises sounded on the monitor and they both looked at it, smiling. 'If Layla is anything like her mother, then it will be because poor little Lorenzo will be continually bossed and teased by his big sister.'

'Are you saying I boss you around?' She sat forwards, leaning into him and brushing her lips over his. 'Tease maybe, but not boss.'

'I like a strong woman,' he said, pulling her onto his lap and kissing her, oblivious and uncaring of their guests. 'But, more than anything else, I love you. My strong woman. The mother of my beautiful twins.'

'And I love the man I married, the father of my babies. I love you to the point of distraction.'

She closed her eyes and he kissed her, hard and passionately. When he ceased the torment, pulling back from her, she could see the love in his eyes and smiled. She was happy, loved and in love—far more than she'd ever dared to hope for that night she'd walked into the hotel bar in London.

'I love you, Kaliana. With all my heart and every day I love you a little deeper. You are my world.'

* * * * *

MILLS & BOON

Coming next month

CINDERELLA'S ROYAL SEDUCTION
Dani Collins

"You're genuinely asking me to marry you. And if I do, you'll give me this hotel and spa, all the property and rights to the aquifer. Everything," she clarified.

"If you'll live in Verina with me and do what must be done to have my children, yes," he said with a dark smile.

She was still shaking her head at the outrageous proposition but found herself pressing her free hand to her middle, trying to still the flutters of wicked anticipation that teased her with imaginings of how those babies would get made.

She veered her mind from such thoughts.

"Why? I mean, why me?" She lifted her gaze to his, catching a flash of sensual memories reflected in the hot blue of his irises.

"I've already told you. I want you in my bed."

"And that's it? Your fly has spoken? That's the sum total of your motivation?"

His eyes narrowed, becoming flinty and enigmatic. "There are other reasons. I'll share them with you, but they can't leave this room."

That took her aback. "What if I don't want to carry your secrets?"

"You're going to carry my name and my children. Of course you'll keep my secrets. Would you like to tell me yours?" He regarded her over the rim of his glass as he sipped, as though waiting for her to tip her hand in some way.

She shrugged her confusion. "I'm not exactly mysterious," she dismissed. "The most interesting thing that's ever happened to me is happening right now. You realize how eccentric this sounds?"

"Eccentric or not, it's a good offer. You should accept it before I change my mind."

She snorted. "You're quite ruthless, aren't you?" She spoke conversationally but knew it as truth in her bones.

"I do what has to be done to get the results I want. You understand that sort of pragmatism, even if you've pointed your own efforts in dead-end directions. I look forward to seeing what you accomplish when you go after genuinely important goals."

"This is my home. It's important to me."

"Then claim it."

A choke of laughter came out of her. "Just like that? Accept your proposal and—" She glanced at the paperwork. "I'm not going to agree to anything before I've actually reviewed that offer."

"Due diligence is always a sensible action," he said with an ironic curl of his lip. He waved his glass toward the table, inviting her to sit and read.

Gingerly she lowered onto the sofa and set aside her whiskey.

Rhys kept his back to her, gaze fixed across the valley as he continued to sip his drink, saying nothing as she flipped pages.

His behavior was the sort of thing a dominant wolf would do to indicate how little the antics of the lesser pack affected him, but she was glad not to have his unsettling attention aimed directly at her as she compared the two contracts. Aside from the exchange of money on Maude's—and the fact that hers finalized on her wedding day—they were essentially the same.

"I want possession on our engagement. If I decide to accept your proposal," she bluffed, fully expecting him to tell her to go to hell.

"Done. On the condition we begin the making of our children on the day our engagement is announced." He turned, and his eyes were lit with the knowledge his agreement had taken her aback. "We'll keep the conception part as a handshake agreement. No need to write that down in black-and-white."

He brought her a pen. His hand was steady as he offered it. Hers trembled as she hesitantly took it.

"Are you completely serious?" she asked.

"Make the change. Sign it. I'll explain why I want you to marry me. You'll accept my proposal, and Cassiopeia's will be yours."

Continue reading
CINDERELLA'S ROYAL SEDUCTION
Dani Collins

Available next month
www.millsandboon.co.uk

COMING SOON!

We really hope you enjoyed reading this book. If you're looking for more romance, be sure to head to the shops when new books are available on

Thursday 9th January

To see which titles are coming soon, please visit

millsandboon.co.uk/nextmonth

MILLS & BOON

THE HEART OF ROMANCE

A ROMANCE FOR EVERY KIND OF READER

MODERN

Prepare to be swept off your feet by sophisticated, sexy and seductive heroes, in some of the world's most glamourous and romantic locations, where power and passion collide.
8 stories per month.

HISTORICAL

Escape with historical heroes from time gone by. Whether your passion is for wicked Regency Rakes, muscled Vikings or rugged Highlanders, awaken the romance of the past.
6 stories per month.

MEDICAL

Set your pulse racing with dedicated, delectable doctors in the high-pressure world of medicine, where emotions run high and passion, comfort and love are the best medicine.
6 stories per month.

Celebrate true love with tender stories of heartfelt romance, fro the rush of falling in love to the joy a new baby can bring, and a focus on the emotional heart of a relationship.
8 stories per month.

Desire

Indulge in secrets and scandal, intense drama and plenty of sizz hot action with powerful and passionate heroes who have it all: wealth, status, good looks…everything but the right woman.
6 stories per month.

HEROES

Experience all the excitement of a gripping thriller, with an inte romance at its heart. Resourceful, true-to-life women and strong fearless men face danger and desire - a killer combination!
8 stories per month.

DARE

Sensual love stories featuring smart, sassy heroines you'd want a best friend, and compelling intense heroes who are worthy of th
4 stories per month.

To see which titles are coming soon, please visit

millsandboon.co.uk/nextmonth